SUPER STORM
SUPER MOON

SUPER STORM
SUPER MOON

A TALE FROM THE SEA

Leslie Stolfe

Columbus, Ohio

The characters in this novel are fictitious though numerous resources and hours of research went into creating a novel that mirrors the events that took place on Long Beach Island from October 2012 to June 2013. Thank you to all the newspapers, magazines, photographers, videographers, authors, news reporters, weathermen and such whose work has helped to make this story realistic.

SUPER STORM SUPER MOON: A TALE FROM THE SEA

Published by Gatekeeper Press
3971 Hoover Rd. Suite 77
Columbus, OH 43123-2839
www.GatekeeperPress.com

ISBN: 9781619847033
eISBN: 9781619847040
Library of Congress Control Number: 2017942390
Printed in the United States of America

DEDICATION

For Willie, the best brother in the universe.
Many years have passed since you've left us but not one day goes
by that I don't miss your smiling face.
Your love for Long Beach Island equaled my own.

For my family, from 2 to 94
you are what I live for,
my crazy dog included.

ACKNOWLEDGMENTS

With undying gratitude to my parents for making sure we've had a vacation on Long Beach Island every summer since 1982. The sweetest memories were made on Stratford Avenue, Kentford Avenue and Coral Street.

Thank you to the many organizations and individuals whose tireless efforts helped restore and rebuild the island after
Super Storm Sandy
wielded her fury upon it.

The United Emergency Services -Firemen, Auxiliary Members,
EMTs, Police and Government Officials
177th and 108th Fighter Wing of New Jersey Air National Guard
New Jersey National Guard
195th NJ Air National Guardsmen
State Police from Louisiana
Alabama Utility Workers
The Army Corps of Engineers
150th Engineer Company
328th Military Police
New Jersey Utility Crews
The American Red Cross
Waves 4 Water
S.T.A.R.T. Stafford Teachers And Residents Together
Jetty Rock Foundation
Alliance for a Living Ocean
Jimmy Ward – LBI Is Alive, Hope For Long Beach Island
ReClam the Bay
I know there are a multitude of Organizations, Companies,
Volunteer Groups and Individuals that I have left unmentioned
and for that I am profoundly sorry.

A SPECIAL THANK YOU TO

Rebecca Gee from Kapler's Pharmacy,
Beach Haven Beach Patrol Chief Mike Lawrence,
and
Father Frank Crumbaugh of Holy Innocents Episcopal Church
who shared some of their experiences with me.
Jeff the Lifeguard -the inspiration for Dillan's unique look and
helpful personality.
Leanne Wuest -owner of The Labrador Store and More, whose
dog Buoy was an obvious inspiration.
Wil, for designing this book's beautiful cover.
And finally, to my cousins Patti, Bonnie and Cathy and friends
Janine, Jackie and Julie who showed a deep interest in the
development of the story.

INTRODUCTION

EIGHTEEN MILES AT SEA, anyone who has ever vacationed on Long Beach Island is familiar with the phrase. For those who come to play, she boasts a multitude of activities. There's boating, crabbing, clam digging and jet skiing on the bay, or surfing, boogie boarding, shell collecting, and, of course, swimming in the Atlantic Ocean. If you simply want to relax and regenerate, there are cream-colored beaches as far as the eye can see. You can sunbathe, read an engaging book while keeping an eye open for passing dolphins, or nap in a beach chair to the mellow sound of rolling waves.

If you're brave and sturdy enough to climb the two hundred seventeen steps to the top of Barnegat Lighthouse at the northern tip of the island, you can take in a three-hundred-and-sixty-degree view of the Jersey coast line. Drive the eighteen miles to Holgate at the southern end and, on a clear night, you can glimpse the bright lights of Atlantic City.

Most people who visit LBI, as it's commonly referred, fall in love with its charm and return summer after summer to enjoy all the treats it has to offer. Children can play at Fantasy Island, a small amusement park and arcade, Thundering Surf water park or Mr. Tee's Putt & Play, one of its many fun-themed miniature golf courses. Parents and their kids alike enjoy late afternoons on the beach, flying kites, throwing Frisbees, tossing footballs or building sandcastles.

The town of Beach Haven has many shops and restaurants that beckon with their souvenirs and delectable pastries and candies. Crust and Crumb Bakery and Country Kettle Fudge are a must for all. Of course, you can't forget to indulge with ice cream; it's a summer staple, after all. There's Barry's Do Me A Flavor and the Showplace Ice Cream Parlor that fill a certain need in young and old alike.

You can enjoy family and friends or complete solitude, do a lot or do nothing at all. Take in its golden sunrises on the ocean or watch in awe as the setting sun paints the sky with fire on the bay. LBI gives you a sense of peace, magic, and endless possibilities.

Such a special place certainly seemed impervious to hardships and misfortunes. Locals and visitors alike were accustomed to the street drains backing up during high tide or heavy downpours. Occasionally, minor flooding might overtake the pizzeria's parking lot, but it was commonplace and manageable. Therefore, in October 2012, when a huge, slow-moving storm was heading for the eastern coastline of the United States, many people were not intimidated. Taking the threat seriously, the governor of New Jersey urged residents to evacuate the island by saying, *"Get the hell off the beach!"* or find themselves trapped and vulnerable to the elements. Ideally, if everyone took heed of the mandate and The Weather Channel's ominous warnings for a post tropical cyclone with hurricane force winds, first responders could remain safely at their stations.

It was during these tempestuous days when the full moon, high tide, and the largest Atlantic hurricane on record met along the Jersey shore and the months of recovery that followed that our tale unfolds – a most unusual time for a love story.

HER

OCTOBER 2012

A DOLPHIN WAS GENTLY nudging me. "Come play," he urged. He dove deep and returned a moment later with a starfish in his mouth. "Come on, come on! Let's play tug!" It wouldn't end well for the starfish, but I pretended to grab for it anyway. The dolphin let go of the mangled *toy* and it floated aimlessly in the water between us. I smiled, grabbed it and swam away with great haste, the dolphin in my wake.

He poked me again with a smooth, firm nose. How did he catch me so quickly? I was about to frolic away once more but was startled by an unfamiliar sound. My fanciful dream subsided as I was guided into consciousness by a low whimpering. I came to with an innate need to gasp for air, choking out fiery seawater in the process. I collapsed back onto the uneven, brick-hard, surface below with tearing eyes, a runny nose and slobbery chin. Jetties were more comfortable than this! Every cell in my body ached. I reached up and touched a bump along my hairline that brought tears to my eyes and traced dry and crusty blood down the side of my face.

In the complete blackness, I could make little sense of my surroundings. The raging wind and pelting rain on the roof and walls almost drowned out the low whining near my ear. My first instinct was to flee but my burning chest and aching muscles wouldn't allow it. If this creature had wanted to hurt me, it could have taken me out when I was semiconscious and fighting for oxygen.

I couldn't fathom where I was or how I had gotten here. Feeling terribly frightened, I came to an unsettling conclusion – I was suffering from amnesia.

After another fit of relentless coughing, I felt a gentle lick on my hand and heard a soft *woof*. The large beast inched closer and settled down along my side. It sighed peacefully as I gingerly placed my arm around its neck. The warmth of its body and its rhythmic breathing escorted me as I floated off on a blissful wave toward slumber.

I was stiff as driftwood when I woke up. I could tell it was daytime by the slim rays of dull light that filtered through gaps in the boarded-up windows. The large black dog stared at me with soulful eyes that somehow registered concern.

"Hey, big guy," I whispered through a raw throat.

I pushed myself up, taking stock of my bones and muscles and studied my whereabouts. I immediately assumed the ramshackle appearance of the room was a result of the violent storm, but as I climbed precariously from a pile of lumber and cement sacks, I realized a restoration project had been underway.

My back ached and my limbs felt weak, but the bump on my head had decreased in size and was less tender, leading me to believe that the pile of construction material had been my bed for way too long. I bent down and petted the dog that seemed to be smiling with satisfaction now that I was upright.

I craved water like a landlocked fish and poked around the rubble in vain, searching for a forgotten water bottle. My empty stomach burned almost as badly as my lungs. I imagined my furry friend must've been ravenous as he watched my every move from his adorably cocked head.

On wobbly legs, I exited through the remains of a door frame and found the dimly lit hall littered with a multitude of complicated-looking tools. With the dog at my heels, I came upon a landing where the stench of stagnant sea water was overpowering. The stairs led to a foyer and adjacent room where a hole in the wall allowed the wind and rain to enter the home unchecked. In the two or so feet of mucky water a large plastic bucket, a soccer ball and various pieces of lumber floated. I wasn't completely surprised by what I'd found, but I was terribly disappointed that the comfy-looking couch was totally trashed. Feeling resigned to the fact that I'd be here awhile, I headed back upstairs in search of food and water.

The next room I came upon had all four walls intact. In the dim light, I bumped into a large table which was covered with clutter, including candles, matches, an oil lamp . . . and a lighter! Once illuminated, the makeshift kitchen revealed gallons of bottled water, two cases of canned dog food, three good-sized bags of kibble, a stack of ramen noodles and a plethora of canned and junk foods. Someone had been well prepared for the storm but then left their dog behind to fend for himself – how horrible! My companion stared at me with pleading eyes as I added water to one of the large mixing bowls on the floor. I heard him lapping as I searched for a can opener. Once located, I opened the dog food on both ends and plopped it into the other huge bowl. After I drank my fill of the freshest water I'd ever tasted, I thoroughly chewed some stale but tasty Wheat Thins and washed them down as gently as possible.

After I refilled the dog's water bowl, I peeked into the mini fridge where any trapped coldness had faded away. Some baby carrots, half a jar of salsa, a chunk of stinky cheese and a few bottles of beer was all there was, leaving me disheartened. Was I seriously hoping for fresh lobster? What was I thinking?

I sat down in a beat-up old dining chair and sighed. How the hell did I get here? My friend lumbered over to me, his hips wiggling and tail wagging like a boat propeller. I reached for his collar and found the tag. It was red and had a white cross on one side, *Buoy* and a phone number on the other.

"So pleased to meet you, Buoy! Thanks for watching over me. If you could only tell me how I got here!"

He placed his head on my thigh and looked up at me with big dark eyes. It was only then that I realized I'd been parading around totally naked. Perhaps I was still in some form of shock. I was uncomfortable having the dog's eyes on me, even if they were adoring me for doggie reasons.

Grabbing the lantern, I wandered further down the hall looking for some form of clothing. I found a small bathroom, just big enough to hold a tub, sink and toilet. Thank goodness someone had the wherewithal to fill the tub with water; it's probably what saved Buoy from dehydration.

Next, I discovered a small bedroom. I wandered around carrying my lamp, taking in the space. The walls were covered with a coral paint, which was brighter where pictures once hung, the ceiling cracked and chipping. Lace curtains hung over a boarded-up window and near it sat a small dresser, items hanging messily from the drawers. I grabbed a blue T-shirt from the dresser sporting *My Dog Digs The Beach* on its front. It looked like my new buddy digging a hole in the sand. I slipped the baggy shirt over my head. Along the opposite wall sat a twin bed covered with tousled sheets, some pillows and a lovely old quilt. I sure wished I'd woken up here! On the far wall, a closet door and a small table which held an old-fashioned telephone, its cord disconnected and frayed. Next to that sat a pretty antique lamp. Under different circumstances one might find this room quite cozy. I dug around in the drawers a bit more, then pulled on a pair of men's cotton boxers and comfy sweats.

Once appropriately covered, I became curious and began to snoop around. What kind of person would abandon his dog in such weather? There were a few personal products on the dresser, lip balm, zinc oxide, sunscreen and nail clippers. Then, I spotted a piece of paper sticking out from under an empty beer bottle. The scratchy handwriting read *Summer 2009-Anna-Big Sur*. I turned it over. On a wide beach, in front of a beautiful sunset stood three figures: my new companion, a perfectly sculpted, bikini-clad model type and the guy.

This had to be him! He was a bit strange looking, especially with the hair. Tall, lean, muscular and very tan. Light eyes underlined with blue zinc paint and dirty blonde dreadlocks down to his biceps. I twirled a piece of my own dark chestnut hair, now crusted with sand and seaweed, and imagined it matted like that and shuddered. What was he thinking? No wonder I didn't see a hairbrush with his stuff! I turned the photo over again, hoping his name had magically appeared – it hadn't.

My next task was to get some more light into the place. I went back to the kitchen window, raised the glass, screen and storm pane. Now, I only had to get the plywood off, but it wouldn't budge as it had been adhered from the outside. I found a Skil cordless jigsaw in the hallway – three minutes of fiddling with it and the battery died. I went back and found a screwdriver and handsaw. After digging at the wood with the screwdriver for a bit, my sore muscles started barking. I told them to be quiet. I needed to get a look outside.

I kept at it for a while but didn't feel particularly strong or energetic, and it didn't take long before I tired out completely. Having no particular agenda, I relinquished my tools and wandered back to the comfortable-looking bed with Buoy at my side. Even though he cuddled up against me, I began to feel rather scared and lonely. As the winds continued to howl and the rain hammered the roof, tears ran down my cheeks and moistened my neck, but I couldn't help giggling as a warm tongue licked them dry.

"What are we going to do?" I asked wearily from under the toasty quilt.

I awoke with a start, sat bolt upright and felt a bit woozy. Being here felt so completely wrong! Perhaps I had a slight concussion and that's why I couldn't remember anything. My furry companion rolled on his back, gazed into my eyes and placed a long, wet lick on my forearm.

"Love you too, boy," I whispered with a resigned sigh. I fluffed the pillow, laid back down and reciprocated with a languorous belly rub. "I bet you're scared too!"

After a bit, we rose and wandered back to the kitchen where I made a snack. I ate green beans from a can and Ramen noodles (edible though not completely enjoyable) that I soaked in some water. I found a few boxes of Blue Dog Bakery treats and gave two to my new companion. I set to work on the plywood just as he began to pace anxiously about.

"Sorry Buoy," I said. "We can't get out just yet," and I placed a pile of paper towels on the floor in case he knew how to use them – he didn't. With nowhere to go and nothing else to do, I applied myself to the task at hand. After a while, I had made a hole just big enough to see the blackest sky and to rid ourselves of a rather stinky dog poop.

I guessed it was the wee hours of the morning when we returned to the bedroom. I found a tube of sore muscle rub on the dresser and applied it to my sawing arm. It throbbed but was worth the pain because come morning I would get a glimpse of my whereabouts and hopefully a clue to my identity.

BUOY

I COULD FEEL IT, a change in the air. Something bad was coming, something dangerous. My hair bristled, my nose twitched uncontrollably as unfamiliar and powerful scents filled my brain with menace. I tried to tell my human, Dillan, with my restlessness, my pleading eyes and by poking his thigh with my nose. He didn't seem to notice as we walked along the shore. He thought I just wanted to play.

I ran alongside Dillan in the sand, watching my ball in his hand, waiting for it to soar. I ran after it, caught it on a bounce and returned to him triumphantly. He continued to run, now in wide circles and I ran after, jumping and trying to get my ball from his hand. I know this game – I went ahead down the beach as always and waited. Soon my ball would come flying to me. Out at sea a light flashed and a sharp crack sounded. I spun to look and felt something sting my butt. I gave Dillan a confused look and sat in the sand facing the sea. My ball went rolling toward the waves. Any other time I'd be on it in a flash. Today, I didn't care.

Something bad's out there, I said to him, but he didn't understand. Dillan sat next to me and scratched gently between my ears.

"What's the matter, Buoy? Your arthritis acting up? You need a good rub down?"

"Woof," I replied.

Soon Dillan's friends came on the beach dressed in their stinky wetties and carrying their water sleds. They seemed so excited and happy. They begged my human to join them in the waves.

"Come on Bro, we've got heavies!"

I didn't want Dillan out there with the dangerous far-off noises and unusual smells, so I whimpered loudly to distract him.

"Maybe later. I gotta get the house secured. I promised Mac I'd do my best to protect his investment."

As his friends ran and plunged into the surf, I struggled to rise and limped my way toward the path which headed over the dune.

Yes, Dillan, my arthritis is acting up and I need a rubdown, a good, long rubdown. Limping unnecessarily was a talent I'd developed when I learned it brought forth great results, just like doing tricks or looking particularly cute. It takes a lot of practice, but comes in very useful. My main goal was to keep Dillan out of the ocean, getting a deep muscle massage was just a pleasant bonus.

I lay on the couch and had just starting relaxing for the first time in days when Dillan stopped my massage to answer his cellphone.

"We talked this to death, Jack," he said. "We're staying!" He put the phone down and began rubbing my leg again. I heard a familiar voice but it sounded different, not as friendly.

"Even if it was up to me, which it's not, I wouldn't let you stay. Have you checked the weather lately? This thing's massive and it's headed directly for us."

"It's gonna turn east; they always do. This could be the best surfing we've had in a very long time!"

"No one will be surfing here, not even our lifeguards, including **you** – so just forget it! I just pulled some of your friends out of the ocean and gave them a talking-to. Listen, you're a good kid, Dillan. I'm just looking out for your safety and Buoy's too. If you stay and get into trouble, we might not be able to get there to help. Plus, I don't want to risk any of my guys' lives to save someone who disobeyed a mandatory evacuation."

I looked up at Dillan with the most pitiful face I could make.

"Damn Jack, you got me. We'll leave, but I've got a ton more work to do to prepare the house. I'm so behind with this restoration already – this just sucks!"

"Thanks for your cooperation, really. It's one less thing I have to worry about. Governor Christie says everyone needs to be off the island by four o'clock tomorrow. If you run into any of your stubborn friends between now and then, please drag them along with you!"

"You're killing me!"

"See you in a couple of days."

"You can count on it. And Jack – be careful."

"You bet, kid."

Dillan ran his hands along my other leg. "I've got to take these tools upstairs to higher ground and pack our stuff. You stay and rest, old buddy."

I tried to doze but his banging around and the whirring wind outside made for an anxious afternoon and evening. We made a quicker than usual jaunt down the block for pee and poop. The grassy park was one of my favorite places. So many smells to explore, but not tonight. Dillan was all business. We jogged home and went to bed earlier than usual. I slept fitfully, in the soft bed, pressed against my human.

By the next afternoon, the rain had started and the wind became even more intense. Finally, Dillan led me outside, into the downpour, and opened the door of the Jeep. He helped me into the backseat and threw the duffle bag in the back.

"Shit! I forgot something. Buoy, stay! I'll be right back."

As soon has he disappeared into the house, I heard a sound riding on the wind.

"Help! Help!" It was a cry too faint for human ears. Dillan wouldn't know. He wouldn't help. He'd drive us away. "Buoy, stay," Dillan had said. Trapped between the devil and the deep blue sea, I looked at the house then looked toward the beach. As soon as his face appeared in the doorway, I jumped from the Jeep and ran as fast as I could. I charged through the deluge, my imaginary leash pulling Dillan close behind me.

"Buoy! Stop! Stay! Come! B-u-o-y!!!"

I heard my human, my best-est friend in the whole wide world calling. I felt so ashamed disobeying him, but I also heard her, who sounded so scared, who needed our help, and this was the only way I could get him there. He kept yelling at me but I kept on running, over the dune, through the sand, out to the crashing waves and into the seething ocean. I was tossed upside down and spun around and around before I could surface. I looked back toward shore for Dillan but I could not find him beyond the pounding waves.

Among the ferocious winds, another weak cry for help reached my ears and then, she was gone as well. I found myself, most frighteningly, alone. I took a deep breath and dove under the water but could see nothing in the churning sea. I swam as hard as I could, paddling under the huge waves as they came at me with unyielding force. I'd never swam in anything like *this* before, and I was tiring quickly. I just wanted to be home, to be by my human's side once more. Suddenly, I sensed she was ahead. I felt a renewed strength and confidence as I swam toward her. She grabbed ahold of me and we swam up, up, up to the surface. I felt her gratitude as we fought the raging currents and made our way to shore. As I collapsed on the beach, the girl at my side, I thought I could hear Dillan, calling me home.

DILLAN

"**B**UOY!!!!!"

For the life of me, I couldn't imagine what had caused him to bolt out of the Jeep. If I hadn't gone back inside to check the power this never would have happened. I ran as fast as I could behind him, screaming for him to stop. For an older dog with arthritis he sure could book it! Being a lifeguard, I was in pretty good shape, but I couldn't catch up to him. Across the street and over the dune he flew. Completely ignoring my commands, he plunged straight to the crashing waves. He'd never done anything crazy like this before. It seemed he was suicidal.

"**Buoy, Come, PLEASE!**" For a second I saw his black head being tossed in the waves, then he was gone. I ran and jumped in but was immediately taken under by the current; I barely made it back to shore. I had to get my board; it was the only thing to do.

I ran back to the house, the heavy wet jeans making my legs feel like lead, and grabbed my board. The street was already ankle deep with water where the storm drains had backed up. I jumped in the Jeep and raced up the street, to the next beach, knowing that the current would carry him that way. I kept my eye out for anyone or anything that might help me rescue my best friend but no one was in sight. Anyone with half a brain had left already. It wasn't like I wasn't warned; we'd had plenty of time to get the hell out, yet here I was and Buoy was . . . .

I started to panic as I ran over the dune. The waves were only about six feet from the dune fence. I stopped for a second to scan the waves while fighting to keep my board from blowing out of my grasp. My heart leapt! – but it was only a dolphin's tail.

"I saw your Jeep. What the hell are you doing?" I heard through the raging wind.

"Jack! Thank God! Buoy is missing – he's out there! He jumped out of the Jeep and, and he just ran . . . ."

"Jesus, Dillan, you're not going out there! I won't let you!"

"Try and stop me!" Before I knew what happened, Jack Foster had slapped his handcuffs on me and had me pinned on the sand.

"Are you *crazy*? Let me go! I have to save Buoy!"

"Listen to reason!" he yelled above the wind. "If you go out there, it's quite possible you will die. How long has he been out there?"

"I don't know – around ten minutes."

"Let's go up another couple of blocks and see if he's made it to the shore. Promise you won't spring when I take the cuffs off."

"Okay, okay!" I huffed defeated.

We drove north in the cruiser for five beaches, checking each as we made our way back. No sign of Buoy – only a rising tide and wind-driven swells.

"God, I am so sorry. I know how much he meant to you. I have no words."

Jack put his arm around me as I shook my head in disbelief. How could he be gone when just a few minutes ago we were getting ready to leave? "Maybe he made it out. Maybe he's found his way home," I uttered sadly.

"I don't know, kid, but I truly hope so. Let's go check, then get you to a safer place."

Jack dropped me at the Jeep and we met back at the inn. There was no sign of Buoy at the house, so I ran around the block searching and calling his name. One last hope: Bicentennial Park. It had been turned into a parking lot for a few emergency vehicles, but Buoy was not sniffing among them, as I'd hoped. I jogged back to the inn, praying for a miracle, but Jack was the only one waiting on the front door stoop.

"Did you remember to turn off the utilities and pack your valuables?"

"Yeah, that's how it happened. I had turned off the water and gas, but went back inside to double check the fuse box. I can't imagine what made him run away. He's never done anything like that, ever." I placed my hand on the railing and sighed. I think I was in shock – it had all happened so fast. Jack put his arm around me and squeezed my arm.

"Dillan, I will keep an eye out for Buoy and spread the word to all the emergency personnel but you have to get out of here. Do you have your wallet, passport, checkbook? Important documents?"

"Yeah, I think I have everything, everything except – " I looked at the empty back seat, my heart broken. I didn't want to leave when there was a shred of doubt in my mind. "I just gotta lock up," I said, distraught.

As I turned the key, I had an idea. If he did make it out, Buoy would come home and I didn't want him locked out in the storm. "Just give me one more minute, Jack." I ran upstairs, threw on some dry clothes and sneakers, then pulled two huge bowls from the buffet. I filled one with water and one with his dry food. I found a couple of 2x4s and Jack helped me wedge them under the front door knobs, holding it opened about a foot. I prayed they would hold against the wind and that no one would rob me blind.

"It's almost four," Jack said, "I hate like hell to do this to you at a time like this, but you need to get off the island. I just got a text that the bay has risen significantly. If the causeway floods, you'll be trapped. You okay to drive?"

I didn't feel okay for anything. "Yeah man, sure. Thanks," I lied. Jack gave me a clap on the back, and I climbed into the Jeep. Too choked up for words, I just nodded my farewell.

"I'll be right behind you."

I watched for Buoy through the driving rain, but there was no sign of my best friend. My brain kept telling me he was gone, but my heart said the opposite.

Jack followed me all the way to the causeway. He didn't trust me, with good reason. I saw him flash the police lights as I headed toward Route 72. My gut feeling was to turn around, to go back and continue my search, but the weather report on the radio spelled disaster and the police barricade made reentering the island impossible.

IAN MACAVERY

JULY 2011

IT WAS COOL AND dim in The Hud, a hole in the wall bar that I came upon nearly twenty years ago when my parents first retired and moved to LBI. I didn't have a drinking problem, but today I had an experience that drove me straight to the bottle. We had driven past the Seafarer's Inn, a property we had recently acquired and headed down to the trailer park to visit Mom. She had been very excited when I told her about our plan to remodel the old inn and move permanently to the island as soon as I retired. My wife Shona and I would live in a separate wing of the inn and rent out rooms during the summer to help with the mortgage and taxes. Our plan for this trip was to review the proposed estimates with our contractors while spending some quality time with my mom.

My mother had fallen in love with the island during her childhood vacations – and I'd done the same. I'd kissed my first girl, drank my first beer and lost my virginity all under the lifeguard stand and the full moon. Yup, it was a magical place. I even met my wife on the beach, the summer before I was headed to college. We kept in touch and years later we wed, surrounded by family and friends, on the Centre Street Pavilion. A seagull crapped on us as we posed for photos, a wonderful sign of good luck. At the time, we didn't believe it, but three children and twin grandsons later, I'd have to agree. We had made it, and it had been an enjoyable ride.

I had a key to Mom's place, but I knocked just the same. Shona was still admiring her rose bushes when she finally opened the door.

"Hi Mom!" I said, feeling relieved. I waited for her to reply, to grab me for a tight hug and smooch on the cheek as she always did, but she didn't. It was three in the afternoon and she was wearing a threadbare nightgown. She looked at me strangely.

"Aren't you going to invite us in?" I asked. She looked at me in a way that made me feel utterly helpless and infinitely sad. "*Mom?*" I asked. The seconds seemed to last an eternity.

"I don't know you," she stated flatly, "Go away."

My world crumbled into pieces, just as it had ten years before when my father suffered a massive heart attack while we were crabbing on the bay. In hindsight, I was glad that I had been there for his last moments but how horrible for my twelve-year-old son who had been enjoying a wonderful day with his grandpa.

Now, I stood on the tiny stoop, staring at my mother and wondering what to do next.

"Hon?" Shona asked as she came up the steps behind me.

"Oh, hello Shona," my mother said suddenly. "Won't you two come in? It's hotter than blue blazes out there."

Once we had brought in our suitcases, had some iced tea with Mom and everything seemed back to normal, I got in the car and drove straight to the bar. I would've poured myself something stronger at the trailer but the only thing I could find with alcohol was a bottle of vanilla. Shona had understood completely and had everything under control.

I said hello to my old pal, Phil the bartender, and had a couple of gin and tonics while the pinball machine binged and bonged and a game of shuffleboard took place beside me. I was trying to get my thoughts together when a young guy with tanned skin and Rastafarian hair came up to the bar.

"Hey Phil," he said to the bartender.

"Your regular, Dillan?" the bartender asked.

"Yes sir, and make sure it's icy cold!"

"As if we serve it any other way here. Put your money away, son; it's no good here."

"Come on, Phil; it was no big deal."

"Saving my granddaughter from drowning certainly was! You'll drink free for as long as I own the place, you understand?"

"If you insist. You're the boss. You're lucky I was closest to the rescue can. Mitch prefers top shelf!"

They both chuckled as the young guy sat next to me.

"Mac, this is Dillan – a true hero! Our little Talia wouldn't be here today if he hadn't been on the ball."

"Just doing my job. Nice to meet you, Mac," he said as he held out his hand.

I had a huge dilemma to deal with and wasn't looking to make small talk, but I didn't want to be a rude prick either. "Hey, man," I nodded.

He took a long gulp from the Heineken bottle and sighed. "God, it feels great in here. It was hotter than the Devil's armpits on the beach today!"

Before I realized it, an hour had gone by, it was dinner time and I had made friends with a kid who was closer in age to my son. I felt pretty sorry for him as he relayed the story of his girlfriends' unfaithfulness and he had me wrapped around his finger long before he revealed he was a licensed carpenter. When he showed me photos of his work on his cell phone, I knew I had found the real deal. Being holed up with his dog and two other lifeguards in a one-bedroom apartment wasn't an ideal situation. When I offered him the inn, rent free, along with a reduced wage for his labor he seemed thrilled. Having someone live at the inn also relieved my worries of theft or vandalism. Dillan would keep his lifeguarding position and do our construction work on the side. It seemed like a win-win for both of us. I would still need to hire electricians and plumbers and possibly roofers, but at least this part of the plan had fallen into place. I'd meet Dillan at the inn the next day and give him the plans my architect had drafted. At the end of the summer we'd see where we were.

Dillan had appeared out of nowhere, taking care of my remodeling problem; now at least I could concentrate on Mom. We knew we couldn't leave her alone. She hadn't even recognized her own son. Maybe I had roused her from a nap and she wasn't quite awake. Maybe she hadn't been feeling well and decided not to get dressed that day, but the state of her living space told us something more was going on. Mom had always been fastidious in her approach to housework and the trailer was, by her standards, a dreadful mess. Piles of newspapers, stacks of mail, mostly unpaid bills and some unopened birthday cards from last month sat on the kitchen table. Dirty dishes filled the sink and the clean laundry was heaped in the basket – a big no-no in her eyes. It had only been four weeks since we had visited last but, apparently, it was long enough for something to have happened.

"Have you been feeling all right, Mom?" I asked as we sat in front of the TV that evening.

"I'm going to bed now," she replied as she rose and headed down the hall.

It wasn't the reply I had been looking for. Shona made sure she got into bed all right and I made a quick trip up to Rommel's liquor store for my wife's favorite wine and something a bit stiffer for myself.

A few days later we took mom to her doctor, came out with a new prescription for Aricept and complete instructions for the other meds she was supposed to have been taking but wasn't. We weren't sure if she had simply forgotten to take them or had just given up because the process was so complicated.

We moved Mom up to our place in Bergen County. She made the adjustment better than we thought she would, but she missed her island home, her little rose garden and her neighbor Lilly. Who could blame her?

Fiona, our youngest, had gone off to college that fall, so with me working extra to make payments on the inn, there was no one around to help Shona during the day. We ended up hiring a sitter, a couple days a week, so she could get out of the house, have a lunch date with her friends, or grocery shop.

Work at the Seafarer's Inn was going slowly, but beautifully. The kid was meticulous in his craft and since I was so preoccupied with work, trying to sell my mother's place and getting her affairs in order, the timeline wasn't a concern. I'd rather Dillan take his time so when we finally moved in, it would be perfect.

By the next summer, things took a turn for the worse. Mom's meds were no longer helping with her cognition. Some days she would recognize us and seem contented, other days she was in a far-off place. She developed a temper that she'd never had before, and we never knew what would set her off. Shona and my parents had always been close so she wanted to care for Mom at home, but she was becoming physically and mentally exhausted. Fiona, who had done well at school, felt guilty being away when her family needed her. Her heart was broken when she came home and saw the changes in her grandma. On top of all that, we had lost two prospective buyers for the trailer.

On a positive note, work at the inn was going along very well. Besides the photos that Dillan frequently texted, I got to see everything first hand when we finally got back there in August. Our wing had been gutted, the rooms framed out, the electricity had been brought up to code and pipes installed for the plumbing. The downstairs laundry room was ready for new appliances. The parlor had new walls and crown molding, the hardwood floors had been sanded and varnished, and a fresh coat of paint brought it all together. Dillan beamed when I told him how happy I was with his work. When we opened the inn, the parlor would be a comfortable lounging space filled with books, board games and wi-fi for our guests. Upstairs, he had been tearing down the walls between the thirteen small bedrooms and combining them to make efficiencies with kitchenettes and spa-inspired bathrooms. He was also repairing the fireplace and replacing the windows as well. I felt badly not paying him more, but he insisted that living there rent-free was well worth it.

"I'm living the dream," he exclaimed, sounding sincere. "In a few weeks, when the season ends, I can really get down to business again. I think she'll be move-in ready by next September."

HER

I SAT BY THE hole in the window, munched on a freshly opened bag of potato chips and waited. The morning dawned slowly, a dull bleak gray. The rain and surging ocean water had finally stopped its clamoring. It seemed the worst was over. The patter of light rain mingled with the lap of breaking waves as they rode in on an occasional gust of wind. Peering out, all I could see was the side of a large building, an expanse of clouded sky, and a portion of flooded road below. I should've picked a better window! I was contemplating my next move when Buoy wandered in.

"What do we do now, boy?" I asked disheartened.

"Woof!" He looked at me with the sweetest face imaginable.

"I guess you're probably hungry, right fella?" I prepared a can of food and added some water to his bowl. "Maybe we should go outside and snoop around a bit?"

I could only imagine what devastation had occurred around us. I felt grateful to be alive and deep down I felt Buoy had something, if not everything, to do with it. A few minutes later, loud and anxious voices sounded outside. I peeked out of my little hole but they were somewhere out of sight.

"Thank God for the Engleside; those bulkheads saved us again!"

"Too bad about the Sea Shell, though. That wave was insane! I never imagined anything like that was going to happen."

"If we weren't holed up right next door, we might have had our first fatality."

"I've got the list of idiots who refused to evacuate and crossed off the ones we've rescued already. We'll get to the rest of them one by one. Oh, and Bob, Dillan's dog jumped in the ocean Sunday and didn't resurface. It would be a miracle if he survived, but please let your guys know to keep an eye out. If anyone finds Buoy's body, I want to be the one to notify him."

"Right, Captain, will do. Poor Dillan, he must be a mess. He loved that dog."

"Yeah, he was traumatized, but unfortunately there wasn't anything I could do to help him. I just gave him a lousy police escort to the mainland."

"I'm sure he understands, Jack. You did what you had to do, given this godawful situation."

"I hope so; the kid's like a son to me."

"I'll get my pups to dig out Engine No.1, then we'll head back to the firehouse. Once we secure it, we'll get on the road and see what we can do to help folks."

"Let's hope we find some roads that are passable!"

The men's voices disappeared in the distance. Buoy sat by my feet and I scratched his head while I mulled over their fascinating conversation. "So, Dillan, huh? Is that your master's name? We should go find those guys and give them the good news!"

I sprung up and headed for the door, hoping the ocean had completely receded from the ground floor. Buoy jumped in my path.

"What's the matter? You don't want Dillan to know you're alive?" I detected that very concerned look in his eye again. "Gosh, Buoy, how can you be so smart? You're worried about *me*, aren't you? I won't be able to answer any of their questions. Who knows what they'll do to me? They might take me to a shelter or a hospital," I said as I touched my temple, "and I want to stay here with you."

I was torn, I really was. This Dillan guy didn't abandon Buoy. It sounded like he was forced to leave him behind, and I couldn't be angry at him for that. "I think we need to put Dillan's mind to rest, Buoy. He deserves to know that you are alive and well. Whatever happens to me, happens."

I edged my way past the dog, who did his best to block up the entire doorway and padded down the hall. I wandered down the stairs for the first time to find a total disarray of furniture covered in sand and debris. Yuck! Alien objects like pieces of dune fencing and half a flag pole had found their way inside. A smashed air conditioner frame protruded precariously from the melee. Boy, I hoped every house wasn't like this one. I was afraid of cutting my feet so I ran back upstairs to look for a pair of shoes. Huge, heavy work boots wouldn't do, but some old beat up Converse with a thick pair of socks would tie up nice and tight. I'd just have to be careful not to trip over the toes. I made my way down the stairs as Buoy flew past me.

"Be careful mutt, you're liable to hurt yourself down there!" He ran right to the front door and sat facing me in the sand.

"What are you doing? Don't you want to go stretch your legs and find those men? They seem to know you, and can let Dillan know that you are safe." He seemed to stare me down. "At least let's find a place to pee that's not in the house." I wondered if it truly mattered at this point. The place was a total disaster.

I made my way past the fireplace and over to the two-and-a-half-foot hole in the wall. Sharp pieces of wood and some insulation were protruding inside. I was about to pull myself up and stick my head out for a better view when I heard a heavy hum. A large military vehicle was heading past and I quickly ducked out of sight. I'm not sure why I was afraid, but I was.

"Maybe we should wait for nightfall, Buoy; then we can explore a bit and figure out what to do next."

I clomped back upstairs and found a shovel among the tools and surfing apparatus. With a little coaxing, Buoy begrudgingly left his guard post and allowed me to start digging. It was going to take a lot of hard work to get the door opened and who knew what we'd find on the other side – probably just a lot more sand. Bit by bit, I dug at the nasty wet sand. Lord, it was heavy!

By afternoon, I was exhausted and filthy from digging. I used a little of our precious water to wash up and lay down to rest. Buoy was happy to accompany me, the full length of his body pressed against mine and his head shared the pillow. He felt nice and warm.

It was early evening by the time we awoke. I had a bit more digging to do and then it was time to explore. I found a leash for Buoy and waited by the hole, listening. There was no sound but what was left of the wind and waves. The coast seemed clear. Buoy acted a bit put out when I snapped the leash on his collar but he sat by the door patiently. I pulled the door firmly inside but it didn't budge. I tried again with all my might and but it only opened a crack. It wasn't going to give up without a fight. It reminded me of a clam, as you're trying to shuck it, clamping tightly for dear life. I grabbed the shovel and wedged it between the door and the frame. I leaned against the handle and pushed with my legs and butt. The door squeaked loudly as it gave way, giving us barely enough space to pass through.

Buoy seemed excited, but I was scared. I knew we couldn't just hide inside forever. Someone would find us, whether it was the police, the army or this Dillan guy. I needed to figure out where I was and what had happened. That way I might remember who I was or at least have enough info to make up a believable story.

No artificial light of any kind made it unusually dark, but when the moonlight peered around the clouds, it was possible to see fairly well. The stars themselves were incredibly bright and even seemed to aid us a bit. The first thing to catch my eye was the utility pole lying next to the house. I guess it was lucky that it only made a hole and not smashed through the roof. To our left was the Coral Seas Motel where I couldn't see any obvious damage. To our right, Coral Street – wide and lined with an odd combination of new and very old homes. A thin layer of sand and small debris covered most of the street but the damage seemed minimal.

As we walked down the middle of the street an undeniable chill entered my body and left me paralyzed. Not far from our house sat a huge, old Victorian with a wraparound porch. Somehow, I knew that inside its dark brown cedar shakes, the rooms were looming with secrets. There were no signs that preventative measures had been made to shore up the home which led to its uninhabited appearance but, oddly, a lace curtain was blowing to and fro in the top most turret window. The brick pathway to the porch and doublewide front door beckoned eerily. For a moment, I wondered if someone inside needed help but it felt like it had been abandoned years ago.

I gave a gentle tug on Buoy's leash and hurried us on our way, making a mental note to always walk on the opposite side of the street. We made a left on Beach Avenue and headed down the road, past Marine, Ocean, Berkley, Norwood, Belvoir, and Chatsworth. Large pools of water sat trapped in the lowest sections of the streets. The constant clinking and clattering of unknown objects blowing in the wind was disconcerting. We snapped our heads occasionally, trying to see what had suddenly given way with a loud bang or dull thud. We continued on for a few more blocks when my jaw fell. It was worse than I had feared!

Some homes had been reduced to a pile of junk and broken lumber. A Jacuzzi tub sat in the middle of the street. One home looked to be in fairly good shape, except that the neighboring home wound up smashed against it. Many homes were missing parts of roofs or entire top floors. Cars were buried under sand and boats had come to rest in the queerest of places. Pipes and wires dangled precariously from the wreckage and more utility poles lay across the street. In some areas, the road had lifted, buckled and crumpled into pieces and the smell of natural gas permeated the air. We even heard the hissing of a broken gas main nearby. This place was a disaster area, and very, very dangerous.

Warily, Buoy and I walked on, afraid of what we may find next. I tripped on something and looked down. It seemed odd to find a mermaid doll half-buried in the sand. I pulled her out and wiped her off. I worried for the little girl who had lost her and probably her home as well. We plodded on, collecting other trinkets along the way: a photograph, a bright pink baseball cap, which I shook out and placed on my head, and a tiny decorative plate. All the while we kept alert for the sound of an engine or the glaring headlights of a vehicle.

We found ourselves on Bay Avenue. I only knew because I dug the sand away from the street marker. It was about three feet high here, but much higher in other parts. Occasionally, we'd see a boarded-up window displaying a threatening message, "GO AWAY SANDY!" Sandy was truly an apropos name for this storm. Sand had accompanied the destruction everywhere.

I felt such sorrow for the people who lived here and hoped none of them had lost their lives in the storm. Unfortunately, as we walked, I didn't see anything that jogged my memory. For all I knew, one of the homes I had seen could have been mine, even the mermaid doll, a childhood favorite. I had no more idea who I was now than when I first awoke two days ago, or had it been three? I wasn't really sure. I was getting tired and I was afraid Buoy was too so we headed home. Even though it was waterlogged, powerless and had a hole the size of a Hawksbill Sea Turtle in the wall, it seemed mighty inviting. The squeaky old bed was a place of refuge, at least for now, and it was beckoning me.

We continued up Bay Avenue till we reached Coral Street. We had just turned up the block when we both heard the now-familiar sound of a military truck approaching. I pulled Buoy against the building, ready to hide us if necessary. I peered around and watched. It turned in just two blocks north of us. I was curious, so we headed after it.

We followed Bay Avenue one more block when we spied a firehouse. It was hopelessly dark, sat in a foot or so of water and seemed abandoned. I felt really weird about its appearance, like this was a complete wasteland. We turned on Amber Street and plodded on. I could see some activity ahead which comforted me a little. I crouched down next to Buoy and draped my arm around his neck. Just beyond a sandy lot full of fire trucks, rescue and army vehicles, the huge truck was unloading people. One, two, three, four . . . eleven folks in all, one small animal crate and a large golden retriever.

I could hear voices but could not make out the words. I'm assuming it was a lot of *thank-yous* and *what-do-we-do-nexts*. Our home, I now found out, was only a block from the rescue effort – a lot closer than I ever imagined!

We made it back safely and for the first time I noticed the sign above our door, Seafarer's Inn. The wooden letters showed little sign of damage while just a few feet away stood the gaping hole.

"This must have been a charming place in its day," I whispered to Buoy.

With some difficulty, I made sure the front door was tightly closed and we headed upstairs in the darkness. I gave Buoy a nice drink of water and poured one for myself. We were good on supplies, but I still craved something from the sea. After fumbling around under the light of the lantern, I found a can of tuna fish – I felt like I'd found buried treasure! Alleluia! I was in heaven.

We headed to the bedroom, where I snooped around a bit more and found an old backpack. I'd make good use of this on our next walk. I attached the mermaid doll to the zipper pull with a rubber band as a lucky talisman then slipped the photo under the wooden frame of the dresser mirror. It was an old black and white shot of a couple celebrating their wedding. They looked very happy and very much in love. I liked it because, for some reason, it gave me hope. My reflection, on the other hand, looked hopeless. I would've wrestled a giant octopus for a hot shower and shampoo!

I took off my clumsy sneakers and my new pink hat and hung it on the bedpost. I didn't know what Ron Jon meant but the hat would keep my hair in check on a windy day. I dug out some fresh things from the dresser. This T-shirt read *SandCastle Construction Co.*

"This is pretty cute, isn't it, Buoy?" I slipped on the big shirt and climbed into bed. "Come on in, big guy. I'll shake out the sheets tomorrow. I'm way too tired to clean your feet now."

Buoy jumped up and lay down beside me and I scratched his head sleepily. "It won't take long before someone discovers us," I whispered to my furry bed warmer. "I just hope I can stay here with you until Dillan comes back home."

"Grrrrr," he replied as he nuzzled my neck.

We laid low the next day, staying out of sight. Occasional gusty winds thinned the last of the dense gray clouds. There was nothing I would've liked more than to rip the plywood from the windows and let some sunshine in. The hurricane was finally gone but left in its wake, unfathomable damage. From the beep, beep, beep of the front-end loaders to the endless parade of utility trucks, I knew their tireless efforts were meant to get the people home.

Each night, Buoy and I would explore, bypassing the creepy house on Coral Street, and collect interesting objects while witnessing the town's progress. We both enjoyed the exercise it provided and – well, I admit – the excitement of avoiding discovery. There must've been a curfew because at night all the hubbub of the day disappeared into thin air. We could hear the occasional police or army vehicle coming from a distance and there was plenty of time and places to hide.

Now that the air was no longer permeated with natural gas, I could smell the fresh saltiness of the sea and I was itching to go see it. I imagined the beach would be devastated, and when we arrived all that was left was a steep cliff. Buoy and I stood on the chopped away dune, looking out to sea in awe of her strength and beauty.

Whoa! Suddenly the sand gave way and I fell straight down into the swirling water below. Before I could surface, Buoy was pushing me upward. Instead of panicking, I just thanked him for his courage and giggled. "How many times do you have to save me, huh boy?" The water felt amazing, cleansing and absolutely renewing! We swam slowly along the coastline until we found a section where we could exit safely.

"I wasn't quite expecting that – pretty darn chilly, but it sure felt great!" I said, as I removed my back pack and sat on the freshly bulldozed beach. "Did you enjoy it too?"

Buoy shook his body from head to tail and back again. He sat down next to me and looked as happy as I felt. I lay down in the sand and looked up at the stars feeling completely relaxed. "I know this sounds totally nuts, but I could stay here forever." Buoy lay next to me, breathing deeply.

After a little while, I felt him poke me with his nose and I heard the hum of a boat – I must've fallen asleep! A bright searchlight was heading in our direction.

"Come on boy, let's get out of here!" In wet clothes, I ran up the newly created dune and back toward the street with Buoy close behind.

The night got only weirder when, after a couple of blocks, Buoy stopped in his tracks and cocked his head. We heard a deep voice singing. "Here's my number, so call me maybe . . . do, do, do. I might be crazy, but here's my number, so call me maybe."

I knew the sound of someone belting one out in the shower when I heard it, but how? I had seen no sign of running tap water anywhere. We walked past the Sea Shell Motel and hid behind the huge pile of debris. Across the parking lot, outside the Engleside, was a Hazmat shower. I'm not sure how it worked but blessed steam was escaping along with the silly song lyrics. I swear I could even smell the shampoo from our hiding place. Just a few seconds later, a fella emerged, wrapped in white towels and carrying a handful of clothes. He hurried off to one of the motel rooms and before I gave it any thought, with Buoy at my heels, I made a beeline for the shower.

Even with the occasional touch up and our ocean dip, I was at the point where I couldn't stand myself. My head felt gritty, my skin dry and my hair was a horrible matted mess. I hadn't had a shower in . . . well, I couldn't remember the last shower I'd had. I quickly stripped off Dillan's clothes and got down to the task at hand. Buoy got the benefit of the steam, a quick rinse and towel dry. I squeezed out my hair, helped myself to one of the complimentary towels and dried off. After checking that the coast was clear, we slipped out of the shower and ran home. It felt fantastic to be so clean and fresh. It felt fantastic to be human again! Soon the darkness would give way to dawn – time to tuck in for the day.

In the afternoon, while I puttered around the house, I heard a new noise. Helicopters were flying nearby. I ran to the kitchen window where I watched three large black aircraft circling. Things were definitely happening, though I had no idea what they were. I so wanted to just step out into the sunlight, walk up a block and visit with the evacuees and rescuers. I wanted to know what was happening. I wanted to be helpful instead of twiddling the days away, but mostly I wanted to meet Dillan. I realized that he'd been in my thoughts ever since I'd learned that he was forced to leave Buoy behind. I hoped he would return soon so his mind would be put at ease and I hoped that he would like me enough to let me stay.

DILLAN

SINCE I HADN'T PLANNED on leaving, I had no idea where to go or what to do. Traffic was heavy in all directions except heading east, so it didn't really matter where I went at this point. I pulled onto Route 9 toward Manahawkin where I decided to stop, get a nice big cup of coffee and make a couple of phone calls. My parents would be relieved to hear that I had given up on my idiotic idea to weather the storm at the inn, but Mac wouldn't be thrilled that I'd left his property vulnerable to the elements. I spotted my friend Mitch's van parked at Bagels and Beyond, pulled in beside it and grabbed my phone. After a quick report to Mac, who was understanding about Buoy and totally cool with me leaving his investment property, I called my parents.

"Hey Mom."

"Hi, hon. I'm glad you called. How's the weather over there?"

"Not great; it's raining pretty hard. I just wanted you guys to know I left the island."

"That's a relief. I'm glad that you saw reason. Where are you going?"

"I'm not sure yet, but I'm gonna see what some of the guys are doing. I'll let you know."

"Well, you and Buoy could always stay here for a while. We haven't seen you in forever."

"I didn't want to go that far, Mom. I have so much to do at the inn and . . . ."

"Is everything all right? You sound upset."

"It's nothing. Look, I gotta go. Mitch is waiting for me in the bagel shop," I lied. I couldn't tell her about Buoy; they loved him as much as I did.

"Okay. I love you, honey."

"Love you more, Mom."

"Dad says he loves you."

"Tell him I love him back."

"Be safe; take care of Buoy."

I tapped the phone to disconnect, and taking a deep breath jumped out of the Jeep; landing in an ankle-deep puddle. Seething with anger, I spewed forth a mile-long surge of profanity that would've horrified my mother. Evidently Sandy, the disgusting mass of swirling gray clouds above me, wasn't done with me yet.

Mitch stood at the counter chatting with Katie, one of our fellow guards. He'd been crushin' on her and often headed over to Manahawkin just to exchange a few words. I'm sure she realized he wasn't only interested in the bagels, as there was a Bagels and Beyond right in Brant Beach. Luckily, a man of few words was just the kind of friend I needed right now.

"Hey, Mitch."

"Dillan, bro! What are you doing on the mainland? I thought you were hunkered down at the Seafarer's."

"Change of plans; you got a minute?"

"Yeah, sure. You want anything to eat? I'm buying."

"Just a large coffee would be great man, thanks."

I told Mitch all about Buoy, my throat tightening with every word.

"Jesus . . . ." he said as he shook his head. "I can't believe it, but you know Buoy is an awesome swimmer. He might have made it out somehow."

"I keep telling myself that, but the ocean was insane. Anyway, it's probably not a good idea to get my hopes up."

"Listen, come with me. A bunch of us are meeting up at Jimmy's mother's place in Cherry Hill."

"Isn't that like an hour away?"

"Yeah, probably more in this weather, but what else do we have to do till this Sandy bitch passes?"

"You sure she won't mind? I mean how many guys are gonna be there?"

"I'm not sure, probably a few. It doesn't matter, she's cool. Have you met Catherine yet? She's quite the MILF!"

Jimmy was the youngest in our crowd, having just turned nineteen. He was one of the guys I'd shared an apartment with when I first moved to LBI and got hired as a guard. He waited tables when he wasn't guarding or surfing. His mother was probably hovering in her middle-to-upper forties.

"Christ, Mitch, you're whacked," I snapped, disgusted.

"Yeah, but . . . oh, never mind. I was just trying to distract you, that's all."

As we left, Katie promised she'd text once in a while to let us know what was happening in Manahawkin. I was hopeful there wouldn't be too much to report from Cherry Hill.

Power was out, trees were down and a whole lot of horny guys were ogling Jimmy's hot mom in the candlelight. Even I had to admit, Catherine was stunning. The gym equipment in their finished basement wasn't going to waste by any means. Occasionally, I would reach down to scratch Buoy's head just to be reminded of the bitter truth. My stomach clenched and my heart ached. It was all I could do to maintain my composure, while inside I just wanted to puke my guts out.

We played poker and drank beer. The guys put away massive amounts of chips and salsa, Oreos and pretzels. They talked about the great time we all had at last weeks' Clam Jam. I just listened. I wasn't up for small talk. After a few beers, everyone had an outrageous surfing or rescue tale to tell. It wasn't the worst place to be, surrounded by friends and camaraderie. Everyone was anxious though, worried about the island, our neighbors who had stayed, our beaches, our way of life. Sandy had already ruined my life and could do the same for many others.

By Wednesday, the worst of Sandy was over. Gary, who insisted on staying above the surf shop, had sent some pictures to our cells. I couldn't believe what I was seeing. None of us could. Dave and Joe's parents had evacuated to stay with family on the mainland, but the guys were just as anxious to get back there as I was. I had to get to the inn and look for Buoy. Even if the chance of his survival was minuscule, and I knew it was, I couldn't stand the idea of him lying there needing my help and suffering alone. He had been my best friend for many years and if his dead body had washed ashore, I needed to take care of him; not leave him there to . . . God knows what.

We thanked Catherine for her hospitality and stepped out into the gray blustery day. Jimmy, to his embarrassment, was banned from joining us, which I felt was probably a very sound decision. We felt pretty badly leaving them with no power, but together we made short work of the downed branches in the yard and driveway. It was the least we could do to thank her. Joe drove with me and Dave went with Mitch in the van.

There were plenty of downed power lines and debris in the streets of Cherry Hill. The good news was that the power companies and clean-up crews were already out there working. Our trip to Manahawkin was slowed by a few detours but we made it safely. I was glad that I had the Jeep because I was of the mindset that nothing was going to stop me. That was until we made it to Route 72. After waiting two hours in traffic, we got as far as Marsha Drive and were abruptly turned away by the National Guard. I tried to plead my case, got damn aggravated and almost ended up arrested.

Luckily, with one phone call the guys had another plan, one I wasn't sly enough to dream up on my own. We headed out to our friend Jake's parents' place in Barnegat Township. Again, the Jeep came in handy maneuvering through the partially flooded and littered streets. Jake had the foresight to bring his small fishing boat and jet ski there and dry dock them before the storm. By the time we arrived, he was tired of being cooped up with his parents and up for an expedition. We hitched the boat trailer to the Jeep and the jet ski to Jake's SUV and headed back to the bay.

Most of the roads were still flooded or covered with piles of bay mud and salt hay. After constantly being diverted by impassable roads, we were lucky to find a place where we could launch the craft. The plan was to pop onto the island, check out our places, take a few photos and meet back at the boat in an hour. We were probably breaking more than one state-of-emergency law but no one seemed to worry about it.

It was our home and we felt we had a right to be there. We suited up, the four of us in the motor boat and Jake on his jet ski.

"I'm going to dock as close to town as possible," Jake said. "I want to talk to Gary and check out the shop for myself."

The water, extremely choppy for the bay, was chock full of floating debris. I could only imagine the amount of crap that had already sunk. As the bow lifted and slammed down repeatedly, we held on, white knuckled, for fear of being thrown overboard. Mitch maneuvered around huge chunks of floating docks and decks, a refrigerator, gasoline jugs and an unmanned Bayliner craft. It was an incredibly surreal and dangerous situation. After a few hair-raising minutes, Jake veered the jet ski north. As he disappeared from sight, I hoped we hadn't made a stupid decision.

Mitch, who frequently boated in the bay, was taken aback by its newly defined shoreline. Finally, we found a dock that had survived and we were able to secure the boat and disembark. My hands were cramped, which made removing my wet suit difficult. As we tossed our wetties onto the dock, the blessed sun came out for the first time in four days. Maybe it was a sign.

The first thing to hit me was the sheer destruction; the second, the absence of humanity. We could hear the rumble of heavy machinery far in the distance, perhaps bulldozers and such. I wasn't interested in taking photos; my only thought was to make it home and find my dog. I ran as fast as I could toward Liberty Avenue where I'd turn right, toward the ocean, and get off the main drag. I came upon a couple of people who were dragging saturated items from their waterlogged homes. Obviously, they hadn't taken the mandatory evacuation seriously. Neither one had seen a black Lab wandering about, but one guy had noticed dog prints in the sand. Both told me they had been afraid for their lives.

My hopes were sinking fast. I barely noticed the homes that were torn wide open, the trailers positioned like fallen dominos, the smell of gas, the boats smashed into people's houses or the fact that I was sometimes running in very deep sand. I had but one mindset: getting home.

I certainly was worried about getting caught, especially after what happened at the checkpoint on Route 72, but I thought it worth the risk to whistle Buoy's call. Occasionally I would stop, take a deep breath and whistle as loud as I could. If he was anywhere near, and able to run, he would've come to me. I had just rounded Dolphin Avenue heading for Atlantic when I heard a growing rumble and turned to see military vehicles approaching from behind. I ducked under a home that had been lifted off its foundation which was probably the stupidest thing I'd ever done. Nothing about this house was stable. A slight breeze and I could've been a goner.

Three huge camo-draped Humvees rolled past me, shaking the ground as they went. I held my breath and slipped out quickly, apparently too quickly because I heard a menacing voice yell, "Civilian, halt!" How would I know there were troops peering out the back? The truck stopped at the end of the block and one soldier jumped out, looking incredibly intimidating, muscle jacked and weapon laden. I made another stupid decision: I ran.

I made it as far as Bay Avenue when a Blackhawk helicopter flew directly overhead. No way on God's green earth they could've sent that for me; still, my heart pounded guiltily. I ducked behind a partially uprooted bayberry bush and looked back at GI Joe, who was talking on his radio. Less than a minute later the convoy returned, picked him up, and drove off. Dear God, that was close! I was just a lifeguard trying to find his dog, not an international terrorist!

I sat, caught my breath and checked my watch. It was already time to return to the boat! Mission not accomplished. Mission failed miserably. My heart sank. As I rose, I spotted something tangled in the mess of roots: a photo. I wiped it free of dirt and sand. A man and woman were proudly holding a tiny baby. Neither of them looked familiar but it was very old. Somehow this delicate piece of paper had survived the storm when I was standing here surrounded by complete devastation. I tucked it in my shirt pocket and headed back to meet the guys, who were all talk as we suited up again.

"Did you see that house up the street with the roof torn off?"

"Hell, that was nothing. There's one on Beck that was torn from its foundation and had ended up across the street smashed into the Miller's house."

"Some lots were completely wiped clean, no evidence of the houses at all!"

"I think I'm in shock."

"I saw a bike rack in the middle of West Ave. I swear it's the one from Pearl Street Market."

"I saw Kelly's vintage Volvo buried in sand and seaweed."

"That sucks for him!"

"I tripped over a dead sea turtle, fell right on my face!" Dave exclaimed.

"That's gnarly, bro. I had a little trouble with the Guard. I ran out of time and never made it to the inn," I added feeling despondent. If a sea turtle couldn't survive......

"No sign of Buoy then, huh?" Mitch asked.

"Well, there were some footprints, but it could've been any dog, maybe even a Search and Rescue."

"Sorry, man."

"Yeah, that seriously sucks."

"Don't give up!"

I held my breath for fear of losing my shit and climbed into the boat. The bay wasn't any calmer, even with the improving weather. We were about halfway to the mainland when we saw a small Coast Guard ship approaching from the south. A booming voice raged over our motors.

"Gentlemen, this waterway is closed to civilians! Make haste to the mainland or you will face charges!"

Mitch recognized the guy and waved.

" – **and be careful!**" he added in a more sympathetic tone.

"My cousin Billy," Mitch said sheepishly.

"I guess *he'll* be pretty busy for a while."

"Yeah, thanks to guys like us," Joe snickered.

As we got close to the mainland it was a relief to see Jake standing by the Jeep waiting for us. He gave us some bad news.

"I took a quick walk with Gary. Beach Patrol headquarters' overhead doors were blown out; it's loaded with sand. I'd say it's toast."

"Damn! What a freakin' shame!"

"And the CHEGG took on three feet of water!"

"I guess we won't be having Wing Night for a while."

"Awe Jesus."

"Shit."

We loaded the craft and returned to his place as darkness was falling. While we ate a hot dinner prepared on the grill, Jake gave us Gary's rendition of surviving the storm and his regret at not leaving. The four of us gratefully accepted the hospitality offered by Jake's parents and spent the night on sofas, beds and recliners.

By morning, social media had spread the sad word, the beloved icon of LBI, the beat-up old hunting shack that sat along the causeway and welcomed folks to the island for countless years, had succumbed to Sandy's wrath. To add insult to injury, no one would be admitted to the island for at least five to ten days. I guess I would be driving home to visit my parents after all. There wasn't anything more I could do here.

Buoy

DANG, I'VE BEEN MISSING Dillan! The girl from the sea has been nice enough but not what I'm used to. She doesn't smell like Dillan, play catch, or give massages like Dillan. She doesn't ask me to do my tricks for treats, like pile cookies on my nose. She doesn't straddle me, wrap her arms around me and rock me gently to and fro. She doesn't kiss the top of my head. How will I teach her these things? I couldn't find my tennis balls or Frisbee and my couch has been soaked with water. I miss Dillan. Dillan was my home.

She has taken good care of me though and has been super cuddly in her own way. We've had fun together. We nap together during the day and at night we go on adventures, sometimes even swim.

We had saved each other from the raging sea and we needed each other. Who else would open my blue can? Who would pour my water? Who would scratch my head? And she needed me too. I had to protect her from all the new humans, noises and smells that had invaded our territory. We'd be best buddies until Dillan came home and I'd guard her with my life.

Every time I jump on the bed, Dillan's scent becomes weaker and my heart heavier. Why isn't he here? One day, while we were napping, I thought I heard Dillan signal to me. I raised my head to find my muzzle tangled in the girl's long hair. Rudely awakened, she sat up, then snuggled back into the covers. I sat there straight as an arrow and cocked my head, listening intently. All I heard was the rumbling of the big trucks, as usual. It must have been a dream, a wonderful dream. I laid back down against the girl and sighed. I miss my best friend.

HER

I HAD BEGUN TO lose track of time, but about a week after I came to in the battered old Seafarer's Inn, I heard the most miraculous sound: church bells intricately chiming, playing a lovely song. It wasn't just the gong, gong, gong that one might expect but two complete melodies floating on the breeze. Buoy cocked his head and listened, seeming to enjoy them as much as I. They made me feel hopeful and less lonely. They rang again in the evening; a bit later I noticed the street lights on the main boulevard had come on. I guess the bells, which must have been coming from the church a couple of blocks away, were electronic. Excitedly, I tried the toaster but no such luck. It would have been nice to toast the stale bread and have something warm to eat. Grape jelly on limp crackers was getting old.

I was glad that Buoy and I had already explored the gift shops and attractions nearby. It would have been nearly impossible to go unseen with the streetlights on. In the wind-and water-damaged shops we'd spied LBI T-shirts and sweat pants, postcards and beach bags. Although I would've loved some girl's clothes, I didn't want to steal anything. At least I'd found out I was in New Jersey, but it didn't help to jog my memory one bit.

The Crust and Crumb Bakery, Thundering Surf Water Park, Country Kettle Fudge and Chowda Shops all looked so sad, battered and broken. (What I wouldn't have done for a fresh bread bowl filled with steaming hot chowder!) A huge pile of debris had been deposited on what looked like a baseball field. I'd sat on a bench and imagined being there before the storm. The sunny weather, the village full of people having fun, enjoying yummy treats and coasting down the waterslides at incredible speed. Families were playing miniature golf and some little imp was trying to fib about his score; older siblings scolding him. Later the whole family would indulge in ice cream cones: mint chocolate chip, butter pecan, cookies and cream. I wish I had been here before this Sandy storm hit to enjoy the crazy melee of summer fun!

Three days later, another storm landed! This time snow fell. It looked like a little dusting of sparkling sugar covering the sand and the waterlogged carpets that the Coral Seas had placed on the curb. I didn't remember the last time I had seen snow. I was wondering if I could be from the south. I wanted to go outside and touch it, to feel its frostiness first hand, but heading out in daylight wasn't without risk. Rescue and recovery activity was going full swing. Occasionally, a parade of huge dump trucks piled high with sand would rumble by and Buoy and I had seen more people with suitcases leaving the Engleside the night before. From my perch behind the bushes at the Windward Inn, I heard the policeman say that he would drive them as far as the McDonald's on Route 72. I guess they had gotten too cold and given up. Maybe they just needed a hot shower, warm meal and some normalcy.

The norm here had become helicopters circling, Long Beach Township and State Police cars patrolling, Coast Guard and State Police Marine ships scouting the shore and bay waters, the National Guard protecting, utility trucks repairing and the constant beep, beep, beep of front end loaders combined with the rumble of bulldozers rebuilding the dunes – a regular military zone! I imagine normalcy is quite undervalued until a catastrophe like this happens.

A cold wind came, bringing snowflakes in through the hole in the wall. I tried to catch one on my tongue. It was silly and made me giggle. I guess this would be as close as I got to the snow for now. I thought about covering the hole with some plywood but thought better of it. Anyone might notice a change and investigate. I had lots of sweatshirts, pants and socks available so I wasn't really that cold. I certainly didn't want to be dragged away for looting or squatting or whatever you call living in someone else's home and eating their food. Maybe in a perfect world it's called dog sitting, but here under this military regime, I was pretty sure it was illegal.

The snow was fleeting. It only stayed on the ground until the next day when the weather returned to a slight chill. Buoy and I continued our nightly explorations in the unlit sections of town for another week or so. We crossed the main drag, headed west and saw that the lights had come on across the bay, a hopeful sign. By now our roads were mostly clear of sand except for some very large hills here and there. The huge piles of useless fixtures, lumber, siding, and appliances that had been placed outside of homes and businesses were disappearing bit by bit. Boats which had moored on land had been removed and even the hot tub on Chatsworth Avenue was gone. Police and utility workers had come from as far away as Louisiana and Alabama to help. It was heartwarming. I wanted to get out there too and decided that I'd set a deadline. If Dillan didn't return in three more days, I would take Buoy and march up the street to the Engleside, where I would introduce myself to whatever authorities might be there.

Over the next couple of days, more and more people returned to the island. I could tell by the number of civilian cars and candlelit windows we passed as we walked. Some rare and lucky homes were being powered by generators.

I had quite the collection of treasures by now. Any item that may have been someone's memento was carried home and stored in our little bedroom. The owners had lost so much. These items needed to survive the storm and not end up in a landfill somewhere. My favorites were salvaged the first night, the blue-haired mermaid doll, the wedding photo and the *I Love You, Mom*, mini plate. I used a safety pin to fashion the tiny plate into a decorative brooch, my one and only piece of jewelry.

That morning as we turned in, I could feel our time was coming to an end. I estimated that I had been here around three weeks. I'd enjoyed playing house with Buoy and after a while began to find fun in our nightly cat and mouse games with the patrolling military. Thank goodness, as far as I was aware, it consisted of more hide than seek! Every day the island was becoming more and more populated. Soon the curfew would be lifted, but was that really a bad thing? If

I just walked out into the daylight would anyone know I hadn't just arrived? Would I really stand out as a stranger or would I blend right in? I could say I was Dillan's girlfriend and had come to look for Buoy. What if Dillan was still with this Anna girl or if they asked me where he was? I felt a sob come to my chest and a tear run down my cheek. Maybe he wasn't ever coming back, maybe he couldn't. As I was nodding off to sleep, Buoy's muzzle on my neck, I decided what to do. I'd keep positive, get to work cleaning out this old inn and just wing it.

DILLAN

RIVING WEST WASN'T WITHOUT difficulty. The storm had left a mess, including thirty-six inches of snow as far as West Virginia. I should have flown, but I thought the drive would give me time to clear my head. I needed to make a plan. Would I return to the island and complete my contract with Ian MacAvery or abandon the project and move on? My parents would probably beg me to stay in Cincinnati but I needed to be near the sea. Perhaps it was time to return to Cocoa Beach. I could meet up with old friends, get my guarding job back, even visit the Keys on occasion. I could go anywhere the water was warm enough to swim. Hell, I'd always wanted to spend some time in Hawaii. Now, I didn't have to worry about quarantining Buoy.

Shit! Goddamned freaking storm! I totally hated Sandy!

Mom and Dad were thrilled with my surprise visit but heartbroken by the bad news. Buoy had been a big part of their lives too. Mom always referred to him as her second son. Dad had spent months helping me to train him when he was a pup and we had taken him on all our fishing and camping trips. Buoy may have been a rescue, but he also rescued us by chasing a hungry bear out of our campsite one year. He was the best dog a family could have. As we sat around the kitchen table, sipping wine and feeling somber, I called Jack but it went straight to voice mail.

That evening, the majority of television channels were still airing the devastation that Sandy had left in her wake. The now-coined Superstorm Sandy had been over one thousand miles wide at one point. It met up with a high-pressure cold front to the north and made landfall during a full moon at high tide. It truly was a raging freak of nature. Over two hundred people had lost their lives, a replica of the tall ship HMS Bounty had sunk off the Outer Banks, killing the captain and a crew member, electrical substations had exploded and fire had wiped out entire communities. I knew first-hand what it had done, both inside and out.

Two days later, as I was just about to force down a bite of Mom's pancakes, Jack finally returned my call. He sounded totally wired, maybe on coffee, maybe still on adrenalin, as he recounted everything that had happened in the few days since I had left. Thankfully, he seemed to have no idea that the guys and I had popped on the island for a quick expedition and I wanted it to stay that way. He and his wife Carole were fine, though their home had sustained some water damage. Beach Haven's public safety personnel had stayed at the Engleside for the duration of the storm where he and the other rescuers had been through some pretty hairy times. Whether in trucks, small boats or jet skis, many dedicated people had put their lives in jeopardy to save others. Luckily none of the first responders had been injured though one of Beach Haven's fire trucks had become disabled in a sand-and water-covered roadway while responding to a structure fire. Jack animatedly described the harrowing rescue of a man who was trapped as a huge wave slammed into the Sea Shell Resort, shattering the floor-to-ceiling windows and pinning him behind the bar. He told me about a utility pole that had fallen against the Seafarer's and made a good-sized hole in the facade. Fortunately, he said, the building, now sporting some damaged awnings and gutters, still looked sound even though the storm surge had breached the dune and carried away my grill and hammock.

Some of the emergency personnel were moving to a more suitable command post at the EOC building, freeing up rooms at the Engleside for displaced locals. The police station, which sat on elevated ground, received no water damage but Beach Patrol headquarters was damaged beyond repair, just as Gary had said, and our barracks on Amber Street had been hard hit as well. The towns which embraced the beach replenishment program had fared better than those who were afraid of losing their million-dollar ocean views. They now had a multimillion-dollar mess.

Jack's duties were many and varied, including carting disheartened locals to a mainland shelter once they grew weary from the cold and lack of normal utilities.

When I finally got the opportunity to ask about Buoy, he mentioned having seen dog prints in the area and had notified the Stafford Township animal control officer who had not yet come across any black Labs. I knew first-hand how treacherous the ocean was that day. Why had I still been hoping? Jack made a point of telling me that he also had his officers, the firemen, EMTs and even the Louisiana state police that came to help keeping an eye out for Buoy and not to rush back. He would call me immediately if there was any word, one way or another. He reinforced the fact that the National Guard was protecting the island from looters (didn't I know it!) and the electricity had not yet been restored to my section of town. So, I conceded to hang out with my folks for a few more days, while keeping an eye on social media and texting with my friends.

I loved my mom and dad. They were wonderful, generous parents so I felt particularly guilty feeling landlocked after only a week. When I was a kid, they indulged me no matter what my fluctuating interests were: the Little League thing, the skateboard thing, the guitar playing thing, the NFL and MLB fan thing, but it was my love for the water that was nurtured most generously.

Back in 1965, my parents had wanted to honeymoon some place exotic but because Dad was still studying law and Mom student nursing, there wasn't exactly an abundance of money. They decided Florida had a lot more to offer than just a warm climate. As the years went by, Dad became a partner and made a pretty good living. Mom worked as a pediatric nurse. In 1985, on their twentieth anniversary, even though they could have gone anywhere, they returned to Cocoa Beach. Sentimentality for them, just good luck for me. That's where, at the age of forty, my mom gave birth to a preemie me. We stayed there for six weeks until I was healthy enough to travel home and returned every year to celebrate my birthday.

I was glad to know the massive hurricane had stayed out to sea as it traveled north past Florida, creating only minimal beach erosion and great surfing conditions in Cocoa Beach – if only Long Beach Island had been so lucky.

I spent my days picking on home-cooked meals and catching up on what's-what with who's-who. I wanted like hell to chow down on Mom's cooking but I just didn't have an appetite. I could tell by the way she looked at me that she was worried. Though I didn't honestly believe it, I told her I'd be fine – in time. I just had so much sorrow and guilt to deal with.

Retirement had totally agreed with my folks. Dad's golf score had improved and he finally had time to build his model airplanes. Mom was thinking about entering some of her hand-sewn quilts in a show and had been teaching a pediatric BLS course for parents at the hospital, just as she had taught me when I first started lifeguarding.

Their major project of late was to find the perfect home in Cocoa Beach and get out of the north for good. We talked about their plan to put the house on the market and they enlisted me to help with a few small home improvement projects to help get the house ready. Mom loved HGTV, but honestly I think they just wanted to keep me occupied so I wouldn't dwell on our missing family member.

At night, I sat on my old bed looking at the basket of dog toys in the corner of my room. Mom had placed four new toys, still with the tags, sitting on top. I thought about how much Buoy would have loved them and how he would look right now lying there chewing on them – the big old mush. My stomach ached. I guess we could donate them to a shelter but I'd leave that up to Mom; there was no rush.

It took some deep thought but I decided I wasn't a quitter. I'd go see how the Seafarer's Inn had fared during the storm. I could have asked Jack to check it out further, but I knew how busy he was. He had made it sound salvageable so, if Mac still wanted me to, I'd do my best to repair the damage and finish the job.

My parents didn't want me driving straight through so Dad booked me a room at the Westin Convention Center in Pittsburgh. He'd been there before and told me I'd love their pool. A good long swim was just what I needed to relax. It had been way too long. I left them with hugs, tears and kisses. I wouldn't be returning for Christmas this year but I promised to visit them, in Florida, in the spring. Until then, I knew I had my work cut out for me.

A day and a half later as I drove east on Route 72, I couldn't help but notice the roadside was littered with placards for contractors. Heading over the causeway that led to LBI, I turned just in time to see the now empty marshland where The Shack had stood. For generations, it had been the unofficial welcome mat for returning vacationers. Apparently, it had been a very well-made hunting shack. What people had seen for the last decade or so were just the walls braced up with randomly placed pieces of lumber. The roof had fallen in some time ago and the floor had rotted away leaving an empty shell. Still it was kind of an icon, which proudly wore a huge American flag or seasonal Christmas decorations. Yeah, it was just a crappy old shack that had been falling down for years but the fact that Sandy had obliterated it made me feel like shit.

The Acme parking lot had been turned into one huge garbage dump. I tried to imagine the amount of money that had gone to waste and the amount of waste the earth was going to have to consume. It made me sick. I had studied a bit about the effects of dumping trash in the ocean. I knew we humans were killing not only the sea creatures but the entire planet as well. I could only hope that this trash would be sorted and the metals and plastics recycled. Still, the amount of liquid pollutants that had entered the bay must have been astronomical. What would it do to the ecosystem of our fragile barrier island?

Many people had already returned to the island. They were driving with purpose, outside examining homes or tossing damaged goods by the roadside – refrigerators, couches, chairs, hot water heaters – anything you could think of. I noticed the California Grill was open, stopped in and ordered coffee. There were a few folks inside; each had an interesting story to tell. They advised me that the Surf City firehouse had cleaning supplies, food, blankets, a hot meal and friendly vibe if I needed anything. I wasn't sure what I needed yet. I had no idea what kind of a mess I would walk into. All I knew was that I needed to investigate the property and call Mac, ASAP.

I made my way down Long Beach Boulevard until it turned into Bay Avenue. I was almost home. Of course, I kept an eye open for Buoy – I couldn't help it. I drove past one of my favorite ice cream joints, The Frosted Mug, just to find a huge pile of trash in front. Damn, I could only hope they'd get the place up and running by summer. There was nothing like an ice-cold root beer float. I turned onto Pearl Street, made a left on Atlantic Avenue, then a left on Coral and parked on the corner. I grabbed my duffle bag and jumped out of the Jeep. There was some residual sand built up along the curb and on the front yards of the neighboring homes – nothing horrible though. Maybe it wouldn't be too bad. As I rounded the corner, The Seafarer's looked okay, except for some loose shutters and ripped awnings. The utility pole that had hit the inn was long gone but the hole in the facade remained. I took in the water line against the house, which was high enough to cause my stomach to sink. "Shit," I mumbled.

I pushed the door open just as a huge dump truck rumbled by. I was shocked by what I saw! The common room was empty. There was no old couch, sand or debris in sight. The baseboards had been removed and the bottom portion of sheetrock cut out. I had no idea what to think. Mac hadn't mentioned anything but perhaps he had sent someone to start the gutting process. Maybe my bros had taken pity on me, knowing a full year of my life had gone down the toilet.

I carried my bag up the stairs and glanced into the kitchenette. There was a hole in the plywood that I had nailed over the window – hurricane force winds, crazy shit. I went to the bedroom to drop my bag and stopped short. I fell to my knees in disbelief and relief. Buoy was lying on the bed and looking at me with sleepy eyes. He bounded off the bed and into my arms.

"It's a miracle!" I cried as Buoy wildly licked my face. He jumped on me, knocking me off balance and laid on top of me, his body wiggling every which way. "Oh my God, I don't believe it!"

I laughed as hard as a person can laugh without busting and then burst into tears, holding my best friend in my arms. As he continued licking my face, I just laid there with my eyes closed reveling in the joy and relief. My best friend was alive and well! When I finally opened my eyes, I almost had a heart attack. Standing over us, looking at me quizzically, was the most beautiful woman I had ever seen. I knew it was too good to be true. I had died and gone to heaven.

"Hi Dillan," she said in a purely melodic voice, "I'm, ummm, Sandy."

I was struck speechless, mesmerized by her blue-green eyes. Surely, she had manifested from my deepest imagination, but Buoy's weight on top of me certainly felt real enough.

"Hey," I choked out, completely flummoxed.

The girl held out her hand and helped me to a sitting position, then she sat cross-legged facing me. Buoy sat, but begrudgingly, his head darting back and forth between us.

"You rescued my dog?" I asked with amazement.

"I think it was the other way around," she said, in a voice that reminded me of tiny chiming bells.

I wanted to ask her questions, but my mind was having difficulty formulating a complete thought as I stared into her sparkling eyes. "What happened?" I ultimately inquired.

"Well, it's the strangest thing. I don't remember – anything. I just woke up here with a big gash on my head and a titanic case of amnesia!"

"Wow! Looks like you had a sand facial!" I said as I pointed to the red scar on her temple.

"Yeah, it seriously hurt at first, but it healed pretty quickly."

I reached over and scratched Buoy on his head, just the way he liked it. "Last I saw him, he ran into the ocean, just as the storm was landing. I tried to find him and I would have kept trying but Jack, the police captain, forced me to leave the island. It just about killed me."

"I really think Buoy had something to do with bringing me here."

"That sounds like him. My buddy – always the hero." I put my arm around Buoy and pulled him close. "This guy has been my constant companion since I was a kid. He helped me through a lot of shit. Oh sorry, I mean . . . stuff." She waved off my profanity with a sunny grin.

"Thank you for leaving the provisions. It certainly made things easier, but I'm sorry there's not much left."

"So, let me get this straight. You've been here – no heat, no electric, or water – for how long?"

"A few weeks, I guess. I didn't keep track of the days. When I first came to, there was a lot of water downstairs and it was pretty desolate around here. Once the people started to return, I felt it was safe enough to go outside, so I watched what the others were doing and I started cleaning the place out."

"You did all that, by yourself?

"Well some, but Henry from down the block showed me how to remove the baseboard and the damaged part of the walls. He's been a wealth of knowledge and it was so convenient to have all the tools we needed right here!"

"The old man from the huge brown house on the corner?"

"Yes, why?"

"That curmudgeon won't talk to anyone. He barely ever leaves his house. He's well-noted for being a hermit and chasing noisy kids away from his property."

"He's been perfectly nice to me. Did you know he's an author? He has published a whole series of murder mysteries. He showed them to me. What a fantastic library he has in his home – I'm so glad he didn't have any water damage."

"I didn't know that."

"He writes under a nom de plume: Michael Stocks."

"Seriously, he's Michael Stocks? Shit, no wonder he never leaves his place; he's famous. He must treasure his privacy. Now it makes a lot of sense."

"At first, he seemed a little flustered when Buoy and I met him, but after we talked a while he was very friendly. He invited us in and gave me a cup of hot tea. Poor man, he hasn't had the happiest life, even with all that success."

"I'm sorry to hear that."

"He was very helpful to me though. He knew enough to take some pictures of the damage here. He said if you want them he'd send them to your phone when you got back. Of course, I didn't know if you were ever coming back."

"I wasn't so sure either, but I'm stoked that I did!"

"Henry even helped me drag the soaking couch out to the curb and, believe me, it was heavy! I was worried about him being so old but he's really strong and healthy. He even swims when the water's warm enough."

"I guess I had the old guy pegged wrong."

"I think so. I'm very fond of him already. I'm sure you'll be too, once you get to know him."

"You certainly have a way with people!" I looked at her thin arms, scratches and bruises here and there. "This isn't easy work. I'm glad you had an instructor. I'm grateful to you and Henry for all the work you've done but most importantly, I thank you for taking care of Buoy. I can't explain how much he means to me."

"Buoy was taking care of me just as much as I was taking care of him. He's great company. I think we've become rather close," she said to me as she winked at him. "I was feeling fairly useless when I saw all the clean-up activity going on. Once I met Henry, I figured why not start right here? When it's done maybe I can go help someone else."

Go? Go? I didn't want her to go anywhere. I just met her. "Well, there's still plenty of work to do here, as you can see. The storm's set me back a few months at least!"

Sandy just smiled at me, her eyes twinkling. "Well, I guess you better tell me what to do next!"

"First things first, I need to call my parents and Mac, then I think we should take a walk around and check things out. I have to let Jack and my friends know that Buoy is alive and well, too; and I think we should go to the store and get some food and see what's going on with the electricity." For someone who couldn't speak a few minutes ago, now it seemed I couldn't shut up. I was rambling and on the verge of making a total fool of myself. Poor Sandy couldn't get a word in if she tried.

Meanwhile as my heart and mind raced, I was finding it hard to believe it was all true. Buoy was alive after all these weeks! He'd been well fed and cared for. Looking completely contented, he lay down next to the girl and placed his head on her leg.

After sharing the amazing news with my parents, I called Jack and Mac. Jack couldn't believe what had been going on right under his nose. Mac didn't pick up and there was no option to leave a voicemail. I'd have to try him again later.

As I headed down the stairs, the real crux of the matter made its way into my brain. Sandy had no idea who she was! Did she have a family, parents or a husband that were worried sick about her? I'd have to check with Jack to see if a missing person report had been filed for the most gorgeous woman in the world, the one who'd been sitting not three feet from me, wearing only my boxers and T-shirt. Unfortunately, it was the last thing I wanted to do.

ALEXANDER HENRY

OCTOBER 2012

THE WIND STOPPED ABRUPTLY but I could still hear the roar of the ocean as I crept slowly out of bed. Honestly, I was afraid to peer out into the doom. I had weathered through hurricanes before, even the Storm of 1962, but this time I was truly afraid. Perhaps because I was an old man now. I should have been ready to meet my Maker. I should have just relaxed and let Sandy have me, but it didn't feel right. There was something more I had to accomplish; I could feel it in my old bones.

I pulled back the heavy drape and looked to the sky. A glorious full moon was beaming down onto the street and neighboring homes, its beams reflecting in the rushing water which coursed along Atlantic Avenue. Only a few inches of the ocean had crept up my driveway. Such was the benefit of living on a slightly elevated piece of land. She *had* known what she was talking about. Maybe the old house and I would be lucky enough to survive this one too.

Just then, a loud crack defiled the silence. A flash of light and simultaneous boom as the service wires were ripped from the connection head on my home. I made my way to the other side of the room and peered outside. As I had suspected, a telephone pole had fallen up the street. Unfortunately, it smashed into the front of the old Seafarer's Inn – only one of many casualties this night, I was sure. I sat in my old cushioned chair and waited. It would only be a few minutes now . . . .

SANDY

WHAT A HEARTWARMING REUNION between a boy and his dog! I didn't know if my heart could stand the extreme happiness engulfing the room. I was so holding back the tears and at the same time fighting a burst of giggles as Buoy's body shook and quivered with pure joy. It was simply a beautiful moment to experience. I reveled in it, even as a bystander.

Buoy watched Dillan's every move, as if he might disappear if he took his eyes off him. It was hard for me to look away as well. He was rather handsome, even though he still wore the weird dreadlocks. Somehow, they suited him. Maybe I was just lonely for human companionship and conversation, but secretly I hoped he wouldn't disappear as well.

Dillan left the room to make some phone calls with Buoy on his heels. I pulled on some of his sweat pants and a zip-up hoodie. I felt uncomfortable wearing his clothes now, as if he might mind. We met at the front door where Dillan hesitated, then spotted the leash I'd hung on the newel post and snapped it on Buoy's collar.

"Sorry, boy. I understand why you disobeyed me now, but I can't take that chance again. My heart won't take it."

I was afraid to tell him that Buoy and I had been swimming a few times and under the cover of darkness to boot. Maybe it was reckless of me but the first time wasn't exactly by choice.

It was sunny, breezy and refreshingly cool. I couldn't wait to show him around and explain all that had been happening the last few weeks. We had so much to talk about. Hopefully he would share his life story with me, even though I was apprehensive to hear about Anna from Big Sur. What if she was still in the picture?

"Why are we going this way?" I asked tentatively as we marched directly toward the Engleside Inn. "Don't you want to see the beach?"

"My friend Jack wants to meet you and see Buoy for himself. He doesn't actually believe my 'cockamamie' story. And we have to check to see if anyone's reported you missing. Jack was going to make a couple calls."

My heart sank like a stone. I had been so happy just a few seconds ago, now it all might suddenly come to an end. "You told him then – that I have amnesia and I've been living in your house?"

"Yeah, but he's cool. He won't make you do anything you don't want to."

I envisioned myself being driven off the island in the back of a Beach Haven police car with tears in my eyes. "I don't want to leave," I whispered. "I really like it here."

"What about your family? You must have someone who's worried sick about you. I know I would be."

Dillan swallowed hard and looked at the ground as he walked. Buoy walked alongside him, with a frisky step, just happy to be by his side. I was really ticked that he shared my secret with the police. It wasn't his secret to share.

"Maybe. I don't know. It's hard to imagine what might be behind me. All I can think about is now and what lies ahead. Does that sound harsh or ungrateful?"

"No, not at all. How can you embrace a past you can't remember?"

Our short walk to the Engelside ended when we spotted Dillan's friend Captain Jack in the parking lot. He and another man were unloading food and supplies from an ambulance.

"Hey Jack!" Dillan yelled.

Jack's jaw dropped when he saw Buoy, whose tail wagged fiercely.

"I don't friggin' believe it!" he said astonished as he bent down and petted him. "I looked all over this island for you, mister! How the devil . . . ?"

"I'm sorry," I said sheepishly. "Buoy and I were holed up at the Seafarer's."

"Captain Jack Foster, this is Sandy – the girl I told you about. She's been taking care of Buoy for me," Dillan added, gallantly coming to my defense.

"Really nice to meet you, Sandy," the police captain said as he shook my hand, holding it a bit longer than necessary. "I don't know how no one noticed you two were quartered at the inn. We'd definitely have invited you to stay here with us!"

"We did all right, once the ocean water drained out. Luckily, Dillan had left the place well stocked with food and water."

"You told me a bit about her, Dillan; but you failed to relay how truly lovely she is," Jack commented, as he scrutinized me top to bottom. "That looks like a relatively new injury," he stated as he gave me the once over. "How did it happen?"

"I'm not sure, but it seems to be healing well."

"That head wound may have contributed to your amnesia. I'd be happy to take you over to the Southern Ocean Medical Center."

I didn't want to go to a hospital, no way, no how! "No thanks, I'm feeling A-okay."

"Well, I can't force you to go, but I would highly recommend you get checked out. Just think about it. Meanwhile, I'll do some investigative work regarding your identity."

"That would be really kind of you."

"Not kind really – it's my job," he replied as he seemed to be seriously studying all the angles of my face. "Would you mind if I took a couple of photos of you for comparison?"

I don't know why I felt hesitant, "Um, I guess not."

"All right, just stand straight, put your hair behind your ears and don't smile."

"Okay." I stood tall but felt insecure and uneasy.

"All right, maybe one profile and one smiling – that's good. Got it. Why don't you bring Sandy by the barracks and we'll scan her fingerprints into the system?

"Will do. Thanks Jack," Dillan said, as he peered into the ambulance. What's all this stuff?"

"Donations for the displaced families and volunteers that are staying here. I'm amazed by the number of people who would put their lives on hold to come over here and help us. It's renewed my faith in humanity."

Dillan offered to help the men carry the items inside but his friend insisted that they had it covered.

"Can I help you with anything?" the captain asked.

"I think you have enough on your plate, Jack. Anyway, Sandy got a jump on things. She's quite the carpenter!"

"Really?" Jack replied, sounding curious. "Maybe that's a clue! Do you need a place to stay while we figure things out?"

I looked at Dillan questioningly.

"Thanks for the offer, Jack," Dillan answered, "but Sandy's more than welcome to stay with us."

"Yes, I'll be staying with Dillan," I added, with a certain sense of relief.

"Sure, that's great. I'm glad you're back and that Buoy's safe and sound," Jack said, as he shook Dillan's hand and clapped him on the back. "I'll do everything I can to get you home again, Sandy. I'll let you know as soon as I have any information for you."

"I really appreciate it, Captain Jack," I said, feeling less enthusiastic than I should have.

"I'll be talking to you both soon," he said, as he returned to his work.

"To the beach then?" Dillan asked as he took my hand.

"Definitely," I replied. Buoy knew what *beach* meant and he strained at the leash.

I was relieved that we were heading away from the policeman. I couldn't bear being taken away after waiting so long for Dillan's return. The way he'd looked at me made me uncomfortable, like I was a criminal or something.

"How long have you lived here?" I asked, as we walked between the Engleside and what was left of the Sea Shell Motel.

"A year and um . . . five months."

"Oh, I thought you were a local. What brought you to the island?"

"Honestly, the ocean. I love the water. Since I was a kid I've wanted to live by the sea. So, I lifeguard and follow the seasons. I stayed in California for a while and almost settled down there. That's when I took up carpentry, but it didn't work out. It seems I wasn't meant to be in any one place for too long. I have to ebb and flow with the tide, I guess."

The dune was in pretty good shape as the Army Corp of Engineers had been hard at work rebuilding the berm. The three of us only had to drop down a couple of feet to get on the newly rebuilt beach. Bulldozers were still hard at work pushing the sand in from the shore.

"I feel that way too, somehow – drawn to the ocean. It just makes me happy," I yelled to Dillan over the din.

We walked along without talking for a while; Buoy acting anxious to get to the water. We took off our shoes, pulled up our pant legs and waded in.

"Aren't you cold?" Dillan asked through gritted teeth.

"A little, but it's refreshing!"

He shivered dramatically. "So, I have to ask: Is Sandy your real name?"

"Gosh, I hope not! Unfortunately, it was the first thing that came into my head when I met Henry."

"Perfect choice!" he yelled as he ran ahead.

I followed behind for a while then ran past them and sat facing the sea. The sun felt warm, the breeze cool – Dillan and Buoy sat beside me. It was nice to finally have him here.

"They told me it was destroyed, but from here, apart from the mountains of sand around it, it doesn't look that bad."

"What's that?"

"It *was* Beach Patrol headquarters," he said sadly. "Wanna go take a look?"

"Sure."

We ran up the dune to the small building. Some of the cedar shakes had been torn away, the overhead door on the south end was opened a few feet and the one on the ocean side was gone entirely. Inside, the walls were tattered and the building empty, except for copious amounts of sand.

"There was a deck," he said looking down at the few pieces of straggly lumber left under our feet. "Every morning we'd meet up here, rehash the Five A's of Lifeguarding and get our equipment and assignments for the day."

We sat on one of the two remaining benches facing the ocean. Buoy placed his muzzle on Dillan's knees.

"I'm so sorry. I'm sure they'll repair or rebuild it. These islanders seem resilient!"

"They're nothing, if not that!" he said as he scratched Buoy behind the ears.

We sat in silence for a few moments before I asked, "What are the five A's of lifeguarding?"

"Oh, that's just something the chief drilled into our brains every day before we headed out. You need to have the right attitude and stay alert; in other words, be confident in your ability and no cell phones while on duty."

"Well that makes sense. You can't be texting or playing games when people's lives are in your hands. What's the rest?"

"To be aware of any changes in the ocean, be assertive enough to manage any situation, and to be able to take action immediately."

"That's quite a bit to manage at once."

"I guess, but after a while it becomes second nature, like breathing."

"There's quite a lot to lifeguarding, isn't there?"

"Well there's a ton of training, both mental and physical: there's lifesaving techniques, CPR, first aid, then there's the fun stuff like the tournaments. You know, it's strange how easy you are to talk to. I feel like you're the only person in the world who won't judge me for being a twenty-seven-year-old lifeguard."

"I just thought of one more A: being altruistic."

"Yeah, you're right. It's a 'give all of yourself' job. Almost like being a concierge for the island."

"I'd say if you're doing what you love and saving lives in the process, then you're in exactly the right place."

"Thanks, I wish Anna had felt that way," he blurted.

"Your girlfriend?" I asked, tentatively.

"My fiancée, for a while. We almost got married but she wanted me to be more, to have more. I wasn't enough for her," he said sadly.

I felt badly for my new friend. Not being *enough* for someone must hurt, but it also means they aren't the right someone. I wanted him to feel more positive so I asked, "How many lives did you save last summer?"

"I pulled out, oh . . . probably around thirty who got into trouble. We performed CPR on two people; one poor guy dropped right on the sand in front of us. He'd had a heart attack, just walking along with his family. We also aided a woman who slipped and cracked her head on the jetty. The highlight of the summer though, was freeing a dolphin that was tangled in a fishing net."

"That's exciting, Dillan. How did you do it?"

"It was strange how easy it was. It just swam out there, back and forth, coming closer to shore each time. We could see the net in the binoculars, so we called for back up and went out on our boards. It swam right up to us, like it knew we were there to help. I totally wanted to pet it, to help calm it down, but I was afraid I might frighten it more."

"They feel like vinyl and firmer than you'd imagine."

"How do you know? Have you touched one?"

"I'm not sure. Maybe I've just read it somewhere, but you should be proud of what you do, Dillan."

"I guess, but more people probably get hurt jaywalking across the boulevard or while riding their bikes."

"I doubt it. I wonder what my occupation could be . . . ."

"Well, it's hard to guess, seeing I just met you, but you have a kind spirit so I'd say you're an elementary school teacher, or a veterinarian."

"Maybe I'm a lifeguard too! I know I love the water, like you."

"It's quite possible. You know, you're unusually easy to talk too. I can't believe I just *found* you living in *my* place with *my* dog! Where the hell did you come from, girl?"

"Your guess is as good as mine, but somehow I feel this is the right place to be. The island's a shambles and I think I can help people. I may be little, but I'm strong!" I flexed my biceps, then grimaced with strain. He dismissed my silliness with a smile and shake of his dreadlocked head.

"If you want to rebuild the island then you need to keep your strength up. Let's go get something to eat," he said, "I'm starving."

We headed back toward the inn and climbed into his Jeep. Buoy didn't mind jumping in the back. He seemed thrilled with the possibility of an adventure. It was an adventure for me also, as I saw more of the recovery efforts as we headed toward town. People voiced their opinions regarding the hurricane with spray paint, plywood and business marquis. In large white wooden letters, *"H O P E"* over the door of the Bagel Shack. Joey's Pizza, *"Water Up To Our Eyeballs."* Outside the Island Surf and Sail shop: *"What doesn't kill us only makes us stronger."* Shoes For U: *"No UGGS for Sandy."* Joe Pop's Bar: *"LBI Is Alive-Jersey Strong."* On a pile of plastic-coated mattresses: *"LBI Strong,"* and the most daunting sign in front of a home: *"Looters will be shot by a local vet!"*

The Island Shop may have been a cool store to find some clothes but the mountain of wood and debris outside let me know they wouldn't be open any time soon. After a while we took a left and headed over a long bridge toward the mainland.

"There will be more of a selection out here," Dillan offered. "What are you in the mood for?"

I knew exactly what I wanted to eat – seafood – but I didn't want to be pushy. "Whatever you want is okay with me."

"I think we should just grab something quick and then get some groceries."

"Sounds like a plan."

"Let me think. There's a McDonald's, Taco Bell, IHOP, Subway or TGI Friday to name a few. Let me know when you see something."

"I think blueberry pancakes sound nice, don't you? Maybe some scrambled eggs and a steaming hot cup of tea."

"IHOP it is."

"But will Buoy be okay in the car?"

"He does great in the car. I'm sure he'll sleep like a champ. I'll save a little piece of bacon for him and he'll be cool."

At the word bacon, Buoy gave a hearty, "Woof!"

I felt terribly uncool dressed in Dillan's oversized sweats and big sneakers. It was one thing skulking around in the dark on a practically deserted island but being thrust into the fold of humanity, looking and smelling like heaven-knows-what made me very self-conscious. A girl my age walked by wearing tight jeans, a leather jacket, a frilly scarf and racy black boots.

"Wow, she looks nice," I uttered to myself as I shrank into the booth.

Dillan leaned in close, "Well if you like that kind of get-up."

"What's wrong with it?" I asked curiously.

"Nothing, I guess. I just think you look super cute in my things, like a little waif or street urchin or something."

Soon our drinks were delivered by a waitress who couldn't stop staring. She placed the coffee carafe and metal tea pot on the table and searched her pockets for creamers. She looked directly at me, "I hope you won't mind me saying . . . "

Oh no, here it comes.

" . . . but you have the prettiest eyes."

I sighed in relief. I was afraid she was going to say that I stunk like B.O. "Thanks, that's really very nice of you."

I can't explain how amazing that cup of tea tasted. It just hit me in all the right places, followed by a meal that transported me to pancake paradise. Dillan watched me intently as I ate the second helping that the waitress had brought – on the house.

"What?" I asked, licking the maple syrup from my lips.

"You certainly have a way with people."

"And dogs," I added, with a silly grin.

ShopRite was a huge supermarket, packed with every imaginable food and grocery item. That afternoon it was a beehive of activity, with people buzzing through the aisles like food scouts gathering sustenance for the hive. Most of the bees looked tired and stressed out.

We wandered through the bakery, produce and deli departments while Dillan placed things in the cart.

"Anything you want, just toss it in," he said lightly.

I was overwhelmed. I couldn't remember seeing such a variety. Honestly, I wanted to try it all but didn't know where to begin. Signs for pumpkin – spiced this and pumpkin-spiced that abounded and Thanksgiving fare was everywhere. I grabbed an apple pie and placed it in the cart.

"Good choice," Dillan commented with a wink.

If he wanted to make me feel comfortable, he was succeeding. Many of the shoppers grumbled that they didn't have much to be thankful for this year but deep down I felt that as long as they were safe there was hope. A home could be rebuilt; a car or boat replaced. It would be a long time before their lives were normal again and I really wanted to volunteer to help.

"What are we going to do, Dillan?" I asked, just as we rounded the corner and came to the seafood department. I didn't wait for his reply but ran straight to the counter, my mouth watering.

"Do about what?"

"Dinner?" I asked, my previous thoughts of helping strangers clouded by the variety of iced yummies in front of me.

"Pancakes weren't too filling, huh?" he chuckled.

"Look! Shrimp, lobster, clams, mussels and oysters!" I exclaimed. "Oh, and squid too!"

"Okay, sounds like a plan but I think tomorrow will be a better day for it. How about something simple tonight like clam chowder? Do you like red or white?"

"We could get both and mix them. I saw it on a sign at the Chowda' shop. Doesn't it sound amazing?"

"Sorry, I keep forgetting that you haven't eaten much these past few weeks. Let's get whatever you want."

"A fresh loaf of crusty bread and butter, with the soup, will be plenty."

We wandered through the rest of the store along with the other bees getting what we needed. A quart of milk, sliced bread, butter, dog food, Milk-Bones, more gallons of bottled water, paper towels, bleach spray and a bag of ice. In the health and beauty aisle, lip balm, moisturizing body wash, deodorant, shampoo, conditioner, hairbrush, comb, toothbrush and razor for me. When there would be water, I wasn't sure but I wanted to be ready! I thanked Dillan for buying all the *necessities* for me.

"I owe you more than I can ever repay you," he said, as we entered the checkout line.

Buoy showed us just how overjoyed he was to see us climb into the Jeep by licking our faces enthusiastically or maybe he was just jonesing for another piece of bacon.

"I'll never tire of that again, buddy," Dillan said as he scratched Buoy's head and planted a kiss on top of his nose.

"I think tomorrow we'll get you some work clothes, gloves and boots," Dillan said as we drove out of the parking lot. "But right now, we have one more stop to make."

I was a little bit confused when he pulled into the Holiday Inn. "What's up?" I asked.

"It's a little surprise. We have a very busy day tomorrow so we'll need a good night sleep – and they have hot water!"

"Are you kidding? I can shower! Oh My Gosh!" I squealed with delight.

"We look a bit like refugees but I'm sure they've seen worse lately."

"What about Buoy? I'm not going in if he's spending the night in the car."

"No, worries! Buoy is a certified service dog," Dillan said seriously, "and I've got the papers to prove it!"

He reached into the glove box and sorted through some papers. "This will be radical. Will you please pick through the sacks and find our dinner, while I check us in?"

"Sure," I replied, wondering exactly what his concept of radical was.

A few minutes later Dillan returned looking like a cat who swallowed a canary. "I'm not big on lying," he said, "but sometimes it's absolutely necessary."

"So, Buoy's not really a service dog?"

"Well he's my best friend, like my kid brother, and he's provided a lifetime of service to my family, so yes, damn it – he is a service dog. Just his papers are fake." Dillan smiled.

"How did you get them?"

"Dad's a lawyer. Sometimes he pulls a string or two. It's mostly harmless nonsense, but it comes in very handy at times."

We walked into the hotel with our grocery bags and service dog. I clopped along ungracefully in my oversized tennis shoes and rolled up sweat pants. Thank goodness, the lobby was empty except for the clerk behind the desk who barely lifted an eyebrow as we paraded to the elevator.

"Guess what?" Dillan asked excitedly as the door closed.

"What?" I asked, as I pulled a piece of bread from the loaf and popped it in my mouth.

"There's an indoor pool! Isn't that boss?"

"Sure," I said with my mouth full, "but I don't have a bathing suit."

I always have a few pair of baggies in the Jeep. You could wear a pair and my t-shirt unless you prefer skinny dipping!"

I thought we'd reached our floor when the door opened, but Dillan held my arm as a smartly dressed man stepped inside.

"Nice dog," he said, "What kind of work does he do?"

"He's a lawyer," I choked out, my mouth still full of chewy bread.

"Please forgive my sister's rudeness. She doesn't like to talk about her medical condition. Buoy's specially trained to sense when her blood sugar's dropping. Basically, he lets her know when she needs to eat."

I made a smug face at Dillan who was having a bit of fun at my expense. As the door opened on the fifth floor, I said, "Come on, Dillan; Buoy's giving me the sign!"

Dillan and the man glanced down at Buoy who was crouched over licking his privates.

We found room 526 and went inside. Its contrast was so great to the Seafarer's that I felt like I was in a totally different world. Off-white walls, blue and green striped curtains and couch, light oak wood furniture, a light blue carpet and seascape artwork. It was all so fresh and new. I dumped my toiletries out on the first bed and asked Dillan if he was hungry.

"Not yet, are you?"

"Not really. Would you mind if I showered first? I'm dying to get in there," I replied as I cringed at myself in the full-length mirror.

"You go and enjoy yourself. Take all the time you need. I'll feed Buoy and walk him, then I'll go for a swim. Come down if you want or just stay in the tub and soak. See how you feel."

"That sounds *radical*," I replied with a genuine sigh of contentment.

I reheated the tub water twice, then decided it was time to get out. No sound by Buoy or Dillan had disturbed my spa therapy. The large fluffy robe was just what I needed to pamper myself further. It swam on me, but I snuggled into its luxurious folds. I found Buoy asleep on the first bed and sat beside him.

"Where's your boy?" I asked the sleepy pup.

He just stretched out and exposed his underbelly.

Dogs are such trusting creatures, I thought, just like dolphins. I gave him a bit of a rub and he looked so peaceful and relaxed. "I'll be back in a few minutes, big guy," I whispered as I went out the door.

I padded down the hall in bare feet and headed for the main floor. I found the pool at the far end of the building covered by a terrarium-type dome. It must have been well built to withstand Sandy's demonic winds. Dillan was the only one there, doing laps like a fish, just cruising along, back and forth effortlessly. I didn't want to disturb him so I left quietly and went back upstairs. I planned on checking out the shows on TV and having some dinner when he returned, but that's not what happened.

DILLAN

I T SEEMED LIKE EONS ago, not just the previous night, that I had been swimming but nothing felt better or helped me focus more, and that's what I needed. Sandy was a spunky whirlwind, and as enchanting as a woman could possibly be. She also had a very real past, one that would eventually catch up with her and probably leave me hanging high and dry.

I was afraid our time together would be short, so I wanted to do what I could to thank her for saving Buoy. She obviously loved seafood so I hatched a plan I thought she'd appreciate. After I toweled off, I searched "clambake" on my phone for some instruction. There were three different types: one cooked in a pit on the beach, (scratch that one, Fire Chief Bob would probably object), one cooked in a big pot on the stove, (scratch that one, no electricity) and one cooked on a grill. That would definitely be doable!

Buoy jumped gently off her bed when I opened the hotel room door. Sandy was curled up and sleeping like a baby even though there was a noisy cop show on the TV. I turned it off and took Buoy out to pee. By now it was ten p.m. and I was famished. When we returned to the room, I warmed the soup in the microwave, buttered the bread, and cracked open a beer.

I wasn't sure if I should wake her or not but knowing how hungry she'd been, I figured I better ask. "Sandy, you want some chowder?" I whispered as I stroked her soft, silky hair. She took hold of my hand and kissed my palm, then rolled over and fell back to sleep. I sat on the couch and ate my pink soup, totally enchanted. This wasn't good, not good at all.

The next morning, I showered and walked Buoy before Sandy woke. When she did, I had a woman's tracksuit and flip-flops waiting for her that I had gotten in the gift shop downstairs. She was thrilled with the simple outfit.

"Thank you so much. I love them!" she chimed.

I watched as she brushed and braided her long amber hair and ate apple pie from the foil tin.

"I'm starved," she stated. "What are we going to eat – I mean *do* – today?"

"We have a few more errands to do then we'll head back to the inn. I'm sure Mac will need me to write up an estimate for the repair of the flood and wind damage. It shouldn't take too long. I can use my original as a reference but I'll have to include the gutters, awnings, missing shingles and that lovely hole in the facade."

"I'll be glad to help if I can. What type of errands are we doing?"

"First things first, we need to feed you. Hungry workers are unhappy workers." After a hearty breakfast in the hotel restaurant, I drove us through the connecting lots and parked in front of Kohl's. I'd never shopped there but I'd heard Mom rave about the ones back home. She said they had *everything*, so one-stop shopping fit perfectly into my plan.

"Here we are, girl; go get yourself some stuff and don't be shy about it. Get everything you think you'll need. It's gonna get chillier, so think warm and cozy."

"You're gonna *leave* me here?" she asked, sounding a bit panicky.

"I have some errands to do and today's projects take time, so to save time you're gonna have to go this alone."

"But Dillan, I don't have any money."

"I'll be back in an hour and I'll be very pleased to pay for them."

"But . . . ."

"I really need my clothes back, so I must insist."

She pouted for a second, then smiled a perfectly luminous smile.

"Well, if you insist!" She turned around, planted a kiss on Buoy's nose and jumped out of the Jeep, "Don't forget me!" she yelled.

"Hardly," I replied, "and have fun." I'd known her less than twenty-four hours and I couldn't forget her if I tried.

I was on a mission. I headed over to Home Depot and parked, then I reviewed the Ballistic BBQ's YouTube video on clambakes again. I picked up thirty-pound bag of Mexican beach stone, a large bag of charcoal, a bag of lump charcoal, a charcoal chimney and a Weber kettle grill. For my new apprentice, I grabbed a pair of small work gloves, goggles, knee pads and some extra masks. Next, Buoy and I headed back to ShopRite. I needed two Styrofoam coolers, bags of ice and massive amounts of shellfish and rockweed from the fishmonger. A man on a mission, I charged through the store; tossing more butter, lemons, garlic, herbs, red potatoes, kielbasa and eggs into the cart. Unfortunately, fresh corn on the cob was out of season but I found it frozen which was better than none.

I was a little late meeting up with Sandy and I hoped she wasn't upset as I searched for her throughout the ladies department. I found her by the sunglasses, her small shopping cart heaping with clothes. "Hello there!" I said as I popped my head around the display and startled her.

"Oh, I'm so glad you're back! What do you think of these?" She put on a black-framed pair that were okay but not quite perfect.

"Hum.....nope." I handed her a metal-framed aviator style. "Try these."

She removed the glasses and again I couldn't help but notice her beautiful blue-green eyes. They were mesmerizing with their tiny flecks of gold.

"Your eyes sparkle like sun pennies on the ocean," I uttered like a besotted idiot.

"My dad used to say something like that, but he said jingle shells."

We both looked at each other in sheer surprise. "What did you just say?" I asked, amazed.

"My dad – I just heard his voice in my head – saying *Your cerulean eyes sparkle with facets of golden jingle shells*."

"Wow, that's beautiful. Do you remember anything else?"

"No," she replied thoughtfully, "there's nothing more. I just wish I could picture him."

"Well, you've had a breakthrough; that's fantastic!" I said, feeling guilty that I didn't really mean it. "Did you have enough time to try on the clothes?"

"Yes, I turned shopping into an Olympic event!" she proclaimed proudly.

"Did you get shoes, socks, um . . . undergarments?" I was afraid to say bras and panties; it sounded way too personal.

"I think I got everything! I got work boots and some Skechers; they're so cute. Two pair of jeans and a sweater, some flannel PJs, a practical coat and hat for working outdoors and a couple of T-shirts and sweatshirts for layering. I think I have a well-rounded wardrobe."

"I think you should get at least one more pair of jeans, another sweatshirt and tee. You'll be getting rather dirty helping all our neighbors gut their homes! I'm not sure when or if the laundromat will reopen. We may have to come over to the mainland for that. Actually, I just thought of something I need. You go get a few more things and I'll meet you at the registers."

I found the bed & bath section and picked out a blowup mattress. I'd be able to use the tire inflator from the Jeep to blow it up. Then I grabbed a pillow and a quilt. It wasn't anything like the ones my mom had made me – Anna had kept the last one – but it would do.

The checkout lady offered us a twenty percent discount if I opened a charge account. "Sure, why not," I said, hoping to be buying Sandy more clothes in the future. Hell, Kohl's had housewares and all kinds of things two people might need. My mind was really drifting when I felt Sandy tapping me on the shoulder.

"Dillan, I'm afraid I got carried away. I don't really need all this stuff. It's adding up to quite a lot of money."

"Well, either you get new clothes or I do, and I'm just as happy with my old things. They're broken in already, soft and comfy, you know?"

"They really were, but these fit better," she said sweetly, referring to the velvety pink tracksuit and the large pile of clothes on the counter.

After a successful shopping trip, we headed back to the island and back to reality. At least the sun was shining and I had a surprise in store to make it more tolerable. We spotted new signs along the boulevard announcing the locations of makeshift FEMA offices. After everything the locals had been through, I suspected a new plight was just beginning. It would last much longer than Superstorm Sandy – the plight of bureaucracy.

We carried the clothes and last night's provisions into the house.

"I don't really like TV," Sandy said, out of the blue.

"Why? What do you mean?"

"Well, I was looking at the different channels last night and most of them were full of violence – really gross, disturbing stuff. Isn't TV supposed to be entertaining?"

"Unfortunately, that's what people like to watch these days."

"Do *you* like to watch those horrible things?"

"No, honestly I don't have time for TV. Once in a while, I'll watch sports or put it on if I can't fall asleep. It usually will help me relax."

"I didn't find it at all relaxing. In fact, I found it quite the opposite!"

"Well, we don't have to watch it at all; though sometimes it comes in handy to check the weather."

"Thank you, Dillan."

"I want you to be happy here," I said. "I've got a few things to do before we get down to work."

"Okay, I'll put the groceries away."

I went back to the Jeep and unloaded the grill, the coolers and clambake paraphernalia. I set the grill up in the tiny front yard and was pouring the first layer of charcoal in when Jack pulled up in his pickup truck.

"Hey Dillan, you got a few minutes?"

"Yeah, I'm just planning out this clambake thing, before we attack the plywood. Come on over!"

Jack drove to the end of the block and parked on Amber Street.

"I have a theory, and you aren't going to like it," he said as he walked toward me.

I raised an eyebrow. "I guess you're going to tell me whether I want to hear it or not, so shoot!"

"Suppose Sandy is the sole survivor of a shipwreck," he stated solemnly.

I took a deep breath as I mulled it over. "I'm sure you've checked with the Coast Guard already."

"Of course. There weren't any distress calls off the island that weekend but what if their radio was disabled?"

"And their cell phones too?"

"Well, it was the storm of the century, my friend – communications were sketchy at best. Maybe it was a small boat, just a couple of kids in a dinghy?"

I'd hardly call her a kid – she was every inch a woman – but to Jack, anyone under thirty was considered just that. "It's possible, but she seems to have more sense than that. Maybe she was surfing and got nailed in the impact zone."

"Perhaps it's more sinister than that. What if she was the object of foul play?" Jack added. "Maybe someone capitalized on the storm, to make it appear like an accident, and tossed her overboard?"

I couldn't imagine anyone wanting to hurt her. "Wow, those are some intense theories. I hope they're both wrong."

"I just find it incredibly strange that no one has reported her missing. She doesn't appear to be someone who would be estranged from her family or without friends and it's been almost a month since Sandy hit us."

Yeah, she hit me all right, with a sucker punch. "The fact that no one's looking for her doesn't make any sense!"

"Listen, Dillan; there is another possibility, though I thought twice before mentioning it."

"What? If you have some idea, tell me."

"Well, there are stories, you know, folklore and legends."

"What the hell are you talking about?" I asked, totally confused.

"Have you ever heard of Little Miss August?"

"Nope."

"Abby's a well-known ghost around here. Hundreds of people claim to have seen the child with long wet hair, wearing a woman's dress, all over Beach Haven. They say she fell to her death from the widow's walk of the family home."

"What's that got to do with Sandy?"

"Well there are other stories too: women who mysteriously appear from the sea . . . ."

"You mean . . . *mermaids*????" I asked incredulously.

"You live here long enough, you'll hear all sorts of strange things."

I gave him the most cynical glare. Did he honestly believe this crap?

"Ha! Got ya. I can't believe you fell for that!" he said, wracked with laughter.

"You know, if you weren't my elder and a police officer, I'd call you a jerk."

"I'm sorry," he snickered. "I couldn't help myself. Sometimes making light of a serious situation can relieve the stress and I've been under an incredible amount of stress lately."

"Yeah, it was *kinda* funny. I almost thought you were serious for a second."

"Listen, Dillan; I'd certainly understand if you didn't want her to be found," he said quietly. "If I was your age and found a woman like that living in my house – wow! I'd want as much time with her as I could get."

"There's just something about her, Jack," I said rather pitifully.

"I can see that; no convincing needed. Just be mindful of your feelings, son. I doubt she's unattached."

"I think it's already too late. Not only is she stunningly beautiful, but she saved my dog's life. What more could a guy ask for?"

"Be careful, Dillan; you don't know anything about this girl."

"I like what I know . . . a lot!"

Jack shook his head and rolled his eyes. "Don't say I didn't warn you. Do you want me to keep an eye on the grill while you take care of your windows?"

"Sure, if you're not busy, but doesn't the police captain have better things to do?"

"It's my first day off in weeks and honestly, I'm exhausted. Carole's up at the Surf City firehouse volunteering in the kitchen. I don't think she wanted me hanging around so she convinced me to stay home and relax. She says I tend to micromanage everything. Can you imagine?"

"Nope, not you!"

"I tried to take a nap, but my brain wouldn't cooperate. I kept mulling over your mystery girl."

"*I* can't get her out of my head for one second," I replied, defeated.

Jack gave me a look that said, *You're in way over your head.* "You have a chair for the barbecue king?"

"Sure." I ran upstairs, grabbed a beach chair and yelled to Sandy, "You ready to get to work?"

"Yes! I can't wait to get some sunshine in here!"

"Oh, by the way," I said, as Buoy followed us down the stairs, "Jack's outside, but he doesn't have any information for you yet."

"That's okay," she replied, sounding almost relieved.

I felt badly leaving Buoy inside, but I didn't trust him not to run away again. Jack and Sandy exchanged greetings as I handed him the chair.

"Once it's burned down to hot coals, just let me know. It's quite a process."

"You got it, kid."

Sandy turned out to be just as strong as she proclaimed. She held the ladder for me and helped me carry the plywood boards to the curb. "I think we should write a message on one," she said as she removed her new work gloves, "something inspirational!"

"Whatever floats your boat, girl!" Wow, talk about putting your foot in your mouth! What an inappropriate reply to make after what Jack had theorized. Luckily, it didn't seem to affect her but I could see a thoughtful expression forming on her face before she blurted out, "*FRIENDS, NEIGHBORS, SHARING, REPAIRING.*"

"I like it," I answered, nodding in agreement. "It's short and sweet, and we're not threatening anyone with bodily harm!"

"Is Captain Jack joining us for dinner?" Sandy asked curiously.

"No, but he's helping me cook up something that I think you might enjoy."

"For me, really? Dillan, you have done more than enough for me. Stop spoiling me already. The hotel, the meals, the clothes – it's too much. I don't know if I'll ever be able to repay you."

"You've already repaid me by saving Buoy but if you really want to help, just stay and be my assistant."

"I do and I will. I'll stay as long as I can, but you know I can't really promise anything. When my memory returns, I don't know what will happen."

"Yeah, I know. Have you had any more memories of your father?"

"No, I've wracked my brain but . . . nothing."

"Well, I'm sure more will come with time."

"Hopefully," she replied with a sigh.

"Hey Dillan, I think the charcoal's ready," Jack yelled.

"I'll be busy for a little bit, Sandy. Why don't you take a rest?"

"I'm not tired and I don't want to just twiddle my thumbs."

"You really want to get your hands dirty, don't you?"

She gave me that out-of-this-world smile and nodded enthusiastically.

"Okay. Go upstairs and straighten up the south bedroom. Just sort the bricks, lumber, whatever you can into separate piles and don't forget your gloves."

"Aye-aye, sir; I'm on it!" she proclaimed as she ran back into the house.

I headed back to Jack and the grill. The charcoal fire had burned down nicely and the briquettes were ashy and super-hot. "This looks just about right," I said to Jack, who was stretching and looking very sleepy.

"That's good 'cause I think the warmth of the fire and the rumble of the dozers lulled me to sleep. What's next, Chef?" he asked.

"We light up some charcoal in this chimney and heat the rocks on the hot coals. Once the charcoal is flaming we pour that on top, then cover it with this lump charcoal stuff."

"*It is* quite the process. You had to buy a new grill and all this?"

"Yeah, but Sandy's worth it."

"I just don't want you to be disappointed when we find out the truth about her. All your aspirations may go up in flames, just like these."

"Yeah, thanks for pointing that out," I said sarcastically. "I know there's a good possibility I'm gonna get screwed and not in a good way!"

"You want what's best for her; don't you, Dillan?"

"Of course. It's a wait-and-see game. I get it." We poured the burning briquettes on top of the stones then spread the lump charcoal on top of that. I popped on the domed lid and checked the video one more time. "This says I have thirty minutes before cook time. I have to go prep the food."

"You have running water yet?"

"Shit, I've been so preoccupied I forgot to turn it back on. Sandy's been using bottled to wash and flush the tank."

"We had a boil water advisory going for a while. I'd let it run a good while before using it on food, to flush out all the contaminants. Why don't we use the kitchen at the Engleside and I'll help."

"That would be awesome!"

"It's the least I can do after forcing you to abandon Buoy. You have no idea how badly I felt about that."

"You were just doing your job, looking out for my welfare; but man, when I was driving over that bridge it ripped my guts out," I said as I kicked at the ground.

"Well, Sandy is our miracle then! Thank God she saved your buddy."

"Yup, I think that's what she is, a beautiful and inexplicable miracle."

I ran inside and told Sandy and Buoy that I would be up the street for a little while. "I need you hungry, so please don't eat anything while I'm gone," I added.

"Who, meeeeee?" she replied innocently.

Damn, she was adorable! "You're killing me!" I yelled back. Jack and I each grabbed a cooler and walked up to the Engleside.

ALEXANDER HENRY

OCTOBER 2012

SHE RETURNED SUDDENLY, AS I had predicted, and with a vengeance. The same complete darkness, gale force winds and driving rain that rammed into my home just minutes ago had returned, leaving me quaking in my stocking feet and shaking us both to our foundations. I plodded quickly back to bed, curled up in a ball and pulled the covers over my head. I doubted I could sleep with the raging winds outside and the fear that raged within. There was only one other time in my life I'd felt akin to this: when *she* disappeared, and left me feeling totally helpless. I had put her out of my mind for so many years, but I found now that she'd survived there, in all her beauty and charm, just waiting for the opportune moment to reappear and taunt me. So she did, as I fell asleep among the rising tide, rattling window panes and the occasional crack of a shingle being torn from my roof.

By the next afternoon, the menacing clouds had thinned enough to allow the sky to lighten to a dull gray. I'd scanned the area from my second-level porch and every window in the house. Things didn't look too bad from here, but I couldn't see the beach. My once oceanfront property had lost its ideal view as the apartment buildings and motels somehow edged between us. I had fought against it, as had many property owners, but we were railroaded by laws we never knew existed.

A couple of blocks north, the telephone pole lay across the street and water had pooled in the area around the Seafarer's. It must have sat a good three feet lower than my place, poor bastards. I hadn't met the man who bought it, but the word at Murphy's was after a remodeling project, he planned to reopen the old inn as a bed and breakfast – tough luck, for sure.

There were piles of sand scattered in the street and a thin coating had been deposited on my driveway. I wasn't sure if the water or the wind had carried it there but I could still make out some of the bricks underneath, so I knew it wasn't very deep. My bottom floor was dry as a bone. Well, almost; a thick cloud of humidity weighed down the air and everything it touched, but that was something that happened quite often and was nothing worth mentioning. I felt relieved; at least I had nothing major to repair before I sold the place. Indeed, last night was the deciding factor which I had hemmed and hawed over for the past few years. She was never coming back. I'd lived here all these years, not even realizing that I'd been waiting.

I went upstairs to my bedroom and inched myself into the depths of my closet. Behind my quiver of mangled old logs and sticks and the tuxedos I'd worn for publication parties, on the uppermost shelf, I found the black and red hatbox. It hadn't been opened in over fifty years. When my first novel was published, I treated myself to a black Portis fedora that sported a red satin lining. Back then, I'd used the box to hold her treasures, and I hadn't cared to view them since. There wasn't much: a photo of us, taken with my father's Kodak Brownie, a few pieces of sea glass, three perfectly shaped seashells, a chunk of driftwood and the now-friable love notes she'd left for me under a rock in front of the St. Rita's Hotel, advising me when and where to meet.

Under it all, wrapped in a silk hanky, was the necklace. A most elegant piece, made of natural treasures, a multitude of tiny shells, bright orange and deep red coral and tiny seed beads wound intricately with strands of gold thread. I'll never be able to forget the first time I saw her: rising out of the water just a few feet from me. Her necklace gleamed in the sun but it was her eyes that stunned me into complete submission. The year was 1950. We'd spent every day of that summer together. I was eighteen and I would never recover.

That evening, I pulled my old recliner away from the fireplace and positioned it near the window for a better view outside. I sipped a cup of steaming black tea and stared out into the darkening street.

I hadn't felt this tired in ages. I shouldn't have been feeling sorry for myself, I'd survived the storm and so had my home, and yet I was feeling defeated. If not for the relief that the tea provided, I may have lost my mind. A propane camping stove would have been lovely back in 1962. Thank the heavens; I was better prepared this time. I didn't do much really, just the bottled water, flashlight batteries, matches, extra kerosene for the lamps, a few chests of ice for perishables and some extra canned food.

The days being shorter didn't help my mood. I felt trapped in a cold and bleak existence. I hadn't felt lonely in a long time; in fact, I usually relished my privacy and solitude but now everything was different. The island felt deserted and I was the only idiot irresponsible enough to stay. I sipped the strong, hot British brew and nibbled on a few Social Tea Biscuits, trying to fortify myself.

The next few nights I did the same. I suppose I was contemplating my next move – would I leave the island or just tough it out? – when through the steam of my cup I saw her. Gliding like a specter under the light of the moon, the long dark hair, the delicate step, the spitting image of my love. How could it be? She'd be my age by now, not the young woman I remembered. I rose quickly to get a better look. Suddenly the room spun out of focus, my knees crumbled and my head hit the floor.

SANDY

I COULD SMELL DINNER long before Dillan blindfolded me and sat me at the kitchen table.

"Wait here, don't move and don't peek!" he exclaimed in his excitement.

He had been so secretive as he and Captain Jack made numerous trips up and down the stairs, while Buoy and I sat sequestered in the bedroom. As he trekked up the stairs one last time, my mouth watered with the aromatic bouquet of steaming seafood and briny seaweed. The aroma took me to a place of extreme comfort and happiness. It took me home – not a specific memory, just a feeling of pure contentment. I reveled in it but there was more. I smelled herbs, garlic and some type of sausage. I drank in the heavenly scent and waited anxiously. I heard the sound of something being poured, then Dillan placed a glass in my hand.

"I hope you like white wine," he said. "They swore this would go perfect with shellfish."

"Oh, you gave away the surprise!" I said jokingly. "Can I take the blindfold off now?"

"Sure, I'm sorry. Ta-Da! What do you think?"

Laid out before me was the most beautiful array of all things delicious. Lobster, shrimp, clams, mussels, small red potatoes, corn on the cob, and sausage were artfully arranged atop a bed of rockweed. The table barely held the platter, a few votive candles, individual pots of melted butter and our plates. A basket that held a head of roasted garlic and French bread sat on an extra chair alongside a pile of cloth napkins.

"This looks and smells radical!" I exclaimed, "I am totally amped!"

Dillan looked at me with his eyebrow raised and a funny grin on his face.

"What?" I asked, "Isn't that how you surfers talk?"

"I suppose so! Well, dig, in!" he said with enthusiasm. "Eat it while it's hot!"

I did dig in, with gusto! It tasted just as good as it looked; each item more succulent than the last. "How did you know how to do this?" I asked, quite unladylike with my mouth full of tender lobster meat.

"YouTube, on my phone. It's got everything. I could probably use it to pick up a trick or two for the restoration work as well."

"You know, it's too bad *I* don't have a cellphone. People's whole lives are on it. It might have answered all my questions!"

"It probably would have," he said matter-of-factly, "but if you did have a phone it probably got lost or trashed in the ocean. Didn't you have anything else in your pockets that might help identify you?"

"No, I didn't. I didn't have any pockets."

"That's too bad."

He didn't seem to be getting the drift of what I was saying, but maybe it was better if he didn't know I'd been flailing around in the ocean naked. If it puzzled me, what would he think?

"Did you buy all these things this morning or did you just happen to have it in the back of your car?" I asked as I peeled the shell from a shrimp and dipped it in the melted butter.

"I bought the grill and stuff, but I borrowed the platter and dishware from the Engleside. They'll do anything for Jack."

"He seems like a very good friend. I'm glad you have someone like that in your life. I hope I do too, somewhere." I said wistfully.

"I'm sure you do! You're such a super lady."

"Thank you, Dillan." I felt a little warmth come to my cheeks just as the last of the sunlight faded from the kitchen window.

"I'm sorry it wasn't warm enough to eat outside. Cooking this on the beach, or while watching the sunset by the bay, would have made it more authentic," he said disappointedly.

"I'm sure it would've been beautiful, but it's November, after all. I'm amazed at what you've done and I think it's perfect just as it is. You're a very kind and generous person to go through all this trouble for a stranger."

"You don't seem like a stranger at all, Sandy. I feel very comfortable with you."

"It's weird, right? Perhaps we were friends in a previous life."

"It's kinda weird, but nice."

I took a bite of corn on the cob and butter ran down my chin.

"You look so pretty in the candlelight," Dillan said, as he dabbed my face with a napkin. With that little grin of his, I couldn't tell if he was kidding or serious.

"I *feel* pretty in my new clothes, thank you," I replied, "but you've spent too much money on me! I really didn't need all this extravagance. A pizza with clams on it would've been just fine."

"Are you *kidding* me? You like clams on your pizza! White pizza with clams and garlic is my favorite! God, this blows my mind!"

I just smiled and nodded as I drank the liquor from a clam, dipped it in butter and swallowed it whole. I couldn't actually remember eating pizza, but I knew I liked it.

"Living like this could drain your bank account rather quickly. You have to promise me that you'll stop spending like this. I mean, I loved everything and I appreciate it all, I really do. I just don't want to become a financial burden to you."

"If I couldn't afford it, I wouldn't do it. I have more sense than that. I live simply and don't have big bills hanging over my head, so the occasional splurge is a nonissue."

"Is that why you do carpentry too, to supplement your income?"

"It's complicated. I started doing carpentry for Anna's sake. Her dad had his own company and I apprenticed there. She wanted me to have a stable income so we could settle down. I was all for it, too. I enjoyed working with my hands – to build something out of nothing. I shouldn't have been surprised that, in the end, it wasn't enough for her. She met a guy who drove a Porsche and owned an advertising agency. I was never going to be that successful, that kind of a go-getter. I liked a simpler life style."

"And this is the kind of life you wanted? Remodeling an old inn and lifeguarding at the Jersey Shore?"

"Yeah, I guess. It's not a bad deal. I met Mac – Mr. MacAvery – at the Hud shortly after I arrived here. We started talking and next thing I knew, well . . . here I am. I get to live here rent-free as long as I do carpentry work on my off-duty hours. I quite enjoy the process of seeing an old house come back to life. The storm has totally screwed things up though. The water damage is extensive but at least the place is still standing."

I was beginning to see tiny glimpses into Dillan's soul and I was getting frightened by my growing admiration for him. What if somewhere out there I had a family that I couldn't remember? What if they were injured in the storm or worse? What if I was the only one who made it? What if I wasn't?

We chatted amicably for what seemed to be such a short time, but two bottles of wine sat empty on the table and the votives were going out one by one. A very well-behaved dog was waiting patiently for his dinner when Dillan said, "I've got just one tiny surprise left. I'll be right back!"

"I'll feed Buoy," I yelled, as he ran downstairs and out of the house. As Buoy gobbled up his dinner, I finished up the last few mussels and felt completely sated.

When Dillan returned, he carried a fancy tray with a tea pot, cups, a milk pitcher and an assortment of tea bags.

"To go with our apple pie," he proudly proclaimed, with a huge grin.

"You have thought of absolutely everything!" I sighed and smiled contentedly, "This has been wonderful."

"Thank Jack next time you see him. He was very helpful."

Hot tea with milk and honey went perfectly with our apple pie. I don't know how it fit in my belly as it was already quite full, but I didn't want to disappoint Dillan. He had gone to so much trouble. I began to feel all warm and fuzzy as I sipped the blissfully hot tea, nibbled on apple pie and gazed across the table at the sweetest guy imaginable. It may have been the wine; it may have been something more.

"Where am I going to sleep, now that *you're* home?" I asked with a wine-induced giggle.

"That's a mighty good question but I've taken care of it. Remember I bought a blowup mattress at Kohl's this morning?" Then he smiled a sly, sexy grin, and reached across the table touching my nose with his finger. "You should keep the bed, most definitely. I'll make do with the mattress."

I had the strangest feeling pounding through my veins, like salt water coursing within a rip tide. I looked at Dillan and wondered, was this truly my heart singing or a more basic instinct?

A little bit later I found myself curled up on the bed feeling lonely as Buoy lay next to Dillan on the floor.

"Are you cold?" Dillan asked from the darkness, in a husky voice.

I wasn't really cold but I replied, "A little."

"Buoy, up," Dillan commanded gently. Buoy jumped onto the bed and lay against me. His warmth and rhythmic breathing lulled me to sleep almost instantly.

Later, in the pre-dawn hours, I climbed out of bed as quietly as the old springs would allow, afraid of waking my two roommates. Dillan and Buoy both breathed deep, slow, rhythmic breaths. I slipped on my new sneakers and went to the kitchen. How lovely it was to have the window exposed so I could watch as the last stars started to fade. So many thoughts swirled around in my head, not unlike the hurricane I named myself after: Who was I? How did I end up here? Might Dillan become my boyfriend? Did I already have another? What was I supposed to do? Suddenly, I felt a soft warm body press against my leg.

"Good morning, Buoy," I said quietly as I stroked his large head, "You need to go out, big guy?" He followed me down the stairs and sat while I attached his leash. He was such a quiet and well-behaved gentleman.

Outside, the sky was just brightening. A few seagulls were flying over the sea. We headed toward the beach to enjoy the still of the early morning. No bulldozers, no army vehicles, not even a patrolling ship was in sight. We walked along the water's edge, dodging the sea foam. As dawn turned into daylight, I watched as sun pennies formed on the ocean's surface. They sparkled and danced, beckoning me to follow their little path of light.

"I think I'm a bit too hungover for swimming this morning, Buoy. Plus, the water's gotten pretty darn chilly."

As we headed up and over the jetty, I spotted a school of dolphins. How beautiful they were as they frolicked and bodysurfed toward shore. They were such curious and fun-loving creatures, peaceful and intelligent beyond human comprehension. They lived in harmony with nature's plan and contributed nothing to the destruction of the planet. In my mind, they were more intelligent than we humans, who seemed hell bent on destroying our only home. I seriously hoped they would last beyond us into the millennia to come. I guess walking along the shore had made me philosophical. The mind roams free when there is such a vast expanse before you. I looked up into the sky and felt very small indeed.

Buoy had a spring in his step, inviting me to run along, so we jogged for a bit, then sat and stared out to sea. The path of the sun pennies had become long and inviting. The dolphins seemed to have followed us along but moved out to deeper water. I put my arm around the old dog, Dillan's best friend and now mine too.

In a flash, I experienced a memory: collapsing on the beach exhausted. Beside me lay the big black dog who had helped me swim to shore. In the pelting rain and roaring wind, he had led me into a house and up the stairs. "You saved my life boy, of that I have no doubt!"

DILLAN

I WOKE UP THE next morning with a start. If I'd been in my own bed instead of on the floor, I may have believed the whole thing was an awesome dream. Buoy and Sandy were not in sight and I didn't hear anything except a laughing gull yakking it up outside.

I took a deep breath and relished the fact that I had Buoy back plus this fantastic new girl in my life. I climbed off the mattress and pulled on my old sweats, the same ones Sandy had been wearing – my mind wandered erotically for a bit and then I felt stupid. She wasn't, and probably never would be, my girlfriend. I looked in the mirror gauging my twenty-four-hour stubble and dreads. As I pulled them into shape, one broke off in my hand. Uh . . . it was probably time for a haircut. I noticed an old photo, bent and cracked with wear and tear, stuck on the mirror. A beaming couple from a bygone era was celebrating their wedding day. Something about them seemed familiar. I wondered if Sandy had known them or perhaps they might even be her relatives. Why else would she have placed it there?

Then something struck me. I went to my duffle bag, searched my clothing and pulled out the picture I had found in the sand and rubble weeks ago. Could it be? Holy shit! They appeared to be the same couple with the addition of a tiny baby. This was a freaky coincidence. I used my iPhone to take quick snapshots of them, then called out to Sandy and Buoy with no reply. As I headed toward the kitchen, my phone started playing Chain Gang by Sam Cooke: Mac's ringtone.

"Hey, Mac. How's it going?"

"You tell me, Dillan. Did you make it back? What did you find?"

"I tried to call you the day before yesterday, but couldn't get through."

 "Sorry," Mac replied, "I've been having issues with my phone service."

I told him about finding Buoy and his surprising new boarder, then got down to the nitty-gritty. He was pretty upset about losing the original wood flooring that I had so painstakingly refinished.

"I feel sick about it, too; but it is what it is. Unfortunately, without power, I've got no way to completely dry the place out.

"I can overnight a kerosene heater to you. Will that help?"

"Yeah sure, the forced-air type should work pretty well."

"All right, I'll order one now. Will you text me some photos please? And write up an estimate for the repairs. I'll need them for the insurance adjuster."

"Yeah, no problem. When are you coming down?"

"I don't know. My mother's very ill. She's in the hospital and they don't know if she'll recover. I don't want to be away if she passes. She deserves way better than that."

"Of course. I understand completely. Is there anything I can do?"

"Actually, there is. Would you be able to go down to the trailer park and check on my mother's place? It's lot 126. We heard the park got hit hard, which totally blows because we were just about to close the sale on her place when this happened."

"God, Mac, that's gnarly!"

"I know it's *only* money in the grand scheme of things, but we really could have used it. Now it's just one more stressful situation to deal with and my plate's loaded already."

As we were talking, I looked around the house for Buoy and my amazing new friend. They were probably taking a walk on the beach, so I jumped in the Jeep and headed south to the trailer park. I already knew it was gnarly there, but had no specifics on lot 126. The Long Beach Township police and the National Guard were still parked at the Sea Spray Motel, allowing access to residents of Holgate only. Fortunately, the officer recognized me and after explaining why I was there, he allowed me to pass. The words NEVER FALLEN were haphazardly painted on a large piece of scrap wood which was set against a flag pole. The American flag hung from above making an encouraging statement.

Lot 126 was one of the few lots which still displayed a marker along with a Coca-Cola vending machine that had partially crushed some rose bushes. Oddly there were still perfect red roses blooming alongside the melee of destruction. What was left of Mrs. MacAvery's trailer was in Lot 127, lying against its neighbor. I wandered through the ripped-open structure the best I could but found little of use. Basically, it was an empty shell except for a few kitchen cabinets and some plumbing fixtures. I took some photos and sent them to Mac, along with a text: *There appears to be nothing left. I am so sorry. Will send pics of the inn shortly.* I was pretty sure the pics that old Henry had taken would be helpful to Mac, so I'd see if Sandy would mind accompanying me there in the afternoon.

I wanted to check out more of the area, but I didn't want to push my luck, so I headed back north and drove to the Beach Patrol barracks. I saw Chief Gavin and Mitch's vehicles on the street, so I parked. I found them inside ripping down sheetrock.

The chief held out his hand as he headed toward me. "Dillan, great to see you! I was so happy to hear you found Buoy. At least something good came out of all this."

Mitch, who was wielding a crowbar, yelled, "Hey, bro!"

"Thanks, Chief Gavin," I replied, as I returned his firm shake. "Buoy gave me quite a scare but he's totally fine. Man, this is some mess!" I said, my gut aching.

"Yeah, you don't know the half of it. We took in about forty-eight inches of water. Both our trucks and the quad are totaled. What was left of the first-aid equipment and supplies are useless. The only things that survived were the rescue cans and boards!"

"I'll be happy to help, sir. Whatever I can do, write me in."

"We're looking for volunteers for the weekends. If we get a few more guys here, we'll have this place gutted in a couple weeks."

"What about the renovation?"

"That will have to wait till we get the insurance money and hopefully some government funding."

"I'll be here Saturday, sir."

"Thanks, Dillan. I knew I could count on you. I'm still saving you a position on the squad for next summer, right?"

"Yes, sir. There's plenty to keep me here."

"Hey, Dillan," Mitch yelled, "Why ya keepin' your new wahine under wraps, dude?"

"Listen, I got to get back to the inn, but I'll see you Saturday."

"Way to shut a brother out," Mitch yelled, as I headed outside. I just smiled to myself and waved back. I wasn't ready to share my wahine with the guys just yet.

Sandy and Buoy were waiting for me on the front steps. I felt relieved to see them, as if they both may have been a figment of my imagination all along. We went inside to scrounge for some breakfast. It paled in comparison to last night's dinner, but over cereal with milk from the Igloo cooler, I told her everything I knew about Ian MacAvery and the Seafarer's Inn.

Before we started working, I took some photos for Mac. It was difficult to see all my hard work just washed away, but at least this time I had a helper and a completely beautiful one at that. I hoped she wouldn't distract me to the point of losing a digit – a carpenter needed his fingers intact.

While we were removing doors, and stacking them on sawhorses to dry, I remembered to ask Sandy about the photo she had stuck on the dresser mirror.

"I don't know them, at least I don't think I do," she said, as I handed her a hinge. "I found it in the sand and it looked like such a happy day in someone's life. It made me feel hopeful and less lonely."

"Well, the funny thing is, I found one that looks very similar. Come on, I'll show you." We ran up to the bedroom and after some scrutiny decided they were the same people. I told Sandy about the day my friends and I voyaged across the roiling bay.

"Wow, to think we almost met weeks ago! I'm sure Buoy would have been happier."

"Would *you* have been happier?" I asked.

After a moment of silence, she replied, "You know . . . I think we should try to find these people and return their photographs."

Oh, nice way to dodge the question, I thought. "That's an interesting idea but they're so old and worn. It's possible they might already be dead. I wouldn't know where to begin."

"How about the Long Beach Island Museum? I saw Captain Jack come out of there the other day, when I was walking Buoy in the park."

"Yeah! You're so smart! A local historian might be able to hook us up!"

"I wonder why Captain Jack was there?"

"It would appear he's into local history and folklore," I answered, remembering his odd comments from the other day. "When we stop in, I'd like to check out the shipwreck artifacts."

"Me too, sounds fascinating!"

We grabbed drinks from the kitchen, thumped back down the stairs and got to work removing the door trim. I told Sandy about meeting up with Mitch at the barracks and how he was interested in meeting her.

"Sure, I'd like to meet him too," she chimed. "Your friends are my friends."

"That's what I'm worried about. Speaking of friends, old and new, would you mind walking over to old Henry's with me? I think Mac could really use the photos he took."

"Sure, I've been meaning to stop by and check on him anyway. I could just give him your number."

"I think I'd like to meet him and thank him for everything he's done to help you – and me, for that matter."

After a short visit with Henry, I decided that he was a decent enough old guy, although I could feel the palpable vibe of protectiveness he was giving off. He'd only known Sandy a few weeks but he acted all fatherly – like I was the proverbial prom date. I gave him my number and he promised to text photos of the sea-soaked antique rug, buckled floors, water-lined walls, saturated couch, end tables and lamps that had been ruined. Most of the other rooms downstairs had been empty. I was glad that I had the wherewithal to lug all the tools and supplies upstairs before I'd left. I didn't want to remember that day but thank God, Buoy sat beside old Henry's fireplace looking completely contented.

The next two days we removed molding and finished tearing out the sheetrock on the bottom floor, including Mac and Shona's wing. The kerosene heater, which had arrived by FedEx, was just what we needed to really dry the place out. I don't know how Sandy kept up without one sigh, wince or complaint of any kind. My arms, back and thighs were aching to the point of Aspercreme and Motrin, but what I really wanted was a hot shower. I toyed with the idea of driving us to the mainland and staying in the hotel again, but I was too tired to move. That night, I passed out on my blowup bed by eight p.m.

Before my usual seagull alarm clock, I was roused by the tune of Chain Gang. I reached across the floor and pulled the phone from the pocket of my jeans.

"Hey, Mac." I answered sleepily.

"Good morning. Did I wake you?"

"It's okay."

"I need a huge favor. An inspector is supposed to stop by the inn this afternoon. I had every intention on being there to meet with them, but my mother's condition has taken a turn for the worse. I really can't leave the hospital and God only knows when we'll be able to get another appointment. Would you be able to come up here and get our mortgage payment book and homeowners insurance policy for their review?"

"Um, sure Mac. Whatever you need – no problem. Where are you exactly?"

"Valley Hospital in Ridgewood. It's about two hours north, just off the parkway."

"I'll be there as soon as I can, but I'll give you a call before we get on the road."

"Will the mystery girl be accompanying you then?"

"I'll ask her. I'm sure she'd like to meet you; I'm just sorry it has to be under such difficult circumstances."

"Well, Mom seems to be comfortable, but she hasn't recognized anyone for the last few months. I'm not sure if it is the Alzheimer's or what, but she really started to slip last spring. It's been tough on all of us, especially Fiona."

"I'd like to meet your daughter."

"She's not at her best, you understand. She may be tearful, or worse."

"Well, we won't intrude. We'll just grab the paperwork and head back, so we don't miss the inspector."

"Okay, talk to you soon."

"Give my best to your family, and hang in there, Mac."

"Thanks again."

I didn't have to bribe Sandy to go along, but she was concerned with her appearance as neither of us had had a good scrubbing with hot water for some time. She looked perfectly beautiful to me. Her skin still had the natural glow of summer and her eyes sparkled with warmth and a lust for life that I found truly inspiring. I could tell she wasn't completely trusting when she lifted her arm, stuck her nose in her arm pit and took a deep sniff.

"I'll need a few minutes to feel human," she said rolling her eyes.

"I tell you what: take your time, freshen up and I'll take care of the fur ball. We'll grab a hot breakfast at McDonald's and tonight we'll stay at the hotel. I think we've earned it."

A huge smile spread across her face. "Yummm . . . Pancakes!" she sighed with pleasure.

"And here I thought you'd be more excited about a hot bath and shampoo."

I had two Egg McMuffins and coffee while Sandy savored her pancakes. Our conversation during the drive was animated and engaging. Who knew a girl asking questions about – well, everything – could be so enjoyable? She laughed at my jokes, she loved my dog and she was so hell bent on helping people. There wasn't anything about Sandy that didn't draw me in. There was no testing the water with this girl; I got sucked into the whirlpool without even realizing it.

When we pulled into the hospital parking lot, I was disappointed that the conversation would have to be put on hold. We walked Buoy around for a bit, let him do his thing, then tucked him in the back of the Jeep where he could stretch out and have a snooze.

When I called Mac from the lobby he said his mom was sleeping so he would bring the papers down to us.

"Thanks again for coming, Dillan," Mac said, as he walked toward us, hand outstretched for a shake. He looked exhausted with pale skin and dark circles under his eyes.

"It's no problem at all. I'd like to introduce you to Sandy, my new, um . . . assistant."

"It's a pleasure to meet you, Sandy. Dillan's told me so much about you."

"Likewise," she said, as she gave Mac a hug. "I'm sorry to hear that your mother's ill. Is there anything we can do?"

"Just making sure the inspector gets these papers is huge help," Mac said, as he pulled an envelope from his back pocket and handed it to me.

I didn't envy Mac one bit. His situation made me think about my own parents getting older. "Can we get you a coffee or something to eat?" I asked, not really knowing what else to say.

"No thanks, but I was wondering – did you have a chance to take some pictures of the damage? Ideally, we should've had some before you started working. I forgot to mention that, or did I?"

"Yes, I got some from Sandy's friend and took some myself. I thought I sent them to you a few days ago."

"Maybe you did. We've spent so much time here, that the outside world seems to have disappeared. Let me check my inbox."

The two of us pulled out our phones and sat in some chairs that circled a baby grand piano. Mac searched his texts and emails while I searched through my photos. Once I located the ones Mac was interested in, I handed him my phone. "I'm really sorry. I guess I forgot to send them. I got them the same day that I went to the trailer park."

"Well at least we have them now," he said, as he slowly scanned through them shaking his head in disbelief.

I caught sight of Mrs. MacAvery stepping off the elevator and went to meet her.

"Hi Dillan," she said pleasantly. "It's so good of you to come."

"It's not a problem. Sandy and I needed a break anyway." I

introduced her to Sandy, who gave her a hug as well. She certainly was a people person.

"Your mom's awake," she told Mac as she bent down and gently rubbed his upper arm. "Oh, are those the pictures from the inn? May I see?"

"Sure, hon, but they're rather upsetting."

She skipped through the photos, shaking her head as well.

"Hey," she asked, curiously. "Aren't these your parents?"

"My parents?" I asked, confused. Mrs. MacAvery had never met my parents.

"No, Mac's parents – on their wedding day. I've seen this picture before at your parents' place and this one. Mac, it's the day they brought you home from the hospital!"

Mac took the phone and scanned the pictures. "Dillan, where did you get these?"

We told them the strange circumstances behind finding the photos, then followed them back to Mrs. MacAvery's room. We met the older Fiona MacAvery and her namesake granddaughter who was attempting, unsuccessfully, to feed the frail woman applesauce.

"Hi, Mom, how are you feeling?" Mac asked, as he gently took her hand. She just looked at him blankly then turned toward us. When she spotted Sandy, her eyes lit up.

"I remember you," she said confidently, "You haven't changed a bit – except your hair. The color's a tad darker, isn't it?"

"Sorry, Sandy," Mac said. "She gets terribly confused sometimes."

"I'm Sandy, Mrs. MacAvery. It's nice to, ummm – see you again."

"Sit here, my dear," Fiona said gently, patting the mattress with her misshapen hand. Sandy sat and smiled warmly at the old woman.

"I used to see you on the beach with that young man of yours. The boys of summer only had eyes for you. Not one of them flirted with any of us gals! It's a good thing I was already promised to Douglass or I might have been peeved!" she giggled. "Tell me . . . where's your beautiful necklace?"

Sandy looked at me questioningly, with a hint of panic on her usually serene face.

"I, *um* . . . only wear that in the summertime," she stated weakly.

Fiona didn't respond and appeared to slip back into her own

silent place. Sandy looked at me again. I just shrugged my shoulders. Then she looked at Mac who did the same.

"Would you like to look at some photographs, Mrs. MacAvery?" Sandy asked eventually. "I think you may enjoy seeing them."

Mac passed Sandy my phone and she held it up for Fiona to see.

Young Fiona, eyes puffy and red from tears and probably lack of sleep, grabbed a pair of glasses from the bedside table and slipped them on her grandmother's face.

"Oh, look, Grandma; It's you and Grandpa!"

Sandy took a hold of the old woman's thin-skinned hand. "Mrs. MacAvery, is this a picture of *your* wedding day?"

Fiona focused on the photo on the phone. "Well, bless your heart!" the elderly woman said as she snapped from her reverie.

"Your gown was so beautiful and your husband, what a handsome man!"

"It was covered with handmade lace and came from my homeland. Douglass almost wore his kilt but it was so hot and all that wool! I told him he might catch a bit of a breeze," she chuckled. "I always loved that photo of us; reminds me of Sunday mornings, walking to church with Douglass by my side. He was a good-looking fellow, strong and broad shouldered but in his Sunday suit, he turned a lot of the ladies' heads. I'd hold onto his arm extra tight on Sundays," she smiled with remembrance. "Are there more?"

"We only found one more, I'm afraid," Sandy replied as she ran her finger across the screen.

"Oh, I'm glad it was this one! I remember that day like it was yesterday, son. You were just the cutest thing I'd ever seen and I couldn't get over those long eyelashes!"

Everyone stared at Fiona in amazement and, besides the continuous beeping of a call bell in the hallway, it was so quiet you could hear a pin drop.

"Mom?" Mac asked, disbelieving.

"Yes, dear, it's only me. Who else would I be, Marilyn Monroe? Come over here and give your mother a kiss."

Mac did just that, and held on for dear life, with tears forming in his eyes.

"Did I ever tell you, on our way home from the hospital the car broke down? I had to nurse you on the side of the road while your father changed the tire. It was so dang hot that day. I remember we had to wash up before your grandfather took that picture of us. Your dad had gotten grease on his good shirt and he made me stand in front of him – see?" She closed her eyes and smiled, apparently in deep remembrance.

Mac pulled out his phone and stepped outside the room. Fiona then embraced her granddaughter and covered her cheeks with kisses. "How was your first year at finishing school, dear?"

"You mean college, Grandma? It was great, but I missed *you* so much. I thought about you every day."

"I thought about you, too, my sweet little thistle. I hoped you were enjoying your lessons and living in the dormitory. Tell me, did you have a compatible roommate? Were the young men agreeable?"

The conversation flowed and Mac and Shona's two sons, their wives and twin grandsons arrived a short time later. Sandy and I moved to the far side of the room while the elder Fiona entertained and mystified us with a lifetime of stories, including one of a simple gift.

"We were on our honeymoon and walking hand in hand on the beach in Beach Haven. Your father bent down and picked up a little shell. It shone like gold and was very thin and fragile looking. *Our love is like this shell*," he said, as he turned it over in his hands. *"Delicate and alive with color, yet strong enough to withstand the changing tides of daily life and the storms that wage as well. Tha gaol agam ort."* I loved when he spoke Gaelic to me. I've missed that so much."

"That's lovely, Grandma," young Fiona commented. "I didn't know Grandpa was such a poet."

"He said I inspired him. He was a strapping man but a big mush on the inside."

I whispered to Sandy, "I think we should be heading back. Buoy's probably ready to stretch his legs and we don't want to miss the inspector."

"I understand," she sighed, with a fulfilled look on her face.

Mac and Shona thanked us again for coming. We said our goodbyes with handshakes and hugs. When Sandy wrapped her arms around the jovial old woman, she whispered something in her ear, too low for me to make out.

"Your visit was such a treat!" Fiona said as she squeezed Sandy's hand and gave me a wide smile. "I hope I'll see you both again soon."

"That would be lovely," Sandy replied.

Buoy was overjoyed to see us, stretch his legs and pee on a hedge bordering the parking lot. I gave him a drink of water and a biscuit before we climbed back into the Jeep.

"That was wonderful!" Sandy said as we buckled up.

"Yeah, but you have to admit, the whole meeting was strange. I was beginning to feel like we were in an episode of *The Twilight Zone*. Mac said she hadn't recognized anyone in months and for some reason she thought she knew you! Then we ended up having *her* pictures and suddenly she's back to normal. I just don't get it."

"It seems pretty obvious to me, Dillan. I believe we just witnessed a miracle."

That afternoon, as we worked on the house and waited for the inspector to show up, I couldn't stop thinking of what had happened at the hospital. Mac's mother seemed perfectly lucid and contented while we were there; I only hoped it would last.

A thirty-something Mr. Zimmerman arrived late and appeared very frazzled. His computer was giving him problems which added to his already stressed-out demeanor. As I accompanied him on his tour, he scratched out notes on a clipboard, took photos, and searched through a messy stack of papers for that all-important form that Mac needed to sign. Once he had finished, inside and out, he said a quick robotic thank you and goodbye.

"I imagine it's emotionally draining work," I said, as I escorted him to his car.

"I've never worked under disaster conditions before. I'm doing the best I can, but everyone wants everything yesterday. I understand and all, I really do, but I'm only one person. I've been working eighteen-hour days since this happened. I'm totally exhausted."

"We appreciate what you're doing. I'm sure all the home and business owners do."

"Thank you. A comment like that goes a long way. I'll send the Proof of Loss to Mr. MacAvery as soon as possible. Oh, tell any of your friends that've applied for FEMA, they've been asking for blueprints. I'm not sure what that's all about, but if they can get their hands on any, it might help speed the process for them."

"Thanks, man. I'll convey the message."

I hammered a makeshift piece of plywood over the hole in the facade and we headed to the mainland for some much-needed R&R. Once we were situated at the Holiday Inn, we fed and walked Buoy, then relaxed in front of a home improvement show on HGTV (one of the channels Sandy didn't mind watching). We'd been so busy that we'd skipped lunch without noticing. Now both of us were ravenous but too exhausted and comfortable to leave the couch. After some discussion, I remembered a pizza joint that Jake had raved about so we ordered a clam-topped pizza, minestrone soup, side salads and cannoli and had it delivered to the room.

I never got tired of watching Sandy eat. She was so excited and easy to please. She was the epitome of a kid in a candy store. Every bite that I took for granted, she savored. It was symbolic of how she lived her life. Whether it was making a new friend, sharing a meal or helping a stranger, pure enjoyment graced her pretty face. She had more spark for life in her little finger than most people had in their whole bodies and it was enchanting.

Once we were stuffed, Sandy went to soak in the tub. Buoy lay on the couch next to me and I flipped through the channels aimlessly. It seemed like only moments later I was awakened by her delicate, musical voice.

"Dillan, you'll get a stiff neck lying like that. I'm done in the bath and I think I may have saved you a bit of hot water."

"How long have I been out, girl?" I asked, as I pushed myself up, sat back against the couch and stretched.

"Well, when you didn't knock on the bathroom door, I figured you fell asleep. I was soaking a while, then I showered and washed my hair. I'd say an hour or so, but definitely not more than two. I totally lost track of the time. I hope you don't mind."

"Of course not. That's why we're here. Are you ready to go to sleep?"

"Well, the bed does look mighty inviting. Who do you think Buoy will choose tonight?"

After a moment of thought I replied, "He'll probably rotate between us. I'm gonna go enjoy a hot shower and hopefully work some of these kinks out of my neck."

I didn't mean to hint that I wanted a neck rub but it sounded that way. I'm sure there was only one thing that would have felt better at this point and I didn't want to hint at that either. This woman deserved much more than that. She deserved a true, deep love – something that takes longer than a few weeks to develop.

"Night then."

I gave her upper arms a quick rub through the thick hotel bathrobe and kissed the top of her head. Her hair smelled faintly of the sea, in a good way. "Don't wait up," I whispered in her ear.

When I came out of the bathroom, after letting the hot water ease my tense muscles, Sandy appeared to be sleeping but once I climbed into my bed she rolled over.

"Dillan?" she asked softly.

"Yes?" My body responded in anticipation.

"Would you like to . . . "

"Uh huh?"

" . . . share some of *your* story with me?"

Internally I sighed with deep disappointment. "Um, sure – but it's not all that exciting," I said as I fluffed my pillow and got comfortable.

"It'll be exciting to me."

"Ok, here goes – The Story of Dillan Eckert, Take One."

I paused and chose my words carefully, trying to sound theatrical. "My parents had tried for years to get pregnant so when it finally happened they didn't tell anyone for the fear of jinxing something. On July 31, 1985, they were celebrating their wedding anniversary in Cocoa Beach, Florida when my mom went into labor six weeks early. She blames it on the blue moon that was hanging over the beach that night. So, I was premature but it didn't affect me in the long run. I did all the normal kid things: collected baseball cards, played video games, joined Little League and swim teams."

"Go on."

"My grandmother died from breast cancer when I was nine and my grandfather died less than a year later. Everyone said he couldn't live without her. I'd spent a lot of time with them and I took it pretty hard, especially because my mom was a nurse. I guess I believed she had super powers or something and I couldn't understand how she'd just let them die. I was really confused and angry for a long time."

"I'm sorry, Dillan. That's very sad."

"Of course, once I got older, I understood; but I'm sure it didn't help my grieving parents at the time."

"You're being too hard on yourself; you were just a child."

"Yeah, maybe."

"Tell me some more."

"All right, let's see. My first kiss was Melissa Bradley in the sixth grade. Two weeks later, during lunch period, I saw her holding hands with a seventh-grade football player. To distract myself from my broken heart, I binged on Super Mario 64."

"Uh-huh."

"I have an aunt, uncle and three older cousins in Texas but I never got to know them very well. I don't think my dad is particularly close with his older brother."

"That's too bad. Tell me more."

I didn't want her to think that I was looking for sympathy, but that's what it sounded like so I tried to be more positive. "Every summer, we'd go back to Florida to celebrate my birthday and take a ceremonial walk on the beach. Mom jokes that I learned to swim even before I could walk. As the years went by, I tried every water sport imaginable: surfing, waterskiing, parasailing, windsurfing, kayaking and paddle boarding. They were all fun but swimming came naturally, just like breathing. When I wasn't in the water we'd go on day trips: Disney World, Kennedy Space Center, Brevard Zoo, The Dinosaur Museum. I enjoyed the excursions, but I was always anxious to get back to the beach. That's also where we found Buoy, so you can see why Cocoa Beach is so special."

"What?"

"Yeah, it's kinda crazy."

Hearing his name, Buoy had left Sandy's bed, jumped on mine and plopped down next to me.

"Dad and I went up to the beach one evening to toss a football around. I spotted him first, just a little black mound in the surf. I totally freaked out when I saw it was a puppy. Dad said we should bury it so the gulls wouldn't eat it. He was shocked when he felt his little heart still beating! We took him to an emergency clinic and they kept him overnight. I couldn't sleep a wink. I just kept praying that he wouldn't die. They called us early the next morning and said he was their miracle puppy! When we picked him up, they were feeding him from a bottle. He was so damn cute and tiny. We took turns feeding him every couple of hours for the next few weeks. It was amazing how quickly he grew after that."

"He's so lucky you found him," she whispered.

"No, I'm the one who's lucky. He's been the best dog imaginable."

"I agree. He's very special. I wouldn't be here today without him."

"I never thought I'd say *this*, but I'm so glad he jumped into the ocean that day," I said, as I reached over and gently scratched Buoy between the ears. There was a pause in the conversation and I thought she'd fallen asleep.

"Tell me a little more," she said, as she rolled on her back and stretched out.

"Um . . . Sometimes during winter break we'd take cruises to the most beautiful islands in the Bahamas. That crystal-clear water, snorkeling with the fishes, it makes my heart sing."

"That's lovely and all the more reason you should continue to lifeguard," she said with a yawn.

I didn't take it personally; I knew she was tired. "Thanks, Sandy. We'll save the grown-up Dillan for Take Two."

"Thank you for sharing," she said as she rolled over.

"You're welcome." I shut my eyes and took a deep, slow breath.

A few short feet away lay the most beautiful person I had ever met, and *she* was interested in my life story. There was only one thing that could make this night any better: that I might somehow wind up in her bed. My mind wandered and my fantasy grew, among other things, to epic proportions. I forced myself to think about hammers (that didn't work), screws (not that either), nails (nope), wood (crap!). Weren't there any tools that didn't have sexual connotations? Sometime later, serene images drifted through my mind; a gentle surf alive with moonlight, palm trees swaying, the epitome of a loving embrace. I was on the edge of sleep when I heard the most beautiful voice whisper, *Aloha au ia 'oe. A hui hou, my darling.*

BUOY

I JUMPED OFF THE couch and onto the bed with the girl. She smooshed the pillow until it was just right, just like I used to dig in the old couch cushions, and she curled up in a little ball. As I lay against her, I felt an unusual warmth radiating from her body and a strange smell perfuming her skin. It was as undeniable and unmistakable as walking into a cloud of skunk spray. Dillan's scent had been changing lately too. How they didn't notice what was happening was beyond me. If ever two humans were falling in love, it was them. I only hoped there would still be room in their hearts for me once they realized it. I spent the night moving from warm body to warm body and hoped one day we could all sleep together in a great big bed made for three.

SANDY

DILLAN CONTINUED TO SPOIL me. I was already looking forward to our next hotel stay, although he assured me that we would have our own electricity and hot water very soon. We just had to stop on the way home and buy some kind of fixtures. As we were checking out of the hotel, Dillan's phone rang. He stepped away from the desk to take the call. I grabbed our duffle bag and Buoy's leash and sat on the couch near the fireplace to wait. After a few minutes, he came back, looking upset. He sat down and took my hands in his. I wasn't sure what had happened. Had Captain Jack found out who I was?

"I have some sad news," he stated. "Fiona passed away last night."

"Oh my, I'm so sorry to hear that! She seemed so well yesterday."

"Mac said she continued to have a great day after we left. She was in wonderful spirits, and had visited with the family all afternoon. Even her good friend Lilly had been able to make it up there. She had her favorite meal of shepherd's pie and ice cream for dinner. After that she told them she loved them all, but she was tired and wanted to go to sleep. Mac had wanted to stay, but she insisted he go home and sleep next to his wife. The nurse found her early this morning, looking totally peaceful."

"Gosh that's awful – but lovely in a way. I'm happy I had the opportunity to meet her."

"Want to hear something weird?"

"I guess."

"The nurse found a shiny yellow seashell clutched in her hand."

"What's so weird about that?"

"Mac had never seen it among her belongings and none of the family would own up to giving it to her."

It was rather a lovely thought – that her husband had come to meet her. "Will we go to the funeral?"

"There isn't going to be one. They had wanted their ashes spread at sea once they were both gone. Mac said they will have a small memorial in the spring."

I was saddened by the news but relieved in a small way. From what Mac had said, Fiona hadn't been herself in some time but yesterday she was beaming with memories and love for her family. She seemed to enjoy her last day on earth immensely. What could've been better than that?

We stopped at The Home Depot and Dillan filled the cart with supplies. He also placed an order for a delivery of sheetrock which would arrive the next day. Once back at the inn, we got down to work, measuring and re-measuring, taking notes and clearing out more debris. It seemed to reproduce on its own. I could tell Dillan was disheartened having to repeat the whole process by the way he kept sighing, but perhaps it was Fiona's death that had hit him harder than he let on. After a bit, Buoy went upstairs to lie down, where it was quieter and more comfortable.

"Is there anything you want to talk about?" I asked, genuinely concerned.

"Maybe I have a little PTSD," he replied, "and I feel guilty about it because I wasn't even here during the storm."

"Anyone who sees this place would feel the same, Dillan."

"I mean, I never gave death too much thought, but almost losing Buoy, then Fiona dying – it makes you see how quickly everything can change."

"I guess the best thing to do is never take anyone or anything for granted. We are surrounded by gifts every day – including our own breath."

"I know we've only just met, but you seem to be the glue that's holding everything together."

"That's a lovely thing to say, Dillan, but you give me too much credit. I'm just a girl – and a lost girl at that. I thank *you* for being so kind and providing for me."

"It's the other way around, Sandy. I thank you!"

He hugged me then and I felt a tear on my cheek. I wasn't sure if it was his or mine.

"Well, let's get back to work," he said with a sniff. "This old inn isn't going to rebuild itself."

"Just show me what to do!"

ALEXANDER HENRY

I WOKE UP ON the hard floor of my living room. I guess I had eluded death yet again. Who knew an oriental rug could feel as hard and cold as a stone slab? Well, it *was* threadbare in spots. Only a few embers remained in the fireplace and the room and my old bones were frigid. I pushed myself up with effort, achy in places that hadn't ached for some time. Everything seemed intact but the back of my very hard head felt sore to the touch. I guess I had fainted, and then I remembered *her*: my Naia.

With every stiff muscle complaining I made my way to the window, still expecting to see her there, but there was nothing unusual or unworldly under the moonlight. Her photo and trinkets still fresh in my memory combined with years of loneliness must have finally caught up with me. It'd been nothing but a lovely, fleeting dream as I lay unconscious. I'd have to get an EKG and my blood pressure checked one of these days. I gingerly bent down, picked up my teacup from the floor and headed for bed.

The next morning, I was visited by a very amicable and youthful police officer.

"Mr. Henry, I saw smoke coming out of your chimney. What are you still doing here?"

"I live here, young man."

"Yes, yes but you should have evacuated with your neighbors. Would you like a ride to the mainland?"

"No, thank you. Everything is in order. Of course, it'll be better when the power's restored."

"Are you sure? Don't you have family you could stay with?"

"No, I don't. Thanks for checking on me but honestly, I'm doing all right – no water damage at all. My fireplace warms my living space and I have a camp stove to heat water and soup."

He didn't appear happy with my decision to stay but he didn't force me to leave either. He referred me to the Surf City Fire Department where they were collecting donated supplies and serving hot meals for the residents and volunteers who came to help restore utilities and clean up the debris. Oddly enough, there were other crackpots like myself who had stayed on the island although, I was informed, most hadn't fared as well.

"You'll have to stay on the boulevard; most of the other roads are impassable. Don't go south; it looks like the apocalypse down there. The sand's waist deep in some places. There's a curfew so don't be out after dark. It's not only dangerous but you could also be arrested for trespassing. We've got lots of help coming in to patrol so don't be intimidated by the National Guard. They may look intrusive but they're here to help us keep citizens safe and the island free of interlopers."

That was a lot to digest – but he had me at *hot meal*.

"By the way, Mr. Henry, if you need anything, we'll be stationed right at the Engleside for a few more days. After that we'll be at the old EOC building."

After the officer departed, I shaved and dressed in attire proper for a gathering. My car sputtered to life and I headed toward Bay Avenue. I thought he'd prepared me for the drive, but I had to pull over and collect myself before I reached the firehouse. I prided myself on being a man's man but I wasn't a machine. The island had suffered a cataclysm – my world in chaotic disarray. As I drove along, I fashioned myself an actor in a disaster film, but no one was yelling, "cut – that's a wrap!"

As I entered the firehouse, I wished I'd had more community spirit over the years. The camaraderie was obvious and the warmth extended to strangers, uplifting. We were all in this together, and together we'd get through it. That was the general atmosphere and it was reassuring. I sat with a police officer from Louisiana, a utility worker from Alabama, a bulldozer operator from the Army Corp of Engineers and an EMT from the Beach Haven Water and Ice Rescue Team.

"When you see the water gushing up out of the manhole covers, you know you're in trouble!" the latter recalled, ominously.

After chatting with them and some very unfortunate residents, I thanked the ladies behind the kitchen counter and headed for the door.

"Would you like to take a box home for your dinner, Mr. Henry?" the middle-aged blonde woman asked as she held out a Styrofoam container.

"I cannot refuse your delightful cooking, ma'am. I thank you wholeheartedly."

"Grab a bag of ice and anything else you might need. There are coats, hats, gloves, bottled water and cleaning supplies."

"Thank you kindly. The food was most delicious," I replied, as I reached the door. Although it wasn't the French fried lobster tail at Howard's Restaurant, I couldn't have enjoyed it more.

I drove slowly down the boulevard, being dodged by speeding military, emergency and utility vehicles while simultaneously avoiding piles of trash, sand and all manner of foreign objects. I'd never been so stressed driving here, not even in the dead of summer when the population swells to 110,000 people. By the time I turned on to Pearl Street, I was exhausted. Straight ahead, the parking lot for the beach was full of sand and the pavilion where I sometimes sat to watch the sunrise had been reduced to a few shattered pieces of lumber. I had more than enough stimulation for one day. I needed a cup of tea and my easy chair.

Every night I had fallen asleep in my chair as I watched the road below for her return. One evening, I stared out into the swirling snow as it deposited a fine layer of white over the street. I realized that my imagination had gotten the best of me and it was time to let her go and move on. Maybe I needed to get out and mingle a bit more.

I had enjoyed the young people at the firehouse. Still, the rumble of the bulldozers, pinging of the front-end loaders and thump-hum, thump-hum of the Blackhawk helicopters was a bit more stimulation than I felt comfortable with. I did relish the thought of another hot meal, but I wasn't up for the journey to Surf City. It may have only been a few miles, but it had felt like crossing the desert without a canteen. I just wanted to sit by the warmth of my fireplace and read.

Two weeks after the storm made landfall, I decided to step outside once more. My items weren't water damaged but I figured I'd take advantage of the continuous parade of garbage trucks and get rid of a few things. Some empty paint cans, a broken air conditioner and vacuum, and a bunch of rusty tea biscuit tins were set neatly by the curb.

I headed back to my bedroom. A part of me wanted to lie down and rest, but I forced myself into the closet and grabbed the old hat box. It was the most difficult thing I'd ever done. Outside I went, with my most prized possession; I placed it delicately on top of the pile. I got my broom from the garage and started to sweep the sand toward the road while keeping an eye on the box. I could take it back inside at any time. I could hold on or let her go.

I hadn't made a dent on the driveway when I felt a nearby presence. I looked up and *she* was there, standing on the sidewalk, beside the treasure box. Still young and strikingly beautiful, I dropped my broom and fell to my knees, clutching my chest.

"Are you okay? Are you having pain?"

I moved clumsily over to the curb and sat down quite firmly, mentally unable to process what was happening. Was I enveloped in a lovely dream or had I died and gone to heaven? I looked up and focused on a face which was in surprisingly close proximity.

"Do you have a cell phone? Should we call 911?" she asked, looking quite panic stricken.

"I . . . I . . .," choked out, staring into her eyes. Then, intrusively as a slap, it registered – the color was wrong. The blue was much too bright, just as her hair was too amber. She wasn't my Naia after all, just a girl who resembled her most acutely.

"Oh, my gosh! Do you know me?" she asked oddly.

"No, no . . . I don't believe I do, but for a moment I thought you were . . . someone from my past," I sighed, as I took my first deep breath. She sat on the curb next to me.

"Can I get you a glass of water? Is there anyone inside?"

"No, no . . . I am quite alone here. I'm feeling better now, but if you don't mind, I think I'll just rest a minute or two. I think perhaps I've done enough work for one day." I wasn't sure if I was disappointed or relieved. The thought of Naia returning to accompany me to heaven wasn't an unhappy thought. We sat in silence for a bit.

"Feeling better?" she asked, hopefully.

"Infinitely. Thank you, young lady."

"That's good. What a relief! I saw you sweeping from down the block and thought – maybe I could help?"

"You're incredibly kind. I've been putting this off for a while; but compared to the rest of the island, I guess a little sand is no big deal."

"I'd *really* like to help!" she pleaded. "It would make me very happy."

"All right then, if you insist. Have a crack at it, miss."

I attempted to stand, only to find her hand under my elbow, steadying me. It was a thoughtful but unnecessary gesture. We both bent to retrieve the broom at the same time and clunked heads. A fit of apologies and flurry laughter ensued. I decided that I felt quite comfortable with this young woman, even with her resemblance to the one who tore out my heart and cast it away like moldy bread. I rubbed my head and walked into the garage for a lawn chair. I placed it so I needn't squint my eyes while my legs were bathed in the warmth of the sunshine. I watched her sweep, and I remembered.

It was a late August afternoon – the day my Naia disappeared. Most of the beachgoers had returned from their day of frivolity in the sun and were readying for dinner. We were standing right over there on the street corner, beside a long-gone row of bayberry bushes. I had nervously rubbed one of its leaves between my fingers and she took my hand to inhale its peppery scent.

"This plant's lovely perfume will always remind me of you," she had said as she kissed my palm and held it to her cheek. She then removed her necklace and handed the precious piece to me as a token of her love and a promise of her return. She held me in a tight embrace, one hand entwined in my hair, the other arm tugging at my back. Fear and determination emanated from her as she rubbed her face into my neck and whispered, "I love you more than all the fish in the sea, all the sand on the beach, and all the stars in the sky."

I had no reason to disbelieve her. I could feel the truth in her rapid heartbeat and in my own. I begged her to let me accompany her, to stand ground with her, to plead our case, to convince her parents that her arranged marriage was a horrible mistake. She insisted there was no need. With a final kiss, she turned and walked away. I watched her for quite a while, until she disappeared into a crowd of people headed into town. She had never told me where she was staying. She hadn't wanted her parents to know I existed, until now.

We were destined to be together; she had proclaimed it over and over during those wonderful weeks of summer. We walked, hand in hand, along the shore as the moon rose; planning our wedding, our home, our children, our summer vacations. We dreamed; with hard work, we would someday own our own place on the island. As we took our morning strolls through Beach Haven's historic district, this was the home she loved the most. It was called The Seventh Sister, the last of a group of homes built by Floyd Cranmer in 1936. The huge three-story, covered with cedar shakes and window shutters stood proudly on the corner. The same one I had lived in, now, for so many years – waiting. I remembered how she sung its praises, the wrap-around porch with its unsurpassed view of the sea, the fact that it sat on elevated ground. "Here we could weather any storm," she had chimed. I had bought it for her as a gesture of my undying love but had convinced myself it was just a quiet place to cultivate my characters.

I felt a tear slide down my cheek and pulled a handkerchief from my trousers. I hoped the girl didn't notice as I blew my nose.

"I've wanted nothing more than to get working since I've gotten here. I just didn't know how to go about it," she said, as she swept vigorously.

"What's your name, miss?" I finally thought to ask.

She paused unnaturally and I could almost hear the wheels in her mind squeaking as she replied, "Sandy."

"How lovely!" And quite ironic, I thought. "How apropos! My name is Alexander Henry. Some people know me as Michael Stocks, but I prefer Henry or Hank."

"Okay, Henry. It's nice to meet you."

As she swept the sand into a pile at the edge of the drive, I heard a garbage truck rumbling up Beach Avenue. I was trying to decide what to do when a familiar looking dog lumbered up the street, greeting Sandy with excessive enthusiasm.

"Oh, Buoy! I'm so sorry! I completely forgot you were sleeping on the stoop. I didn't even tell you that I was leaving."

The dog, which I'd seen during walks with his owner, was unable to contain the excitement of their reunion, and upended the treasure box with its wagging tail. We both ran to the hatbox and nearly clunked heads again.

"Oh, my!" she proclaimed, as she delicately lifted the necklace from the ground before the dog could trample it.

"Sit, Buoy! Sit!" she commanded, and he did. "This may be the most beautiful thing I have ever seen," she said, sounding quite awed. She handed it to me then and quickly scooped the rest of the items into the box, catching a glimpse of the photograph. She looked at me with questioning eyes. It was over a pot of tea and a tin of sugary biscuits that I told her my story and she told me hers.

JANINE

NOVEMBER 2012

I SAT AT MY best friend's kitchen table, the room bright and sunny. Outside, her block looked oddly untouched, as if the hurricane had never happened. I sipped a cup of her famous coffee. Just pour in the beans and push a button – the Italian espresso machine did everything except drink the coffee for you. The superb brew was always a bonus that came with visiting Suzanne, but today, as all last week, I was alone. I felt the tears come to my eyes again and sniffed hard against them. I was tired of crying, and leaving my home wasn't the only thing I felt incredibly saddened by.

I'd been in Suzanne's home for just over two weeks, when she and her menagerie of pets returned. If she hadn't had them to consider she may have ignored the evacuation order as well. I was truly happy that they were safe and her home wasn't damaged. Somehow it gave me hope that things wouldn't be too bad when I finally got back to my own place.

Unfortunately, I was shocked as we drove south along Long Beach Boulevard and Bay Avenue. With mouths agape, we witnessed every type of destruction imaginable, leaving me to fear the worst. She stopped her car when the road ended abruptly, the pavement lifted and deposited in my little front yard. The bottom floor of the duplex was wide open, the window glass gone, sections of walls washed away. Oddly a curtain still hung, blowing in the breeze. Any trace of my personal belongings had been carried away in the current.

My son and I had spent every summer here when he was a child, while my husband worked as a cardio-thoracic surgeon at Columbia Presbyterian. Brian thought it'd be a great investment property. Most weekends he'd come down and we'd be the perfect family. Later, I realized it was simply a perfect place to tuck me away while he screwed around with anyone who'd have him. I got the duplex in the divorce settlement, while he kept our estate in Westchester and the cabin in the Catskills. At least until now, I had the rental money to pay the taxes; now I had nothing. Suzanne hugged me as I tried to contain my sobs and she immediately offered to convert her barroom into a makeshift apartment and invited me to stay until all was made right. I loved her and appreciated her opening her home to me; honestly, I had hoped for another invitation, one to stay with my son and his family, but that hadn't happened.

I had always thought that my son and I had a close relationship. I thought I had done pretty well as a single mother, especially with my parents' help. They cared for him while I worked and supported us with love and a strong sense of family values.

My son, Liam, graduated college and left home for a few years. He rented a place with a friend, did his share of partying, got a job with a car insurance company and grew up somewhere along the way. After a while, he realized his father was not going to shell out cash willy-nilly, so he moved home to live rent-free and build up a bank account. I was happy to have him home even if he still tracked in copious amounts of sand, left his balled-up socks on the living room floor and dirty dishes in the sink. I was happy for the company. After a couple of years, he met his wife-to-be and almost every weekend she'd come from the mainland and stay with us. I thought it was because she loved the beach so much, but I think it had more to do with the fact that she was not allowed to share her bedroom at her parents' home. I figured they were adults and smart enough to make responsible decisions.

From time to time they asked me to tag along on their excursions, but I felt it was more of a polite invitation than an actual desire for my company. The weekends were the only time that they could get together and I didn't want to interfere in their budding relationship.

Oddly, when my son did propose, he asked his stepmother – not me – to help him pick out the ring. I had nothing against the gorgeous young woman who married my ex-husband; in fact, on the rare occasion we happened to meet, she was very pleasant. Still, my balloon of self-importance imploded when my son danced with her as his second mother during their wedding reception. That was not a title I was willing to share with anyone.

When I found out my first grandchild was a girl, I was ecstatic! Finally, there was a little girl in the family. I was anxious to buy frilly clothes, dolls and girlie things. I pictured myself babysitting, reading to her, coloring, creating arts and crafts together and sharing my love of baking cookies and cupcakes with someone who might enjoy it as much as I do. As she grew older we'd go out to lunch, enjoy movies and peruse the shopping malls together. I was sure she would love me most deeply. Of course, I would have loved a little boy just as much, and when my grandson came along two years later, I felt exactly the same way.

It wasn't long before my dreams slipped away. I felt like an outcast. If not for an occasional family birthday party or holiday dinner, we never would have seen them. Numerous misconceptions had led to hurt feelings, hurt feelings to a lack of communication and that only led to deeper and deeper wounds. A person can only be turned away so many times before they will stop asking to be included in someone's life. At first, I convinced myself that it was only my imagination. "Once she gets to truly know me," I said. "They are really busy," I said. "Both parents work," I said. "The kids are in daycare," I said. I offered to babysit any time and was crushed when they mentioned that the woman who lived in the apartment below was a handy resource. They barely knew her, and had never even asked me.

When Ellie was nearing her first birthday, I offered to have a party. I was such a proud grandmother that I longed to share her with friends and family who hadn't had the opportunity to meet her. I was thrilled to actually feel like a part of the child's life, if only for a day. It was great fun planning, shopping, baking, cooking and decorating for my precious little one. The party was a success, and I had tons of photos for my scrapbook.

For her second birthday, I started planning early and enjoyed every minute of it. An Under-the-Sea party sounded perfect. I designed and made the invitations and decorations. I planned the menu and the table-scape. I taught myself to use a piping bag to decorate the cookies and made fondant sea creatures to top the cupcakes. I was in my glory doing all this for my grandbaby and the day went swimmingly! Such joy I experienced seeing her little face shine with excitement. It made my heart sing.

Shortly after that my grandson was born. My parents and I were notified a day later and asked not to come to the hospital. "Wait till we're home a few days," my son said. He should have just stabbed me in the heart. I'm sure it would've felt the same. We did meet little Connor later that week and it was a lovely visit. He had the longest fingers and toes I had ever seen on a baby! My son and his wife were a bit tired but well, and my granddaughter Ellie was playful and full of energy as usual.

A few weeks later, I called to see how things were going. My son said they had just returned from the hospital where my grandson was treated for a life-threatening brain infection. He'd spent three days in the Pediatric ICU. I know I should have been more understanding that I hadn't received a phone call, but again my heart crumbled. At least the baby was out of danger and able to come home. Only time would tell if he would suffer from any residual brain damage. Selfish me wondered who babysat with Ellie. Maybe this time it was a blessing being left out. I didn't have to suffer with worry but I didn't have the opportunity to pray for his healing either.

After that, the children were under lock and key for a while. We didn't see them until November when Connor was christened. There was a lovely service and reception but only the godparents were allowed to hold the baby. His great-grandparents and I had to love him from across the room.

Right after the new year, I started planning Ellie's third birthday party. The cold winter months to come seemed less bleak with the promise of an engrossing and pleasant task. Disney's Tangled was all the rage and seemed to be a fitting theme for a little girl with long blonde hair. I ordered the paper plates, napkins, cups and balloons.

I made tissue pom-pom decorations with Rapunzel and Flynn Rider that I printed from the computer and colorful flag banners to hang about the room. I ordered a golden fringe curtain which was reminiscent of Rapunzel's flowing golden hair to hang behind the party table and made a tower from foam board and colored paper to hold the cupcakes.

Unfortunately, during a rare phone conversation with my son, I was told that I wouldn't be allowed to host the party. "It's not what we want for our daughter," he said. I felt my throat closing up and tears fill my eyes. It wasn't the first time my son had made me cry but I certainly wanted it to be the last. I couldn't imagine why someone would not want a lovely party for their little girl, why my son could not see what it meant to me to give her a special day. When he was a child, I was the most important person in his world. He'd follow me around the house like a puppy dog. Now that he was an adult, it seemed I had no place in his life at all.

I don't like being hurt by someone I love. I don't like the way it rips apart the soul you've fought so hard to protect. The rest of the world is out there to test and torment you; your family is there to love and nurture you. I wondered what the hell I'd done wrong. With those last tears, I envisioned not the adorable little towheaded three-year-old that wouldn't let me out of his sight, but his father, the man who had emotionally abandoned me long before standing at the church altar proclaiming, "I do."

Shortly after that, I cleaned out my house – the closet in my son's old room, the storage areas. I took all his photos off the wall, including ones from the wedding. I found old homework papers, art projects, shop projects, baseball cards and figures, crayon-drawn greeting cards, paperback books, even his high school graduation gown. It all went in the trash, everything except a tiny porcelain plate that had come from an elementary school fundraiser. The school had asked for five dollars per child and in turn they could pick out a gift from the catalog. He had chosen a little plate for me, appropriately sized for a Barbie doll. On it, the words *I Love You, Mom* in blue. Red and yellow flowers encircled the words along with tiny butterflies and a bird. He had been so proud when he'd given it to me. Around the plate was a thin brass wire frame which allowed it to stand. It sat on my bedside table for years and even in my deepest pain, I couldn't bear to part with it.

Nine months later, it was gone, along with my house and most everything in it. I was living in my best friend's home, helping care for her three dogs, two cats and five birds in an effort to make myself useful. I kept my cell phone close by at all times, waiting for that call which would reunite us. After some happy tears, my granddaughter would come on and sing "Twinkle, Twinkle Little Star" and whisper, "Love you, Grammy; 'night-night!"

DILLAN

DECEMBER 2012

I HAD MY WORK cut out for me at the inn, but Sandy helped keep me on track. She was always right there to lend a helpful hand: take Buoy for a walk, pick up some groceries, or grab some coffees to get us over the afternoon hump. I was amazed how much we could accomplish in a day. Exhausted, we were usually in bed by eight or nine o'clock. Our sleeping arrangement was rather unconventional, and I was *almost* too tired to fantasize about ravishing her as I gazed up at her quilt-covered form lying in my bed.

Once I had replaced the electric boxes and received the necessary Certificate of Occupancy, things got a whole lot easier. The power and hot water were a godsend and not only for personal hygiene reasons!

I felt amped being so productive and even better having both Sandy and Buoy in my life. In my mind, she was quickly becoming part of my family and that was a dangerous thought, for there was absolutely nothing holding her here. Her past could catch up with her at any minute or she could just as easily decide to move on to bigger and better things. I couldn't help but wonder how no one had come to claim her – she was so amazing, not to mention stunningly beautiful. Somewhere, someone must be grieving, assuming she was dead; and yet, to date, no missing person report had been filed. It just didn't make sense. So, I treasured every moment with her and Buoy too. I became very aware of the present and wanted to be living in it. I felt different inside, better – more relaxed and fulfilled.

I was a bit apprehensive taking her along when the lifeguards met up at the patrol barracks. Of course, she wouldn't have it any other way. What guy wouldn't enjoy the cocky feeling he'd have showing off such a special woman to his friends? Unsurprisingly, they all took to her rather quickly, including Katie. I was relieved she had another girl to talk to as they spackled and sanded – as a bonus, it left her unavailable to the guys.

"That's quite a catch you've made, Dillan," Chief Gavin said, as he shoved some old insulation in a trash bag. "I hear she rode in on the storm. I bet that's quite a story to tell."

"I'm sure it would be and I wish she could tell it, but she's suffering from amnesia, sir."

"That's got to be tough. Jack said no one's even been looking for her. If there's anything I can do to help, let me know."

"Thanks, I really appreciate it. If we think of anything, we won't be afraid to ask."

Another week had flown by and we'd been up and working since dawn. I told Sandy she should put her feet up while I ran out and grabbed our lunch. She looked a little put out but then headed for the stairs taking the most recent copy of *The SandPaper* with her.

The weather was chilly, but I decided to hoof it as it would give her a longer break. As I walked past Kapler's Pharmacy, I noticed the windows were freshly decorated and the door propped open. A handful of people were working inside. Kapler's had always been a cool place to shop, not only because of the convenience factor but because the staff was friendly and beyond helpful. Whether I had a sunburn, hangover, upset stomach, stuffed up nose, bug bites or sore muscles, they offered not just a bottle of pills, but advice: keep the aloe vera in the refrigerator, a cold compress first then warm for strained muscles, darken the room and put a cool cloth on your forehead, drink extra water, try a cool mist humidifier, and no matter what you read – very hot water, not urine, is the best treatment for jellyfish stings! I loved the fact that it was a family-owned and community-driven business. Spend any time there and you could easily see they really knew and cared about their customers. The store had been gutted, Christmas lights hung, and folding tables set up with what appeared to be products salvaged from the storm.

"Hey there, Dillan; come on in!" I hadn't realized that I had been gawking and stepped inside. "I was very happy to hear you found your Buoy!" Pharmacist Roberts said.

"Thanks, it was a bit of a miracle, sir."

"I've asked you to call me Tom."

"I know but my parents instilled this respectfulness thing. It's hard to let it go."

"How did the inn make out in the storm?"

"Probably better than you guys. Thankfully, there weren't any appliances or much furniture on our bottom floor. It's coming along though. I see you're on top of things here."

"As best as we can be, I guess. We're having the Soiree tonight before the tree lighting ceremony. Why don't you come by and bring your new friend. The whole town's been talking about her. We'd like to meet your Sandy."

Really? I guess everyone in a small town would be interested when a mysterious stranger washes up on their beach. "The tree lighting, huh? I've been so busy, I forgot all about Christmas!"

"I think a lot of people have. That's why we've got something special planned this year. It's our hope to bring people together and help foster the healing process. We're serving hot drinks and snacks and there will be music and such."

"Sounds like just what this town needs!"

"But here's the best part: if you purchase a stocking for twenty dollars, you can fill it with anything you like. All the money is going to benefit the Beach Haven Fire Company and the first aid squad."

"That's a great idea!" I reached into my pocket and pulled out my wallet. "I'll take two! Here's forty dollars. I don't want you to run out of stockings before we get back."

"Well, I'm not sure we'll have a great turn out. Spirits are low and it's quite cold out. I'm surprised the tree lighting is even taking place this year, but we're hopeful."

"One should never lose hope, especially at Christmas," I replied as I felt Sandy's glowing personality inspire me. "I'm sure Sandy will love this idea. She's got more spirit than anyone I know!"

"We'll see you later then and tell all your friends."

"You got it."

I jogged up the street to the Bagel Shack and ordered two coffees and four slices of pizza. O'Malley's Pizza next door was left non-operational, but conveniently had been borrowing Bagel Shack's ovens in the afternoon, a big win-win for us. Bagel sandwiches in the morning, pizza in the afternoon. I spread the word about the Soiree to the staff and patrons then hightailed it back to the inn. As I rounded the block, I noticed the church bells were playing a Christmas carol and I began to hum along.

I carried lunch up to the kitchen, found it empty and walked down to the bedroom, thinking Sandy might have fallen asleep. Buoy was lying in the bed alone. Sandy was nowhere in sight. I roused Buoy from his sleep and stuffed down a slice of pie as we headed for the Jeep.

JACQUELINE ROSE

DECEMBER 2012

GRANDPA ASKED ME TO pick up a few groceries. Although the Bagel Shack was selling some basics to employees and the public at cost, we needed a few things besides milk, eggs and bread: Ovaltine, prunes, Raisin Bran, ice cream, peanut butter, and jam to be exact. Our Acme was still in bad shape, so I made my way to the mainland's ShopRite. The jam was the hardest thing to pick out and place in the cart. That was always Meema's thing, to make homemade jam every year.

God, I missed her a ton, but Grandpa still seemed devastated a year after Meema's passing. She'd left this world just moments after the life-sustaining machinery and medications had been removed from her body. I knew *that* was no life, lying there in an ICU bed, being poked and prodded, her butt wiped and throat suctioned by nurses and techs, male and female. She was by far the most modest woman I'd ever met and must've been mortified knowing strangers had cleaned her after she'd soiled herself. Did they see her as the loving, amazing woman she was, or just an empty vessel that once housed someone's wife and grandmother?

I had my share of screw-up's in my teens, but finally got it together when Grandpa called informing me that Meema had suffered a stroke. They'd been there for me, no matter how screwed up I'd been, and now I was going to be there for them. I left art school, moved to the island full time and got a job waitressing at The Chicken or The Egg.

I'd go with Grandpa to visit Meema at the nursing home sometimes, but it was horrible seeing her like that. She couldn't get out of bed by herself and had to get around in a wheelchair. She didn't have the strength to wheel herself about so she stayed wherever she'd been parked until someone moved her somewhere else. She could talk a bit, but mostly preferred to listen. She could nod, smile, laugh and still give me the "I love you so much, no matter what you've done" gaze. I'd look up and down at my arms and know she was referring to my tattoos. She had no idea about all the other shit I'd done and I was extremely happy about that. Asking her to still love me after that would be asking a lot. She and Grandpa were from another time when things were simpler and people were different. Life wasn't as complicated as it is now. I'm not sure she'd understand why I had done what I'd done and with whom. A lot of it was a blur now anyway, hazed over by my drug-clouded memory.

I'd enjoyed spending the summers on the island when I was a kid, when my mom would drop me off and disappear for months. Each year I'd wonder why she'd never come visit and as I grew older, I'd wonder if she'd ever come back for me at all. Eventually, I wished she wouldn't, but the day before school started she'd show up with whatever guy she'd currently taken up with and drag my ass back home. It didn't matter that my dad was off fighting a war somewhere. It didn't matter because he'd run off and joined the Marines months before I was born. He was too young and irresponsible to become a father, Mom said, but he was mature enough to wield a firearm and protect our country – go figure!

When I was a kid, he would occasionally send a Christmas gift or birthday card from some foreign port of call. Life on a warship meant being on the move, I guess. There was never a return address or phone number included. Until I heard from him again, I always assumed that he had been killed in the line of duty. It was a horrible way to think, but what recourse did I have? The worst part was I'd never even heard my father's voice.

On my fourteenth birthday, my mother splurged and got me these kickass biker boots that I'd spent months begging her for. After a pizza delivery and a slice of store-bought cake, she handed me a shipping box that had come from my father. I opened it up with such excitement. Inside, wrapped in French newspaper was a Fairytopia Mermaidia doll. **A kid's toy!** I was fourteen and he sent me a toy for a little girl. I searched through the box hoping, as in the past, for a photo, phone number or a return address and found nothing! I threw the box, with the doll in it, across the room and stormed out of the house. I lit up a cigarette and walked a few blocks, past the deli, the pharmacy, the smoke shop and entered the tattoo parlor. My new boots must've made me look older because when I said I was eighteen they didn't question me. My first tattoo was on my hip: a very sexy blue-haired mermaid. Five years and twelve tattoos later, Meema was dead, my mom had all but disappeared and my grandparents' house was in ruins.

It was hard to leave Grandpa and the island behind but after sixteen months, he insisted that I go back to school. "I love you my dear, but please, **go live your life**," he'd said. "I'm an old man and I am content to just putter about. My doctors say I am healthy enough to take care of myself and I will, I promise."

When I heard about Hurricane Sandy, I begged Grandpa to leave the island. He said he'd ridden out many hurricanes in his lifetime and he refused to leave, saying he promised Meema that he would always take care of the house. When the storm turned inland and was heading straight toward the island, I called the Beach Haven police and asked them to please check on him. Luckily, they got him out of there and took him to the Engleside before the storm surge destroyed the house and washed away everything in it.

This time, because the CHEGG was a literal wash out, I got a job at The Bagel Shack and was sharing an efficiency at the Engleside with Grandpa until we could make other plans. As I carried the groceries toward our room, a part of me wondered if he secretly hadn't wanted to die in the storm. He had been so depressed since Meema passed. To join my grandma and go down with the ship may have been his plan all along.

SANDY

DECEMBER 2012

DILLAN GAVE ME THE most wonderful surprise: Christmas! When I got back from Henry's house there was a spruce tree in the living room. It wasn't decorated, just standing there, plain and simple. The crisp smell of evergreen was wonderful.

"Where've you been?" he yelled from upstairs. "Your pizza's cold!"

"Sorry! I ran over to check on Henry and he insisted I share his tuna sandwich. He's such a sweetheart and I feel badly that he lives there all alone. Are you mad?"

"Of course not, a bit worried maybe, but it gave me time to run up to the Ship Bottom firehouse and get the tree. Do you like it?"

"Are you kidding? I love it! It smells so fresh and alive!"

"I'm not so sure about the alive part, girl – at least not anymore. Do you have any memories about Christmas?" he asked as he came down the stairs, Buoy bounding behind him.

"No, nothing in particular. I know what it is, of course, and that it makes me feel happy and thankful."

"Well, that's good enough. There's something going on in town tonight that I think you'll like. Get out of those work clothes and put on something clean and warm. We're gonna welcome the season in properly."

Dillan drove us to Kapler's Pharmacy, not because we couldn't walk but he didn't want to leave Buoy home or tied to a bench outside. The back of the Jeep was well-equipped with a squishy doggie bed and blanket. He told me this was one of his favorite stores before the storm came. The way he described it and their sister store, Regenerate, led me to believe that I'd like it too because many of their items were made from recycled products – Dillan knew how I felt about waste and pollution!

The store windows were lavishly decorated with three-foot-tall cupcakes, giant brightly wrapped candies, Christmas trees, a red-and-white striped North Pole, a poster-sized letter to Santa, some playful elves, and games and toys. People were just starting to wander in, carrying Christmas stockings or getting them at the door. Even with the ripped-out walls, exposed ceiling above and sub-flooring below, it was a warm and welcoming place. A multitude of Christmas lights and sparkling stars hung from the wood beams and the smell of popcorn and hot chocolate wafted through the air. Dillan handed me a stocking.

"Go fill 'er up, girl; anything you want."

He gave me a mischievous smile as he headed for the tables at the far end of the room.

Christmas music added to the holiday spirit as I perused the available goodies. A little of this and that, odds and ends that survived the storm: shampoo, coloring books, some kid's watercolors. I saw a dog toy and grabbed it for Buoy. Poor guy, he was missing all the fun waiting out in the Jeep. I saw nail files, some hand creams and brightly colored nail polish. The first two were practical, the latter not so much. Even while wearing work gloves, nail polish didn't stand a chance on my fingertips. A pack of pencils decorated with dinosaurs and an Old Barney pen that lit up when you clicked it for Dillan – whimsical and useful. I got two toothbrushes – one for each of us – and a musky-smelling shave cream for Dillan. I found some delicious-smelling raspberry bubble bath for the tub and matching body lotion. Now that we had hot water, I'd have to treat myself to a spa evening. I got a little folding mirror, a mascara, lip gloss and blush. On the next table was a bright orange *BEACH HAVEN* shoulder bag. It was just the right size to hold my new treasures and I loved it. I spied a collection of small photo frames. One had a seagull glued on top and I immediately thought of Henry – no, probably not a good idea to resurrect that photo from the hat box. I'd have to find him something else.

I headed for the dessert table at the back of the store. It was kind of Henry to offer me half of his sandwich and pickle earlier, but my stomach was far from full and grumbling loudly. I was so excited about going out that I had forgotten all about the pizza sitting on the kitchen table. I spied some cupcakes and cookies that were sitting there just begging to be eaten when an older woman spoke to me.

"Hot chocolate, miss? I made it myself!" she said proudly.

"Oh yes, thank you! That sounds lovely."

"Would you like a little extra chocolate in it?" she asked, giving me an exaggerated wink.

"Okay, sure. Why not? That sounds wonderful."

"How about a squirt of whipped cream? That will make it very festive."

"Yes, please! Sounds perfect," and it was – delicious, delectable and yummy. About half way through my second cup I began to feel oddly warm.

Dillan caught up with me, sipping a cup of coffee and carrying his bulging stocking. We continued searching the outer row of tables for a gift for Henry, while bumping into some of Dillan's friends and acquaintances. I was introduced as "my friend Sandy" and welcomed by all, including the staff of the store who were doing everything they could to be hospitable and spread holiday cheer.

"Hey, Dillan, what is this stuff?" I asked, handing him a small bottle labeled Poo-Pourri. He glanced at it, smiled and added it to his stocking. Maybe it would be my Christmas gift!

At the back, on the table in the corner, I finally found something for Henry: a selection of Yogi teas, each for a specific malady. There was Lavender Honey for stress relief, Sweet Tangerine for positive energy, Mint for regularity and Lemon Ginger or Peppermint for digestion. I wished they had one for a broken heart. I wondered what flavor that would be – probably chocolate. Maybe I should just take him some of this wonderful hot chocolate, I giggled to myself. After what seemed to be a considerable amount of consideration, I grabbed the stress relief and positive energy boxes and moved on.

"I think I'll have another hot chocolate – it's kick-ass! You *really* should try this!"

Dillan took a sniff of my cup and then a sip. "Girl, you've been had," he laughed. "Let's get you something to eat."

"No, I haven't!" I said stubbornly. "At least I don't remember it, and I think that's something a girl would remember!"

Dillan almost choked on his coffee he was laughing so hard. I chuckled too, wondering what I said that was so funny.

All the treats were free and I didn't want to leave anything untested. I savored a cupcake, two cookies, three chocolate candies and a banana while sharing the occasional bite with Dillan.

"Having fun?" he asked.

"Oh, yes! I'm having a fantastic time. Everyone seems so happy. It's the first time I've felt this much hope – joy even."

"Well, that's the magic of Christmas," he paused, "and Baileys!" he chuckled. "I'm gonna get you a coffee. Then I'm taking you to *church*!"

"Church, how lovely! Could we ask Henry to join us?"

"I don't see why not. I think it would be just the thing for him – get him out and mingling a bit."

"Cool! I mean, rad. Oh . . . whatever!" I giggled.

After some gentle coercion, Henry agreed to accompany us. He disappeared from the kitchen for a moment then reappeared all bundled up in an expensive-looking but musty-smelling wool coat and scarf. I guess he hadn't had the opportunity to wear them for a while. Dillan and Buoy led the way as we walked to the LBI Museum.

"I thought we were going to church," I commented as we climbed the stairs.

"Well, it was a church at one time and it still has the pews and stuff."

Henry stepped in front of us and held open the door. "And a Christmas tree!" I added. "Do we have any ornaments for ours?"

"Not yet, but we'll get some."

"I'd be happy to share mine with you," Henry offered.

"Thanks, Henry!"

"Do you mind if we sit in the back?" Dillan asked. "I'm not sure if dogs are allowed."

"Well, he is a service dog; don't forget."

"Most people in town love him, but they don't know that."

A crowd was growing, as many of the people from Kapler's were walking in along with a half-dozen or so people carrying musical instruments.

"Oh, this does look like fun," I squealed.

"That's the Lighthouse Brass Band," Henry said. "I heard them play at the park last summer."

Once the big old room was full, the reverend pulled out a book, but it wasn't the Bible. It was *The Night Before Christmas*. With a wonderfully expressive voice he read in a lovely Cajun dialect.

The kids were bouncing up and down on their parents' laps and people really seemed to be engrossed in the story.

"Do you know it?" Dillan whispered.

"Who could forget Santa?"

"I'm sure you were always a good little girl. Probably on top of the nice list."

His lips gently grazed my ear as he spoke and I felt something amazingly wonderful inside. I pushed myself up in the pew and found my hand pressed against Dillan's thigh. It was firm and warm and I didn't want to move it away.

When the story was over, the band began to play Christmas carols. Dillan sang along tentatively, while I sang along with the ones that had an easy refrain. I had never really heard him sing before. Obviously, he didn't realize what a nice voice he had because he really held back. It wasn't until the end of the program and singing "Twelve Days of Christmas" that he and Henry really belted it out, and I'm not sure if it was in a good way! Every two pews would stand when their refrain came along, each group becoming more boisterous and animated than the last. I couldn't wait until it was our turn to sing *eight maids a milking*! How hard we laughed as we milked our air cows! The rows would pirouette at *nine ladies dancing*, and jump into the air at *ten lords a leaping*. If it wasn't so hilarious, I might have been worried that someone would get hurt. *The French hens* clucked *and the turtle doves* cooed. It was total joyous mayhem. Henry was a good sport keeping up with us and Buoy let out a howl at the end that pushed people over the edge with laughter. It took a few minutes for everyone to simmer down enough to listen to the mayor's closing words, "God bless us, everyone!" Still feeling joyous, we all filtered out onto the porch and the cold night air.

"Come on; let's go get a good view of the tree!" Dillan said over the chatter. He took hold of my hand and smiled. He seemed to really be enjoying himself. Buoy followed along as I grabbed Henry's elbow to help him down the stairs.

"Are you having fun, Henry?" I asked.

"Yes, it's quite a hoot! A good thing for the town, I think."

We followed the people across the street to Bicentennial Park where the Christmas tree waited under the gazebo. Somehow the structure had survived the storm, maybe just for this purpose. I could feel how important this evening was to the people. It really filled their hearts with hope and a sense of normalcy. It was a tradition and it was being upheld. It was hard to put a value on that, but I think the term would be *priceless*.

After the Mayor welcomed everyone with a holiday greeting and few encouraging words, the countdown began: "Ten . . . nine . . . eight . . . ."

As I stood, the anticipation building, I wondered if Dillan would take my hand again – and he did, but not until the tree exploded with a multitude of colorful lights. Everyone clapped and cheered but we just stood there, silently holding hands, gazing at the tree. I felt a tear form in my eye. It was a happy tear but a confused one as well. I wasn't sure what I was allowed to feel, because these feelings could certainly betray me later. I was most likely setting myself up for a gigantic fall.

A convoy of colorfully decorated fire trucks arrived, sporting wreaths, tinsel and strings of lights. After a toot of the siren, out jumped Old Santa himself. Everyone cheered and the kids ran to greet him. Someone started singing and it wasn't long before most everyone joined in: "*Jingle Bells, Jingle Bells . . . .*"

Dillan spied Chief Gavin and his wife in the crowd and went to say hello, while Henry and I watched as Santa handed candy canes to the excited children.

A gentleman about Henry's age walked up to us, a gloved hand extended. "Excuse me," he said tentatively, "I really hate to bother you, but I was wondering – would you happen to be Michael Stocks?"

Henry looked at me as if I might offer some advice. I just gave him the "it's up to you" look. I knew he was a private man and prized his anonymity, but I also knew how lonely he had been all these years.

"My name is Alexander Henry," he replied, shaking the man's hand, "but some people know me as Michael Stocks, yes."

"I'd heard a rumor that you lived here among us; how exciting! My name's Hanson, Lucas Hanson. I'm living right over there, at the Engleside. It's certainly a thrill to meet you."

"Likewise, pleasure to make your acquaintance."

"I love your books, especially the ones set here on the island. I used to read them aloud to my wife when she was at the nursing home . . . God rest her soul. She seemed to enjoy them as well."

"That's very kind of you, Mr. Hanson."

"Please call me Lucas. Except for a few of your books that I squeezed into my suitcase, my whole library got destroyed along with my home," he added, sounding discouraged.

My heart went out to him.

"I'm so very sorry to hear that. Please, call me Henry, if you like. That's what my friends call me."

Mr. Hanson's face lit up just like the Christmas tree. Henry smiled at me then and I knew the friend he was referring to was me. It warmed my heart in the sweetest way. They chatted amicably as the singing rose in volume and kids began to run around, burning off some of their sugar-fueled excitement.

"I've read them all – your books – at least twice but with my memory these days, I'm always surprised by *who done it!*" Mr. Hanson said with a chuckle, and I laughed along with both of them.

DILLAN

SANDY, BUOY AND I headed across the street to Henry's house to pick out a few decorations for our tree. She was surprised and delighted with the large selection he had spread out in anticipation of our visit. The kitchen table was set with an elaborate tea set and cookies but the rest of the main floor looked like a pop-up Christmas store in the mall. The couches, chairs and desk were all covered with worn boxes of Shiny-Brite ornaments and antique-looking Christmas paraphernalia. Ten plastic storage boxes, still half loaded with strings of lights, garland, wreaths and bows, were strewn around the library floor. Sandy kept oohing and aahing over every little thing. She was as excited as a child on Christmas morning.

"Take whatever you want," Henry said, almost sadly.

"We don't need too much, Henry. Just a few decorations for the tree would be fine," Sandy said while inspecting a fragile ornament.

"Well I hope you'll take more than that. What do I need with three nativities?"

"I was wondering that, too," I added curiously. "You don't seem like a hoarder; the rest of your home is so neat and uncluttered."

"Dillan, I can't believe you said that!" Sandy scolded.

"Sorry! I was just making an observation. Henry could decorate ten homes with all this."

"Well, Sandy can probably guess why," he said with a loud sigh.

"Was it because of Naia?"

"Every season I'd make sure the house was properly decked out, in case she returned at Christmas time. I wanted it to look just the way we had imagined it would."

"Who's Naia?" I asked.

"My one and only, the love of my life," he said sadly. "I'm not sure why but Christmas always hits me hard, even after all these years."

I was sorry I'd asked. I could tell it brought back painful memories for the old guy.

"Oh, Henry," Sandy said softly as she walked over and gave him a big hug.

"I'll be happy if you take it, take all of it. There's never been a Christmas celebration here. I would go to parties and dinners with my publishing company and agent, but I was always home for Christmas – alone and waiting."

Dear God, I felt so badly for him. I had him pegged all wrong. He wasn't really a curmudgeon, just a broken-hearted, lonely old man.

"I have an idea!" Sandy sang in a voice that I'd come to know so well. "Why don't we have Christmas dinner here this year? Dillan's not going to visit his parents and you two are the only family I know. We could invite Mr. Hanson too. Please say yes, Henry," Sandy pleaded. "I think it would make for a lovely day."

"It's a tad out of character for me," he hemmed and hawed, "but I guess if it means that much to you. I'm not much of a chef so I'll need some help with the preparations."

"What do you think, Dillan? How hard can it be?" my little do-gooder asked.

"Sure, I'm in. If I can pull off a clambake on a Weber grill, I can certainly roast a turkey."

"My mother made the best dressing when I was a lad," Henry added. "It had celery, onions and loads of butter. The edges were crunchy but inside it was so moist and flavorful. I can almost taste it. I bet I have the recipe around here somewhere. She wrote down all my favorites thinking someday I'd have a wife who'd cook them for me."

Jesus, Henry's life was worse than a Hallmark special on TV. "It sounds delicious, Henry. If you can come up with the recipe, we'll try to recreate it."

"Gosh, I hope you find it," Sandy added, sounding hungry. "It sounds mouthwatering."

Sandy filled one storage bin with decorations and then we had tea at the huge old kitchen table. The poor guy must've been hoping to have a lot of children with this Naia woman. I wondered how anyone could ditch such a nice guy. While we ate our cookies, and planned the Christmas dinner, Henry searched for his mother's recipes. He found them in an old Betty Crocker cookbook, handwritten on yellowed paper and held in place by a rusty paper clip.

"My mother gave this to me when I moved out on my own. I don't think I've ever opened it!"

"Now's as good a time as ever," Sandy replied encouragingly.

"Looks like we'll have a real old-fashioned meal if we use that cookbook. What year is it from anyway?" I asked.

"Let me see," Henry said, as he looked for the copyright. "1950."

"I don't think the basics ever change," Sandy said. "Here's to new friends, old recipes and happier holidays!"

"Hear! Hear!" Henry agreed, tapping his china cup first with Sandy's and then with mine.

"Ditto!"

I must admit, I hadn't given Christmas much thought before the previous day's events. We'd been so busy that I assumed we'd rather ignore the holiday and stay the course but suddenly the Christmas spirit had engulfed Beach Haven like a thick layer of sea fog. Now, I found myself almost as excited as Sandy. Her childlike wonder and gift for bringing people together made me feel all warm and cozy inside, like Mom's hot cocoa, served with whipped cream and a peppermint stick on a cold snowy afternoon in Cincinnati. Finding a gift shouldn't be too hard for someone who owns so little, but I wanted it to be very special and personal. Maybe I could search the internet for a colorful tool chest and have it monogrammed for her. Unfortunately, there was one problem. She didn't know her *real* name. Well, maybe someday I'd be blessed with a miracle and be able to give her mine.

We decorated our tree with Henry's ornaments and tinsel and were happy with its old-fashioned simplicity. Sandy hammered a nail into an exposed stud and hung up a mangled wreath, while I hung one on the front door.

"Why did you take the most decrepit decorations when he had so many?" I asked.

"Because I wanted to use the best ones at his house. I'm hoping he'll let me decorate it for Christmas, but I think we really need to get him a tree, don't you?"

"Yeah, sure. Can you imagine that poor man decorating that huge house every year in the hopes that this Naia woman would show up?"

"Yes, and it breaks my heart. I think he should have some happy Christmases to remember, don't you?"

"Sandy, I swear you are the most kind-hearted person I've ever met. I feel so selfish next to you. I wish I had your knack for knowing exactly what to say and do."

"I don't give it much thought," she replied. "Anyway, you keep people safe and save lives for a living. I'd say that's pretty special."

"I wonder what you did before. I bet you were in the Peace Corps or were one of those nurses that travels around the world donating her vacation time to makeshift clinics. Whatever it was, I'm sure you were dedicated to helping people."

"Speaking of which, I read in *The SandPaper* that the animal shelter needs food and dog walkers. They're collecting food at Uncle Will's Pancake House and . . . do you think we could go play with the animals sometime?"

"I think we can do whatever you want."

"Good, because I have a plan."

"I'm not surprised."

It was getting dark as Sandy, Buoy and I walked up the block to the Engleside to find her new friend, Mr. Hanson, and invite him to our Christmas celebration. At the main office, Patrick, the clerk, told us he was staying in room 112. We walked around the front of the building and across the crushed-shell coated parking lot to his room in the corner. Through the window, we could see him sleeping in a comfy-looking armchair. We hated to wake him but I knocked tentatively. He rubbed his neck, got his bearings and came stiffly to the door.

"Hi, Mr. Hanson. It's Sandy. I met you last night in the park."

"I couldn't forget you, miss. What can I do for you?"

"These are my friends, Dillan and Buoy," she replied.

"How do you do? Is he friendly?" he asked, motioning to Buoy.

"Sure, he loves a good scratch behind the ears," I said.

As Mr. Hanson pet Buoy's head, Sandy inquired, "I'm sorry it's such short notice, but we wanted to invite you to Henry's house for Christmas dinner. I hope you don't already have plans."

"Really? How exciting! He's such a fascinating fellow. I hope your invitation includes my lovely roommate."

Sandy and I looked at each other surprised, "Yes, sure. Of course it does!" she said.

"I don't believe we have any plans, but I'll have to check with my special girl. I'd really like the opportunity to get to know Mr. Henry better."

"Okay then," Sandy said, "If we don't hear from you before then, please come by Christmas morning, about ten. It's the brown house on the corner of Coral and Atlantic. We'll make a whole day of it!"

"Should we eat breakfast first?"

"No, definitely come hungry!"

"Sounds most delightful! Thank you very much," Mr. Hanson yelled over the crackling of our footsteps as we trekked across the parking lot. "God bless you!"

"I wasn't expecting that!" Sandy said as we crossed Atlantic Avenue and headed south.

"I'm glad he has a special lady. It gives me hope for myself."

"Don't be silly!" she replied as she elbowed me gently in the ribs, "any woman would be crazy not to fall for you, even with that ungodly hair!"

"What?" I asked, feigning surprise. "You don't like my hair?"

"Well, it's growing on me a little, but I don't really like it, no."

SANDY

ONE OF OUR FAVORITE places to get a hot breakfast or lunch was the Bagel Shack. Its bright Caribbean pink color and huge wooden H O P E letters over the door stood out in this battle-weary war zone. Almost every other morning the three of us would walk or drive up, depending on the weather, and get something yummy and energizing to start our day. My favorite was bacon, egg and cheese on a poppy seed bagel. Dillan loved the everything bagel with plain cream cheese. They also had crumb-topped coffeecake, muffins, and cinnamon buns smothered with cream cheese frosting when we felt the need for something sweeter. Dillan introduced me to coffee, which I don't think I liked in the past, but with the right amount of sugar and cream it was pretty good. We'd always get large so it would keep us revved up while we worked.

We met a lot of people while waiting in line: construction guys, utility workers, locals and even National Guardsmen. Everyone was so friendly, perhaps because we had so much in common to discuss: mold, insurance, trash, rewiring, recovery. One of the National Guardsman in line behind us recognized Dillan and asked, "Hey, bro, is that your dog outside, the one you lost?"

Dillan shrank back at first, then held out his hand. "Yes, sir; I found him!" he said as he shook the serviceman's hand. Dillan leaned in behind me and whispered, "Among other things."

"I'm happy for you. I have a German Shepherd myself, back home. I could not let you pass that day. You understand, right?"

"Yeah, we're cool."

When Dillan paid the bill, he gave the checkout girl an extra twenty dollars to put toward the serviceman's check. As were leaving the little shop, one of the employees shouted, "Excuse me, miss?" Dillan and I both turned around thinking we'd forgotten something.

"That doll, on your bag – where did you get it?"

"I found her in a sandbank down near Holgate," I replied.

Her hand flew up to her mouth gasping. "Oh, my God!" she squealed. "I never thought I'd see her again! Can we talk, please?"

"Sure, of course," I replied, feeling elated. "I'll meet you outside."

We left the tiny shop and unhooked Buoy from the bench. He wasn't used to being tied but he took it well. He was the unofficial greeter of folks as they waited in line and everyone seemed to enjoy him.

The college age woman came from around back. She was wearing a bright pink Bagel Shack T-shirt which contrasted with her tattoo-sleeved arms and silver hoop nose ring. Her long black hair tinted with purple was pulled back in a high ponytail and she carried a grey hoodie. Though she was doing her best to look tough on the outside, she was as sweet as pie when she spoke.

"I think that might be my doll," she said with a huge sigh.

"Really?" I asked, anxious to hear her story.

"Excuse me," Dillan said, as he handed me my sandwich. "Buoy and I'll head back and get started. Take your time."

"Thanks, I'll see you in a little bit," I replied thankfully. "Why don't we sit over there at a table so we have a bit of privacy?"

"Sure, that's cool," she answered.

We headed around the side of the building to a little alcove. We sat in the sunshine at one of the round concrete tables. For mid-December, it was quite comfortable. She placed her jacket on the bench and sat on it.

"Your boss okay with you leaving?"

"Yeah, no problem. I was due for a break anyway."

"Can I buy you a coffee or something?"

"No, thanks; I'm good."

I took off the backpack and unwound the rubber band that held the mermaid to the zipper pull.

"Out of all the stuff I'd left at my grandfather's house, it's crazy that she's the one thing that turned up!" she said, sounding ruffled.

"I found her right after the storm while exploring. I was very worried about the owner. I pictured her as a little girl."

"My dad sent her to me when I turned fourteen. I hated her then, thinking it was a totally uncool gift for a teenager."

"Well, I guess it was thoughtful of your dad to send something, even if it was inappropriate. I'm sure he meant well."

"Yeah, I know that now, but then . . . it sent me off on a serious rampage. I got my very first tattoo that day and I didn't stop for years."

"Oh, that's too bad," I said but luckily I quickly recovered, "Not that they aren't nice tattoos. I happen to love whales and dolphins but that shark . . . it really looks menacing!"

"Yeah, that's the infamous Mary Lee. You ever heard of her?"

"No, but I think I've seen her in my nightmares!"

"I've got a cool jellyfish over here," she said pointing to the back of her right upper arm. "I've designed them all myself except the mermaid – *this mermaid*," she said, shaking the doll. "She's my first and favorite. I'd have to drop my pants to show you that one."

"Maybe another time," I said with a chuckle.

"Yeah . . . def. She's a little on the sexy side. My grandmother never saw her. My grandfather never will either."

My mind pictured a topless little mermaid striking an erotic pose and I shivered involuntarily. "Were you raised by your grandparents?" I asked.

"Partially. My grandmother passed away about a year ago and Grandpa, well he never fully recovered. I guess that's something that you never recover from. Now he's lost their home on top of everything else! I don't want him ending up in an old folks' home somewhere. There's all this paperwork and endless phone calls, but nothing seems to be happening. God, I get so frustrated sometimes that I just want to scream or punch someone!"

"I'm sure you're not alone there! I can't imagine how hard it is for you. Where are you staying now?"

"We're at the Engleside and it's great but we can't stay there forever. I guess we can only take it day by day. It's impossible to plan ahead, although it would be nice to have some idea what will happen."

"I met a nice man at the tree lighting ceremony who was staying there."

"Oh, I flippin' missed it. I had to run to the laundromat in Manahawkin and met a friend there. She really needed someone to talk to, so I couldn't just ditch her. I just caught the fire trucks driving away. The tree's really pretty though."

"It was good for the people, I think. How about your mom? Is she still living?" I asked hesitantly.

"Gees, I hope so! She's totally unreliable though. She moves around a lot. I'm not even sure if she's in the same place. She *did* try when I was a kid, but she'd never come close to winning The Mother of the Year Award."

"Your dad?" I asked hopefully.

"I've never met my father, never even talked to him on the phone. He was in the service and traveled around a lot. The last birthday card I got from him was three years ago. I still can't imagine why he never wanted to meet me. I don't even know if he's still alive."

"That's awful," I replied honestly. My mermaid girl hadn't had a happy childhood but at least the visions of a drowning child had vanished from my mind. We chatted for a while when she asked, "So what's it like dating a lifeguard? There are so many cute ones every summer."

"Dillan? Oh, we aren't dating. We're just friends. We work together – in construction," I added.

"Could've fooled me. I noticed the way he looked at you but it's none of my business," she said as she rose. "I have to get back to work. Thank you for saving my doll. It's all I have of my father and it means a lot to me. I'm Jacqueline Rose, by the way."

"You're welcome, Jacqueline Rose. I'm Sandy and I'm so happy she found her way home. I'm sure I'll see you again."

"I hope so!" she yelled back as she ran inside.

I was very happy that I'd found the owner of the mermaid doll, even though she wasn't at all what I'd envisioned. She was interesting to say the least, with her oceanic life tattoos and body jewelry. I replayed her words over in my head as I ate my egg, cheese and bagel sandwich and came to one conclusion. From a fractured and less than perfect childhood emerged a talented, strong and fiercely dedicated young woman, I assume in part due to the gift of loving grandparents. I wondered if I'd had the same and I couldn't imagine otherwise.

Though we were busy planning our Christmas party, ripping down walls, and shopping for gifts for Dillan's parents, I really wanted to foster some relationships among my new friends. I asked Dillan if it would be all right to talk with Captain Jack about finding Jacqueline Rose's father, and he felt that Jack would be more than happy to help. We braved the cold weather that day to walk over to the police station but Jack wasn't on duty. As Buoy led the way back home, our heads bent low against the damp wind, Dillan called Jack on the phone and I overheard the one-sided conversation.

"Hey, Jack. Are you busy?" he asked.

"Would it be all right if we stopped by?"

"No, I'll let her tell you herself."

"Okay, see you in a few minutes."

We rounded the corner and the three of us jumped into the Jeep. It was a relief to be out of the icy cold wind.

"Jack wanted to know if you got your memory back."

"Do you think it's odd, that I'm not more curious about my past?"

"I think I'm glad that you're not," Dillan replied.

"Even if my memory does return, we'll always be friends, Dillan. I'll never forget you or Buoy and my time here."

I saw Dillan slump in the driver's seat. Remaining friends didn't appear to be what he had in mind. I didn't know what else to say so we rode in silence for the half mile it took to get to Jack's house. In the tiny development of cookie-cutter cottages, Jack's stood out naked among all the Christmas pageantry. He met us at the door looking tired and stressed but invited us in warmly.

"Come in out of the cold, guys," Jack said. "Carole, the kids are here."

"It's nice to see you two. Let me take your coats. Now, what can I do for you, Sandy?" he asked eagerly.

"Well, I hate to be a bother but I'm looking for a missing person."

"That's certainly ironic," he chuckled. "Let's hear."

He tossed our coats over a dining chair and led us to the living room.

"The place looks great, Jack. You'd never know you had water damage," Dillan offered.

"We're luckier than most. Servpro was enough to do the job."

Carole yelled from the kitchen, "Would you two like some coffee?"

Dillan looked at me and I nodded. "That would be awesome, Carole," he replied. "If it's not too much trouble."

"I really like your décor. We should paint the parlor this color, Dillan. I think Shona would love it."

"Thanks," Jack replied. "It's all Carole's doing. She has a knack for decorating. So, you've got my curiosity piqued; who's this person you're looking for?"

As I was telling him about Jacqueline Rose, I realized that I didn't even know her last name.

"That's not a problem," Jack said, "It's a small town."

Soon his wife entered with a tray of coffee and biscotti. Dillan jumped up and took the tray and placed it on the coffee table. Carole, who also looked quite peaked, sat next to her husband and poured. It appeared they were just getting over some nasty bug.

"It's nice to finally meet you Sandy," she said. "Jack's told me a lot about you."

"It's my pleasure. Your husband's been very kind."

Jack said he'd seen Jacqueline Rose waitressing at the CHEGG some time ago and was wondering if she had transplanted from some place called Seaside Heights. "I know, she looks *different,* but she really is the sweetest girl. She didn't ask me to try to find her father but she seemed distraught that she'd never met him. She told me he joined the Marines before she was born, about twenty years ago. For all she knows he could have been killed in the line of duty. There's also the possibility that he survived, married and has five other children. Who knows? There's not much to go on."

"So, you don't have a name or age, anything like that?"

"Jacqueline Rose's mother wouldn't talk about her father. I'm assuming he was young when he cut and ran, probably not old enough to handle the responsibility. Jacqueline Rose said she'd received a few cards and gifts over the years. They were mailed from foreign countries, with no return addresses."

"Sounds like quite a mystery!" Carole commented.

"Maybe we should ask Henry to help?" Dillan offered jokingly. "He's a mystery writer after all."

"There may be a good reason why the mom didn't want to tell her daughter much. He may have been an abusive asshole. Her mother's still living?" Jack inquired.

"Yes, and her grandfather."

"Do you really feel it's a good idea to foster an introduction after all these years?"

"Well, she's had quite a difficult life. If he turned out to be a decent man with a good excuse for not reaching out to her, then yes."

"Okay, I'll see what I can do, but if he turns out to be a creep or a felon my lips are sealed."

"I totally agree with that."

As I sipped my coffee and looked around the room, I noticed there were no signs of Christmas anywhere – no tree, wreath, cards, lights – nothing. Either they had been so ill that they hadn't felt up to decorating or they probably weren't Christian – maybe they were even atheists. The possibility that anyone could be atheists, when you looked into the vastness of the night sky, confounded me.

"I thought I'd bump into you guys at the tree lighting ceremony the other night," Dillan said.

"No, we decided to go to the movies in Manahawkin. What was it called, hon?"

"*Silver Linings Playbook.*"

"Was it good?" Dillan asked.

"Typical rom-com," Jack answered flatly.

"No it wasn't," his wife countered. "It was quite well-written and acted. I love that Bradley Cooper!"

"You and every other woman," Jack added with a chuckle.

"I don't think I've ever heard of him. Is he cute?"

"*Cute?* Last year he was *People*'s Sexiest Man Alive. He could rock my dinghy any day!" Carole said playfully. "Haven't you seen *The Hangover*?"

"She's got amnesia, Carole; remember?" Jack rolled his eyes at his wife.

"I'm so sorry; I forgot for a moment. It must be awfully frustrating for you."

"It's hard to explain. I remember things, just not how I fit into the scenario. I'm enjoying the present very much, though. In fact, you two missed a lot of fun the other night. We had the best time singing Christmas carols in the museum; didn't we, Dillan?"

"Yeah, but the best part was when Buoy howled at the end. He cracked everybody up."

"He's a good ol' boy, your miracle dog . . . no thanks to me."

"What do you mean, Jack? There was nothing more you could've done. That's all in the past now anyway," Dillan said.

"Well that whole time, while I was following you to the causeway, I kept thinking there should've been."

"You're being awfully hard on yourself, hon," Carole consoled as she placed her hand on his leg and gave it a little squeeze. "Buoy and Dillan are fine. Right, boys?" she asked.

"We're better than fine. We're fantastic. Right, pal?" Dillan asked Buoy as he scratched his head and checked his watch. "Oh, wow! Look at the time. We'd better get going, Sandy, if we're gonna make it to the animal shelter before they close."

"Do you think we can spare the time away from the inn?"

"No prob, sweetheart," he joked. "We're going to be volunteer dog walkers, as if walking Buoy isn't enough for us," Dillan chuckled, as he reached down and rubbed Buoy's chest.

"I just figured it was a way to help. I haven't met any cats yet, but I sure love this guy. He saved my life!"

"That explains why he jumped into the ocean that day. I only wished I could've helped somehow," Jack uttered sadly.

Buoy must have known Jack was talking about him because he walked over, sat beside him and placed his muzzle on his leg.

"We can stop at ShopRite and get some more dog and cat food on the way," Dillan offered, which surprised me because we'd already dropped off a good-sized donation at Uncle Will's Pancake House.

"That's so nice of you two," Carole said. "If we give you some money, will you take a donation for us?"

"Of course."

Carole elbowed her husband who pulled out his wallet and handed me a fifty-dollar bill.

"I hope that helps," Jack said.

I'm sure it will, and thanks for your hospitality," Dillan replied.

"And for offering to help find Jacqueline Rose's father," I added gratefully.

"It's our pleasure," Jack said. "If this guy's respectable, then he deserves to know his daughter – even if she is as colorful as a cartoon character."

"Oh, Jack," Carole sighed, sounding embarrassed.

As the three of us climbed into the Jeep, I asked Dillan if he noticed anything strange about our visit.

"Only that they both looked so exhausted. Do you think they're getting over the flu or something?"

"I wanted to ask, but something told me not to pry."

"That's never stopped you before," he said jokingly.

"Don't you think it's odd that there weren't any Christmas decorations?"

"Well, not everyone's into it as much as you are."

"I don't know; it just worries me. Maybe we should drop in on them again soon."

"I think that's a good idea, girl. Maybe we could invite them to our Christmas dinner?" Dillan offered.

"I was just going to suggest that! I'm sure Henry wouldn't mind. The more the merrier, right? Maybe we should ask now. You know it's only a couple of weeks away."

"Yeah, you're right. Let's go back."

We hopped out of the Jeep and headed toward the door but I stopped short as Dillan grabbed hold of my arm.

"Look," he whispered.

Through the window, I saw an upsetting sight. Carole was on her knees, her arms wrapped around her husband and her face pressed against his chest. Jack appeared to be sobbing.

"Jesus, that's gnarly. What should we do?" Dillan asked.

"I think we should leave," I replied sadly.

"Any other day, I'd say I need a beer," Dillan said as we climbed in the Jeep, "but this requires whiskey. Would you mind if we stop at The Hud on the way home?"

"Where?"

"The Hudson House. I know the bartender and his wife pretty well. They're good people."

"A glass of wine sounds perfect right now. My hands are still shaking."

Dillan reached over, took my hand in his and gave it a squeeze. "We'll find out what's going on. Maybe there's something we can do to help."

DILLAN

THE TIME FLIES BY when you are working twelve-hour days, six to seven days a week. Sandy gave me little time to rest but that didn't mean I wasn't enjoying every minute. I never realized how much work went into Christmas and I developed a whole new respect for my mother's efforts, especially when I was a kid, to have everything just right. She must have been completely exhausted by the time Christmas morning arrived each year. God bless her.

I'd been super busy and missing my usual workouts but still got plenty of exercise. What with lifting and lugging construction supplies, running on the beach with Sandy and Buoy, dog walking at the shelter and jogging uptown to pick up breakfast, lunch or odds and ends, I was still in pretty good shape. I did miss swimming though and couldn't wait for the hot weather when I could swim for hours along the coastline.

With Sandy's help, I got my parents' gifts purchased and shipped off to Cincinnati on time. Usually I would make every effort to be home for the holiday, but they understood our workload. Their curiosity was piqued regarding Sandy and they were anxious to see Buoy again after his brush with death, so I planned to make good on my promise to hang out with them in the spring. Hopefully, Sandy would still be with me and would want to come along, but it was impossible to plan that far ahead. For now, I was trying to live in the moment.

A week before Christmas, a large delivery truck pulled up in front of the inn. It carried our order from the Tuckerton Lumber

Company. Now, we could really get down to business. After Christmas, we could finish the downstairs repairs. The thought of progressing to the upstairs left me disheartened. Once another bedroom was finished, Sandy would probably toss me and my blowup mattress overboard.

About an hour later, a moving van pulled up. I was happily surprised to see that Mac had sent us a gently used couch and rocking chair and a new stainless steel oven and a mid-sized refrigerator. It was thoughtful of them and went a long way toward making the place more functional. I was pretty sure that Sandy would love the opportunity to actually cook and not just microwave our meals. Not to mention, that actual living room furniture would be one hundred percent more comfortable than reading the *Beach Haven Times* on the john.

As the week rolled on, the one thing that I couldn't shake was the memory of Jack and Carole appearing so distraught as we peered through their window. I remembered how worn down they'd both looked and hoped neither of them was battling some horrible illness. Jack, being a strong man and an authority figure, probably wasn't comfortable appearing weak, so I wasn't sure how to offer my assistance.

Jack and I met, of all places, standing in line at an ice cream truck. I was on a quick break from my first day sitting wood for the BHBP. Jack, being a police officer, was curious about any unfamiliar face in his community and had welcomed me to town. I must have looked like a troublemaker because he used the opportunity to reinforce the noise ordinance, no alcohol in public and with the Fourth of July right around the corner, the no fireworks law. We kept bumping into each other and once he realized I wasn't in town to wreak havoc, we became friends.

Inappropriate as it might be, I had texted him the day after our visit and asked them to join us for Christmas. His first response was an immediate and definite *No, thank you*. Later that afternoon, another text: *Carole says we'd love to join you for Christmas*. At least that was a good sign. I could only think of one other person who might have known something and that was the fire chief. Jack and Bob were good friends, brothers in service to the community. Jack had mentioned boating and fishing with Bob and occasionally they would all go out to dinner or a play at the Surflight Theater. Last year, they even went on a cruise to the Bahamas together. If anyone knew what was going on, it would be Bob.

Sandy and Buoy were over at Henry's finishing up the decorating, so I threw on my jacket and jogged a couple of blocks toward the bay. The fire station was still a mess from the storm and when I peered in through the bay door there was no sign of movement. I did, however, spot a light coming from down the hall. I tried the main door. It was locked so I knocked – no answer. I knocked harder – still no answer. I was just about to give up when the chief's car pulled into a parking space on Bay Avenue and Bob climbed out.

"Hey, Dillan. Have you come to volunteer?"

"Um, I don't think I'd make a very good fireman."

"No," he laughed, "I mean with the cleanup. We have a ton of work to do to get this place ready for the turkey dinner in February. We need every able-bodied person in the community to chip in, and I hear you're quite the carpenter."

"Sure, Sandy and I would be happy to help," I replied, because I knew she would.

"Good, I appreciate it. Now, what can *I* do for *you*?" he asked as he unlocked the door.

"Would you have a couple of minutes to talk?" I asked, as I followed him down the hall.

"Of course. Sorry about the condition of my office; the only things that survived were my collectibles. Thank God, they were up on high shelves. Some of these babies are irreplaceable."

I looked at the two shelves of miniature fire trucks lining the walls. They went around the entire office. There must have been over a hundred. "Wow, this is some collection! You must really love being a firefighter."

"Well, the pay sucks but the reward is priceless," he laughed. "I was relieved to sell the farm market two years ago. Now, I can completely dedicate myself to my families."

"Families?" I questioned.

"Sure, my brothers and sisters here, and my wife and kids at home."

"Oh, right – got it!"

"There's no closer bond that's not made of blood," he replied, looking pensive.

"I wasn't here for the storm, but I heard your company did an amazing job."

"I'm certainly proud of them. We rescued over one hundred people."

"I'm sure your training and leadership had a lot to do with it."

"Thank you, Dillan. That means a lot. So, what can I do for you?"

"Well, it's Captain Jack. I know you two are friends and I was wondering if you might know what's going on with him."

"What do you mean?"

"Well, he seemed visibly upset about something the other day. I'd like to offer my help, but I didn't want to pry."

"He hasn't told you then?"

"Told me what?"

"I know you mean a lot to him and vice versa or otherwise I wouldn't say anything." He seemed to be thinking it over, as if he might be betraying Jack's confidence.

"Go on, I can keep it to myself."

"It happened quite a few years ago, before he and Carole moved here."

"I always assumed they were locals."

"No, they transplanted to the island, to get away and start again. You can't let on that you know. Do you understand?" he asked firmly.

Holy shit, he was making it sound like Jack had killed somebody. "Yes, I promise, of course."

"Jack and Carole had a daughter. She died on Christmas Eve when she was only six years old."

"Jesus! No wonder they looked so wrecked last week. How horrific!"

"The child had some form of freak accident. He never told me the details, but he blames himself."

"Oh my God! I had no idea!"

SANDY

THE TWO WEEKS BEFORE Christmas were crazy busy, what with planning the menu, buying the food and gifts for the party, decorating Henry's place and walking our new buddies at the shelter. I fell in love with a particularly well-mannered senior pup and knew the perfect person to adopt him. The fact that this pit bull's name was Sherlock totally sealed the deal for me. I just had to convince Henry that he needed a companion, and if my plan worked out as well as I hoped, he'd have more than one.

SOCAS was not only a fun place to volunteer but also a place to rejuvenate the spirit. I loved playing with the dogs in the yard, showing them love and affection and exercising them by playing catch with balls and Frisbees. All except a few shy buddies enjoyed the socialization. I would sit next to their cages and read to them in a calm, gentle voice which helped to ease their anxiety. The kitties were nice too; they would rub their little faces on my leg and climb into my lap for a gentle petting. We'd often find this one tiny black cat curled up next to Sherlock, and we nicknamed her Mrs. Holmes. The shelter wanted to send her to a home with a cat-friendly dog or adopt her out with one. My plan was to get Henry out there to meet them both right after Christmas.

On the morning of the twenty-first, we had just made our plan for the day when four of Dillan's surfing buddies showed up at the door.

"Have you heard the 411?" Mitch asked excitedly.

"No man, we've been too busy working. Some improvement, huh?" Dillan asked.

"Yeah, looks great but here's the kicker, bro. There're some serious northeast winds right outside your door."

"God, I haven't been surfing in eons. Not sure if I remember how," Dillan joked.

"Well, don't miss this opportunity, dude. Pull on your wettie, grab your sled and come on. It's gonna be crazy!" Joe added enthusiastically.

"I don't know. We've got a lot planned for today."

"Don't get clucked, bro!" Gary goaded. "We've got some promising combo swells forming."

"Promising what, I get cactus juiced?"

"Jesus, Dillan. What's happened to you? You used to be fearless," Jake commented disappointedly.

"Hardly," he replied. "I was always more kook than Kelly Slater."

"Shit, man, you were improving. Some days you were really going off!"

The guys left grumbling but excited to face the challenges of the heavy surf. Dillan, I realized, had made a choice, and had chosen my company over his buddies and the thrill of a great ride.

Christmas Eve we spent at Henry's. The three of us prepped all the food for the next day. There was a recipe in the old cookbook for Christmas pudding but the ingredients didn't sound very appealing. We diced the celery, onions and herbs for the dressing, made stock for the gravy by cooking some extra turkey wings and blanched the green beans. As Dillan and I set the dining room table, Henry was the odd man out, but I guess no one could ever fill Naia's shoes. At least he wouldn't spend Christmas alone this year; he'd be surrounded by friends. In just a few short weeks, I had come to love Henry as a father and I couldn't bear to see him so lonely.

Before we left, the pumpkin and apple pies were out of the oven cooling and the bubble bread, the one modern recipe I *had* to try, was set on the counter to raise overnight. We didn't expect Lucas and his lady friend or the Fosters till about ten so we told Henry we'd be back at the crack of dawn to stuff the bird and continue the job. Brunch would be scrambled eggs, bacon, fruit salad, mimosas and bubble bread. Melinda, a check-out lady who worked at ShopRite, had given me the recipe. She said the ooey-gooey breakfast rolls were absolutely amazing, especially if you added extra raisins and pecans.

Dillan, Buoy and I walked home tired but happy. He took my hand as we crossed the street and didn't let go. As we walked the otherwise deserted avenue, I thought I heard sleigh bells ringing in the distance. The magic of Christmas, it seemed, was not just for little kids.

"Let's keep going," I said as we reached the inn. "I'd like to see the tree again." All was right with the world as we walked, hand in hand, up the block and into the park. Buoy made us do the usual perimeter check and then we sat on a bench close to the gazebo.

"Isn't this perfect?" I asked with a sigh.

"You certainly are," he replied in a smooth bass voice which stirred me deep inside.

We were just about to kiss when I felt a cold chill come upon me that forced me to stop. "I'm sorry, Dillan; I can't."

"I know, I know – there might be some guy out there who already has your heart."

"If it was free to give, you would already have it, but it's not fair to either of us if we move ahead without knowing."

"You're right. I'm sorry," he said as he let go of my hand.

"So am I."

The next morning, we woke before dawn. Laden with packages, a new squishy dog bed, and Buoy in tow, we entered Henry's kitchen at five-thirty. Buoy didn't appear to think kindly of being awakened and dragged out of the house so early, but it was only a few short minutes before he was curled up on the bed in front of Henry's fireplace. Dillan stoked the embers to get it warm and cozy for our pup. I plugged in the Christmas tree and turned the CD player on very low. Henry's vast collection of Christmas music would add a wonderful ambiance to the day. Buoy was asleep almost immediately and I imagined Sherlock lying by the fire with the little black kitty curled up beside him. It made me sad to think of them at the shelter and all the other pets that didn't have loving homes for Christmas. They all deserved to be well loved, warmly snuggled and treat filled.

Henry came down, awakened by the smell of brewing coffee but he still preferred to make a pot of tea. I hoped he would like the ones under the tree that I had picked up at Kapler's. We stuffed the bird with our homemade stuffing, rubbed butter all over the skin and sprinkled it with salt and pepper. Though the double wall oven had seen better days, it was just what we needed for this big meal. Dillan used his strong muscles to slide the heavy turkey in and then we started on breakfast. I fried up a ton of bacon, while Dillan whisked up two dozen eggs with some milk.

By nine-thirty, Henry was ready to put his feet up for a short rest; that's when I popped the bubble bread, which had risen over the rim of the tube pan, into the oven. I went to join the guys in the library and peeked out the window before I sat down. The island seemed deserted.

"I quite like holidays; they're so peaceful and relaxing," I sighed, as I sat in a comfy chair. You would have thought I cracked the funniest joke ever the way Dillan and Henry laughed.

"I'm thinking you're wrong, girl," Dillan finally got out. "This is much more exhausting than an average day working at home."

His words didn't escape my ears. The inn was now *home*. A few short minutes later, we heard a rap on the door.

"I'll get it," Dillan said, as he stood and squared his shoulders. "You two rest your legs."

"Be my guest, Dillan," Henry replied, "I'm glued to this chair for at least another thirty minutes."

"Not me, I'm right behind you," I said, wondering why he would act so odd. Together we welcomed Jack and Carole at the door, who thankfully appeared to be on the mend. Dillan uncharacteristically gave them both a bear hug as they entered then offered to take their coats and packages.

"Merry Christmas!" Carole said. "Something smells absolutely delicious – doesn't it, hon?"

"Yeah kids, smells tasty," Jack added as he hugged me warmly.

"That's the bubble bread. It should be ready shortly. Dillan will show you into the library while I do some last-minute stuff."

"Can I help with anything?" Carole asked sincerely.

"No, thanks. Go on in and I'll bring in a fresh pot of coffee in just a few minutes."

Dillan led them down the hall and returned a short time later. "Okay, they're formally introduced, what's next?" he asked.

"They can sip on coffee or mimosas while we make the eggs. I guess we should wait for Lucas and his lady friend though. They should be here any time now."

We took a carafe, orange juice and champagne into the library and joined our guests. It felt quite nice to sit down with a hot cup of coffee and tuck my legs up under me for a couple of minutes. I was still worried about what we'd seen through the Foster's window, but I could hardly bring it up; instead I asked, "Have you had a chance to look for Jacqueline Rose's father?"

"Well...," Jack began, just as we heard a rap from the doorknocker.

"Excuse me – our other guests have arrived."

I hopped up and Dillan followed me to the door. When I flung it open with a *Merry Christmas,* I was surprised by the familiar, yet uninvited face that appeared there. It was Jacqueline Rose and behind her stood Mr. Hanson. *She* was his special girl! How amazing! I was surprised; I hadn't put two and two together before. I gave her a great big hug.

"Hello, mermaid girl!" I exclaimed. "This is a wonderful surprise! I had no idea Mr. Hanson was your grandfather."

"And I had no idea who I was spending Christmas with," she laughed. "Grandpa just told me he had met some new friends and one of them was a famous writer."

"Come in, come in," Dillan said warmly. "It's nice to see you both again."

Lucas gave me a hug and handed me a bottle of wine. "I'm sorry we couldn't bring more," he said humbly.

"Don't be silly; it's very thoughtful of you."

Dillan took their coats then led Mr. Hanson to the library.

"This is Alexander Henry's home," I told Jacqueline Rose. "He's written a bunch of mysteries under the pen name Michael Stocks. We met your grandfather at the tree lighting ceremony and they seemed to hit it off."

"I'll be thrilled if he finds someone to spend time with. The four walls of our motel room seem to be shrinking every day. Hey, what's that delicious smell?"

"It's called bubble bread and it's almost ready. It's my first time making it, so I hope it tastes as good as it smells!" I said nervously.

Just then, the timer rang, so I pulled out the bread which had grown enormously and was a glorious golden brown. Following Melinda's directions, I tipped it out on to a foil-covered platter. The hot caramel-like sauce oozed down all over the rolls like lava on a volcano.

"You can have the first taste," I said, as I pried one of the soft rolls loose and placed it on a plate. I wanted to make sure she got the best part so I plopped some of the nuts, raisins and gooey stuff on top. She blew on it, then took a dainty bite from the fork.

"Oh, my! It's amazing," she said as she popped what remained on her fork into her mouth. "Was it very hard to make?"

"Not at all. You'd be surprised how easy it is. Come on down to the library. I'll introduce you to Henry and the others, then please help yourself to the coffee and mimosas on the table. Breakfast will be ready in just a few minutes."

Being a hostess felt exciting and nerve wracking. I wanted everything to be perfect. Having Jacqueline Rose with us seemed like a little extra Christmas magic that made the day even more special. I hadn't been able to forewarn Henry about her nose ring, purple hair streaks and tattoos, the latter mostly covered except for the hibiscus flower peeking out from under the cuff of her plaid flannel shirt. He took it quite well for a man his age and was as polite and welcoming as anyone could be. I wasn't sure what would happen when I introduced her to Jack, but seeing him turn as white as a sheet wasn't it. He stood and shook her hand, looking most uncomfortable.

"Nice to meet you all," Jacqueline Rose said pleasantly, as she made her way to the coffee carafe.

"Dillan and I need just a few minutes, then please join us in the dining room."

"Sounds lovely. I'm quite famished," Henry replied.

"Me too!" added Mr. Hanson.

Once back in the kitchen, I exclaimed, "What a happy coincidence! I truly like Jacqueline Rose."

"That was an interesting twist all right," Dillan replied, as he took the eggs out of the refrigerator and gave them a quick whisk. "One thing I learned as soon as I moved here is that Beach Haven is a very small town."

I leaned in close to whisper and took in his musky aftershave. "I wonder if Captain Jack's made any progress on our little investigation. I hope he won't mention it today unless there's good news."

"If I get him alone, I'll ask," Dillan replied.

"Good. Let's get this breakfast served up so we have some time to relax and open gifts before we serve dinner."

"Dang, girl. Are you trying to kill me?" he joked.

I know I must have opened Christmas presents in the past, but I was so excited I could hardly contain myself. As we all relaxed in the library, Christmas carols playing, a nice crackling fire in the fireplace, the tree twinkling and Irish coffee all around, I reflected on my life, what little I could recall of it. Dillan was responsible for everything that I had: my food, my clothes, my comfortable bed. He said I more than earned my keep with all the work I did at the inn, but I felt he was overly generous. He indulged my every whim unquestioningly. He had planned on paying for the entire Christmas dinner as well but Henry wouldn't hear of it. I felt badly that he offered to pay for the party I insisted we have, but he was adamant and honestly seemed to be enjoying himself. The only one looking uncomfortable was Captain Jack, who appeared to occasionally squirm in his seat.

I climbed under the tree and pulled out the few gifts that were there. Had we known Jacqueline Rose was coming we would have gotten her something more suitable, instead of the modest scarf we had chosen for Lucas' lady friend. I'd make sure to give her the receipt so she could exchange it. Henry gave Lucas a complete collection of his signed works and he couldn't have been more thrilled. Dillan and I gave Jack and Carole a gift card to Pinziminio Trattoria Restaurant. Everyone received a Jetty brand UNITE+REBUILD T-shirt from Santa. Buoy was overjoyed with his can of tennis balls and a bag of USA-made jerky treats. We gave Henry an IOU for a lunch or dinner out and the teas, which he said looked quite delicious. We gave Lucas a VISA gift card, not very personal but practical. Henry gave the Fosters a bottle of brandy. They gave him a gift card to Buckalew's, and us tickets to two fundraisers. The first was a rock concert called The Sandy Blows Benefit at the Ship

Bottom firehouse and the second was a movie screening of East Coast Rising at the LBI Foundation of the Arts and Sciences. I was already looking forward to our nights on the town. I gave Dillan the pen, pencils and shaving cream from Kapler's, plus a large perfectly shaped snail shell that I found on the beach.

"I'm sorry there isn't more," I said as he opened the package.

"Don't be silly, girl. I love it. All the best gifts are from the sea. It gave us you."

"Here! Here!" Henry said.

There were still two gifts behind the tree. The larger one was very heavy and had a handle protruding through the wrapping paper. The tag read, To Sandy -From Dillan. When I opened it, I was very touched. It was a wooden treasure chest with my name painted on it.

"Did you make this?" I asked Dillan.

"Yes, but it wasn't easy to keep it a surprise."

"It's beautiful."

"Open it up."

Inside were an assortment of tools, each one labeled with my name. "Wow, Dillan. I love it!"

"With all the volunteering we do, I figured you could use your own set."

Who ever thought a girl could get choked up about tools? I jumped up and gave him a hug. "It's very special. Thank you," I said with a catch in my throat and tear in my eye.

"It turned out to be heavier than I expected, but I'll carry it for you when we go out."

I pulled the last present from way in the back. It was also for me. "Come on. Open it, Sandy," Henry urged gently. I slowly peeled away the paper to find a familiar old red and black hat box.

"Oh, Henry . . . I can't."

"But you must. It's perfect for you."

I opened the box. Wrapped in red tissue was Naia's gorgeous shell necklace and a little card. "Open the card later, my dear," Henry said.

"Are you sure?" I asked, holding up the beautiful piece of jewelry.

"I couldn't be more certain," he replied with a wink.

"Thank you, Henry," I said, after taking a deep breath. "Thank you everyone and Merry Christmas. Now let's go check that turkey, shall we, Dillan?"

Dillan pulled the turkey out of the oven, placed it on a carving board and tented it with foil. Then he read the gravy directions out loud. It had called for the giblets to be included but after a close inspection this morning, we decided to toss them out. No one felt particularly hungry, so we decided to have another drink with our guests while the turkey rested.

By the time we returned to the kitchen, everyone was feeling quite relaxed. Even Jack had stopped looking like he wanted to bolt and run any second. The men shared in the carving process, no digits lost, after watching a demonstration on YouTube. I reheated the mashed potatoes over a bowl of steaming water while simultaneously sautéing the green beans with some butter. The sweet potato casserole was keeping warm in the oven as was the stuffing we had removed from the bird. Since no meal would be truly complete without seafood, our guests enjoyed a jumbo shrimp cocktail as we dished up the meal.

Dillan, Henry and I paraded into the dining room with our feast and set the platters on the table.

"May you enjoy the food as much as the company," I said, feeling a bit tipsy.

"To all my new friends, I thank you for being here today," Henry added.

"Merry Christmas," Dillan said.

The wine glasses clinked and "*Hear, hear!*" was heard all around.

"Made with love. Definitely made with love," Lucas said, as he savored every bite.

It was a very good day.

CAPTAIN JACK FOSTER

DECEMBER 2012

IT WAS THAT TIME of the year again and it started long before Black Friday. As the years passed, I hoped things would get better, that I would stop being angry at my daughter, at God and myself. They say that time heals all wounds; that's total bullshit – it doesn't.

I hated it, all of it: every commercial, holiday special on TV, the carols on the radio, the lighted trees, decorations, cards, ornaments, wrapping paper, bows, gift bags and tags. Everywhere I turned, I was swallowed up by its suffocating presence. When I lost my daughter, I also lost my faith. I felt broken and painfully hollow. I had a treasure who was taken away by a stupid, senseless accident. Carole told me Sara was too young to go ice skating but it was her best friend's seventh birthday party and she was so excited about it. I assured Carole with the proper protective equipment she would be safe. I was wrong. She was standing along the wall and never even had a chance to get the helmet on. A child fell and slid across the rink, her legs sliding into my daughter's lifting both her feet off the ice. She landed on the back of her head. Even though her skull had cracked, it didn't help reduce the pressure from the intracerebral bleeding. Twenty days later, on Christmas Eve, we let her go.

Every year at Christmas time, I am transported back to the Pediatric Intensive Care Unit to relive that ungodly wretched day. Carole, early on, blamed me but no more than I blamed myself. I was a police officer who couldn't even protect his most cherished daughter.

I somehow felt betrayed by my innocent sweet Sara, not only for wanting to go to the party but for leaving us alone to deal with the grief of her absence. I rationalized that she was a happy, active child, full of love and adoration for us, not to mention furry kittens, colorful My Little Ponies, princess dresses and tiaras, and a particular story book filled with dolphins, whales, seals and polar bears. She loved life and should never have been blamed for leaving us. It wasn't her fault for being in exactly the wrong place at the wrong time. Was it fate? Was it a punishment for something I'd done in the past? If I heard one more well-meaning person whisper *It was God's will,* I probably would have punched them in the face. It wasn't God's will to take my beloved six-year-old away; there was no God.

Our daughter's room remained untouched for years. I would often go there when Carole was asleep and talk to Sara. I would sit on her bed and remember her playing with the little toy animals she loved so dearly. As the image before me faded from view, I imagined her in heaven, snuggled in the embrace of a gigantic, protective polar bear.

One night, I had a glorious dream. I was standing on the shore, looking out to sea. The scene was washed with a bright but calming light which paled the natural colors. I turned to see my Sara standing on the sand, but she wasn't alone. There was another young girl on her right, standing slightly behind her. I only glanced at her quickly but she appeared to be the same age and build, even the same red hair color. Sara was dressed in an outfit I remember well: white sparkly sneakers, pink leggings and a ruffled sweater. She didn't say a word but just stood there, waiting, looking peaceful. I ran to her, dropped to my knees and wrapped my arms around her. "You're alive! You're alive!" I sobbed over and over. My words grew garbled and became louder and louder until I woke myself up. I was angry that the dream ended so quickly. I was disheartened that Sara hadn't spoken. Who was the other little girl with her? Was she a guardian angel? A spirit that helped guide her into my subconscious?

I didn't tell Carole about the dream. I didn't want to upset her. I thought about it over and over and could come to only one conclusion: It was Sara's way of telling me that she was all right. She was peaceful; she had a companion who was looking out for her and guiding her. She appeared to me in a place that I loved and felt comfortable in. She was telling me it was the place we needed to be, to heal.

Once we'd left Westchester County and moved to Long Beach Island, things got a bit better. We were welcomed warmly by the citizens of Beach Haven and became part of their community more quickly than I'd imagined. We'd make time to walk on the beach each day to talk about our loss and our feelings. I would often imagine Sara right there with us, the three of us holding hands and dodging the incoming sea foam.

I've been the police captain for four years now. This place suits us well. Even after that mother of a hurricane, I'd never want to leave this place or any of its quirky residents. We are a family.

Christmas was rearing its ugly head again and we were having a particularly bad day when Dillan had called and asked to stop by. I welcomed the thought of a diversion and something else to focus on for a while. I assumed Sandy had some sort of breakthrough and maybe we would finally have something to go on, but she had come for a totally different reason.

I'd seen the girl before, this Jacqueline Rose she was interested in. She was the kind of kid who stuck out in our little town. I hate to profile people, but I did wonder where she came from and what she was doing waitressing at the CHEGG last year. I was informed by the owner that she'd spent summers here when she was younger, was nothing but polite and punctual, and the customers loved her. In fact, he recalled, the only time she had missed a shift was when her grandmother had died.

The next morning, I decided to stop by the Bagel Shack for a bit of breakfast and feel her out. I stepped into the line, but was ushered ahead – such are the perks of being the police captain. Unfortunately, she wasn't behind the counter. After I ordered my coffee and breakfast sandwich, I asked to speak to the owner privately. I had only one question, "What's Jacqueline Rose's last name?"

A quick DMV check and I found her mother in, of all places, Seaside Heights. I really was surprised at my own dumb luck but sometimes initial hunches, no matter how unfounded, can pay off.

After the forty-mile drive, I took a quick tour around town. The coastline, boardwalk and many of the attractions were in varying states of disrepair, not unlike our own island. I had seen their damage on the TV reports – the iconic roller coaster I had ridden as a teen was nothing but an unappealing sculpture of bent-up steel.

I found Ms. Hanson's apartment situated over a kitschy gift shop and knocked on the door – no answer.

"Ms. Hanson? This is Captain Foster of the Beach Haven police," I paused, waiting, but received no response. "I'm here about your daughter – Jacqueline Rose." I heard footsteps and the locks being undone. A woman, who appeared to be in her late thirties/early forties opened the door looking panicked and tired.

"God, is she all right? Tell me she's all right!" she squealed.

"Yes, she's fine. I just have a couple of questions."

"Is she in some kind of trouble?" she asked worriedly.

"No, ma'am. Nothing like that. I guess I'm actually here about her father."

"Did she ask you to find him?"

"Would you be willing to give me his name?"

"Is he under some sort of investigation?"

I couldn't be forthright with the woman, and it bothered me. "I'm sorry; I'm not at liberty to say. Is it true he was in the Marines?" I asked in an effort to divert her questions.

"Well, I'm not positive. I told my daughter her father was in the Marines to explain his absence plus he'd said he was thinking about joining. A friend of mine who worked on a cruise ship sent her gifts from abroad to make him appear more authentic."

"I'm sorry, I don't understand."

"Would you like a cup of coffee while I explain?"

She'd suddenly become very accommodating. "Sure, Ms. Hanson, that would be nice."

"Please, call me Erica."

She offered me a seat at her tiny kitchen table which was only slightly bigger than a TV tray.

"Sorry about the mess," she said, as she cleared a place for me to set my cup. "I've been working double shifts at the restaurant and I'm usually too exhausted to clean up when I get home."

"No problem."

"I lied to Jacqueline Rose about her father because I didn't want her to know I had no idea who he was," she freely admitted.

"But, surely you had some idea, unless you were roofied or something. Please tell me it wasn't anything like that."

"No, I'm sure it wasn't. From what I remember, he was super sweet, shy even."

"If I had a dollar for every time I heard that," I said, shaking my head.

"I was young – in college at the time. There was this beach party, not far from here. All the local and summer kids were going. There was a bonfire and tons of alcohol, anything you wanted, really. A lot of the kids, I never saw before. I remember it quite vividly, considering I had a few drinks in me."

"Go on."

"Everyone was having a blast, acting crazy, and dancing around the fire. I noticed him sitting by himself, just drinking a beer and staring at the sea."

After a long pause she added, "I hate thinking about this."

"Take your time," I replied, though my interest was piqued. We sipped our coffee in silence for a bit before she continued.

"He was a clean-cut type of guy, almost nerdy, but so handsome. I felt brave because of the rum and Cokes, so I went over and sat by him in the sand. He was friendly and we talked for hours, so it seemed. He said he was thinking about becoming a Marine. One thing led to another and before I knew it we were lying under the boughs of a wild beach rose. You can guess the rest."

"So, what happened to him?" I asked, feeling more than a little bit curious.

"I never saw him again. I spent as much time at the beach as I could and went to every party I heard about, hoping to meet up with him again. I asked around in case anyone knew him, but I only knew his first name. No one had any idea who he was."

"Please don't think I'm presumptuous, but I must ask: is it possible that another man could have been her father?"

"No, not a chance. I wasn't promiscuous. I was just so taken with him. When I found out I was pregnant, I was almost happy about it. I was positive we'd meet again before the summer ended."

"I'm so sorry, Erica. What year was that?"

"Nineteen ninety-two," she paused, visually upset by the memory. "It wasn't easy, you know. My parents had such high hopes for me. They couldn't understand why I'd quit school to have a baby. Right before she was born, they talked me into giving her up for adoption, but once I saw her pretty little face, I couldn't go through with it. In hindsight, I probably should have. I was a horrible mother."

"Well, I don't know about that," I said, "She seems to be doing all right."

"So, you've talked to her then?"

"No, I haven't, but she appears to be a responsible kid. She's got a job and she's taking care of her grandfather."

"Poor old Dad. I heard he's living in a hotel."

"I believe his home was severely damaged by the storm, yes."

"I'm pleased that he and Jacqueline Rose are close. Funny how things work out."

I wanted to tell her to go see them for herself. Maybe whatever had divided them could be repaired, but I had other things on my mind.

"You said you only knew Jacqueline Rose's father by his first name. What was it?" I asked with trepidation.

"Jack," she replied with a loud sigh.

DILLAN

I HAD NEVER MET a girl who came close to Sandy in selflessness and gratitude. It was as if she existed just to be helpful. It was more than admirable and in my eyes, it made her seem as close to perfect as a human could be. When we were together, which was most of the time, I felt as if all was right in the world. It was a completely new and overwhelming feeling for me and I knew what it meant: happily ever after or ball-breaking misery till the end of my days.

She didn't have to say a word, but I could tell she had some something up her sleeve as we headed toward the Sea Oakes Country Club in Little Egg Harbor. Our Christmas gift to Henry was a nice lunch out and we decided to invite Lucas to come along.

"I know where we're going," Lucas said, as we pulled onto Railroad Avenue. "We used to golf here years ago."

"You and your wife?" Henry asked.

"Oh, yes, we had some wonderful times here, especially when the big bands came to play. We always had to watch our pennies so we were never members, but we would come for a hoot now and then. It seems strange to be here without her."

"I'm so sorry for your loss. I don't think I ever told you that," Henry said as we got out of the car.

Though it was an upscale place, thankfully the lunch menu wasn't too fancy. There were burgers, a nice assortment of sandwiches and some interesting-sounding pizzas available. It was just my kind of food. Everyone else seemed pleased with the menu too, especially Sandy, who was gushing over the idea of a lump crab cake with Old Bay aioli.

After we ate our fill, Sandy said, "Dillan and I are going to take a walk around the place and check it out. We'll be back in a little bit."

"Okay, you two enjoy yourselves."

"Take your time," Lucas added.

"So, what's your plan, girl?" I asked as we left the room.

"What are you talking about?"

"I know you're up to something."

"I just thought the two of them should get better acquainted. I mean, they're neighbors and I think they'd make good company for each other."

"Did you know Lucas used to golf here?"

"No, that wasn't part of the plan. I felt badly about reminding him. I thought the afternoon might backfire."

We grabbed our coats and headed outside. The sun was blazing brightly in the clear blue sky but the wind made it downright cold on the golf course.

"I bet they hold weddings here," I mused, as I pictured her in a form-fitting, neckline-plunging white dress. With the sun adding greatly to its sheerness, it was more reminiscent of a lacy negligee.

"It looks that way. Nice place for one – in the summer."

"Do you think you might be married?"

"Wow Dillan! That's some question," she replied as she kicked at the ground. "Deep down I feel like there may have been someone special, but married? I have no idea."

"I'm sorry I asked," I said, discouraged.

"I wish I knew for sure. Living in limbo is difficult."

For you and me both, I thought with mounting frustration. As we reentered the dining room, the old gents appeared to be getting along swimmingly.

"It's never been the same since Jack's Bakery closed," Lucas said. "Sunday mornings I'd go up there and get these lip-smacking sticky buns for my Helen and Jacqueline Rose. That little girl was so adorable with that sticky goo all over her face and fingers, until the time she stuck one of them dang raisins up her nose."

Henry laughed, "Now she's covered in tattoos instead."

"Who coulda guessed that?" Lucas replied, sounding disappointed.

"It could be worse, Lucas. She seems to love you very much *and* she's a good girl."

"You're right. I hope someday she'll find a fella who can look past them."

"Did you ever go to Romeo's for their Sunday brunch? The crepes were delightful!"

"Yes, we'd go for Helen's birthday; she loved it. We also liked Otts. We'd eat on the patio Saturday mornings. Every summer we'd talk about how heavy the tourist traffic was getting on Long Beach Boulevard."

"Yes, the dreaded weekend influx. Do you remember crossing the street without fearing for your life?"

"Now, those were the good old days!"

I glanced at Sandy who was beaming with satisfaction.

We were on the way home when Sandy asked, "Would you mind if we made a stop? I think I left my scarf at the animal shelter a few days ago."

Blindsided! I never even saw it coming. The doggie bed that we'd left at Henry's wasn't really for Buoy after all. If Sandy had her way, poor old Henry would soon be a proud pet parent.

"It's fine with me," Henry replied. "I've got nowhere to be."

"Me either," added Lucas. "We could drive around all day if you'd like."

"Okay, SOCAS it is – but I have to warn you, gentlemen; there are a lot of sad and lonely animals there."

Sandy reached over and smacked my arm.

I'd been trying to help, but it had come out all wrong. "You know, if Buoy wasn't so old and set in his ways, I'd be tempted to get him a playmate."

"I had a dog years ago," Henry said wistfully.

"So did we," Lucas added. "Best boxer ever born."

"Mine was a mixed breed, some sort of terrier, I think."

Sandy didn't have to say or do much after that. The conversation flowed from one dog story to another. Henry had even taught his dog to surf with him. By the time we pulled into the parking lot, I knew she had Henry right where she wanted him, with seemingly little effort. She was like that, a regular Mary Poppins.

"Did you know the police and National Guard helped the animal cruelty investigator rescue over eighty pets from the island after the storm?" Sandy offered.

"Why would people leave behind their helpless animals?" Henry asked sadly.

"I'm sure there were some people who didn't have a choice," she replied, coming to my defense.

"Oh, sorry, Dillan. I didn't mean you, son."

"No offense taken, Henry."

"Why don't you come in while I look for my scarf?" Sandy coaxed.

I held open the door that led to the reception area and we all filed inside. No one was behind the desk, though we could hear plenty of barking from the kennel area.

"Hello – Joanie? Anyone here?" Sandy yelled.

"Be there in a minute."

Joanie appeared from the back room, looking out of breath.

"Sorry guys! I was just sorting some of the food donations. You've come to walk the pups?"

"No, not today. We came to look for my scarf and thought we'd show our friends around," Sandy chimed, giving Joanie a little wink. "Guys, this is Joanie. A wonderful advocate for homeless pets."

"Nice to meet you, gentlemen. I didn't notice a scarf but you're welcome to look around."

"Would you like help with the food?" I asked, knowing how heavy the big bags must be for Joanie, who was about ninety pounds soaking wet.

"I won't turn help away, if you're offering. We're taking some of the donations over to Barnegat to distribute it among the public. A lot of our neighbors are having a hard time after the storm and we don't want them surrendering their pets because they can't afford to feed them."

"I hope that doesn't happen. There are so many homeless ones already," Sandy said sadly.

"Well, it's the ugly truth, I'm afraid. Feel free to introduce your friends to the fur babies."

"Thanks, Joanie."

"No, *thank you*, Sandy!"

Knowing Sandy, I wasn't shocked by what I saw when I returned from the back room, but I was impressed. Henry was petting Sherlock; this old white and brindle pit bull and Lucas was holding Mrs. Holmes, the little black cat. She had the adoption forms on the counter and ready to be filled out.

"What have we here?" I asked, knowing all too well she had used her magical powers of persuasion yet again.

"Sherlock and Mrs. Holmes are going to their forever home," she said with tears forming in her eyes. "Henry's going to give them a very happy life."

"And I'm going to help," added Lucas, as the little cat rubbed her whiskers along his jaw.

SANDY

JANUARY 2013

EVEN THOUGH DILLAN PROBABLY would have preferred a cold beer and sports via the big screen at the Hud on weekends, he offered to work by my side as I volunteered with various organizations. There was no question that he stayed close because he felt responsible for me but, deep down, I knew he enjoyed the feeling of contributing just as much as I did. It was easy to find a place to swing your hammer, work your muscles and use your utility knife; all you had to do was listen while you were out and about.

The Jetty Clothing Company had formed a non-profit organization and had been working with a newly formed group of volunteers called S.T.A.R.T. to help gut homes, reduce the spread of mold and save homeowners money – money that was coming in much too slowly. We had heard about the wonderful things they were doing for the community, so I really wanted to pitch in with the teachers and residents who made up the group. I met a lot of new people from various walks of life, but sadly no one recognized me, nor I them.

On the second Saturday after the new year, during a particularly long day of back-breaking work at the Beach Haven firehouse, Dillan said, "You make me proud on so many levels – little of it having to do with your pretty face," and he kissed me on my rather dirty cheek. He really was the sweetest guy and I couldn't help falling in love with him.

Oh, God! I *really was* falling in love with him. I had a sudden urge to grab him by the dreadlocks and press my lips firmly against his. The kiss would be hard and deep and lingering. It was all so agonizing. I watched him intently as he loaded our tools into the Jeep and sighed.

I was making tuna fish sandwiches and reheating clam chowder for lunch one afternoon when Dillan popped his head into the kitchen.

"I heard about something you might be interested in, girl."

Why did he always call me *girl*? Was that surfer lingo? – "What is it?" I asked curiously.

"The Alliance for a Living Ocean is holding a program in Tuckerton on the twenty-third. It's about the challenges of cleaning up the bay, rebuilding the dunes and preparing for the next big storm."

"You know, I haven't even been thinking about the ocean. All the garbage and chemicals that ended up in there, those poor fish and animals. Gosh, I feel so selfish."

"Don't be so hard on yourself. We've been busting our butts doing other things, but it's not too late to help out."

"I'm in, definitely!"

"Okay, we'll have dinner out first and make a night of it."

"Can we go somewhere that serves seafood?"

Dillan gave me a look that screamed, "DUH!"

***

I had been anxiously waiting to use the benefit tickets that Captain Jack and Carole had given us for Christmas. The Surf City Fire Company was hosting the benefit that would address the almost 400,000 dollars' worth of damage the Ship Bottom Fire Company had accrued from Sandy. I couldn't remember seeing one live band, let alone seven! I danced around the inn now and then as we worked but I became embarrassed when I caught Dillan watching me. The day before the concert, we were heading back from Home Depot when Dillan pulled the Jeep into the Kohl's parking lot.

"Why are we stopping?"

"I thought you might like to get something to wear tomorrow

night," he said as he parked the car and pulled his new Kohl's credit card out of his wallet.

"Why?"

"Most girls like to dress up for a night out, don't they?"

"You want me to wear something *different*?"

"I want you to wear whatever you're most comfortable in. Your work clothes are stained and worn and I just thought you might like something new, that's all."

"Oh, I thought you'd be embarrassed by me if I went like this."

"Even if you were wearing my old sweats and hadn't showered in a week, I couldn't be prouder to be by your side."

"I think I can do a bit better than that," I said as I grabbed the card, jumped out of the Jeep and ran into the store.

The next day, it was business as usual but by late afternoon I was getting excited. "What time are we leaving?" I asked through my mask, as I sanded down some spackling compound.

"It's going to be set up like a club so let's not go too early," Dillan replied, "It won't get rocking till after everyone's got a buzz on, plus I want to make a grand entrance with you on my arm."

"You know it's not an official date, right?" I yelled through a little cloud of white dust.

"Yup, I know. Just two friends enjoying a little fun for a good cause," he replied disappointedly.

Once Dillan had sealed up the paint cans and we washed the brushes and putty knives, we had leftovers for dinner. I was so excited that I didn't have much of an appetite. Dillan went to shower as I cleaned up the kitchen.

"How do you wash that hair?" I asked later as he came down the hall with a towel wrapped around his head.

"Very carefully," he replied with a laugh. "You really aren't digging my dreads, are you?"

"No matter how many times you ask me, I'm still going to give you the same answer." I replied flippantly, as I headed toward the bathroom to shower and get ready for the benefit. When I went to step into the tub, I jumped and almost screamed. Thankfully, it wasn't a furry little creature but just another chunk of Dillan's hair that'd broken off. I picked it up as if it were the nastiest thing imaginable and dropped it in the garbage can.

I washed the dust from my hair, then scrubbed with raspberry shower gel and shaved my legs, which I considered a difficult and tiresome chore. I especially didn't want any nicks today because it was my first time wearing a dress. I found the sleeveless, deep blue piece on the sale rack for an excellent price, so excellent in fact that I hightailed it right over to the shoe department without feeling too guilty.

After I dried my hair, I pulled on the silky dress. Its delicate fabric reminded me of water flowing over the rocks in a waterfall. I spun left to right and watched the layers of thin material follow my movement. I placed the extraordinary necklace Henry had given me around my neck and looked in the mirror. It *did* look perfect, just like he said, and for once I felt very pretty. Perhaps my dress was a bit *too* short and a bit *too* low cut, but it was *too* late to do anything about that now! I put on a little lipstick, mascara and blush then gathered up my courage. I made sure Dillan wasn't around when I came out of the bathroom. I didn't want him to see my outfit before we got there.

When we arrived at the Surf City firehouse, we had to park a few blocks away because there was such a good turnout. Dillan reached under the seat and pulled out a bottle of liquor.

"What's that for?"

"Fortification."

"What do you mean?"

"These things tend to be better with a little buzz."

"Can I have a sip?"

"Sure, girl. If you think you can handle it. Just remember what a lightweight you are."

"What do you mean?"

"I mean, after a couple glasses of wine you're sawing wood!"

"That's not true. I didn't fall asleep at Christmas and we were drinking all day."

"No, but after we got home and we had some of this, you were rockin' Bruce Springsteen's 'Santa Claus is Comin' To Town' pretty hard, remember?"

"I don't know what you're talking about."

"Dancing half naked around the Christmas tree?"

"Nope, not a clue."

"I'm not surprised," he said laughing. "Let's not repeat that tonight, okay?"

"Whatever!" I took a big gulp of the whiskey and proceeded to cough as it burned its way down my throat. "I don't remember it tasting like this." Dillan just rolled his eyes and shook his head.

As we walked back towards the firehouse, I saw Dillan tuck the bottle into the waistband of his jeans. I guess he wasn't fortified quite enough. It was crowded and noisy as we entered the hall. The band was playing that funky music loud enough to vibrate the blue and white balloons and strings of white lights that decorated the place, not to mention every cell in my body. The sensation seemed familiar and exhilarating. I must've been to shows like this before.

I wanted to get closer to the band to see if anyone was dancing. I let Dillan slide my coat from my shoulders and I slipped away. I wove my way toward the front of the crowd feeling inspired by the beat. The band stopped playing and everyone yelled and applauded. The MC stepped out, thanked Shorty Long and The Jersey Horns and announced a band called Eleven Eleven. Strange name for a band but the music was good. "Do, Do, Do – Do, Do, Do, Do . . . ." A very catchy song had me tapping my foot and nodding my head along with the others in the crowd who were sipping drinks and eating snacks.

"I thought I lost you," Dillan yelled over the music as he came up behind me and put his hands on my shoulders.

"I thought this was a dance," I yelled back, looking at the empty dance floor.

"It's an old song called 'Semi-Charmed Life.'"

"Do you think anyone is going to dance?"

"It's by a band called Third Eye Blind."

Was he not hearing me or was he intentionally changing the subject?

I stepped out of the crowd and started dancing in the small open space in front of the makeshift stage. People moved back to give me more room. The song had a lot of energy and I let it wash over me. I shook my butt; I shook my boobs – I danced like no one was watching. Dillan caught my eye and I watched as the Jack Daniels bottle slipped from his hand and smashed into pieces on the floor. Dang, I wanted more of that! A fireman appeared and cleaned up the mess. Dillan's mouth hung open as he stared at me, but I was having so much fun that I just kept dancing. The song flowed seamlessly into another and more people joined me on the floor. Before long, most of the room was dancing except for a few wallflowers.

I was having a fantastic time. I made my way over to Dillan, who had gotten a beer from somewhere. I wagged my finger at him, beckoning him to dance with me. Reluctantly, he allowed me to pull him onto the floor.

"What's the matter?" I asked.

"I have two left feet!" he yelled as he moved around a bit.

"Oh, come on. Just relax and have fun. Pretend like no one's watching."

"No one *is* watching me," he replied, "'cause they're *all* watching *you!*"

"There're a lot of girls out here. It's not just me."

"None as spectacular as you are."

I just shook my head in disbelief and kept dancing. After a few minutes, the tempo shifted and the music became more romantic.

"*Hey, where did we go? Days when the rains came . . . ,*" the guitar player sang.

Dillan grabbed me by the waist and pulled me hard against him, then we rocked back and forth. He spun me around and sang, "You-u-u . . . my brown-eyed girl."

"They're blue," I yelled back, giggling.

"Don't I know it!" he said as he spun me again.

I was having the best time ever but I was also very hot and thirsty. We walked over to the kitchen window where Dillan bought me a ginger ale and a big chocolate chip cookie.

"This is awesome!" I yelled, holding up the cookie. "Want some?"

"Yeah, I want some. I want it all, every last morsel!" he teased.

Dillan grabbed my hand, then kissed it, and took a huge bite of the cookie.

"I'm afraid I have some competition tonight. These guys can't stop staring at you. Do you have to be so beautiful?"

"I don't know. Maybe you shouldn't have bought me this dress. If I'd worn my old jeans no one would have noticed me."

"Do you honestly believe that?"

I nodded my head.

"You are *so* wrong, girl!"

I excused myself to go to the ladies' room which was down a hallway at the far end of the room. Unwilling to let me out of his sight, Dillan followed me to the hallway entrance and waited.

Inside, I straightened my dress, checked my makeup and blotted a bit of sweat from my nose and forehead. I stepped out of the bathroom and bumped head-on into a very large and hard body. A huge dude in a Hawaiian shirt took hold of my upper arms and squeezed them tightly. I was so shocked that I didn't even think to call for help. He pushed me up against the wall and put his face close to mine.

"**LEAVE THIS PLACE!**" he growled menacingly.

I was so frightened that I closed my eyes.

"**DID YOU HEAR ME?**" his words boomed over the music.

I nodded as I couldn't force any words to come from my throat.

"**GOOD!**"

He gave me a shake, then I felt his grasp loosen and release me. I slowly opened my eyes and sighed with relief. He was gone, but he'd left my heart beating more wildly than the drums on stage and angry red grip marks on my arms.

With tears in my eyes, I ran back to Dillan, who was standing right where I left him.

"*Did you see him*?" I asked, totally freaking out.

"What's the matter? See who?"

"The big jerk in the Hawaiian shirt!" I yelled back while scanning the room.

"No, did he hurt you? Are you all right?"

"Let's go home, Dillan!" I grabbed his hand and pulled him toward the coat check.

"Sure, okay. As long as you tell me what's happened!"

DILLAN

S ANDY SEEMED TERRIFIED AND couldn't stop shaking on the way home.

"Why would anyone want to hurt me?" she asked, "What could I have done?"

"Sandy, please – just tell me what happened!" I implored, feeling so freakin' useless and frustrated beyond words.

Finally, after calming down a bit, she told me about the jackass who scared the shit out of her. I was fuming and wanted to go back and look for the asshole, but Sandy just wanted to get home. I had a myriad of thoughts running through my mind and none of them were pleasant. Was he just some drunk jerk or could he possibly be someone from her past? If so, why was he so angry and threatening?

When we got back to Beach Haven, I pulled in front of the police station and parked. I reached over, took her hand and squeezed gently. "We're going to get to the bottom of this. He was probably just drunk and no one to worry about," I said, trying to console her.

A cop who was sitting behind the counter stood up and welcomed us. His badge identified him as Officer Alfred Washington.

First thing first. Though it was late, I asked if Jack was on duty. The twenty-something cop walked down the hall and returned with Jack, who was looking incredibly astute for the late hour.

"Is everything all right?" he asked worriedly. "Jesus, you smell like whiskey!"

"Not exactly; some lowlife just accosted Sandy at the Surf City firehouse."

"What? At the *firehouse*?"

"Yeah the Sandy Blows concert was there tonight. You and Carole gave us the tickets," I replied.

"Well, it *was* really fun until . . . ," Sandy added.

"Come down to my office and have a seat. Would either of you like some water?"

"Yes, please," Sandy replied, still looking slightly shaken.

"None for me, thanks."

"All right now," he said calmly as he drew the water from the cooler and handed Sandy the cup, "tell me exactly what happened."

Sandy gave a good description of the blatantly obvious guy who somehow walked past me completely unnoticed. I felt like an idiot and a failure. She still had pink marks on her bare arms where he'd grabbed her and they looked like they would bruise. I was enraged at the thought of anyone hurting her. I felt like I could explode.

Jack jotted down a description of said asshole: six-foot-six, muscular solid build, large strong hands, like vices, black wavy shoulder-length hair, large brown eyes, dark skin, possible Polynesian descent, wearing a brightly colored Hawaiian shirt and dark jeans.

"I didn't see his shoes," Sandy said flatly as she slumped back in her chair.

Jack took pictures of her arms and asked me to please relax as he observed my hands clenching and unclenching rapidly.

"I'm heading up there right now. You two go home, try to relax and get some sleep. I'll do my best to bring this jerk in."

"Thank you, Captain Jack," Sandy said as she gave him a hug.

"If I apprehend him I'll give you a call, otherwise I'll buzz you in the morning," he said as he climbed into his police car.

I looked north as we pulled onto Bay Avenue, and Jack was long gone. Selfishly, I wondered if I really wanted him to find this moron. If it meant Sandy's past was catching up with her, then no. I hoped it would remain a mystery.

The next morning, even though it was Sunday, we were up earlier than usual. Over coffee, I discovered that neither of us had slept very well. Every time I had started to drift off, I dreamt that some thundering Tiki god was squeezing Sandy's arms until she screamed in pain. I'd startle, then check that she was safe before I'd close my eyes again. I was envious of Buoy, who had buried himself under the covers and lay next to her.

It was mid-morning; we were on our second pot of coffee and still rehashing the night's events, when Jack finally called. I put him on speaker phone and set it on the table so we both could hear.

"Sorry, guys; no luck. By the time I got up there the show was wrapping up. There wasn't any sign of your assailant and there weren't many people left to question. I found one kid who saw someone matching his description outside, peering into parked cars. When I asked him why he didn't notify the police, he said he didn't think the guy was breaking any laws."

"That's it then?" I asked.

"I'd alerted the Long Beach Township police last night and we're running an APB. I'm really sorry, Sandy. How are you feeling this morning?"

"A little shaken up. My arms are sore but basically I'm fine."

"We'll do everything we can to find this guy. This might sound insensitive, but I have to ask: Could he be someone from your past?"

"Seriously, Jack?" I asked, perturbed.

"Dillan, it's certainly a possibility that he might know her. When he said, 'leave this place' did he mean leave the concert or leave the island?"

"Your guess is as good as mine, Captain Jack. There was nothing familiar about him. I should think I'd remember an abusive boyfriend and if he did know me, why didn't he just drag me outta there?"

"That's a good question. I'd say he wanted to avoid a scene. No one's reported you missing and now someone mysteriously shows up and attempts to put the fear of God in you."

"You're frightening me a bit," she replied.

"Jack, what's the next step?"

"Keep your eyes open and call me or 911 right away if you spot the guy or notice anything suspicious. Don't confront him yourselves."

"We can do that," Sandy said with a sigh.

"Alright, kids. We'll keep in touch."

"Oh, Captain Jack, I know you're busy, but I wanted to ask if you'd had a chance to look for Jacqueline Rose's father." There was a long pause.

"Jack are you still there?" I asked.

"Yes, I'm here," he replied, "I wasn't going to mention anything, because there's still DNA samples that need collecting, but I think I may have located him."

SANDY

ONE COLD, DREARY MORNING Jacqueline Rose appeared at our door. She was wearing a huge smile and rosy cheeks which were partially covered by her black, purple-streaked, wind-whipped hair. Buoy barked and wagged his tail in welcome as she fought against the gusts, which attempted to steal her large portfolio as she wrangled it into the door.

"Hey, it's great to see you!" I said happily. "Come on in. How are you?"

"I'm great! I have some fantastic news!"

"Come on upstairs and I'll make us something hot to drink. Dillan . . . Jacqueline Rose is here!" I yelled. "Would you like coffee, tea or hot cocoa?"

"Hot cocoa would be great, thanks. I only had to walk a block and a half, but it's freezing out there. That damp ocean wind cuts like a knife, right to the bone."

"What have you got there?" I asked curiously as I warmed the water for the Swiss Miss.

"It's my artwork – things I've done over the years. I thought you might like to see them before I leave."

"Leave? You're leaving?" My initial thought was that I would miss my new friend but then I thought of Lucas and wondered how he would manage without her.

"Yes, and I have only you to thank."

"Me, why me?"

"Because of your admiration and encouragement. I was teetering with going back to school or just giving up, but I took to

211

heart everything you've said these past few weeks. I decided to go back, but only after Grandpa gave me his news."

"News? What news?"

"He's moving in with Mr. Henry."

"What? Really?" I asked excitedly. The pieces were coming together more easily than I'd anticipated.

"I think it's a great idea!" Dillan said as he entered the kitchen, wiping his hands on a rag. "Henry lives all alone in that big old house and he and Lucas seem to get along so well."

"They really do. I haven't heard Grandpa laugh so much in ages. They're talking about writing a book together and they want me to design the cover! Mr. Henry said I can stay at his house any time I want. I'll even have my own room. Can you imagine?"

"That's so awesome! I'm thrilled," I added as I squirted some whipped cream on top of the cocoa and handed it to my talented friend.

"Oh, yum! Thanks."

Dillan started clearing the clutter from our kitchen table. "I'd love to see your artwork," he said. "Sandy told me that you designed your own tattoos; they're amazing!"

"Thanks," Jacqueline Rose replied as she held up her hair so we could examine the back of her neck. "I don't think you guys have seen this one."

"Oh, how cute!" I said about the seal who was holding a paintbrush in its mouth.

"I met Seaquin at Jenkinson's Aquarium. She actually paints pictures to help raise money for their conservation efforts."

"How cool is that? I'd love to go there sometime."

"You really should, Sandy. It's not a huge place but they do some great work there. I try to go a couple of times a year."

She unzipped the large case and showed us her wonderful collection of art.

"I've always loved to draw and paint. It was my best subject in school."

"I wish I had your talent," I said honestly, as she flipped through her impressive body of work.

"Have you ever tried?" she asked.

"Well, not that I can remember, but I haven't had much free time since I arrived here."

"Well," Dillan added, "If Mac agrees, maybe the two of you could paint a mural on one of the walls before you leave."

"Oh my gosh! We could do an ocean scene with creatures like your tattoos. What about the two suites with the adjoining kids' bedrooms? Those would be perfect!"

"That sounds like fun!" Jacqueline Rose said. "I'm not leaving for a couple of weeks so there's plenty of time."

"It'll be so unique. Mac and Shona will love it!" I said, beaming with excitement.

Dillan got the okay from Mac, who sounded very enthusiastic about our project. After we finished painting the walls a beautiful azure blue, Jacqueline Rose came by with her diagrams and a large assortment of acrylic paints and brushes. She explained her idea to us then sketched out the designs on the walls with a pencil. It didn't take her long at all, I guess because she had been drawing sea creatures for so many years. The murals contained all forms of ocean life from the most common to the exceedingly rare.

Dillan and I applied the base colors and Jacqueline Rose came after us and painted all the shading and detailing. The creatures were realistic yet softened somehow so they appeared to have a dream-like quality. I could just imagine little children falling asleep to the sound of the waves, little starfish above their heads and baby belugas and dolphins playing alongside their beds. She gave them such happy, expressive faces, yet they didn't look cartoonish. Any child's imagination would be piqued, staying in these rooms.

By the end of the day we were done and the walls had turned out beautifully. Jacqueline Rose insisted we sign our names on the bottom corner, next to hers. It was such a feeling of accomplishment. Out of some bottles of paint and a mutual love for the ocean came two beautifully detailed murals that would transport many little children under the sea.

As we were washing out the brushes, Jacqueline Rose burst out, "Oh my God, I was so focused on the project that I completely forgot to tell you something!"

"What?"

"I had a call from your policeman friend, the one we spent Christmas with. He said a man claiming to be my father had been inquiring about me."

"Really?" Dillan responded, feigning surprise.

"That's some news!" I added, "How do you feel about it?"

"Nervous, excited, scared. It's complicated."

"Would you want to meet him?" Dillan asked.

"Captain Jack said if I had any desire to meet him I should have a DNA test done."

"Are you going to do it?"

"I already did. He came by the Bagel Shack the other day and swabbed the inside of my cheek. It was quick and painless."

"I'm excited and nervous for you!" I said as I gave her a big hug.

"Captain Jack spoke with my mother. Given our history, I wasn't surprised when he told me she'd been lying to me my whole life. My father never sent the cards or gifts. She'd asked some friend to do that. Apparently, he never knew I existed, until now."

"What?"

"It all sounds so mysterious, doesn't it?" Jacqueline Rose asked, "I wonder how he found out?"

Dillan gave me a raised eyebrow that I promptly ignored and I just shrugged my shoulders, "Who knows?"

"I'm so angry at Mom, I can't even call her for an explanation! I might say something that'll make our relationship even worse."

I placed some cookies on the table, thinking chocolate couldn't hurt in a situation like this.

"Well, your life's certainly taking some interesting turns, that's for sure," Dillan said as he dunked an Oreo in milk and popped it into his mouth.

"What if the guy's a drinker or a crackhead? I hope he's not some loser just looking for money," she said, sounding disheartened.

"I understand what you're feeling, but I think you're doing the right thing. You've grown up to be an intelligent, compassionate and responsible person. Perhaps your father is one too."

I think it's a chance worth taking," Dillan added. "You'll never know the truth unless you're brave enough to meet him."

"Thanks guys."

CAPTAIN JACK FOSTER

JANUARY 2013

JACQUELINE ROSE HAD FREELY given me a sample of her DNA. She was impressively brave or incredibly stupid to be willing to meet the man who fathered her twenty years ago. I grabbed a glass of water, sat at my office desk and powered on my computer. I absentmindedly ran my fingers through my hair as it booted up. Since meeting with Ms. Erica Hanson, I couldn't get her story out of my head: the summer of 1992, the beach party at Seaside Heights, the booze, the sex. It all seemed a little too familiar.

I ignored my work e-mail and went directly to the Family Genetics website. The home page claimed that DNA testing had a 99.99 percent accuracy in paternity cases – very little room for error. I logged in with my password and scrolled through the results. They confirmed my suspicions. I had found Jacqueline Rose's father. He wasn't a crackhead, felon or an abusive asshole as I had initially expected but a reputable guy: *a police captain.*

I took a long gulp of water and sat back in my chair as my heart pounded like a jackhammer. I had a child – a beautiful, vibrant, artistic *living* child. She could never replace our glorious little Sara, but I certainly had room enough in my heart for her. It would be an even bigger shock to Carole and I prayed that she would feel the same.

That night after dinner, I broke the news to Carole and for the next two days I watched as the emotions that inspired her tears changed from shock to anger, from anger to acceptance and from acceptance to hopefulness. Jacqueline Rose was not her biological daughter but she was downright determined to welcome her into our lives with an open mind and open heart. As I held her in bed that night, I couldn't have been any more certain that I'd married the right woman.

"When are you going to tell her?" Carole asked, as she poured my coffee the next morning.

"*How* do I tell her?" I asked, "What is she going to think of me?"

"What's her *mother* going to think?"

"God, I can't believe that she didn't recognize me when I went to interview her."

"You said she'd been drinking and it *was* twenty years ago."

"It seemed fairly clear in her mind even with the twenty-year gap factored in."

"What do you remember about it?"

"I'd spent a couple of weeks in Seaside that summer with friends from school. They had a typical agenda: surf, meet girls and get laid. I wasn't much of a surfer *or* a womanizer, but I went along to relax after a stressful semester."

Carole poured herself another cup of coffee, added milk and stirred absentmindedly. "So, you got drunk and had sex with a stranger on the beach?" she asked, sounding like it was the least possible thing in the world.

"What college-aged guy wouldn't, given the opportunity? I'd always been a bit of a geek, but I was more than ready to join the ranks!"

Carole shook her head and rolled her eyes. I knew she could never imagine *me* being nerdy.

"Remember, when we first met, I told you that I'd almost joined the Marines?"

"Right, you were having a hard time finding direction and had no idea what you wanted to do with your life."

"My dad was constantly pressuring me to join one of the armed services. He thought it'd make a *man* out of me. That summer was my breaking point."

"So, you got drunk and lost your virginity?"

I just shrugged my shoulders. Everyone at the bonfire was drinking or on MDMA. I just got plastered. I remember finding a phone number written on my hand the next morning. I should have called, at least to make sure she got home alright."

"Your whole life may have been different if you had made that call."

"Yeah, that's a mind-boggling thought. I feel guilty that I didn't know about Jacqueline Rose though. I would have helped support her, emotionally and monetarily."

"Hindsight is twenty-twenty but of very little use to anyone, so stop beating yourself up. You can be a part of the girl's life now. She still needs a father no matter how old she is."

"She definitely could've used a father; I mean look at those tattoos. What's that all about?"

"I'd say it started as a cry for attention."

"And apparently it grew into an addiction. Thank you for understanding, Carole," I said as I took her hand and gave it a squeeze.

"We have been through much worse."

"Yes, we certainly have."

"I love you."

"And I love you."

I had some decisions to make. There was no doubt that I'd be paying Jacqueline Rose a visit but I also owed Sandy a huge debt. Without her inquiry, I never would have known that I had a daughter. Now, when I thought about Jacqueline Rose's face I could see a resemblance. We had the same dark eyes, the same black hair, even the same chin. It was hard to admit that I was slow noticing the clues in her name. Jacqueline for Jack, Rose for the beach rose under which she was conceived. I liked it, for in a minuscule way I had been part of her life all along.

I decided to a make a visit to the inn and give Sandy and Dillan the improbable news in person. As I turned the corner at Murphy's Market, it struck me how much I missed that grocery store. It was so conveniently situated between work and home. They had a great variety for a mom-and-pop store and never charged me for a hot cup of coffee in the morning. Fresh baked bread, check. Bottle of wine for dinner, check. A nice steak or fresh clams, check. I looked forward to its reopening. It couldn't be soon enough.

I turned onto Beach Avenue and spotted my friends walking Buoy in the park. They made such a good-looking couple; I truly hoped, yet doubted, things would work out for them. The appearance of the creep at the benefit only confirmed my suspicions that things were way more complicated than Dillan wanted to believe. I made a left onto Amber, pulled a U-turn, and parked. In the summer, parking spaces on the bed and breakfast-lined street were rarely available, but in the off season, especially a cold January day, the block looked deserted.

"Hey kids!" I yelled as I hiked across the park with its gusty winds and thin winter grass.

"It's good to see you," Sandy said with a sincere tone as she offered me a hug.

"It's good to see you kids, too."

"How're things?" Dillan asked, his hand outstretched.

I gave him a firm shake and clapped him on the back. "I've got some news," I replied as I reached down and scratched Buoy's head.

"Did you find the schmuck who accosted Sandy?"

"No, sorry, it's not that."

"Something about my past?" Sandy asked worriedly.

"No, it's not that either. Let's go sit on that bench so we can talk."

"This sounds important," Dillan said, as he took Sandy's hand and followed me.

"It's about your friend, Jacqueline Rose," I said as we sat. "I've found her father."

"Holy crap, that's awesome! I hope he didn't turn out to be a criminal like you feared."

"Yeah, what's he like?" Dillan inquired.

"He's a lot like me," I said, feeling my throat tighten a bit.

"You mean he's a police officer?" Dillan asked.

I shook my head and rubbed my palms on my jeans. "No, honestly – it's me."

Dillan and Sandy both looked at each other, astonished.

"That's impossible!" Dillan said.

"I know what you're thinking and no, I didn't cheat on my wife. It happened before I met her."

"That never crossed my mind," Sandy replied as she wrapped her arms around me. "It's a miracle. I can think of no finer person to be a part of Jacqueline Rose's life!"

I still can't believe it. Can you tell us how it happened?" Dillan asked.

"I'm sure you don't need the details, Dillan, but a drunken beach party, if you must know. I only met Erica once and I never knew about the baby."

"Wow, sounds like an ad for condoms!" Dillan blurted out.

"Dillan!" Sandy scolded.

"Sorry – just saying."

"You know her better than I do. How do you think she'll take the news?" I asked anxiously.

"It will definitely be a shock at first, but I'm sure things will work out great."

"How's Carole doing with all this?" Dillan asked.

"Much better than expected. That's why she's the love of my life," I said proudly.

After I talked with Dillan and Sandy, I headed over to the station and started my shift in the usual way, by receiving change of shift report and if there were no pressing issues, reading my mail. I'd just finished with report when there was a rap on my door frame. There stood the unique Jacqueline Rose, my biological daughter.

"Come in, come in," I said nervously, as I jumped up and showed her a seat.

It happened so quickly and not at all as I had planned. I wanted to ask Jacqueline Rose out for lunch or at least for coffee, in a comfortable place, where we could sit and really talk about how everything came about. I wanted her to believe that I was sincerely interested in her welfare and just as sorry for not having been part of her childhood.

"I hope I'm not bothering you," she said as she sat, "but I'll be leaving soon and I wanted to know if there was any more news about the man claiming to be my father."

"Leaving?" I asked, feeling a myriad of emotions.

"Yes, I'm returning to school in New York this semester."

I wondered if telling her would change her plans which I did *and* didn't want to do. I had been really looking forward to getting to know my daughter.

"Yes, there's news and it's quite unbelievable, but I assure you that the DNA samples quite confirm it."

"Who is he then, someone famous? Is it Jon Bon Jovi? Mom was quite a fan back in the day," she said excitedly.

"No, it's me. I am your father."

"That's not funny. You're supposed to be a professional. How can you make a joke out of something like this?"

"I assure you, Jacqueline Rose," I said firmly, "this is no joke. It's the God's honest truth."

At that she promptly fainted.

SANDY

JANUARY 2013

ONCE JACQUELINE ROSE HAD accepted the fact that Captain Jack was her biological father, we decided to have a little get-together to celebrate. She was still angry at her mother for lying to her and hadn't even told Erica that her father had miraculously surfaced after twenty years.

It was cold and damp outside but everyone was well fed and comfortable, sipping brandy, and relaxing in the library. I sat back in my cushy chair by the fireplace and looked around the room. It had only been about a month since we'd celebrated Christmas here and yet so much had changed. Lucas had already moved in. How convenient it was for everyone, including the owners of the Engleside, who needed every room for the insurance adjusters, FEMA representatives and contractors who had flooded the island.

Sherlock and Mrs. Holmes were curled up together on the doggie bed. Though Buoy had met the pair a few times before, he stayed close to Dillan's side, still not sure what to make of the interlopers. Jacqueline Rose, Captain Jack and Carole were involved in a deep conversation about her art school and Henry was in his recliner, looking comfortable and satisfied. He lifted his brandy snifter, toasted me silently and we smiled. There was a wonderful feeling bubbling up inside of me. As I shifted my gaze from person to person, I felt like I was fulfilling my purpose, until my eyes landed on Dillan.

The next evening, we were planning on using the second set of tickets that Captain Jack and Carole had given us for Christmas. This event was a screening of a short film called *East Coast Rising*, a surfer's point of view on Hurricane Sandy. It was being held at the Long Beach Island Foundation of the Arts and Sciences building in a town called Loveladies. I was a bit nervous about attending, as I was concerned the giant Hawaiian might rear his ugly head. Well, he wasn't exactly ugly, but he was mean and intimidating. Jack, who was still perplexed by my own mystery appearance on LBI, was looking for answers. He promised to have some undercover men inside and would stakeout the building.

"Do you think my blue dress will be appropriate for the fundraiser?" I asked Dillan as we painted.

"Sure, as long as you cover up your breasts. Do you own a decent sweater?"

I was shocked by his bluntness and almost dropped the wet paintbrush.

"Not one dressy enough. How about a scarf?" I grumbled.

"I guess, as long as you look a bit more modest tonight."

"I thought you liked the way I looked at the dance."

"I did, but so did every other guy there."

"Yeah whatever," I mumbled, annoyed. "So, what are you going to wear?"

"A dress shirt, tie and kakis, I guess. I have a suit somewhere, but I think it's back in Cincinnati."

I couldn't help but giggle. The thought of Dillan in a suit and those crazy octopus dreads was quite a vision.

"What's so funny, girl?

Two can play at this game. "I'm picturing you in a suit with that hair!"

"Yeah, all right. I concede. It's time for them to go. I'll go to the mainland next week and get a haircut but I'm gonna warn you, I'll look like a shorn sheep."

"Your head will be cold too!"

"I'll just wear a beanie till it grows a bit."

"You'd really do that for me?"

"Seriously, it's been a long time coming. I only wore it this way for convenience."

I wondered how much sand, dust and paint particles were lingering in those matted locks of dread.

"You know if you don't want to wait, I could do it," I offered, not wanting to lose the opportunity to rid him from the kraken perched upon his head.

He looked at me skeptically.

"How hard could it be? Snip them off, shave your head? I think I can manage."

"I don't know," he said squinting at me.

"It's no trouble. We've got all afternoon."

"Well, if you insist, but only if you promise to save as much hair as possible."

Once we finished painting, we had lunch and then took turns showering. Soon there would be many available bathrooms to choose from – we were just waiting for the fixtures to arrive – but for now we were still sharing. While Dillan scrubbed his scalp and conditioned his hair, I dried mine and put on clean jeans and a T-shirt. I grabbed the latest copy of *The SandPaper* and headed down to the couch. Buoy jumped up beside me and laid his head on my thigh.

"How ya doing, big guy? I bet you're ready for spring. I know I'll be happy to get in the ocean again."

I was only a few pages in when Dillan yelled, "I'm ready!" from the top of the stairs, sounding not-so-ready.

"Come on, Buoy; let's go do some damage," I giggled excitedly.

Dillan was sitting at the kitchen table looking glum. There was a comb, brush and scissors sitting on a towel waiting.

"Okay let's get this over with," he grumbled anxiously.

I grabbed his phone from the table and said, "Smile!"

He made an exaggerated grimace.

"We need a before-and-after so we can see which looks better," I giggled.

"You come over here," he said, "and we'll take a selfie together."

I handed Dillan the phone and placed my cheek against his. I noticed him breathe in heavily.

"You smell nice, like raspberries and the open sea."

He kept taking photos till we agreed on one that we were both satisfied with.

"Are you sure about this? 'Cause once I start, there's no going back."

"I've never been more sure of anything," he said as he sighed and closed his eyes.

I took the towel from around his neck and blotted his hair and scalp some more. The towel was fairly saturated and I didn't want it lying on his shoulders. "I'm going to get a dry towel; don't move a muscle."

"Not a chance."

When I returned a few moments later, I found Dillan dunking cookies in a glass of milk.

"I needed some fortification," he said with a mischievous grin.

"I'm surprised it wasn't Jack Daniels."

"I broke the bottle, remember? I haven't bothered to get another one. Anyway, these are just as good. Not as good as Mom's homemade chocolate chip, but good."

I lifted the damp dreads and wrapped the fluffy towel around his neck.

"That's nice," he said, as he played with his phone looking for some music. Once he found something relaxing he set the phone down and closed his eyes. As I gently moved the misshapen, uneven chunks of hair, looking for a plan of attack, Dillan leaned back and slid down in the chair.

"I think I'll just cut them off about two inches from your scalp, and see if I can comb out what's left."

"Well you got me here, so now I'm putty in your hands."

I delicately snipped each tangled mass of hair and deposited it on the table. I stopped counting after twenty. Once they were all removed, I walked around the table to take a good look at my work. Poor Dillan, now he looked even sillier.

"Are they all gone?" he asked sleepily as he straightened himself up.

"Yes, they died a peaceful death, but unfortunately this is just the beginning."

"This chair is killing my back. Do you think we could move somewhere more comfortable?"

"Maybe we could sit in the parlor with me on the couch and you on the floor?"

"Yeah, let's try that."

"Could you grab some conditioner and another towel please? I need a couple cookies before we start."

"I told you!" he replied smugly.

After my snack, the three of us headed downstairs to the sitting room. It had no resemblance to the sand-and muck-filled room I'd found when I first arrived here. Buoy immediately jumped onto the couch. I grabbed the end cushion and dropped it on the shiny new floor.

"Sit," I said, pointing to the floor. Buoy jumped from the couch, cocked his head and waited for a treat.

"Oh sorry, not you, big guy. I mean your daddy."

I sat on the couch and Buoy joined me. Placing my legs astride the cushion, I pointed to the floor again.

"Come on, let's get this over with. Unless you just want me to shave your head."

"Alright, but be gentle," Dillan replied timidly.

He sat on the cushion, set the phone on his leg and leaned back. I must admit that his choice of music was quite peaceful. I placed the other towel over my lap and squeezed some conditioner into my palm. I rubbed my hands together then tried to gently work the cream into the tangled masses of hair. After a few minutes, a tiny moan of pleasure escaped Dillan's lips. It flustered me. I continued to work the cream into his hair while gently pulling the loosened strands. Very, very slowly they gave way.

I heard Dillan's phone hit the floor; he made no move to retrieve it. I continued to work gently as the time flew by. I found myself quite unexpectedly massaging Dillan's scalp. The pressure of his body pressing against my legs had become intense and overwhelming. I felt tingly and aroused and lost. Dillan pushed hard against the back of the couch. My fingers slipped tenderly along his scalp and through the silky shorn locks. I laid my head back against the couch and just disappeared. We were swimming in the ocean – we were free. Dillan moaned again, only much louder this time. With a quick forceful motion, he stood up, left the room and stomped loudly up the stairs. A moment later, he stomped down again and walked out the front door, slamming it behind him – leaving me confused and lonely in his wake. His actions created a tidal wave of sadness and uncertainty within me.

I gave Buoy a scratch on the head and walked upstairs. My legs were achy and wobbly from being in one position for so long. It was getting late and I wasn't sure if I should dress for the movie screening or not. I had no idea where he'd gone or when he'd be coming back.

I decided to get ready just in case and I was sitting at the kitchen table sipping a cup of tea when I heard his phone ringing downstairs. Hopefully he was trying to reach me. I ran down and grabbed it from the floor. Captain Jack's name was lit on the screen. I answered, fearing something might be wrong.

"Hello, Captain Jack?"

"Hi, Sandy. Is Dillan there?"

"No, he stepped out and forgot his phone."

"Oh, I just wanted you to know that I got a couple of my off-duty guys to go to the screening tonight. I'll stakeout the parking lot and they'll be inside to keep an eye on things."

"That's really nice of you, but I'm not sure if we're going. Dillan kinda stormed out and hasn't returned."

"Did you have a fight or something?"

"No, not exactly. Maybe a misunderstanding. It's kinda personal."

"Alright, no further questions. Just have him call me when he gets in."

"I will, and thanks for trying to protect me. Personally, I hope the creep's long gone."

"Probably some random jerk who came over for the concert, got plastered and thought you were an old girlfriend or something."

"*Maybe I am,*" I said sadly.

DILLAN

I FOUND MYSELF SITTING at the kitchen table, a towel full of matted hair lying before me. Sandy was standing behind me, snip, snip, snipping away and plucking the dreads from my head, one by one with a certain victorious pleasure. Each time she dropped one ceremoniously on the towel, it was as if she was yelling *SCORE!* without uttering a word.

I knew she never loved my hair. In fact, once she found a chunk of it on the kitchen floor and screamed because she thought it was a dead mouse. After closer examination, she picked it up and chased me all around the inn, finally succeeding in bouncing it off my face. We laughed until we cried. I almost went to the mainland the next day for a cut, but I couldn't do it. By keeping my dreads I was holding on to my pre-Sandy life, a life to which I might someday return. I felt somehow keeping the hair might make the transition easier, but deep down I knew that was bullshit. With or without it, when she left, I'd be a gnarly mess.

When she offered to cut it herself, I knew it was the right time. Losing my dreads was a small price to pay for the momentary experience of having her fingers gently entwined in my hair. As she lifted the locks and moved them side to side, sparks shot through my veins. Her breast occasionally grazed the back of my head as she reached forward to drop a piece of hair on the towel in front of me, sending shivers down my spine. She thought she had won the battle but, secretly, I was the winner. It started out feeling quite soothing but quickly became a flame that made my jeans unbearably tight. I had to slide low on the chair just to hide my discomfort under the table. Damn her, she was torturing me with her gloating playful innocence.

By the time my dreads were all shorn, my back and my bulge were causing increasing agony. I had to move to release the pressure. When Sandy suggested we move downstairs, I was relieved, to say the least. She asked me to get some supplies and I used those couple of minutes to calm down, readjust and stretch my back. Glancing in the bathroom mirror, I almost gasped at the mangled porcupine looking back at me. I hoped it would look better once all the nubbins were worked loose but if it didn't at least I'd be enjoying Sandy's touch for a little while longer.

Downstairs, she was the boss of me once more, ordering me to sit on the floor. I did as she commanded with no reservation. The deep soft cushion under me and the couch behind my back didn't compare to the feeling of having her legs wrapped around me. I was in trouble and she hadn't even started.

I closed my eyes and took a deep breath. The music from my phone was acoustic guitar, accompanied by ocean waves, wind chimes and an occasional birdsong – just the thing to make me forget it was January in New Jersey. I didn't need help with relaxing or fantasizing. This was going to be better than a perfect surfing day. The music was to relax *Sandy* and it did. I believe after a while she forgot she wasn't in love with me, because the way she caressed my head and played with my hair told me otherwise. It was as if all the barriers of not knowing who she was and her mysterious past melted away and there was no other possibility than the two of us belonging together.

Her touch was soft and slight at first, gently working the conditioner in, then pulling and tugging at the strands. It may have become annoying and uncomfortable to any other dreadlocked head, but to me, it was paradise. It took hours to work the ends loose, though it seemed like a very a few short minutes. Once they were all free, she ran her fingers through the locks and caressed my head with a gentle massage.

I was so lost in her touch that by the time I realized I had another erection, it was too late. My body seized and, **oh God**, I erupted in my jeans. Torn with the desire to jump on her and make her mine or to flee in embarrassment, I chose to flee.

Finding myself in the Jeep, my first instinct was to drive to the hotel and swim for hours. I was so embarrassed, insecure and angry! Not angry at Sandy but at this crazy situation that I found myself in. I loved her but she kept me at arm's length. She led me to believe that she had feelings for me but wouldn't – no, couldn't – act on them. It was torture to be so close but not to have her, physically or emotionally. If she said that she loved me but wanted to wait for marriage to have sex, I could deal with that. Suddenly, reality thundered in again – she might already be married. It was so easy to forget when the two of us had been keeping house for months. What if the Hawaiian moron showed up at the fundraiser? What if he was from her past and he grabbed her and ran? What if she disappeared and I never saw her again?

My second idea was to jog, just get out of the car and run on the beach for miles but I was wearing jeans and work boots. Things weren't going my way, perhaps there was a reason. I took a deep breath, got out of the Jeep and counted to ten. I crossed the street and banged on Henry's front door. A minute later he opened it.

"Hey Henry."

"Good afternoon, Dillan. To what do we owe this pleasure?"

"I wanted to ask your opinion about something."

"My word!" he exclaimed. "Did Sandy finally have her way with you?"

"*Excuse me?*"

"Your hair. Either you have it artfully concealed under your cap or it's been shorn."

"Oh, it's gone alright, but that's only part of the problem."

"How about a cup of hot tea? I find it helps clear the mind and soothe the soul."

"Holy cow!" Lucas exclaimed as he entered the kitchen. "What happened to your hair?"

"Sandy finally talked some sense into the boy," Henry said, with a nudge to my ribs. "Come on then, young man; remove your cap for inspection."

"Yes, let's take a gander."

I pulled the beanie away and stuck it in my jacket pocket.

"You have a handsome face, a nice strong jaw line," Henry commented.

"I agree," Lucas added, "a good decision over all, though I think a barber could tidy it up a bit."

"I have one in Manahawkin where I get a hot lather neck shave and a shoulder massage with my cut."

"I think I've had enough massages for a while," I uttered ruefully.

"Have a seat, my boy," Henry said kindly.

"Those places still exist?" Lucas asked, as he sat across from me at the huge kitchen table.

"Yes, definitely! It reminds me of the barber my father took me to when I was a boy. It was our ritual, he and I. If I was a good lad and didn't squirm too much, I'd get a stick candy."

"The good old days," Lucas said. "Can you still get a shoeshine?"

"Now you're pushing it, my friend. I think those days are long gone."

Henry made a pot of tea while we were making small talk but once he poured, he asked me what had me so upset.

"Has Sandy ever mentioned how she feels about me?"

"Sometimes we chat about things," Henry replied, noncommittal.

"I'm in love with her."

"Who isn't?" Lucas added with a laugh.

"Not funny, old man," I replied.

"It's hard not to be." Henry added, "She has a certain something. It's hard to place one's finger on it – she reminds me of my Naia."

"You think she's going to disappear from my life too?" I asked fearfully.

"I don't think she'll want to."

"Maybe Naia didn't want to leave you either," I added, considering their story. What if something had happened to her?

"I have one bit of advice," Henry offered. "Enjoy every minute with her as if it were your last."

I took a deep breath as that ugly thought settled in.

"I know it's not my place to say, but you and Sandy seem a perfect match," Lucas added encouragingly.

"I *am* inclined to agree," Henry stated firmly.

"What do you suggest I do? I want to marry her."

"That *is* a conundrum now, isn't it?" Henry said pensively.

"She has no family, no identity. Too bad she can't just start afresh," Lucas stated.

"I'm afraid it doesn't work that way," Henry replied. "This is terribly complicated. I believe you must slow your relationship down. Make the most of each day, but don't add unnecessary pressure. She has a strong moral backbone that should be respected, but in the same instance we shouldn't assume that her prior life was perfect."

"No one has a perfect life," Lucas added sincerely.

"If she *does* possess commitments, when her memory returns, they might be altered."

Henry had given me enough hope to keep from going mad.

"Thanks guys," I said as I stood. "You've given me something to think about. I have to go get presentable. We're going to Loveladies tonight, to another fundraiser."

"Keep a close eye on her and have an enjoyable evening, my boy," Henry said, as I ran down his front steps, taking his advice to heart.

I entered the inn feeling sheepish and worried. Sandy must be thinking I'm a childish idiot! I didn't mean to storm out; I just had to get away. Buoy was still lying on the couch but jumped down to greet me when I looked in the doorway.

"Hey buddy!" I said as I gave him a good scratch between the ears. Buoy walked behind me and pushed his way between my legs. I bent down, wrapped my arms around his middle and gently rocked him back and forth. Henry's words, "Enjoy every moment" would become my mantra.

I ran upstairs, Buoy directly behind me. Sandy was sitting at the kitchen table, sipping tea and looking glum.

"I'm sorry I ran out like that."

"I think I understand."

"I get too frustrated sometimes. I needed to have some breathing room."

"Is everything okay now? I mean, are we good?" she asked, sounding worried.

"Of course, we are. We'll always be *good friends,* if nothing more," I conceded.

"Good."

"Good enough," I replied. "I see you're ready to go. If we leave soon, we'll still get there in time."

"I kinda lost interest. Would you mind if I stayed home?"

"I was looking forward to the movie, but I wouldn't enjoy the evening without you." It didn't sound like things were as *good* as I hoped they'd be.

"All right, I guess it could be fun," she said with her deadly smile.

"I'll be ready in ten minutes. I just have to take a quick shower and shave."

"Oh," Sandy said, handing me my cell, "Captain Jack called for you. He'd like you to call him back."

SANDY

I WASN'T UPSET AT Dillan for leaving; it was my own fault. Who knew running your fingers through someone's hair could be so magical? I got carried away by a tsunami of emotion that was as troublesome as it was blissful. I'm sure he was aware that my feelings for him were growing, but I couldn't shake the horrible gnawing sensation that I was promised to someone else.

I went to the bedroom, wrapped the scarf around my neck and draped it as artfully as I could to hide my cleavage. Being self-conscious, I was now uncomfortable with the length of my dress as well. I didn't want to be inappropriately dressed for a formal event, but it was the only dress that I had.

"I'll feed Buoy," I yelled as I walked past the bathroom.

"I'll take him out as soon as I'm dressed," Dillan answered through the door.

A few minutes later, he walked into the kitchen wearing his most formal attire. In his hand, he held a knit cap.

"So, what do you think?"

"You look, um . . . dressy," I said generously.

"I mean my hair!" he said, pointing at his cocked head with eyebrows raised.

Here and there the strands were sticking upright at strange angles.

"I think it needs a touch up, but all in all it's a great improvement."

"My head actually hurts. I guess because the hair's been in one position for so long."

Or maybe you're hinting that you'd like another scalp massage, you beach bum! "Sorry about that," I said. "I'm sure the pain won't last too long."

"It just feels strange, that's all. I think the beanie will help. Come on, Buoy; let's go to the park, old buddy. Be back in a few, then we'll hit the road."

"Okay, I'll be ready and waiting."

"You look really pretty, by the way," he added.

"Thanks," I replied as I tried to stretch the hem of my dress to meet my knees.

On our way to Loveladies, we passed through the many towns of Beach Haven. Our inn was nestled among the historic homes in the Queen City of Beach Haven. Next came North Beach Haven, then Beach Haven Gardens, Beach Haven Terrace, Beach Haven Park and finally Beach Haven Crest.

"Why are there so many different Beach Havens?" I asked Dillan. "It's so confusing!"

"I don't know. It seems strange, doesn't it? I mean how many Beach Havens did one island need?"

"Seems like the settlers didn't have much imagination," we joked.

As we approached the causeway, thankfully the names became more distinct: Spray Beach, Brant Beach, Ship Bottom, Surf City, Harvey Cedars and finally Loveladies. The Foundation of the Arts and Sciences building was on the left with a large parking lot in front. With only a few open spaces, it seems we had gotten there just in time. As we were getting out of the Jeep, Dillan got a text message. He checked his phone and took my arm.

"Jack's sitting in his truck with a good view of the main doors. Two of his men are inside mingling. There's no sign of your assailant."

"That's a relief. He was probably just some drunk jerk who mistook me for someone else. I don't know why we thought he'd show up here anyway."

"Just taking precautions. This won't be anything like the last fundraiser. I'm sure it's a borderline artsy-fartsy vibe in there."

"You mean snobby and snooty?" I asked, giggling.

"Probably not that bad. I heard a bunch of surfers are coming tonight. We're a fun crowd, but I doubt anyone will be gyrating on the dance floor," he said, sounding a bit judgmental.

The large open room was set up with small tables covered with red tablecloths. White paper lanterns hung from the ceiling and live mellow jazz music filled the air. We made our way over to the bar area where Dillan purchased two orange armbands for twenty dollars. I ordered a glass of white wine and he asked for a beer from the keg. The art gallery was full of mingling people, some whom I recognized from our weekend activities but many that I didn't. We wandered about the room, admiring the art and photographs that were up for silent auction and greeting friends along the way. I couldn't wait to see the island come back to life in the spring with its beautiful hydrangeas and roses that graced the photos before me. I could almost feel the heat from the fiery sunsets on the bay and the wind which held aloft a myriad of colorful kites.

Dillan took my elbow and leaned in close. "I see one of Jack's guys over there," he whispered.

"Oh, yeah," I nodded as I sipped my wine. I recognized Officer Washington from our trip to the station after the incident.

"I was having such a good time; I forgot I should be worried."

"Sorry, girl. I thought seeing him would calm your nerves."

"The wine and Nicotine & Brown are doing a great job of that."

"Let's get some snacks into you so the wine has some competition."

"I won't fall asleep during the movie, if that's what you're afraid of."

"I think I smell *seafood* . . . ," he said enticingly. Indeed a few people had entered the room carrying trays of delectable appetizers: cocktail shrimp, scallops wrapped in bacon, mini crab cakes and seared ahi tuna.

"I don't think I'll have to twist your arm," he said as a woman stopped next to us with her gleaming tray of delightfulness.

I just beamed at him as I popped a scallop in my mouth and stacked some goodies on my napkin. "Just in case you don't make it around to us again," I said to her with my mouth full. Dillan took a few morsels too.

As I looked around the room, I realized that I hadn't need worry about the appropriateness of my dress. There was a wide variety of clothing from suits and ties to jeans, flannel shirts and beanies. Women wore anything from jeans, sweaters and boots to cocktail and formal dresses with high heels. There was no apparent stuffiness. Fancy and casual, young and old, all mingled politely.

"I've developed a new appreciation for 'chicken of the sea' since you appeared," Dillan said as he admired his tuna steak appetizer. "I'd eat the canned stuff in a pinch, but now I can't seem to get enough."

"It's delicious, right?"

"Yes, but you have to be careful about how much you eat because of the mercury."

"Mercury?"

"Yeah, you know . . . it's poison."

Immediately I smacked the tuna steak out of his hand and watched in amazement as it sailed across the room. My shock turned to embarrassment as it bounced off the back of a smartly dressed man.

"What the heck is wrong with you, girl?" Dillan exclaimed quietly in my ear.

"It's poison! It's probably what's making everyone sick."

"Everyone who?"

"I don't know, well – anyone who eats it!"

"I think you're overreacting. The FDA says we can eat it in moderation."

"That sounds like bull shark to me."

"You mean bullshit?"

"Yeah, whatever!" I huffed.

"I'm so glad that guy's wearing a heavy jacket. If he felt anything hit him, he didn't let on!" Dillan said laughing.

"I can't believe I did that! What's wrong with me?"

"Probably just nerves. Let's go get a refill. More wine should help."

After a welcoming announcement and thank-you to the artists who had donated their work and the Mud City Crab House for catering, we were invited to grab some popcorn and have a seat.

The Jetty Rock Foundation was hosting the event to raise money for the Waves 4 Water Disaster Relief Team, who in turn funneled the funds back into the community with the services we needed most.

"Isn't it great how so many people stepped up to the plate to help rebuild the island?" a gentleman was saying as we sat at one of the tables.

"Yes, locals and strangers alike. People from all over the country. It's restored my faith in humanity," one woman replied.

"The surfing community certainly has had a huge part in all of it," Dillan said, as I gave a little wave to one of volunteers I recognized from S.T.A.R.T.

"It's great to see the young people so involved in their community," an elderly man added.

"We should've brought the guys," I whispered to Dillan.

"You're right. I think the fellas would've enjoyed this."

The lights dimmed and we arranged our chairs for the best view of the movie screen. It opened with waving dune grass and seagull calls. "*This morning I formally declared a state of emergency in anticipation of Hurricane Sandy . . . . ,*"

I felt an involuntary shiver ripple up my spine and I was glued to the screen within seconds. I was still engrossed in the film when Dillan leaned in.

"I gotta pee. Will you be alright?"

"Yes, of course. Go on," I whispered.

Seconds later, an incredibly strong hand clamped over my mouth and squeezed my cheeks tightly. I tried to pull away but there was enough strength in that one arm to immobilize me. I felt his face press forcefully against the side of my head before he grazed his lips against my ear. It made me shudder.

"GO HOME, KAIMANA!" the now familiar voice snarled deeply. **"I WON'T WARN YOU AGAIN!"**

Just as suddenly, he released me. I was afraid the scream that had been trapped in my throat would escape and frighten everyone. My heart was pounding as I spun around but, unbelievably, he'd vanished. Was everyone so engrossed in the movie that he went completely unnoticed? How was that even possible? I looked around the room for the police officer and spotted him leaning casually against the wall by the closest exit. Was I losing my mind? I stood up shakily, smoothed my dress around my legs and walked determined over to Officer Washington.

"Hey," he said quietly, "you're blowing my cover."

"Didn't you see him?" I asked as I rubbed my sore jaw and looked around the room, still quaking.

"What are you talking about?"

"The guy who grabbed my face!" I felt tears of disbelief forming in my eyes. "He was just here two seconds ago! God, I thought he was going to break my cheekbones!"

"I don't know how to respond to that, miss. When I saw your boyfriend leave the room, I moved closer. I had my eye on you the whole time. I haven't seen anyone tonight matching the description that the captain gave us and I certainly didn't see anyone accost you."

I spied Dillan coming down the hall and sighed with relief. I shrugged my shoulders and shook my head as I held back tears, reaching out for him.

"What happened? Is everything alright?" he asked as he took my hands.

"You won't believe it! I'm beginning to question my sanity. I want to go home!" I sputtered through a painful jawbone.

"I'll get our coats. Stay close to the officer," Dillan said, "then you'll tell me what happened in the three minutes that I was gone!"

I felt lightheaded and confused. Dillan sounded angry; maybe he didn't believe me either. What the hell? Was the brute invisible?

As Dillan helped me on with my coat, Officer Washington said firmly, "Let's go speak with the captain." The other plain-clothed officer was right behind us as we stepped out into the cold night air. Captain Jack was not in his truck, but he appeared from behind the building a moment later.

"Are you two alright?" he asked, breathing heavily.

"Not really!" Dillan replied in a frighteningly angry voice.

"Please tell me you saw him!" I begged.

"Yeah, kinda hard to miss," Jack replied.

Oh, thank God! I was terribly relieved that someone else had finally seen him! "I thought he was going to shatter my cheekbones," I said, holding back the tears.

"Where were you two?" Jack asked his men accusingly.

The officers responded simultaneously and everyone began talking at once. My head began to spin realizing with this second attack that this was no case of mistaken identity. Luckily, Dillan had my hand and was near enough to lean on.

"He's a big son of a bitch – just like Sandy described him. He booked it over to Tidal Drive and got in a black Escalade. He's headed south on Long Beach Boulevard. I've alerted the Long Beach Township police."

"Do you think they'll catch him?" I asked hopefully.

"They'll be watching the main road and entrance to the causeway, so with any luck."

"What if he just parks in a garage somewhere and hangs low till the next time he wants to terrorize her? I mean, who knows what he's capable of?" Dillan asked as he squeezed my hand a bit too tightly.

"A huge guy in a black Escalade – sounds like a professional bodyguard," the nameless officer commented.

"No shit, Sherlock!" Officer Washington chastised.

Jack pulled a small flashlight out of his pocket.

"I swear, I never took my eyes off her!" Officer Washington replied resolutely.

"Me either!"

"I'm sure an Escalade will be easier to spot than a six-foot-eight sumo wrestler, so get out of here!" Jack barked sarcastically. "If you spot him, don't engage. Tail him from a respectful distance."

"Yes, sir!" the officers replied in unison as they hurried for their car.

Jack put his finger under my chin and gently lifted my face so I was looking at him.

"Close your eyes," he said gently.

He shone the beam on my face. My cheek and jawbones were still aching. I was sure I'd have bruises.

"Can you see any marks?" I asked.

"Oh, yeah. I see something that never should have happened. Would you like to go over to the medical center and get checked out.

"I don't think anything's broken but some ice would be great."

"This whole thing is bullshit!" Dillan said as he released my hand. "I'll go get some ice from the bar, then I'm taking you home."

I gave him a little grin which made me wince. Jack said he'd stay with me in the Jeep until Dillan returned. Once we were alone, Jack said, "If I hadn't seen him with my own eyes . . . I don't know, Sandy. This is one of the strangest cases I've ever worked on. Are you sure there isn't anything you've forgotten to tell me?"

"I keep trying to remember exactly what he said – wait! He said something like, *Kai-ma-na*. He called me Kaimana!"

"Can you remember it word for word?"

I thought for a moment and heard the growling cadence, "He said, 'Go home, Kai-ma-na. I won't warn you again,'" I said, sniffing. "Do you think that's my real name?"

"Apparently he thinks so. At least now we have *one* clue to the girl who's appeared from nowhere."

As Dillan approached the jeep with a small bag of ice, Jack climbed out and clapped him on the shoulder. "I'll follow you two home," he said resolutely and headed for his truck.

"What, I don't understand," Dillan said as he handed me the bag and started the car, "with Jack watching the doors, how did the asshole get inside in the first place?"

My head was spinning. "Maybe there's a back door?"

"Must've been. Sounds like he'd be too big to climb through a window."

Who was the thug and why was he so hell bent on getting me to leave the island? He obviously knew me, but as I searched the hidden recesses of my brain I found no traces of him or my alleged name. The only memory I *could* recall were my father's words, "Your cerulean eyes sparkle with facets of golden jingle shells," a treasure that I found comfort in from time to time.

I could see the stress and concern still etched on Dillan's usually relaxed face and thought it best not to speak as we drove. I closed my eyes and gently moved the ice from cheekbone to cheekbone. I took some slow, deep breaths to help me chill but couldn't ignore the cruel voice in my head or the disgusting feeling of his lips pressed against my ear. Without warning, I was thrown forcefully against the car door. An instantaneous flash of images had me flying out of the vehicle and feeling the weight of the Jeep as it crushed me, but as we screeched to a halt, we remained upright and belted in safely. As the Jeep rocked on its wheels, I heard a distant voice, the words making little sense.

"*Are you alright?*"

"What?"

"*Are you alright?*"

"We missed the end of the movie," I said as I burst into tears.

DILLAN

I HAD ALMOST BRUSHED off our first encounter with the Hawaiian asshole as a case of mistaken identity. Now I had to face the dilemma once again, only this time there was little doubt he had the right target. It was hard to imagine Sandy doing anything to piss someone off to that extent. Even more mystifying: how could the huge oaf make his way through the art gallery and none of us had spotted him? Once I heard the words *professional* and *bodyguard* my mind became bombarded with possible scenarios: runaway daughter of rich controlling parents or – something more sinister – fleeing wife of an evil crime lord? I was hoping my imagination was in high gear fueled by anger, frustration and my own appreciation of intense action films.

The ride home seemed to take forever, what with enduring Sandy's silence and keeping my eye on Jack who was following behind. We had gotten as far as the causeway when the huge Escalade ran a red light and came straight at us. I slammed the brakes to the floor and swerved hard to the right, tires squealing.

"Holy shit!" I yelled as we came to a jolting stop facing north on the one-way avenue. "Are you alright?"

Sandy didn't respond, just sat there in apparent shock. I restarted the Jeep, pulled off the road into the gas station on the corner. Thank God it wasn't summer when the traffic is incredibly heavy or we might have found ourselves in a head-on collision. Once we were parked, I reached over, pried Sandy's clenched hands apart and stroked them gently with my thumbs. "Are you alright?" I asked again, more calmly.

"We missed the end of the movie," she said flatly. Then she started sobbing – women!

I had completely forgotten about Jack, who pulled up beside us and climbed out of the pickup.

"Are you hurt?" he asked worriedly.

"No, but we're a bit shaken in here."

"I followed him to the bridge but that bastard was flyin'! Wish I'd been driving my cruiser."

"Aren't there any other cops around?"

"They must've been on a call."

"Do you think he was waiting for us?"

"My gut feeling is he found an unexpected opportunity to put the fear of God into you. If he had wanted to hit you, he would have."

Jack got a call on his phone and after a couple minutes of silence he said, "No shit! That's certainly surprising. Sounds good."

He hung up and returned his attention to us.

"We've got a match on the plates. Asshole lives right here in Manahawkin! One of my guys is on his way to pick me up – we're gonna pay him an *official* visit."

"Please be careful, Jack," Sandy choked out between sobs.

"Always," he said as he leaned in to look at her.

"Can you stop by the station and fill out a report on your way home?"

"Can't that wait till tomorrow? I just want to make her a cup of tea and tuck her into bed."

"We've got tea at the station, even the herbal stuff. It won't take very long. Just tell Officer Powell exactly what happened in your own words. I'll fill in the blanks later."

"You alright with that?" I asked my shivering, tearful friend.

Sandy just nodded.

It was about one a.m. when we finally got to bed. Still visibly upset, Sandy cuddled up with Buoy while I undressed. We had hashed out every possible scenario why someone might be harassing her and came to no conclusions. None of this guy's actions made sense.

People have often concocted crazy stories to get themselves out of trouble, starting as far back as "the dog ate my homework." Perhaps Sandy had been faking her amnesia all along. Was she trying to hide from an obsessive lover by creating a new identity? Perhaps she was in the witness protection program and something went awry. I hated that I questioned her character, even for a split second. As I flipped off the light and got into bed, I could feel any chance of happily-ever-after slipping away with the receding tide. I was just starting to drift off when I was awakened by a sniffle and a loud sigh.

"Sandy?"

"Yes?"

Somehow I found the courage to ask, "Would it help if I held you?"

"I would like that very much."

I climbed into bed next to her, lay down and pulled her toward me. My arm was wrapped around her shoulders, her damp face rested against my chest. Buoy didn't budge.

"I'm so, so sorry," she sobbed. "I'd never knowingly put you or any of my friends in danger."

Any thought of her lying quickly evaporated from my mind.

"I'm worried about Captain Jack and just imagine if we'd had Henry and Lucas in the car!"

"Everything's going to be alright," I said with unfelt certainty.

I had just started stroking her hair when she uttered, "He called me Kaimana. My name is Kaimana."

I felt my anger and frustration reaching epic proportions and summoned all my self-control to continue with a soothing voice.

"I'm still going to call you Sandy, if you don't mind."

She nodded and whispered, "Okay."

I could have easily held her all night but my phone rang. Reluctantly, I climbed out of bed and pulled it from my jeans pocket, praying it wasn't bad news.

"Jack, what happened? Did you find him?"

"Not exactly. The Escalade was in the driveway but the owner is an elderly man. Apparently, it had been stolen and returned without his knowledge."

"That seriously sucks. I was hoping we could put an end to all this."

"We're going to dust it for prints, so maybe we'll get lucky. Sorry I called so late, but I didn't want you waiting till morning."

"Thanks, Jack. You're a good friend."

"My guys will be patrolling your street frequently, so lock up and try to get some sleep. I'll call you in the morning if we get any leads."

As I climbed into bed, I found that Sandy had rolled on her other side and was now essentially spooning my dog. Slow deep breaths were coming from both of them. I stared motionless at the ceiling. This guy was becoming a serious threat and I had no idea what to do about it. Suddenly I realized something. The Hawaiian Neanderthal had never let Sandy speak, so he had no idea that she'd lost her memory. No wonder he was getting irate to the point of T-boning us! As I was finally drifting off, a semi-conscious fantasy began swimming in my head: we were rolling naked in the sand, under the midday sun, with Buoy keeping guard.

The next couple of weeks went by without the slightest disruption, of course we were on the alert for said asshole, but he never appeared. The inn started to show some real progress once the bedrooms were reconfigured. I couldn't have been more pleased with the way the suites were looking. We had even started working on Mac and Shona's private living space. Though I was happy with the way it was coming along, the thought of finishing the project had me edgy. On so many levels, I wondered what my future held.

After a particularly achy night, I trekked up to Kapler's to get some IcyHot and was reminded by the elaborate window display that Valentine's Day was looming its precarious head. Yes, I loved Sandy but how could I possibly show it? Especially how she, in no uncertain terms, disentangled herself from my limbs and ran out of the bedroom the morning after we shared the bed. At least Buoy had stayed behind to comfort my wounded ego as I languished in the scent of her pillow.

I headed over to the cards, picked one out for my parents and made my way to the more romantic section. After reading quite a few, I decided that there was nothing appropriate for our unconventional relationship. Not too many people would send a card that read:

FORGET THE SCHMUCK
FROM YOUR PAST LIFE,
GIVE ME YOUR HEART,
I'LL MAKE YOU MY WIFE.

Sadly, there was no way we could have a traditional Valentine's Day with XXX & OOOs, flowers and candy. However, I still wanted to do something special for her and I'd have to be very sly about it! As I wandered toward the cash register, I spotted a rack of stuffed animals. A baby seal was poking out between a dolphin and a stingray. It reminded me of Jacqueline Rose's tattoo and I quickly hatched a plan. I'd take Sandy to the aquarium in Point Pleasant and we could have a nice lunch while we were out. I felt rather brilliant as I walked home. I ran upstairs, passing Sandy on the way to the kitchen, and could barely control my expression which beamed with excitement and smugness.

"Ready to get back to work?" Sandy asked while she stared at me with a curious eye.

"You know it!"

As I removed my jacket, my painful shoulder reminded me that I had completely forgotten the IcyHot. Way to go, Ace.

Sandy didn't mention Valentine's Day once, even though we had seen signs of the holiday uptown: an arrow pierced heart here, a bow-wielding cupid there, huge red roses in the florist's window. She spent extra time at Henry's probably trying to distract him from his own heartbreak. I felt guilty knowing that I still had a small chance at happiness, even though Henry didn't. Well, at least now he had furry and human companionship. I quite liked his pitty, Sherlock. He was noble and calm and so eager to please. He and Buoy were making great strides at getting along and we'd often take him up to the beach with us when we ran. The two dogs would sit and rest when they got tired and wait for us to jog back. It was becoming quite the Milk-Bone-fueled routine.

The fourteenth of February began just as any other Thursday, but shortly after we started work, I let out an exasperated groan. "Shit!"

Sandy came in to investigate. "What's the matter?"

"The blade broke on my saw," I lied.

"Can you use something else?"

"No, this is the only one for the job. I'm going to have to go out and get a new one."

"Okay, I'll stay here and carry on."

I wasn't expecting that response which threw a monkey wrench into my plan.

"Why don't you come along? We can have lunch out."

"I haven't showered or anything. I'm a mess."

Jesus, she was usually much more accommodating.

"Okay, you shower. I'll walk Buoy and check Home Depot's website for the part.

"Are you sure? We have a lot to do today."

"Yes, Yes, I'm sure. It'll be fine. Let's just get out of here for a while."

"All right, you're the boss."

As I walked Buoy, I met up with Henry at the park. He and Sherlock had copied our pattern of walking around the perimeter before going into the grass.

"Hey, Henry!"

"Hello, Dillan. How convenient to meet you. I was going to pay you two a visit on my way home."

The two dogs did what dogs do when they meet. Even after all these years, I'd never become comfortable with that whole ass and ball-smelling routine. God, it was gross.

"That's cool. Sandy should be out of the shower in a few minutes."

"Well, no need of me interrupting your day. I just wanted to give her this," he said as he pulled an envelope from under his coat.

"Oh, a Valentine card. I'm sure she'll appreciate it."

"Do you two have any special amusements planned for the day?"

"Well I wanted to keep things low key, so I'm just taking her to Jenkinson's Aquarium. It's a surprise."

"A sound decision, young man. She'll be thrilled!"

I wasn't sure how Buoy would feel about the aquarium inhabitants, so I thought it best not to pull the service dog card this time.

"Could you possibly take Buoy out a couple of times, if you are going to be around?"

"Be glad to. Maybe I'll even bring him over for a visit. I think he and Mrs. Holmes are becoming quite fond of each other."

"Yeah, they were getting cozy by the fireplace the last time we were over."

When Buoy and I got back to the inn, I followed him into the parlor where he got comfortable on the sofa. I placed Henry's card on the mantle for later. I sprinted upstairs to change clothes and literally bumped into Sandy who was bending over the dresser drawers. Fortunately, or unfortunately, depending on whose viewpoint you take, I knocked her onto the blowup mattress and landed on top of her. I couldn't help myself and kissed her spontaneously. She kissed me back just as passionately then slapped my face, hard.

"Ow!"

"Oh my God! I'm so sorry! I didn't mean to do that!"

Buoy entered the room as I righted myself and rubbed my cheek.

"I deserved it, I guess."

"No, you didn't. It was just as much my fault."

"Seriously, I was way outta line. I don't know why I kissed you like that. Are we okay?"

"If you can forgive me for slapping you."

"Yeah, we're good. No hard feelings. Let's just get out of here."

"Aren't we taking Buoy to Home Depot?" Sandy asked as I said good-bye to him at the door.

"He's so warm and comfortable here and I don't want to rush lunch because I'm worried about him being cold in the car."

"I don't understand why we're taking a long lunch when we have so much to do anyway?"

"Because we deserve a break. You've been working incredibly hard for weeks now. Let's just enjoy an easier pace today."

"Whatever you say."

We left the island and headed west on Route 72. When we drove past Home Depot, Sandy exclaimed, "Dillan, you just missed the turn around."

I already had a plan for that. "Oh, I forgot to tell you, they're out of stock at this store. We have to drive up to Point Pleasant."

"Oh, how far is that?"

"About an hour."

"Oh, okay. Do you mind if I shut my eyes for a bit?"

"Of course not, girl. Give those baby blues a rest."

As we drove, I had been keeping a wary eye out for the black Escalade, just to remember it had been stolen. Not much chance the Hawaiian God of Anger would be using that vehicle again. Thankfully, the trip went smoothly and we arrived at the Lakewood Township exit without incident. A few more turns and I pulled into the parking lot of the large pink building with the Caribbean blue logo. How perfect! She awoke looking directly at the Jenkinson's Aquarium sign on the side of building. I was anxious to see her reaction which was incredibly juvenile but heartwarming.

A huge smile lit up her face, "Oh my gosh! We're *here*? How did you know I wanted to come here?" she asked as she stamped her feet and grabbed my face, kissing my cheek with uncontrolled excitement.

"A little seal told me. Come on, let's do this!"

I jumped out of the Jeep and met Sandy who took my hand. It would seem I had made a very sound decision.

After I purchased our tickets, we wandered hand and hand into the exhibit. The first tank was a simulated coral reef. Sandy ran up to the glass, pulling me along.

"Hello Nemo," she cooed, making fish lips at the clown fish.

"Do you *know* Nemo?"

"Well, not personally," she giggled. "That's what it says on the sign. Aren't they the cutest?"

"Yeah, I guess they are."

She oohed and aahed her way through the bottom level like a child ripping open presents on Christmas morning. I honestly didn't take notice of the fish or displays, as I was basking in the self-satisfaction of pleasing her. Her joy was palpable and infectious.

Even the employees smiled as she darted about the room, reminding me of that school of silvery fish in the *Nemo* movie.

"Can we sail through once, then drift along at a slower pace?"

"It's your day, girl. You take the helm."

"Ohhhh, this is going to be so much fun!"

SANDY

FEBRUARY 14, 2013

I KNEW IT WAS Valentine's Day but I didn't let on. Had I ever had a valentine? I couldn't remember. Did I know the day was for lovers and filled with cards, candy, flowers, jewelry, romantic getaways and sometimes engagements? I sure did. Did I love Dillan? There was no denying it, but it was best to keep my mouth shut and ignore it – for now.

As we drove along the highway toward Home Depot, I felt so torn. Just by being near Dillan, I put him in danger. I closed my eyes and tried to clear away the images that kept flashing through my mind. Dillan barging into the bedroom and knocking us both onto the blowup mattress. He kissed me and without thinking, I kissed him back – fiercely. Suddenly, I felt the powerful grasp of the Hawaiian God's hands in my hair and the weight of his body pinning me painfully against jagged rocks as he drove his tongue into my mouth. When I slapped Dillan's face, I imagined I was slapping *Waimoku*. Suddenly remembering his name felt like being smashed by a towering wave and the brute force he'd used, trying to persuade me, left me frightened beyond words. I shivered as I played the scenario over and over in my head. Searching my memory for the missing pieces, I heard him repeatedly moan my name as he ground his manhood against my most sensitive areas. "Kaimana, give up this folly of a fairy tale – ***You will be mine!***"

I wanted to share my memories with Dillan, but they were fragmented and made little sense. What if I wasn't as innocent as I presume? What if I'd led Waimoku on, only to reject him? Could jealousy be what fueled his insane behavior? After serious consideration, I decided to wait and see if more memories would bubble to the surface.

Surprisingly, I fell asleep in the car. Dillan, apparently unafraid that I would slap him again, woke me by kissing my forehead. Instead of Home Depot, I found myself looking at a pale pink building with a Jenkinson's Aquarium sign! The broken saw blade was a total ruse. I hadn't felt so excited and carefree in ages. I forgot my worries, grabbed Dillan's hand and rushed in to explore!

"I wonder if they had much damage from the hurricane," I asked as my eyes adjusted to the dimness inside. All around were rippling lights – reflections of the water in the floor-to-ceiling tanks. "This is *so* cool! Thanks for bringing me here!"

"It's my pleasure, girl. I'm happy you're happy."

"I'm not happy; I'm ecstatic!"

I ran from tank to tank, taking it all in. There were huge stingrays that soared through the water like seagulls soared through the sky, glowing moon jellyfish that beat like a heart to propel themselves, their transparent insides rippling with flashing lights and eerie looking sharks with empty black eyes and hungry-looking mouths that I'd hate to meet up with in murky water.

"None of them are man-eaters," Dillan said as he read the sign.

"How about women-eaters?"

"I doubt they're that particular. They're pretty cool in a tank but in the ocean, they'd seriously creep me out."

"I think they get a bum rap. The ocean is *their* home and we invade it when we swim, surf and jet ski. They only attack humans because they think we're seals and they're hungry."

We stood silently for a while, holding hands and staring, mesmerized by the sharks' rhythmic movements. When I had my fill of the shivery stuff, I pulled Dillan over to the Kuda seahorse tank. Four ponies were attached to the seaweed by their curling tails and a few more were hovering around gracefully.

"Now these little guys are my friends."

"How do you know?"

"I can just feel it. Look! They're coming to say *Hello*!"

"That's weird," Dillan said as, one by one, they moved gracefully toward us.

"They seem to like you too," I laughed. "They're so pretty! I love the way their tiny fins vibrate. They remind me of hummingbird wings."

"I wonder if they greet all the visitors like this?"

"I'd like to think not," I replied as I ran my finger along the glass, pretending to pet one. "I hope we're special."

"You're pretty special, no doubt about that. This big one looks like he wants to wrap around your finger."

"I wish I could stick my hand in there and see if you're right."

"You don't want to get us thrown outta here before we get started. Do you, girl?"

"I was just kidding, silly. I can contain myself. "Can we sail through once, then drift along at a slower pace?"

"It's your day, girl. You take the helm."

I took a deep breath and looked around the room. There were only a few other visitors in sight. I loved the relaxing atmosphere and the feeling of escaping reality for a while. For some reason I felt comfortable, even safe among the creatures of the deep. Even the sharks didn't seem so scary after a while – they weren't man-eaters after all.

Dillan followed me to a pirate ship in the middle of the room where we climbed onto a dock and looked down into an open tank where turtles basked on rocks and swam among beautifully colored koi fish. Life-size artificial trees and a rocky waterfall made visitors feel like they were outside.

Across the room were African penguins, swimming and playing behind a glass enclosure. Their home was a simulated beach that mimicked their natural habitat. The staff had decorated the rocky walls with handmade paper valentine hearts. Some penguins were swimming while others played with toys like balls and baby rattles.

"Aren't they sweet?" I asked as I climbed into a plastic bubble at the base of the display and watched the penguins swim around me.

"You seriously have the heart of a child."

"And I hope it stays that way. I wonder why they are wearing those beaded bracelets on their little wings."

"The sign says they help to identify them, along with their distinct personalities. Otherwise they look pretty much identical."

"I see." I touched the glass where one, wearing pink and purple beads, was ogling me. I assumed she was a girl. "She seems friendlier than the others." I guess I spoke too soon because before long there was a line of the little buggers swimming over to check us out. "Aren't they adorable?"

"Yeah, they're pretty cute," Dillan conceded.

"These are Jonesy, Dunlop, Kringle, Saba, Shadow, Agulhas and this one is Zaina," a girl wearing a blue Jenkinson's polo offered.

"I wish we could take them all home."

"I don't know what they would do to our *new* floors," Dillan laughed.

"Did you know that African penguins are endangered in the wild and ours are part of the African Penguin Species Survival Plan?"

"It's great that you're trying to help them," I said, "but terribly appalling that they've come to the brink of extinction."

"I know. Climate change, loss of habitat and food sources and pollution all play a role in their decreasing population." The girl just shook her head sadly. "We're doing what we can," she said. "Upstairs in the education area you'll see more about it and also International Polar Bear Day which is in a couple of weeks."

"Thanks. We'll make sure we check it out," Dillan replied.

It hurt to think we humans knowingly contribute to the destruction of the planet and all its awesomely diverse and beautiful creatures without a second thought. Instant gratification for our bloated egos and the quest for the almighty dollar seem to be what motivate most people these days. We were given the task to nurture and protect our fellow inhabitants, but in our selfishness and greed, we've failed miserably. Even with the organizations trying to help, the future looked bleak for us all.

After I nonchalantly wiped a tear from my eye, I took a deep breath and pretended not to be affected by her words. Dillan had gone through so much trouble to show me a wonderful day that I didn't want to spoil it.

We moved on to a wooden sign painted with the body of a seal. There was a hole where its face should be. I went behind and stuck my face through. Dillan snapped a few shots as I made some funny faces.

"I don't think these are quite right," he said, looking at the phone. "Why don't you try making a seal face?"

I had to think about it for a second then I opened my eyes wide and stuck out my bottom lip.

"That's it!" Dillan said. "Perfect!"

We moved on to a large tank that appeared to be empty. Suddenly, out of nowhere, there was a dark form moving toward me. It stopped abruptly and looked me straight in the eye.

"I think that's Luseal," Dillan said. "The sign says she's blind."

"Oh, one eye does appear reddish, poor baby but if she's blind then why does she seem to be looking at me?"

"Nothing surprises me anymore. Maybe she senses your presence."

"Hello, Luseal. You seem like a friendly girl." She rubbed her face against the glass repeatedly. "Do you think she's okay? Maybe she has a toothache or something." In a flash two other dark figures appeared at the glass to greet us.

"Coral and Seaquin," Dillan said. "This *is* getting pretty strange."

"Seaquin? Isn't she's the one Jacqueline Rose has tattooed on the back of her neck – the one that paints artwork for charity?"

"Yeah, you're right."

"Maybe they're just super hungry and looking for a handout," I said as we watched their silly antics.

"Yeah, but this one's kissing the glass. I think she wants me."

"Well then, she has good taste," I giggled. "Please take some more pictures. I never want to forget this day."

An employee saw us trying to do selfies with the seals and offered to take some photos. She got some great shots of us with the seals bobbing in the water behind us. In one shot it looked like Luseal was trying to hug me. After a short time, more visitors came to watch the seals so we said good-bye and moved on. We passed a very colorful gift shop and went upstairs where we found Pacal and Lily the pygmy marmosets who were busy grooming each other.

"Have you ever heard of a marmoset?" I asked.

"Nope."

"Then it's a first for both of us. How about a saddleback tamarin?"

"Not that either. My parents took me to zoos and aquariums when I was a kid, but I don't remember these. I do remember gorillas, orangutans and spider monkeys though."

"I wonder why his name is Stinky?"

"Seems pretty self-explanatory," he chuckled.

We moved on and came to smaller tanks filled with snakes, salamanders, toads and colorful poison dart frogs. "They're so cute. How could they be so dangerous?"

"It's the toxin on their skin. It develops from their diet of mites, ants and termites. Their bright colors warn predators not to eat them," a cute guy, whose name tag read *Armand*, answered.

"Oh, thanks! I'm learning so much and totally enjoying the aquarium."

"We've got a lot to see here. There's about eighteen hundred animals and three hundred different species. I've worked here four years and I still learn something new every day," he said with a friendly smile.

"Did you have much damage from the hurricane?" I asked.

"It's quite a long story but I'd be happy to tell you about it if you have time."

I glanced over at Dillan, who was in the shadows looking at the snakes. He stepped toward us and said, "Yes, of course *we* have time. *We're* very interested."

I sat on one of the benches and Dillan sat next to me.

"So, we had quite an operation here," Armand continued. "Many of us volunteered to stay during the storm but only eight were chosen for their specific capabilities. Each one had a role to play, if needed, along with overseeing the general welfare of our animals. I was really worried because everyone here at Jenks is like family, animals included."

"I can imagine."

"We were concerned mostly for the tank-bound animals. They need filtered, re-oxygenated water to survive. If the power went out, they would be in danger."

"Yeah, of course; what did they do?"

"The staff hung glow sticks through the gift shop and up the stairs so that rescuers could find them if necessary and they set up a command center on the top level. They kept things as normal as possible for the animals by keeping to their daily routines. The power went out Monday evening and around seven-fifteen the storm surge breached the retaining wall and flooded the basement with five feet of water and sand!"

"No!" I was enthralled.

"Unfortunately, yes. The surge took out a quarantine room, the vet rooms and the life support system. Everything but one holding tank was destroyed and washed out into the parking lot."

"Holy crap!"

"It also triggered the sprinkler alarm which made it quite noisy for a while. It was then they decided to move all the penguins upstairs to a small quarantine room for safety. The lights were out so they wore headlamps while moving the penguins. It was quite frightening for everyone."

"The animals must have been very stressed, poor creatures."

"Scarlet and the other parrots acted a bit weird because they could sense the storm even before it arrived and the penguins showed some signs of stress just from being confined in a small area. They fought amongst themselves a bit but it was more like a family quarrel than an all-out brawl. Luckily, the upper floors were untouched, and in the end no animals were injured."

"That's a miracle!"

"Yes, we thought so too."

I felt Dillan prying my hand from his. In my rapture, I hadn't realized I'd been squeezing it with all my might.

"That's quite a grip you've got there, girl," Dillan said as he flexed his hand. "All that carpentry has made you strong!"

The employee smiled and continued, "While repairs were being made in the basement, we spruced up some of our exhibits with fresh paint. Doesn't it look great?"

"It's wonderful. I really love it. I could see myself working here too."

"You should fill out an application! I'm sure they'd be thrilled to have you. I'm Armand, by the way."

"I'm Sandy," I said, reaching toward him for a shake, "and this is my friend, Dillan."

"Hey," Dillan said.

Armand looked warily at my outstretched hand, then bowed as he took a step backward. "Nice to meet you both. If you have any more questions or need anything, feel free to ask. I'll be here till closing."

"Thank you, Armand," I giggled. "It was a pleasure talking with you."

"Oh, did you see Ace, our sea turtle in the Local Fish tank?" Armand asked in an afterthought.

"No, we must have missed him."

"Actually, she's a female. She may have been lying on the bottom by the pile of rocks. She was rescued from freezing to death in New York Harbor in 1995. She's pretty cool."

"Thanks, we'll be sure to check her out," I replied, as he gave a little wave and walked away.

"Looks like you've made *another* friend," Dillan whispered in my ear.

"I hope you're not jealous, just 'cause he's human."

"No, because he couldn't take his eyes off you since we got here!"

"What? No way. You're imagining things."

"Come on, you have to know how completely hot you are. You're like a magnet for guys – and apparently sea creatures as well."

"I'll stick with the sea creatures; you're more than enough as far as guys go."

"Thanks – I guess."

We headed over to the touch tank which held horseshoe crabs, starfish, skates and sea urchins for close-up, hands-on inspection.

"Hey, did you know starfish are supposed to be called sea stars now?" Dillan asked as I dipped my hand in and gently picked one up.

"Seriously? Ohhhh, look at their little tube feet," I said as I flipped it over. "They're fascinating and they tickle!"

"You remind me of this saying I heard that kinda struck a chord. It goes something like this: *'There are two ways to live your life. One's as if there's no such thing as miracles, the other's as if everything is.'* I think you're an everything girl."

"Thank you. That's the nicest thing that anyone's ever said to me."

"Well, since last November at least," Dillan said.

"No, I'm sure – since ever," I responded and placed a kiss on his cheek.

"Are you an everything guy?"

"I'm beginning to be."

"Good!"

After we got sufficiently acquainted with the creatures in the tank, we wandered around the top floor. Louie the salmon-crested cockatoo was loudly squawking, with the occasional *Hello* thrown in. Brilliantly colored Macaw parrots were ambassadors from the rainforest. A Pine Barrens display housed local creatures including owls, salamanders and corn snakes while across the room some alligators, who didn't seem to savor their food one bit, were being fed in a sand pit.

Suddenly, it was time for the seal feeding so we headed across the hall to the viewing area. All the seats were empty, so Dillan and I sat front and center. A thirty-something female trainer came out carrying three buckets of fish and instantly Seaquin, Coral and Luseal slipped out of the water and onto the tiled deck. Megan introduced herself and welcomed us in a friendly but professional way. She told us about Luseal being rescued from the Point Pleasant Canal in 1991 by the Marine Mammal Stranding Center in Brigantine. She'd been injured, possibly by a shark, and was found to be blind in one eye. Because of her blindness, they feared a similar incident may reoccur and decided not to release her back into the wild. Coral and Seaquin were half-sisters who came from California to keep her company. They ate a diet of mackerel, capelin, squid and herring three times a day.

The girls must not have been very hungry because they paid more attention to us than to their trainer. After a while, Megan scooped the fish out of the water, disappeared and returned with three new buckets. When she still couldn't get the seals' attention, she came out to speak with us.

"Hey guys!"

"Hi," we replied in unison.

"The seals are acting rather strangely. Usually it's gobble, gobble unless they don't feel well."

"I really hope they're not sick," I said.

"They've been acting normal all morning, so I don't think that's the issue. I was wondering if you'd like to come around back."

"Seriously?" This was totally awesome. "Of course! We'd love to!"

"This is a total exception to the rule, but I just have to see why they're acting so peculiar."

I took Dillan's hand and pulled him along in my excitement. Once we stepped on the deck, the seals slid up out of the water. They scooted toward us, barking loudly.

"Don't be afraid," Megan said, "They're not being aggressive, just curious."

Within a few seconds the *girls* had surrounded us and quieted down.

"It's so strange. They generally don't seek the attention of strangers to this degree."

"Sandy has a way with animals – and humans as well," Dillan explained as the seals gently nudged us with their whiskery noses.

"Do they want us to pet them?" I asked.

"They are definitely showing signs of affection. Just move slowly so you don't startle them."

"I think Buoy will be jealous when he gets a whiff of us later," Dillan said.

"Sorry, I should've put you in waders before I brought you out here. I didn't know they would be quite so attentive. Are you fishmongers or something?" she joked.

"No, but Sandy eats her fair share of the stuff!"

"You like it, too. Remember clam-topped pizza?"

"I give, girl. Do you think they can smell it through our skin?"

"We believe they have an acute sense of smell out of the water but that doesn't seem likely. Do you want to try feeding them? I have to make sure they get their vitamins."

"I'd love it!" I said.

"Sure," Dillan added.

Megan explained the feeding technique and showed us the different commands to use for certain behaviors. When Luseal, Coral and Seaquin performed the behavior to her satisfaction, we rewarded them with a tasty fish or squid.

After they did their fair share of showing us their bellies, rolling over, saluting, waving and speaking, *we* were rewarded with *raspberries* and kisses. Once they had finished their buckets of seafood, we watched as Megan gave their teeth a quick brushing.

"This has been a fantastic experience," I said to Megan as I reached down to pet the girls one last time before saying good-bye.

"I am glad that you enjoyed it. We can always use someone who relates well with the animals. You should think of putting in an application."

"You're the second person who's told me that today."

I left the seals feeling a bit sad that I couldn't spend more time with them, but I wanted to walk through the aquarium again at a slower pace. I didn't want to miss a thing. I was already hoping Dillan would bring me back another day. After a trip to the restrooms to wash our fishy hands, we came upon bearded dragons, Slash, the honeycomb moray eel; Popey, the blue-tongued skink; Eddie, the Burmese python; Ray-Ray the southern stingray; and a Nautilus whose ancestors had inhabited Earth for 500 million years. Talk about a miracle!

I couldn't have spent a happier Valentines' Day than I had with Dillan at the aquarium. We stopped in the gift shop on the way out and Dillan surprised me with some awesome souvenirs. As we headed back toward the parkway, I was wondering what I could do to help our endangered friends.

DILLAN

FEBRUARY 2013

SANDY LOVED THE AQUARIUM, so in a roundabout way I was able to show my love for her. No flowers, no card or romantic mush. She positively glowed with excitement from the moment she awoke in the parking lot.

My idea for a special lunch had been replaced by a second tour around the aquarium. Though I was downright starving by late afternoon, I had to admit I really enjoyed the aquarium too, right down to being kissed by my new friend Luseal. Unfortunately, we didn't get to see Seaquin paint on canvas, but I did find a few pieces of her artwork for sale in the gift shop. I purchased one on the sly along with a silver seahorse ring, while Sandy was occupied looking at the mugs, glass jellyfish figures, books, stuffed animals, T-shirts, jackets and a plethora of colorful souvenirs. It wasn't my scene, but it helped the aquarium stay afloat, so to speak. I was happy to contribute by insisting Sandy pick out a few things. She balked, of course, but once I explained how the proceeds helped benefit her new friends, she caved with a smile on her face.

Luckily, we came upon the Sweet Shop on the way out and bought two warm, chewy, salt-laden pretzels, which tasted fantastic – probably since I hadn't eaten since breakfast. We shared a bag of almond butter crunch and some gummy sharks on the ride home. I would have preferred to take Sandy out for a lobster dinner but she said she felt guilty leaving Buoy for so long and would be happy with a cup of soup. I guess the excitement of the aquarium was too much for her and therefore I was epically stoked.

Buoy greeted us at the door with his usual wiggle butt and wagging tail. It wasn't until we flipped on the lights that we noticed we'd had a visitor. Sandy gasped and I just shook my head in disbelief. In the middle of the parlor sat a table draped with a red cloth. In the middle sat a bouquet of red roses which were flanked by two tall candles. The table was set formally for two, complete with champagne glasses and a chilling bottle of the good stuff.

"Dillan?" Sandy asked timidly.

I just shrugged my shoulders and shook my head. Standing against the vase was a note card written in a scrolling font. Sandy grabbed it and read it out loud:

Since you stepped from the melee of the storm and entered our lives, the world has become full of possibilities once again.
Dinner came from The Gables – just reheat and enjoy.
With sincere gratitude to our young friends,
Henry and Lucas
P.S. Buoy spent a comfortable afternoon with his new companions.

"I swear I had nothing to do with this!" I yelled as I ran up the stairs after her. "I'm as surprised as you are."

"Let's just get the food. I'm starving!" she said, acting unnerved.

She grabbed the two salads from the refrigerator. My mouth watered as she drizzled her spring greens, roasted beets, goat cheese and caramelized walnuts with dressing. I followed suit and we headed back downstairs.

"I think the guys are trying to tell us something," I blurted out as we sat at the lavish table. Immediately I realized my mistake, but Sandy only squared her shoulders and handed me her champagne glass. I popped the cork and poured.

"I'm sure they meant well and I appreciate their thoughtfulness, no matter how uncomfortable I feel right now," she said with a resounding sigh.

"I'm sorry you feel that way," I replied, as my appetite vanished into thin air.

"Dillan, God forbid, *Wai* . . . that fudge-nut turns out to be my husband! How would you feel then?"

"What did you just say?"

"I said *fudge*-nut. Believe me, I was thinking much worse but the alternative just feels so crass flowing from my lips."

"You could drop the F-bomb around me any time and I certainly wouldn't think any less of you."

"Thanks. I'm just *super pissed* that somehow he's managed to ruin my perfect day!" she exclaimed before draining her glass and holding it out for more.

"There's no way you could be married to that idiot."

"We don't know that! Anything is possible!"

"I've only known you for a few months, but I feel like I've known you all my life. I know you're way too smart to get involved with someone like that."

"I really hope you're right!"

***

Saturday was jam-packed. We had signed up weeks ago to serve the meal at the Fireman's Annual Turkey Dinner and we were also slated to run a 5K in the morning.

The "Let's Get Sandy -Run for a Cause" was being held at the Ethel Jacobsen School. Ever enthusiastic and full of energy, Sandy was excited to be a part of the latest fundraiser. The 5K was for all ages and abilities – walk, jog, run, push your stroller, bring your dog – whatever your preference, you were welcome. The three of us jumped into the Jeep on yet another cloudy morning and drove up to Surf City. We signed up with the other three hundred or so runners and bought a couple of Waves 4 Water/Jetty water bottles.

I always had a bit of a competitive side, as did Sandy, but since we felt guilty leaving Buoy home alone again we decided to just walk for the fun of it. We fluctuated between jogging and walking, laughing and talking and saying hello to friends and strangers along the way. I can't deny I was itching to sprint ahead as the runners passed us, but spending quality time with my companions was way more fulfilling than the thrill of competition.

As the rosy color bloomed on Sandy's cheeks, a feeling of total wellbeing spread over me. I found myself blissfully happy. We were about three-quarters of the way through when Buoy let out a loud howl and sat down abruptly. He held up his paw and Sandy gasped and swooned. I caught her and helped her sit on the ground. The masonry nail which protruded through the top of Buoy's paw had probably been buried in the large pile of nearby sea grass. He looked at me helplessly but still seemed in better shape than Sandy, who was as white as a sheet and a bit green around the gills. I offered her a drink from the water bottle and told her to take some slow deep breaths.

"Oh my God," she kept repeating.

"He's going to be alright, but we need to take him to the vet. Can you walk with me back to the Jeep? I'm going to carry him and I don't want to worry about you fainting!"

"You're right," she said, obviously trying to regain her composure. "Sorry, I acted like a maniac."

I made sure she was steady, then hoisted Buoy up, trying to be as gentle as possible. I must have been running on adrenaline because it wasn't until I got him into the back of the Jeep that I realized how winded I was. I dialed Stafford Veterinary Hospital as I climbed behind the wheel. Sandy attempted to comfort Buoy from the back seat as I explained the situation to the clerk. Within a few minutes we were heading over the causeway.

The folks at Stafford Veterinary Hospital were beyond wonderful. They ushered us into the exam room immediately, and Dr. Herd couldn't have been more impressive.

"Okay boy, let's have a look," he said as I set Buoy on the examining table. "I bet that hurts a lot. We'll take him to the surgery suite and remove it, clean it up and see if he needs a stitch or two. Then we'll chat."

"He seems nice," Sandy said as she took my hand. "I hope our baby's going to be all right."

Our baby. What a radical concept. I wasn't ready for a kid quite yet but I couldn't imagine having them with anyone else. "I always thought of him as more of a BFAM."

"What's that?"

"Oh – brother from another mother."

"I can see you two as brothers. The resemblance is uncanny. I hope I'll get to meet your parents someday."

"That's rad because I'm planning on visiting them in Cocoa Beach this spring, and I was really hoping you would join us."

"Ohhh Florida: sunshine, warm water, your family. That sounds fantastic. I'd love to go!"

"Awesome!"

Dr. Herd came back about thirty minutes later with Buoy in tow and a smile on his face. "Who knew that extra webbing between his toes would be good for something other than swimming," he said jokingly. "The nail punctured it and missed the pads completely. We cleaned it well and administered an antibiotic and pain med. It should heal quickly as long as he doesn't mess with it too much."

"Thank goodness!" Sandy chimed.

"Thanks, Doc."

"No problem, guys. The bootie's to keep it clean as well as deter any licking, but we'll send you home with a cone in case he misbehaves. Check the wound twice a day for redness or drainage."

Oh no, not the dreaded cone of shame! Buoy wouldn't be too happy about wearing that.

"It's been awhile since his initial visit, so I gave him a complimentary physical. He seems good on all other accounts, our miracle dog," Dr. Herd revealed as he wrote on Buoy's chart.

"Miracle dog?" Sandy asked.

"Well sure. Have you ever seen an eighteen-year-old Labrador in such awesome physical condition?"

"Eighteen?" she asked, sounding quite shocked.

"Well, that's what this young man tells me, though honestly I find it hard to believe."

"I double-checked with my parents and they agreed. We found him the summer I turned nine."

"I had no idea he's so old – and he saved me from drowning

during the hurricane. That makes him doubly amazing!"

"So, he's a hero to boot! That's mind-boggling!" Dr. Herd exclaimed. "The extra webbing between his toes probably helped him in that department. I've never seen a dog's paw stretch so wide. I hear amazing pet stories all the time but this one takes the cake."

"So, he's good?" I asked, relieved.

"He's better than good. Barring any issues, he doesn't need to come back until his yearly, which is in August. We'll do a geriatric blood panel and heartworm test then. Of course, give us a call if you have any concerns with the paw."

Sandy offered to work the dinner without me, but Buoy was acting fine so we asked Henry and Lucas if they would dog-sit for a few hours. I was ready to carry him if need be but he walked normally down the block and tackled the stairs with no obvious discomfort. Once inside, he happily trotted toward the library with Sherlock and Mrs. Holmes bringing up the rear. An abundance of pet beds and toys had accumulated over the last few weeks making the room appear unusually messy. We were a little apprehensive about leaving him, but Henry promised to call if he chewed at the bootie or acted "the least bit strange."

The first thing we noticed as I opened the door to the firehouse hall was the smell of Thanksgiving as it wafted past us and into the street. People of all ages were bustling about and setting the many tables in the newly remodeled room. With its freshly painted walls, new flooring, wall sconces and window treatments, it was a massive improvement since the last time we were there.

"The room came out wonderfully!" Sandy said as we were greeted by a fully uniformed fire chief.

"There's no way we would've been ready without volunteers like you two. Thanks for your help and for coming back again today," Bob said as he shook our hands.

"Sure, it's the least we can do."

"I'll introduce you to Elsie. She'll assign you a section and put you to work."

After a quick check of her clipboard, Elsie gave us two tables of eight in the middle of the room and asked if we would be willing to work for the first half of the service. We said, "No problem," and loaded our trays with baskets of rolls, bowls of butter pats and creamers, and relish trays filled with olives, carrots and celery sticks.

"From what I hear this is a serious tradition," Sandy said to Elsie and the other ladies behind the counter.

"Yes, this is our ninety-sixth year. I've been in the auxiliary for twenty-five and held this position for the last fifteen. My husband and son are both firemen. It's in our blood."

"I'm glad we could be a part of it," Sandy added, "and it smells amazing."

"Thanks. People really seem to enjoy not only the meal, but the chance to catch up with their neighbors. Some will bring their own bottles and need glasses; otherwise we have water, soda, coffee or tea. Once you get those set out, come back and I'll give you the fruit cups."

We had just finished loading our tables when I noticed Tinder, a kid from the beach, setting out napkin-wrapped silverware on a small table along the wall. I hadn't seen him since September and was hoping he and his family had weathered the storm well.

"Hey dude, how goes it?" I asked as I came up behind him.

"Dillan, hey!" He spun around and gave me our special handshake. "Are you serving too? That's so cool. Whoa, what happened to your hair?"

"Just time for a change. See that girl over there?"

"Yeah, she's hot."

"Okay, how old are you?"

"I just turned twelve, why?"

"Never mind." I guess his hormones were already on red alert. "That's my friend, Sandy. She chopped my dreads."

"Can she cut my hair too?" "

"Oh, come on. Seriously dude?"

"What?" he replied with a bit of an attitude.

Some of the younger firemen we'd met before had gathered around Sandy like moths to a flame, and I forced myself to look away.

"How did you make out in the storm?" I asked.

"We stayed with my grandparents' for a while before Mom and Dad got back to check on our house. I was afraid they'd come back and say it was gone, but it was all right! I stayed at my grandparents' a long time though. They said it'd be *too traumatic* for me to come home too soon."

"I can understand that. I'm glad you're okay. I better get back to work before they fire me."

"Very funny, dude. See you on the beach!"

"You got it."

Within minutes, our two tables were almost full. Sandy and I got busy carrying out gravy boats and plates piled high with steaming hot turkey, mashed potatoes, green beans, stuffing and cranberry sauce. Everyone appeared upbeat, talkative and hungry.

"If this is any indication, looks like we're going to have a huge turnout," the chief said as he approached me carrying a stack of Styrofoam takeout containers. "We've already got more tickets sold than last year. I hope we don't run out of food!"

No shit, I thought. I was totally banking on eating tonight!

"I do hope we're planning on eating before we go home," Sandy whispered in my ear as she slid past me on her way back to the kitchen pass-through.

"You bet, girl. The smell's driving me crazy. I keep expecting Mom to walk out of the kitchen."

As people pulled bottles of wine and beer from shopping bags and began to share, the hall took on the air of a Sunday family dinner and I began to feel a little homesick.

Coffee was offered again at the end of the meal to go with an impressive assortment of homemade desserts. We grabbed trays of the precut layer cakes, Bundt cakes, strudel, fruit pies, cream pies, cupcakes and cookies. I had all I could do to keep from grabbing a slice of lemon meringue pie and absconding with it.

A line was forming near the door so folks reluctantly left to make room for their neighbors.

"We have more dine-ins than takeout this year," Elsie said as we grabbed some more turkey dinners. "I guess some of these poor folks don't have a kitchen or dining room to eat in right now."

"I'm sure the firehouse is more comfortable than a lot of their homes," Sandy replied sadly.

"It's great to see their faces though. I'm glad they've come out to support us."

I spotted Katie and Mitch sitting at a crowded table across the room and, when she wasn't looking, Mitch gave me a huge grin, nod and the thumbs-up sign. I wasn't sure if that meant they were finally dating or he was just stoked about sharing a table with her. I gave him an up-nod and continued serving.

"Dillan, do you know that woman over there?" Sandy asked quietly, as she placed two hot gravy boats on the table.

"No, I don't think so. Why?"

"She looks so sad, as if she's about to cry."

"She does look miserable, doesn't she?"

"I'll try to speak to her in a bit. She looks like she could use a friend."

We made another trip to the pass-through where Sandy grabbed a waiting tray and headed back. I waited for one of the sous chefs to fill mine with hot meals. Upon returning to the tables, I found Jack and Carole buttering rolls and looking hungry.

"Hey guys, great to see you!"

"Sandy just told us about your haircut," Carole said, "a vast improvement, I'd say."

"Thanks. She's a wiz with the shears. It seems like ages. How have you been?"

"Things are good," Jack replied, "falling into place. Jacqueline Rose keeps in touch. I wasn't sure how it was going to play out, but she's a great kid."

"Whoever would have imagined?" Carole said wryly.

"Certainly not me," Jack added, "but honestly we're thrilled to have her in our lives!"

"We think she's pretty special too," Sandy said, as she placed a heaping pile of food in front of Carole. "I hope you're hungry," she said, "but seriously, try to save room for dessert. They're all homemade and look so yummy."

"I'm sorry, but the only *Kaimana* I've come across is Don Ho's daughter. There's also a resort in Honolulu by that name –

no missing persons, though," Jack said, sounding defeated.

"I kinda hoped something would finally turn up," Sandy said with a sigh.

"So was I, but I'm not giving up," Jack said.

"I'm sure you'll get some answers soon, Sandy," Carole added.

"How's the pooch?" Jack asked, as he cut into a thick slice of turkey.

"He stepped on a nail during the 5K this morning, so he's chillin' over at Henry's place."

"Ouch! Poor Buoy, he can't catch a break!"

"He took it like a trooper. The vet said he'll be fine."

"Are Lucas and Henry coming to eat?" Carole asked.

"They didn't mention it when we asked them to doggie sit, so I doubt it," Sandy answered.

"I'll give them a call," Jack said, "maybe they'd like takeout."

"That's a great idea. By the time we finish here, it'll be past their dinner time."

Our tables changed diners three times as the hours flew by. When a fresh group of volunteers showed up, Elsie relieved us of our duties. Instead of eating there, we purchased takeout dinners so two less people would have to wait. I was stoked to see there was one slice of lemon meringue left and I got it! My mom always made the best lemon meringue pie from scratch and I used to lick the beaters covered with sticky meringue. Funny how food can make you feel so homesick.

"I feel so badly for the people who have no homes to eat their meals in," Sandy said as she put on her coat.

After hearing bits and pieces of people's conversations all night, I felt grateful that we were doing so well. "We're lucky we could do the work ourselves or our place might be in the same condition as theirs. There are only so many contractors in the world."

"And insurance representatives," Sandy answered as we headed for the door.

"Don't get me started on the way they love to take your money but don't want to honor your claim."

"And those people who will use a tragedy like this to take

advantage of poor folks who are desperate and trusting and have no clue that they are being scammed."

"This talk is getting me depressed. Let's go get Buoy so we can eat. I'm starved."

"Me too. I'm so hungry, I could eat right here on the curb."

As I held the door for Sandy, from the corner of my eye, I saw a large dark figure disappear around the back of the firehouse. I took her arm and pulled her toward the Jeep.

"Hey, what's the hurry? Is something wrong?"

"No, sorry. Nothing's wrong," I lied. "My stomach's overtaken my manners."

I parked in my usual spot and we ran the dinners up to the kitchen.

"I'll go get Buoy."

"And I'll pour us some wine. Don't let the guys chew your ears off."

"Don't worry. I'll be right back, but don't wait for me – start eating."

I made sure to lock the door on my way out and jogged down the block. I knocked, the dogs barked and Henry opened the door. Buoy wove himself between Henry, Sherlock and the front door to get to me. I loved the way he was always so excited to see me – five minutes or five hours made little difference. Once Mr. Wiggle Butt had calmed down, Henry said, "Jack and Carole came by with meals for us. We shared a bit of the bird with the pets and had an amicable chat."

"They're good people."

"Would you like to join us for a nightcap?" he asked.

"Next time," I said sincerely, "but since we're alone, I wanted to ask you something."

"Sure, son."

"A while back you told me I should slow things down with Sandy, and then you two set us up with that romantic dinner."

"Oh, well yes. That's true, but I said *you* should slow things down. It's a different ball of wax coming from us."

"Well, I appreciate the effort, but I'm not sure it worked."

"All in good time, Dillan. All in good time."

"I hope you're right. Anyway, I have a turkey dinner waiting and I'm starving. Thanks for keeping an eye on Buoy."

"Anytime, son, and next time you come by, feel free to let yourself in. There's no need for the formality of knocking. You're family now as well."

"Thanks, Henry. Catch ya soon."

"Good night. Please give our regards to Sandy."

As we crossed Coral Street, Buoy started barking frantically. He took off running and yanked the leash out of my hand. I ran after him, calling, but he disappeared around the corner. I started to panic remembering the huge shadowy figure at the firehouse. If he was so rough with Sandy, what might he do to my dog?

When I got to the corner, Buoy's barking had stopped; the street and Bicentennial Park were deserted. I called again as loudly as I could. I wasn't sure which way to run so I whistled loudly and prayed for a response. The seconds seemed to take hours; then out of the darkness, I saw movement ahead. What a relief it was to see Buoy trotting proudly toward me, with only a slight limp. I bent down and placed my arms around him.

"Why do you have to do shit like that? You scared the crap out of me – you stupid old mutt!" I gave him a good scratch behind the ears, some kisses on the head and stood up. It was then I noticed something small hanging from his mouth. He didn't want to give me his special prize at first but with the command "drop it," I took a piece of torn fabric from his mouth: a colorful Hawaiian print. Did this asshole only own one shirt? I took a firm hold of his leash, pulled out my phone and called Jack.

Back inside the house, Buoy was still anxious and excited.

"I'm not sure if he's happy to see me or the smell of the food is driving him crazy," Sandy said as he ran circles around her legs. "You want your dinner, boy? Can we give him a tiny bit of turkey?" she asked as she dumped a can of food into his dish and mashed it up with a fork.

"Henry already gave him some," I snapped unnecessarily as I hung my coat on the back of the chair.

"Dillan, what's the matter? Did I do something wrong?"

"Jesus, Sandy, I'm sorry. I was just worried about Buoy all day and

I felt guilty leaving him and I haven't eaten. It's no excuse," I said as I grabbed my glass of wine and chugged it.

"It's all right. Sit down and relax. It's been a long stressful day."

She didn't know the half of it. I checked the bandage on Buoy's paw as she pulled a plate out of the microwave and set it on the table.

"I'm sorry," I said again. "There's a lot on my mind. I didn't mean to be short with you."

"I understand," she replied sounding hurt as she dropped a few pieces of turkey in Buoy's bowl. He looked up at her gratefully before scarfing it down. If she only knew what he'd done to deserve it! But I wasn't about to frighten her.

"I'm assuming Buoy was okay and behaved with Sherlock and Mrs. Holmes.

"Yeah, he was good," I replied as I refilled my wine glass and swallowed a big mouthful. "The guys enjoyed their dinners and a visit with the Fosters."

"It was thoughtful of them to do that."

Sandy came and sat at the table with her plate and for a while we gobbled our turkey dinners in silence.

"I missed Thanksgiving with my parents," I said, trying to drown out the thoughts of the schmuck outside who obviously knew where we lived. "I didn't think it was a big deal at the time."

"I'm sure they understood. There was a lot going on here in November."

"It was the first time I missed it. I bet they were disappointed." I ran the last piece of turkey through the remnants of gravy-soaked potatoes and ate it, feeling full and uneasy. When I sighed, Sandy reached over and placed her hand on mine. "I miss them sometimes," I said quietly.

"That's certainly nothing to be embarrassed or ashamed of. There's nothing more important in this world than family. Somehow I miss mine too, even though I can't really remember them."

I immediately realized what I had said. "Jesus. Sorry for being so thoughtless."

"Don't be silly. Never hide your feelings from me. They're safe here," she said, as she touched her heart with one hand and squeezed my hand with the other.

I spent a fitful night on the blowup. Every time I'd look up at the bed, Buoy would lift his head as well. I knew he was keeping one ear and one eye open, so to speak. I got tired of tossing, turning and worrying so I got up and walked around the inn, checking the window locks and looking outside. As I passed the kitchen, the moonlight illuminated the fabric scrap hanging from my jacket pocket. I stepped into the kitchen to tuck it back inside.

"Having trouble sleeping?" a deep voice asked.

I jumped from the bed, awakened by the nightmare – my heart somehow lodged in my throat. As I sat there calming down and catching my breath, Sandy sighed and rolled over. Buoy stretched out and farted. It was just one of many long nights looking up at the ceiling.

Buoy had been limping a bit after chasing the Neanderthal, but was prancing around like a pup a few days later. His paw had healed completely, leaving no sign of the wound. As I gave his leg a good massage, I happily realized he hadn't demonstrated any symptoms of arthritis in months.

I wasn't sure how Sandy, whose work ethic made mine look lax, would feel about taking more time away from the inn, but we'd had a productive week and deserved a break. Wanting to share an integral part of the Long Beach Island experience with her, I lined up a surprise for Saturday.

Fantasy Island was holding a celebratory re-opening of the arcade for the local kids. I knew she'd enjoy the games and being around a bunch of noisy, excited land sharks. I, too, hoped to check on a few of the boogers who hung out on my beach last summer. We passed the familiar plywood sign that read, *Sandy, You'll Not Stop Our Summer* as we headed for the back of the line. I guess they'd been right, as they were well on their way to recovery. While we waited, we distracted ourselves from the cold, misty day by talking about the summer.

"There are a lot of those bushes with big purple flowers," I told her.

"Oh, hydrangeas?"

"Yeah, I don't pay too much attention to that kind of stuff but I think they came out in the spring."

"I am seriously looking forward to some sunshine and getting in the water again," Sandy said as she shivered.

"Me too, now that I'm thinking about it. I guess I've had my mind on other things lately."

"Tell me more," she said eagerly.

"We get the most awesome full moons here. Sometimes they're red and look like something out of *Star Wars*. What's really boss is going up in the lighthouse when the moon is full."

"Oh, that sounds like fun."

"Did you know you can see Atlantic City from Holgate?"

"No, I'd like to see that – you gamble much?"

"No, I work too hard to throw my money away. I mean, I might go with a couple hundred, have a nice dinner and play the slot machines, but I'd never think of it as more than a day of entertainment. I haven't been down there yet. I think there's a boat called the *Black Whale* that takes tourists down in the summer."

"That might be something fun to do."

"Yeah, we'll check into it. The Marine Mammal Stranding Center is near there. You'd really like it. They do rehab with injured seals and turtles and stuff like that."

"I read about it at the aquarium and I've seen articles in *The SandPaper*."

"Right, they helped with one of the seals. We'll go someday."

"Cool. What else?"

"Well, when the season starts, ice cream trucks stop at the beach every hour or so. The drivers walk over the dune and ring bells to get your attention. A kid named Tinder, would usually stop on his way and ask if we wanted anything. Sometimes, he'd just surprise me with a King Cone! I saw him last weekend at the firehouse. He's a good kid."

"All this talking about ice cream is making me colder," Sandy said as she rubbed her arms to warm them up. I pulled her back against me gently and wrapped my arms around her. "Better?"

"Infinitely."

"He has quite a crush on you."

"Who?"

"Tinder. He asked me if you'd cut his hair," I laughed.

"Does he have dreads too?"

"Nope, not at all."

"I hope I get to meet him sometime. Tell me more about the summer," she pleaded.

"There are fireflies at night."

"I like those."

"And dragonflies."

"They say the fairies ride them."

"Could be, but I've never seen one. You're a strange and wonderful girl," I said as I pulled her a little closer.

"Well, this is Fantasy Island. I'd like to imagine fairies live around here."

"Spreading pixie dust?"

"Not exactly. They live in small gardens. Some spread good magic and some create mischief."

"I know what kind of fairy you'd be."

"Yeah?"

"A do-gooder one."

We finally reached the stairs where a bunch of red, white and blue balloons tied to the banister kept blowing into our heads. Loud mechanical music, the whoop-whoop, ding-ding and clang-clang of the machines poured from the building. It was a child's paradise. As the kids ahead of us entered, they were given a free POP ticket for the summer season.

"Dillan?"

"Yeah?"

"Are you excited about going inside?"

"Into the arcade?"

"Yeah, of course. Where else?"

"Um . . . ," I whispered in her ear as I pulled her hips back tightly against me.

"Oh my God! You're such a fiend," she scolded as she quickly extricated herself from my embrace.

"Nope, just one hundred percent, all-American male," I retorted.

She rolled her eyes at me. "I know we're almost to the door

but would you be really disappointed if we left?"

"No, not at all. Did you have a more adult type of fun in mind?" I asked hopefully.

"Yeah, I'm more in the mood for a cup of tea by the fireplace with Henry and we can take Buoy over too."

"Well, it doesn't sound as much fun as what I was envisioning but we can do this another day. Maybe when it's warmer and the Ferris wheel's running again."

SANDY

EARLY SPRING

DURING THE FIRST WEEK of March, the appliances and fixtures for the kitchenettes and bathrooms arrived, along with new furniture for the reception/parlor area. Every day we would see another space come one step closer to completion.

"It's come a long way in four months," Henry said as I gave the guys a tour of our latest accomplishments. "You kids must have been working like beavers."

"Or carpenter ants," Lucas added with a snicker.

"Good one!" Dillan chimed from the upstairs hall, where he'd been staining some molding.

"Seriously, it's marvelous work. Have you given any thought as to what you'll do once it's completed, dear?" Henry asked.

"Not as much as I should be. I keep avoiding it. Perhaps I'm waiting for a sign or something."

"You mean divine intervention?"

"Something like that, Lucas. It's hard to explain. Sometimes I feel like there are larger forces at work and my choices are not my own to make."

"I can understand that point of view but honestly, after living a long life, I think it's malarkey – no offense meant."

"I don't want to leave Dillan," I whispered in Henry's ear. "I just don't think it's fair to him if I stay."

"Would you leave the island – leave *us all* behind?"

"I have no idea what to do, where to go, or how to find the answers."

"Perhaps you'll attain some clarity while you're vacationing. A change of scenery would often help me with writer's block."

"I really hope that works," I said as I gave him a hug.

"You know you can always stay with us," Henry said. "Dillan, too, for that matter. There's more than enough room for everyone."

"Oh, thank you, Henry. You are an angel."

"We think you're the angel, my dear."

I slipped my arm through his and led him down the hall, "Now, I want to show you guys the MacAvery's wing. It's coming together beautifully."

After we toured the spaces that would become Mac and Shona's master bedroom and bath, the guest bedroom, the kitchen, living area and the enclosed porch, I took them upstairs to see Jacqueline Rose's murals in the kid's bedrooms.

"They're marvelous and I'm not just saying that because she's my granddaughter."

"I wholeheartedly agree, Lucas. She's a fine artist. They're so realistic, yet each character appears to have a distinct personality," Henry replied.

"They look like they have secrets," I said.

"I think they appear to have wisdom," Henry added, "as if they know they're in exactly the right place."

I got his not-so-subtle message. When we finished the tour, I offered to fix sandwiches for everyone, but the guys refused graciously as they were on their way to the Greenhouse Cafe and then grocery shopping.

"No need to show us out, kids. I'm sure you're itching to get back to work."

"See you guys later. Be careful going down the stairs," Dillan replied.

"Thanks for stopping by!"

"You know," I heard Henry say to Lucas as they reached the foyer, "I might try my hand penning a romance. I'm thinking of calling it *PLEASE STAY*."

"I heard that!" I yelled.

"Sounds like another best seller, Michael Stocks!" Dillan yelled.

If Dillan wasn't enough to keep me on Long Beach Island, Henry surely was. What an empty life he must've had, never marrying or having children. I had only the slightest memory of my own father but I hoped he was like Henry. I didn't want to leave Beach Haven but how could I move on romantically with Dillan without knowing the truth about my past?

Damn this *Waimoku the Terrible*! If he revealed himself again, I'd demand answers instead of being intimidated. I'd bite his hand; I'd stamp on his foot; I'd kick him in the nut-sack if I had to!

When the MacAverys made a trip down to check on our progress, they raved about the quality of Dillan's craftsmanship and the artistic beauty of Jacqueline Rose's sea life murals. By the time we finished the tour, Shona was glowing with excitement. "It's so beautiful! I can't wait to decorate and become an innkeeper!" I felt my heart sink like an anchor because I'd been imagining the same thing.

"It looks even better than the photos you've sent," Mac said. "How fortunate we happened to meet in the Hud that afternoon!"

"I'd have said yes to anything that got me out of my living conditions at the time," Dillan replied with a laugh.

"As I remember, you were feeling a bit like a canned sardine."

"It was tough. Buoy wasn't happy, either. This job's been a godsend on so many levels."

"For us as well. We couldn't be happier with the work you two have done."

"Thank you for allowing me to stay here with Dillan," I added.

"I don't know how he could've done all this without you," Mac said. "You must've been a quick learner."

"I think I just really enjoy helping people."

"Hey," Shona said, "We noticed Kubel's Too was opened when we drove by. Why don't we celebrate with dinner and drinks?"

* * *

On March 17, we were picked up by a small pink bus and taken, with a handful of others, to Nardi's Tavern and Grille. Recently reopened after the hurricane, the restaurant was hosting a St. Patrick's Day bash.

As we sat at the bar with Dillan's friends, listening to a band called The Love Puppies, I wondered if Waimoku might show up. My eyes darted about the room anxiously as I mentally prepared for a confrontation. Who did he think he was, kissing me so forcefully?

After an hour or so, a band called Richie and The Allstars came on stage and took over. By now, most people were pretty lit and brightly colored feather boas, long green beaded necklaces, large leprechaun hats and silly headbands were being passed amongst the crowd on the dance floor. *Restore the Shore, I'm Not Irish But Kiss Me Anyway, Unite+Rebuild* and *LBI is Alive* T-shirts were proudly worn by many.

Dillan, who'd had a few too many Irish whiskeys, asked me to dance, which was crazy fun. When the music slowed, he held me close, but I never took my eyes off the crowd. If the huge moron did appear, I didn't want Dillan, someone who had probably never punched anyone in his life, getting between us. When the night was over, I half expected to find Waimoku waiting on the party bus, but he never showed, leaving me oddly disappointed. I guess my time for cowering was over. I'd had enough of *not knowing* and I needed answers if I was ever going to find peace and be with the one I loved.

* * *

Before winter had set in, we'd planted dune grasses with the ALO to help stabilize the dunes and, on a sunny day in January, we assisted some wonderful volunteers with a beach cleanup. It was on our fourth time working with the ALO that my third mini-miracle occurred. I stood looking at an American flag waving proudly atop a piling out in the ocean and wondered how it got there. Some brave soul must have swum or boated, then climbed the thing. It made a certain statement, perhaps proclaiming the tenacity of my new neighbors and the American people on the whole. I headed toward the trash can carrying a handful of deflated balloons, a broken bottle, a chunk of brick and a six-pack holder. I reached it at the same time as another woman.

"I absolutely hate knowing what this does to the marine life," I said.

"I agree, but I like to think that every piece we remove helps."

After a few moments, I recognized her as the woman from the fireman's dinner who had disappeared before I had a chance to speak with her.

"I'm Sandy."

"Janine," she replied. "Nice to meet you."

"Isn't the ALO a wonderful organization?"

"Yes, I've been volunteering for years."

"My friend Dillan and I are newbies. Didn't I see you at the turkey dinner last month?"

"Yes, it's a tradition. Did you enjoy it?"

"You bet! The turkey was even moister than the one we made for Christmas. How did you make out in the storm?" I asked, trying to feel her out.

"I lost my home and my car. I mean, what's left of it's still there but I don't know if the duplex is salvageable. I'm still waiting to hear from the powers that be. It's so frustrating – I don't know what to do. I was one of those idiots who wouldn't leave and I had to be rescued when the bay water flooded my home. I felt so stupid and embarrassed putting those poor men in danger! I'll never be able to repay them."

"I heard that they rescued quite a lot of people."

"They were amazingly kind, considering! I stayed at the Engleside for a couple of days then hitched a ride with some soldiers who took me to my friend Suzanne's place in Harvey Cedars. Luckily, she had given me a key just in case of an emergency."

"How did she make out?"

"She had enough sense to go to the mainland, but her home wasn't damaged at all! I've been there ever since. I quite enjoy her company but I can't impose on her forever." She gasped suddenly and tears welled up in her eyes.

"Janine, are you, alright?"

"Your pin," she said sadly, "I had a little plate just like that. My son Liam gave it to me for Christmas when he was seven."

I could see how upset she was as she reached into her coat pocket, pulled out a tissue and blew her nose.

"Really? Would you like to talk about it?"

"The turkey dinner was particularly difficult this year because I was alone. I usually went with my son."

"Oh?" I asked delicately.

"Well you know the old saying: *A son is a son, til he takes a wife but a daughter's a daughter for all of her life.* Sometimes I wish I'd had a daughter."

So, Janine shared her story with me, on that breezy April day sitting on the shore.

"I felt from the beginning that my daughter-in-law and I didn't really mesh, but it wasn't because I thought she'd make a poor wife. We were just different people who saw the world in a different way. I always imagined my son's wife would become my *daughter* and I'd hoped that over time she'd come to know and love me, but that was a pipe dream. We only became less and less agreeable toward each other. I'm sure that's why I was super excited about having a granddaughter. There was no reason for her not to love me. I wanted to share her life and shower her with love and affection, but they won't let me. They keep my grandchildren under lock and key. I was even told that I was pressuring them and to stop asking to visit! Is that any way to treat your mother?"

I took hold of her hand and she started sobbing. "I am so, so sorry, Janine," I said as I leaned closer and rubbed her back gently.

"My son has broken my heart into a thousand pieces. I just don't know what to do. I'm afraid to talk to him; afraid he'll say something thoughtless and make me cry again. Shouldn't he know me better than anyone? Shouldn't he understand my desire to be a part of his family? I just don't think I can go on like this for much longer. I miss my grandkids every single day."

"Do they live far away?" I asked, wondering if that could be part of the problem.

"They're only an hour north on the parkway. That's nothing to me. I'd be there in a heartbeat, if they'd only ask."

My heart was aching for her fractured family. She seemed like a lovely woman who would do anything for her son and his family. I couldn't imagine how it felt to live so close to the ones you love, yet be excluded from their lives. I wondered if the bulk of their issues could revolve around misconceived notions and unfulfilled expectations, especially if they both had totally different views about what life was *supposed* to be like.

"One day I was feeling so hurt that I threw out all of the childhood drawings and school projects that I'd saved, not to mention the stuff he'd left behind when he moved out: the baseball cards, books, video games, some artwork he'd purchased. I felt so lonely and discarded at that time. I even took their wedding photos off the wall."

I didn't know what to say, so I just took her hand and squeezed it.

"I was immediately sorry after I threw it all away. I mean most people aren't as sentimental as I am, and I know I hold on to the past too tightly, but those were the best times, weren't they?" she sniffed.

The little plate that I'd found and turned into a pin was the only thing she had left of her son's childhood – the one time he had loved her like she'd wanted to be loved. "I'm not sure," I replied honestly. "Maybe the times ahead could be even better. I mean, I hope they can."

"Not for me," she said sadly, "I've missed out on so much already. I've never been asked to babysit or tag along anywhere or spend a weekend. I am a grandmother in name only; inside I am an empty shell. Some wounds will never heal."

"I don't believe that, not for a minute," I countered. I took off the makeshift pin and secured it on her scarf. "I found this in the sand near Stratford Avenue and I believe miracles happen every day."

She smiled and hugged me tightly. "Thank you so much, Sandy."

Dillan and the rest of the crew gathered on the beach hauling their buckets and bags of trash. "Anyone interested in some chowder?" he asked. "I hear the CHEGG has finally reopened!"

"Come on, Janine," I urged. "Let's talk more over a cup of New England clam chowder. Dillan's been waiting for that place to reopen. He says their chowder is *boss!*"

There was quite a crowd at the CHEGG, but that didn't deter us from getting in line. There was no table for fifteen, so we split up and sat as tables became available. I sat with Janine at a table for two in the back, which couldn't have worked out better. Dillan sat nearby with five of his friends.

I liked everything about the place, from the quirky chicken paintings, huge Barber Shop sign, New Jersey-shaped sculpture made from license plates, wall-mounted surfboard and all things fowl decorating the room. The room was noisy to say the least, even with so many of the patrons stuffing their faces with delicious-smelling food. I perused the vast and varied menu and looked over at Dillan with a befuddled expression. He jumped up and sauntered over.

"Order whatever you'd like, ladies. I'm buying."

Janine said, "That's really nice of you but . . . ."

"No buts about it," Dillan interrupted. "It's my pleasure. Any friend of Sandy's is a friend of mine."

"There's so much to choose from and it all sounds so good. I want it all," I said playfully.

"We'll come again, girl. There's always next time."

"Promise?"

"I promise. They make a mean breakfast, too. I'm all over the *Local Yolkal.*"

"Let me see," I said as I read the menu. "Oh, here it is, under combinations: Two eggs, two strips of bacon, home fries and toast with your choice of pancakes or French toast. Sounds perfect!"

"Yeah, but since you're a CHEGG virgin and knowing your preference for seafood, I think you should try the Buffalo Shrimp with the mild sauce," he offered. "You'll love it, but make sure you get some New England clam chowder too. I think it's one of the best on the island."

"I agree," Janine said, "It's one of my favorites."

Dillan gave my forearm a gentle squeeze then went back to sit with Mitch and the gang. Janine and I ordered from a broad-shouldered, dark-skinned waiter with a thousand-watt smile.

"Good afternoon, ladies. Do you have any questions about the menu?" he asked politely.

"I don't; do you, Janine?"

"No, the menu and I are well acquainted."

"I have a non-menu question." I piped.

"Okay, shoot."

"Why do you look so happy?"

"Me? Many reasons, but mostly because we got the restaurant finished on time and I've got my old job back."

"I always thought being a waiter would be hard work," Janine commented.

"Our place is always packed so it's non-stop but I love meeting new people and seeing familiar faces year after year. It builds biceps, abs and glutes too!" he added, flexing and squatting.

We both giggled as he went to place our order. Once he'd returned with our mugs and a pot of coffee, I finally got to hear a little more of Janine's story. She broke down numerous times during our conversation but always quickly recovered.

"I swear: one of these times I won't be able to stop crying. I'm just going to cry until I disappear into a puddle. I only get to see them every few months, but every time they would bring up moving to Florida. I would wait and wait for that visit and then they would ruin it. It's hard to explain how it made me feel, but it was almost like they were doing it on purpose to hurt me. They know how much I love those kids. They know they're what I live for, and if they moved away, well . . . I'd have nothing."

"Did you ever tell him how you feel? Did you ask to see your grandchildren more often?"

"Oh my God, yes. It seemed the more I asked, the more he pulled away. If I called, he was too busy to answer or return it. I tried three times one week. I actually got worried that something terrible had happened."

"Seems inconsiderate of him."

"He told me once that 'he didn't even have time to talk to his high school friends anymore.' That was supposed to make me feel better? I am his mother! If he doesn't need me, at least he should respect me."

"So, what do you think the problem is?"

"I don't know where to start. I'm sure his wife doesn't like me and maybe I didn't give her enough reason to. I tried but maybe I saw her as the enemy all along. She was taking my son away and he was all I had. I had no husband, no other children. When he moved an hour away to live with her, it wasn't the end of the world, but when they wouldn't let me help with the babies, it completely broke my heart. They grow up so fast, you see. The time for cuddling is so very short. I was deprived of a grandmother's right, I think, and

I will never get that back. My own grandmother and I were very close. She died when I was only ten."

The tears started flowing again and I couldn't imagine all the bottled-up emotions this poor woman had inside. It appeared like a whole lifetime's worth. With each sigh she uttered, I imagined her pain and I began to wonder about my own relationship with my parents. Had we been close? Did I appreciate them? Had I disappointed them? Did they love me unconditionally? Were they even still living? My one and only vague memory of them was of my father's voice. It was loving and kind and full of adoration. With this new awareness, I began to feel guilty having not done more to find my true identity. I'd become *Sandy* quite easily and I really liked her. As far as I knew, she and I shared the same personality but what if that whack on the head had changed me? What if before the storm I was a different person?

It seemed just moments later the waiter returned with the check. I was so engrossed in Janine's saga that although I had eaten, I had barely thought to taste the food. She seemed like such a lovely person. I couldn't imagine how her son or anyone, for that matter, could treat her so callously. I knew there must be some horrible misunderstanding that drove the wedge between them. Maybe all they needed was a little outside intervention – some tiny catalyst to start the healing process.

"Oh Sandy, look at the time! I have to head back to Suzanne's. She's visiting her daughter and I told her I'd take care of the animals. Some zookeeper I am! She'll kick me out if I'm not careful."

As she put on her scarf she saw the pin, smiled and sighed. "I can't thank you enough for finding my little plate. I love my son so much."

"I'm very glad I found it too! I wish you the best of luck, honestly." I stood up, gave her a huge hug and walked her over to Dillan's table.

"Can you please give Janine your number in case we need to get in touch?" I asked him.

"Of course."

"You can always reach me on his phone. We're oddly inseparable," I whispered in her ear.

"Thank you for the meal, Dillan. It's been lovely meeting you two."

"No problem, Janine. Knowing Sandy, I'm sure we'll see you again!"

"You've been awfully kind listening to me carry on this way," Janine said as I walked her toward the door, "Perhaps you're heaven sent?"

She offered me a wistful smile then rushed back into the world, but not before she'd shown me pictures of her family and told me where they lived. Seemed this angel had a mission.

DILLAN

APRIL/MAY 2013

AS THE DAYS GREW longer and warmer, the island took on a renewed energy. More and more people were coming across the causeway to check out our progress, look for summer jobs, volunteer for beach cleanups or book weekly or seasonal rentals. LBI depended on the influx of humanity that happened every season for its survival and as the weekends became more crowded, I could sense the anticipation of a successful season growing. It felt like everyone's hard work was going to pay off.

Even though Sandy and I hadn't been sharing the bed, there was an unwelcome step backward in our relationship when we had to vacate our bedroom to renovate that area. We hadn't ever made love, but I couldn't imagine loving anyone more. Now I couldn't even gaze upon her as she slept in the moonlight, something I found solace in when I had trouble sleeping.

Mitch and Dave came by in early April and helped us install the whitewashed cabinets and black granite countertops in Mac's wing. We then moved the range downstairs to join a French-door refrigerator, dishwasher and range hood that had arrived via delivery truck. Their kitchen completed, sans the tile backsplash, was fairly magazine worthy.

Mitch had been smiling like a Cheshire cat all day, and was stoked to report that he and Katie had taken their relationship to the next level. "Don't lose hope, bro," he said when Sandy had taken Buoy to the park. "Patience and persistence pays off!" He pried the tops off a couple of Heinekens and, handing one to me, suggested the four of us hang out at the Hud sometime. After a couple glasses of wine, Katie could nonchalantly ask Sandy about her feelings and report back. Taking a large gulp of beer, I wondered if I wanted to know the truth about anything.

"You've been living together for months, dude. What's takin' so long?" Mitch asked, sounding annoyed.

"It's complicated."

"I'd wait a good long time to tap that," Dave said.

"Hey, that's the love of my life you're talking about."

"Last summer, Anna was the love of your life," he retorted.

"I couldn't have been more wrong about her, but that bullshit pushed me to the East Coast, where I was meant to be. Don't know how else I would have gotten here."

"Your woman rode a hurricane to get to you," Mitch announced, as he set his empty bottle down. "All this romance talk is making me horny. Let's finish this up so I can go meet Katie."

All the walls were primed and we were waiting for Shona to text us with her color choices. We'd apply the crown molding and baseboards after we finished painting, tiling the bathrooms and the kitchenettes. Barring any catastrophes, the place would be move-in ready on time. It's a good thing Shona wanted to do her own decorating or it would have made the inn feel even more like home than it already did. Wonderful memories of simple times: sharing a bottle of wine and a pizza or home-cooked meal, a neck rub, the haircut. The occasional kiss on the cheek and the time we practically made out (totally worth getting that slap), chasing each other around, just being crazy, having fun. The inn had become a labor of love that would be difficult to leave.

We had our share of bangs and bruises which included sore muscles from squatting and lifting and stiff necks from painting the ceilings. These were aches and pains of accomplishment and nothing that a hot bath, muscle rub and Motrin couldn't handle. I actually whacked my thumb with a hammer as I watched Sandy bend over to retrieve a roll of painter's tape that had rolled under the couch. Another time, while standing on a stepladder, I hit my head on a beam trying to get a glimpse down her shirt and, most recently, I stepped in a paint tray as I watched her strip down to her tank top. I told myself I was keeping an eye on her so she wouldn't hurt herself but the truth was I couldn't take my eyes off her. Any appearance of her lightly bronzed skin made me lose my mind. Her perpetual tan led me to wonder if she might also be of Polynesian descent, making the connection between her and the evil demigod more plausible. Unfortunately, even with Jack's help, we were no closer to the truth than when he first appeared. He seemed to apparate like a wizard from the Harry Potter movies.

By May, most of the shops and restaurants had reopened for the season: The Hand Store, Murphy's Market, Acme grocery, Bay Village, Uncle Will's Pancake House, The Chowder Hut, B&B Department Store, Buckalew's Tavern, Panzone's Pizza, and my favorite, Subs and Such. *You Can't Beat Our Meat*, they boasted and I had to agree. The Italian combo with roasted red peppers rocked! Sandy said, "If I had to get shipwrecked somewhere, this was the perfect place. Not only have I found a family, I've gained a whole new appreciation for food." She loved the Down East Lobster Roll and Old Bay Fries at The Blue Water Cafe and the Buffalo Shrimp at the CHEGG, but she swore that the clambake I made for her was the best thing she'd ever eaten!

On the first perfect beach day, we took a break from work hoping for a good long swim. Sandy, whose bikini had practically driven me to my knees, was afloat only fifteen minutes before she fled the cold water for the warmth of the sun, sand and a beach towel. She insisted that I get my wettie and have a paddle with the guys, but I knew I wouldn't enjoy myself while she and Buoy sat and waited. Every minute away from her left her vulnerable not only to the Hawaiian jackass but any other male, age fourteen and over, who passed by.

Though we hadn't seen the Hawaiian scum in months, I always *felt* him nearby, lurking in the dark and around every corner. He'd appeared in my dreams more often than not, usually dragging a screaming Sandy out the front door of the inn as I stood paralyzed. Sometimes, with his massive leg, he would give Buoy a crushing kick in the ribs, just to be a dick. I'd watch in horror as my buddy crumpled to the floor, whimpering in agony. That's about the time

I'd wake up with my heart pounding and I'd have to walk across the hall to make sure they were safe. I guess my subconscious was simply reiterating how helpless I felt against this ghost from the past – the butt-crumb who knew Sandy's secrets, the a-hole who held all the cards. I was looking forward to leaving that threat behind as we planned our trip to Cocoa Beach, where we'd hang out with my parents and enjoy Florida's comfortably warm, familiar waters.

We wouldn't finish work on the inn until we returned from Cocoa Beach, but the end of the project was looming. Months of hard work had somehow flown by and suddenly the time I had been dreading was upon me. *Would Sandy stay with me?* I'd grown so accustomed to having her by my side that I felt like a different person – a more amped, chill, hopeful, complete person. With Sandy's encouragement, I found I could rebuild a crumbling brick fireplace, plant a fairy garden and bake chocolate chip cookies from scratch, just like Mom's. I felt that with her by my side, there wasn't anything I couldn't do – even shoot the curl, given the opportunity. If she left, I knew my life would suck for a very long time.

SANDY

MAY 2013

THOUGH MANY OF OUR island neighbors were still reeling from the effects of the Superstorm, we could see a light forming at the end of our post-hurricane tunnel. Suddenly, the thought of happy vacationers staying in our home had become foreboding. Even though Dillan had a contract with Mac, I found myself asking if we could take day trips instead of working. We visited the Marine Mammal Stranding Center, took a fishing charter from Viking Village, visited the Popcorn Park Zoo, climbed to the top of Barnegat Lighthouse, toured the Tuckerton Seaport and wined and dined at the Renault Winery. Dillan was more than happy to do all those things, leaving me feeling somewhat guilty. We'd have to work extra-long hours when we returned from Florida to make up for my procrastination.

I was hoping Jacqueline Rose would be coming home at the end of the semester, but in an effort to catch up, she might have signed up for summer classes. Her artwork was beautiful, her spirit inspiring and I truly admired her determination. After she'd met Jack, things just seemed to fall into place. Somehow that experience meant both closure and new beginnings for both. I was hoping the same luck would follow me as we headed upstate to find Janine's son.

Dillan wasn't happy about me wandering around some distant condominium complex alone, so he engaged a real estate agent to show him some available units. This way, he'd remain *undercover* while I carried out operation *Family-101*. We joked about being spies or detectives and Dillan kept calling me Felicity Shagwell, whoever she was.

From talking to Janine, I'd learned that there was a playground near her son's condo. I theorized that on a beautiful Saturday afternoon, it was bound to be teeming with children and their parents. Chances were slim they'd be the particular parents I'd wanted to meet, but I felt it was worth a shot. Anything to help mend the gap that had torn Janine's family apart.

Dillan parked in the shade in an unnumbered space. I jumped out and grabbed my purse and books from the back where Buoy waited, eager to lick my face. "Thanks, big guy. I love you too," I said as I scratched behind his ears. We were early for Dillan's appointment, so he decided to take Buoy for a walk around the complex. We headed down the hill together. "Wish me luck," I said, as we came to a split in the road.

"I'm not sure you'll need it, seeing the way you have with people, but good luck, girl. I hope you find them and work your magic."

Dillan had google-mapped the complex so I knew exactly were the playground was. He turned around and headed back the way we'd come and I followed the main road around to the left. In a few minutes, the trees gave way to a fenced-in area which housed a wooden jungle gym, a blacktopped area and a large patch of fresh new spring grass. There were a handful of parents and children there, each occupied with one activity or another.

Just as I reached the fence, a child fell from her bike and cried out. As the father ran to her aid, a toddler took off in the opposite direction, directly toward the gate. I jogged toward the opening and scooped the boy up just seconds before he would have reached the road.

"Excuse me," I yelled. "Does this belong to you?"

In that split second, when the look on the man's face registered, I knew exactly what it felt like to be a parent.

He grabbed the girl and ran toward us. "Hey, that's my son!" he yelled in a panicked voice.

I carried the towheaded boy into the fenced area, placed him down, closed the gate and made sure it was latched.

"Well, he could've been a pancake!" I replied more concerned than accusing.

"Oh my God! I thought you were trying to kidnap him."

"Nope, I was just walking by as he hightailed it right through the gate."

As the excitement of the moment began to settle, I realized I had struck the jackpot. How serendipitous it was when I recognized from Janine's photos Liam, Connor, and Ellie. The beautiful little girl was staring at me with big blue eyes and rubbing her elbow.

"Thank you," he said with a deep sigh, heavy with gratitude. "I wish these people would make sure the gate is latched. I'm going to insist there be a huge sign attached to it. I don't care how aesthetically pleasing it is to the masses!"

"I'm glad I was here to help. I imagine it's hard keeping track of two little ones."

"You don't know the half of it. These two don't stop till they drop!"

"Do you think anyone would mind if I sat over there and read my book?" I asked, motioning to the empty wooden bench near the jungle gym.

"Of course not."

"What kind of story do you have?" Ellie asked.

"Well," I said as I reached into my Beach Haven bag, "I have a grown-up book about a lady who works in a bakery and a couple of books about the ocean and the mysterious creatures that live in the sea," I said with flair as I showed her the covers.

"Are there mermaids in your book? I love Ariel. She has no voice but then she sings."

"I'm not sure. Do you want to read them with me?" I asked.

"Ellie, I'm sure this nice lady just wants to relax. Why don't you go play with some of your friends?"

"But Daddy!"

"I don't mind, if it's okay with you. My name is Sandy, by the way."

"I'm Liam; nice to meet you."

I was desperate to engage him in conversation but Connor was pulling him toward the swings. Thankfully he noticed my Beach Haven purse.

"Beach Haven!" he remarked, "Have you been?"

"I'm living there right now."

"Really? I heard it's pretty terrible since the storm. My mom lives there. My childhood home was badly damaged."

"I'm sorry to hear that." I couldn't resist, so I asked, "Is she staying here with you then?"

"Oh no. She's down there living with a friend."

"That's too bad. Maybe she could have helped you with the kids!"

"I don't know. Maybe she could have, but we just don't have the room."

"Is Grammy gonna come live with us, Daddy?" Ellie asked excitedly.

"No, Grammy lives at the beach. You know that. It's a long way away."

"I like the beach. I like building sandcastles and swimming and finding shells and everything.... but I miss Grammy," Ellie said thoughtfully. "My Grammy likes to bake us cookies."

"Cookies!" Connor added with a smile.

"Grandmothers are great at baking and coloring and playing too," I added encouragingly.

"I want to play with Grammy!" Ellie proclaimed, stamping her foot.

"Grammy!" Connor mimicked.

"Sorry," I said to Liam. "I didn't mean to start a war."

"It's not the start of anything. More like an ongoing battle," he said as he picked up the tot.

"Oh, that's unfortunate. I don't remember my parents, but I hope we weren't at odds with each other.

"Why don't you remember your mommy and daddy?" Ellie asked, puzzled.

"I got a big bump on my head. It made me forget a lot."

"Amnesia? That's got to be tough!" Liam commented.

"I *imagine* my mother and I are kindred spirits. I know in my heart we'll be reunited someday," I said wistfully.

"Well, I'm so busy with my routine that sometimes I forget Mom even exists – and she's probably just sitting around waiting for me to call," he added sounding miffed.

Ellie climbed on the bench and started perusing one of my books.

"If you did call her once in a while, it'd probably make all the difference."

"My mom loves us," he said, as he playfully jostled the toddler to and fro. "She just doesn't understand how busy and stressed out I am. She expects us to drop everything and fit her in. I swear we don't have a spare minute."

"Maybe you could let her help with the kids once in a while. An occasional afternoon of you-time might reset your psyche."

"It sounds good but seems impossible. You know how long an hour drive is with two kids?"

"An hour?" I answered sheepishly.

"Yeah, but it's an hour that we aren't doing laundry, dishes, paying bills or vacuuming up crumbs."

"My point exactly. That stuff will always be there, but your family won't. It's good for kids to know there are others that love them as much as you do. You could always invite your mom up here." I could tell by the look on his face that I had touched a nerve and was beginning to feel like I was pushing the limits of polite conversation.

"She and my wife are like oil and vinegar. Liz has little patience for Mom. She finds her impractical and melodramatic." He leaned in a bit closer, "She doesn't even want her to come here," he said quietly so the kids wouldn't hear.

"With a little coaxing, oil and vinegar can make a great salad dressing." I said encouragingly.

"You have a positive outlook about things. I do miss my mom once in a while, but this is a crazy, busy life and the days fly by. I can't believe how big the kids are already. Seems like yesterday Ellie was a baby. Now look at the little monster she's become!" he said jokingly as he messed her long blonde hair.

"I'm not a monster, Daddy. I'm a mermaid princess," she countered as she pushed his hand away, "Connor is the little monster!"

"Monster!" he parroted.

"He says a lot of words for a little guy."

"Daycare has got its good points. Unfortunately, it's not like anyone raises their own kids anymore."

"Were you brought up in daycare too?" I asked, fishing.

"Nope. My parents divorced when I was a kid but with the child support, alimony and rental income from our duplex, Mom only had to work part time."

"Your father was part of your life?"

"Not so much, but my grandfather was a great father figure. He spent a lot of time with me when I was a kid."

"Is he still living?" I asked.

"Yeah, both my grandparents are and they're in pretty good shape too."

"They must adore their great-grandchildren. How lucky they are to have each other!"

"Well, like I said, we're very busy, so we rarely get to visit."

"That's really a shame. I can't think of anything more important than family."

"Such is the way of the twenty-first century."

I felt a little tug on my arm, "Will you read to me?" Ellie asked. "Please."

"Sure, as long as it's okay with your daddy."

"Yes, of course. I'm going to push Connor on the swing for a few minutes. I'll be right over there, Ellie."

"Okay, Daddy."

"Do you know my Grammy?" Ellie asked as soon as her dad was out of earshot.

How perceptive children can be. "Yes, I do. She told me that she loves you to the moon and back one hundred thousand times."

"Me too!" Ellie said.

Although we enjoyed reading about the ocean, the beach and the creatures that lived there, Ellie was obviously disappointed that there were no mermaids in the books. I explained that these were books about real living things not make-believe ones. She just shook her head defiantly. "Mermaids are real!" she said, slamming the book closed.

"How do you know?" I asked curiously.

"Because my Grammy told me so! She said when mermaids play dress-up, seahorses wrap themselves in their hair and around their fingers and they play fetch with the dolphins and they sunbathe in moonbeams!"

"I guess you must be right, Ellie. Tomorrow when I take a walk on the beach, I'm going to look for one."

"You won't see them unless they want you to. They're magic, silly."

I reached into my purse and pulled out a large scallop shell. "Would you like this?" I asked. "I think it might have belonged to a mermaid. I found it on the beach near my house."

Ellie giggled uncontrollably. "That's what mermaids wear to cover their boobies!"

Janine's grandchildren were truly as wonderful as she described but unfortunately my little chat with her son hadn't gone as well as I'd hoped. He certainly didn't seem to experience an epiphany or say anything that made me feel that things would improve. He had lots of excuses and rightly so. Life was like a marathon; you ran or you didn't keep up. I didn't want to find myself in that crazy race. Though I would miss my new little friends, I was ready to go home to island life and island time.

DILLAN

LATE MAY 2013

I HAD HOPED WE could take in some sites at Baltimore's Inner Harbor on the way to Florida, but the many day trips we'd taken had put us behind schedule. I wasn't sure why Sandy suddenly wanted to experience every local attraction she'd read about in *The SandPaper*, but I was afraid she planned on leaving and never coming back. Perhaps I shouldn't have obliged her so freely. Now we had to drive south directly to have a decent amount of time with Mom and Dad. I certainly didn't want to disappoint them by cutting our visit short.

When I pulled my duffle bag out of the closet, I came across Seaquin's artwork and the seahorse ring I had hidden there after our visit to the aquarium. Weeks ago, at CVS, I had printed out some photos, including a fantastic shot of Luseal kissing Sandy and stuck it in the corner of the frame. I'd been waiting for the right time to give them to her, but it had never come. Now would be as good a time as any. I placed the gifts on her bed so she'd have a surprise when she returned from the B&B Department Store.

I shoved some shorts, trunks, tees and tanks into the duffle bag along with sunscreen, a baseball cap, zinc oxide, flip-flops, and boxers. I threw one of Henry's mystery novels in, just in case I got tired of the water – though I couldn't imagine that happening. I heard Buoy bark from downstairs signaling Sandy's return.

"How'd you make out?" I yelled down the stairs.

"I got some nice things – perfect for Florida and I went into the How To Live store," she replied as she came up. "It's really cool!"

"Good to hear they've overcome."

"Yeah, they had a waterline of forty-two inches painted on the display window and a huge painting titled *Love Song For Long Beach Island* that would be perfect for the parlor.

"How much?"

"I don't think it was for sale but it would've been a lovely way to welcome the guests. The owner's an artist and writer who designs her own books and greeting cards. They are so sweet and inspirational. They really make you think about what's important in life. I think I'd like to try writing poetry."

"I'm sure you'd be great at it. You can do anything!"

"I appreciate your faith in me. I hope you don't mind, but I bought myself a pair of earrings – they just sort of spoke to me."

"Listen girl, anytime something whispers, *buy me*, feel free to get it. I can't ever repay you for everything you've done for Buoy and me."

"They didn't say *that* exactly, it was more like, 'Don't we look cute?'"

"Well, whatever they said, I'm more than happy to oblige. You could buy yourself ten pair of earrings and I wouldn't mind in the least."

"Thank you, Dillan. Aren't they adorable?" she asked as she pulled the dangly seahorse earrings out of the bag. I shook my head and rolled my eyes as they matched the ring exactly.

"Don't you like them?"

"Great minds think alike," I said, as I grabbed her hand and led her to the bedroom. I picked up the small gift box and handed it to her. After we finished laughing, she kissed my cheek and I placed the ring on her middle finger.

"What am I going to do with you?" she asked.

"What are you going to do without me?" I replied in a serious tone.

"I have no idea," she said, sounding worried.

"Just stay," I said, taking her hand and looking into her beautiful blue-green eyes, "*Please*."

She shook her head and shrugged her shoulders, "I don't know if I can."

"Here – there's something else," I said as I flipped over the 11x14 framed piece of art.

One glance of the large colorful brushstrokes and she burst into tears – nailed it! She grabbed a hold and held me tight but after a bit her happy tears turned into sobs of frustration.

"I have to take a walk on the beach – alone. I have to think. I'll be back in a little bit."

"At least take Buoy with you. I'd feel better," I said, knowing she'd have some protection and would have to return if only to bring him home.

"Of course. I just need to clear my head."

Later that evening, I watched casually as Sandy packed her duffle bags, hoping that she wouldn't take all her meager belongings.

"Are you excited about the trip?" I asked.

"I'm happy to be meeting your parents, but I'm not sure what they'll think of me."

"What do you mean? They'll love you."

"Not if I end up breaking your heart, they won't."

"Then don't do it."

She sat and motioned for me to sit next to her on the bed. "I'm sorry but there's something I haven't told you," she said in a whisper.

I felt my heart sink. This was it. She was leaving and never coming back. "Do you know who you are?" I asked as my throat tightened.

"No, but I had a memory. I hated it and so will you."

I took her hand. "I guess you'd better get to the gnarly truth then."

"The Hawaiian jackass . . . I remembered something about him."

"Is he your *boyfriend*?"

"No! I don't know. Maybe. I hope not!" she sputtered.

"What do you remember?"

"His name is Waimoku. He's kissed me once – and not very gently."

"Gentle *would* seem out of character. When did it happen?"

"I don't know exactly but we were somewhere tropical, lush – standing in a waterfall."

"Sounds like a honeymoon."

"*Please!* You said I'd have enough sense not to marry a creep like that, remember?"

"You're right, I'm sorry. That was a combination of jealousy and anger speaking. Can you tell me how it happened?"

"He pushed me against the rocky ledge and pressed the length of his weight against me. I can remember the pain of the rocks as they dug into my back. He used one hand to hold my arms over my head, and the other he wound in my hair leaving me completely immobile."

"Bastard!"

"That's too kind."

"Alright – fucker!"

"Yeah, a real one."

"Did he stop . . . after that one kiss?" I asked fearfully.

"I *really* hope so, but I'm not sure. That's all I can remember, but I've had some other, less intrusive memories."

"Why haven't you told me?"

"It's nothing big, just sometimes when I'm drifting off to sleep I hear my father's words in my head. At least I feel like he's my father. I don't even know for sure."

"What is he saying?"

"Sometimes he says, Manaʻo Nani, sometimes he's saying Aloha."

"You mean like in *hello*?"

"No, like in *good-bye*," she said with a sad finality.

I hated to admit it, but I'd been keeping a secret too. "I have a confession also," I said sheepishly. "I saw this Waimoku A-hole outside the night of the turkey dinner."

"What??"

"Buoy chased him around the block and ripped off a piece of his stupid Hawaiian shirt."

"He was here! Why didn't you tell me?"

"Probably the same reason you didn't tell me about your memory."

"*I was afraid it would upset you,*" we both said in unison.

"I *could* be from Hawaii," Sandy stated bluntly, "but how did I end up here?"

"A miracle?" I replied.

"A lot of miracles never get explanations," she said with a sigh.

"Hawaii is worth checking out. Anyway, I've always wanted to go there."

"You'd take me there?" she asked, sounding astounded.

"Don't you get it? There's nothing I wouldn't do for you. Once we get back from Florida, put the finishing touches on this place, and I get paid, we'll make a plan for Hawaii."

"I love . . . thank you, Dillan," she said, "You're my best friend."

"And you mine. Let's get some sleep so we can get an early start."

SANDY

COCOA BEACH

LATELY AND ESPECIALLY AFTER what just happened, my insides had been feeling like a storm-churned sea. I needed fresh air, sand and a distant horizon to help clear my head. As I grabbed Buoy's leash from the newel post, I looked at the seahorse ring Dillan had placed on my finger. If he ever uttered the words *I love you*, I'd cave like a sandcastle left to defy high tide. I clipped the leash on Buoy's collar and headed outdoors. We crossed the street at the Coral Seas Motel and were at the dune a few steps later. I kicked off my flip-flops and left them behind. When we reached the crest, we were immediately refreshed by a cool breeze and salty air.

I looked north and south. Except for a few surfers, the beach belonged to us. We walked across the soft sand, down to the water's edge where it turned firm and chilly under my toes. I took a deep breath and let the dull rumble of the waves relax me. Some little crabs were scurrying about a pile of seaweed, almost begging us to chase them. Buoy stuck his nose down to smell them, barked, then looked at me for instruction.

"Let them be, friend. They mean us no harm." What a wonderful world mantra that would be. Out at sea, a pod of dolphins followed the shoreline north and I thought about the fish they ate, poisoned with mercury and a thousand other pollutants.

Again, I was saddened to think that humans could be so completely selfish, short-sighted and idiotic. If we were the first species on the planet to disappear, wouldn't every other creature be better off? I sighed deeply and Buoy looked up at me. My own problems seemed minuscule compared to that of mankind. Then I thought of Henry and all the wonderful people I had met – strangers and locals who, working together, found the strength to clean up, rip down and rebuild. New friendships were formed; new bonds were made. Gratitude prevailed over desperation and despair. Animal lovers donated time and money to care for unwanted and lost pets. Dedicated people from the ALO were doing their best to make the beaches cleaner and the ocean water healthier. The aquarium was helping to keep the endangered African penguin and poor polar bears from becoming extinct. There were decent, caring people in the world and I wanted to find my place among them, by being part of the solution.

Buoy and I continued along, stepping over an occasional jellyfish, our feet graced by sea foam that washed up then quickly disappeared. After we passed the second jetty, we spotted a school of stingray gliding in the surf close to shore. We watched as they moved so gracefully north, then turning, and south again. I wasn't sure what was causing their activity but my guess was it had something to do with food. Sandpipers ran to and fro at the water's edge, dipping their beaks in the sand, searching for some tiny morsels. Black-headed laughing gulls hunkered down against the breeze, while young herring gulls loudly pestered their parents for a meal.

I sat in the sand and stared out to sea, Buoy at my side. Four brown pelicans flew south over the water. I began to feel more peaceful and centered – such was the magic of the ocean. We stayed until the setting sun reflected a bright scarlet on the wispy clouds above, then headed home. I still needed to polish my toenails and pack for what I hoped would be a wonderful vacation. Though we'd made pleasantries on the phone, I wasn't sure how Dillan's parents felt about my enigmatic past or the fact that we'd lived together for almost seven months.

The longest car trip I remembered taking was when we went to see Fiona in the hospital. That paled in comparison to the eight hours we drove the first day heading south. Luckily, Dillan took pity on us and made frequent pit stops.

"It feels good to stretch my muscles," I said as I bent side to side, then touched my toes a few times after climbing out of the Jeep.

"Good thing we have Buoy along or I wouldn't be stopping so frequently," he teased as he helped Buoy out, then gave my shoulder a gentle squeeze.

"Ohhh, that feels good," I responded automatically. He immediately handed me the leash, placed both hands on my shoulders and started giving me a neck massage.

"Oh my gosh . . . that's fantastic," I cooed as Buoy stood there, looking up at me pitifully. "I'll massage your old bones on the next leg of the trip," I promised him.

"How about *me*?" Dillan asked. "I'm the one who's got stress knots the size of boulders! It's not easy keeping my eyes peeled for Waimoku while avoiding all the other idiots on the road."

"I'll give you a neck rub before bed."

"Promise?"

"Yes, I promise."

"That's boss!"

We stopped in Florence, South Carolina and got a room at the Country Inn Hotel. We took Buoy for a good walk, then had a swim in the outdoor pool to really stretch our muscles. Once Buoy was fed and settled in our cool room, we realized we were starving. We inquired at the front desk, where they recommended the Red Bone Alley Restaurant which was only a mile or two down the road. I had a hard time deciding between Low Country Shrimp and Grits and the Blackened Shrimp with cornbread. Dillan had no trouble choosing the Blue Crab Cakes, which he hoped would ease the disappointment of missing our stop in Baltimore. By the time we finished eating I could barely keep my eyes open.

"Would y'all like coffee or dessert?" our waitress asked in a friendly southern drawl.

"None for me, thanks; I just want a comfortable bed."

"How about you, sir?"

"No thanks. I'm just looking forward to a comfortable bed *and a massage*."

"Dillan!"

"Okey-dokey, then. I'll be *right* back with the check," she said, giving us a wink.

"I just wanted to remind you of your promise," Dillan added with a smirk.

When we opened the hotel room door, I was relieved to find Buoy looking peaceful and contented. He glanced our way and wagged his tail, thumping the bed loudly.

Dillan picked up the leash, "I hate to do this to you, old friend, but one more pee before bed. We'll be right back."

"Are you going past the vending machine?"

"What's your desire, ma'am?" he asked in a pretty good southern accent.

"Anything sweet, I don't care."

"We could've had dessert at the restaurant."

"I know, but I feel uncomfortable leaving Buoy alone for too long in a strange place."

They returned to find me post shower, with towel-dried hair, lying comfortably in my bed. "Beat you," I said, feeling oddly victorious and ready for sleep.

"I got you a pecan log and a couple of strawberry cookies from the lobby."

"Mmmmm, both sound yummy, but I don't need all that. Will you have something?"

"How about we eat the cookies while they're fresh, and save the candy for tomorrow?"

"Sounds like a plan."

***

" . . . ndy . . . andy . . . Sandy?" I heard from miles away.

"Huh?" I opened my eyes to see Dillan's freshly shaved face two inches from mine.

"Are you asleep?"

"I was!" I answered grumpily. I'd passed out while Dillan was in the shower and didn't even hear him come out of the bathroom.

"I didn't want to wake you, but I was hoping you didn't forget about my neck massage. I'm still awfully stiff and my muscles are all primed from the hot shower."

Shoot! I bet his neck wasn't the only thing that was stiff. I didn't want to renege on my promise, but I didn't want to start something that would probably end up leaving us both frustrated or worse.

"Um . . . do you think – ?"

He cut me off, interjecting, "I'll behave, I swear. No tricks. I won't even attempt to kiss you, though I can't promise I won't be thinking about it."

Dillan lay face down on the bed next to me, forcing Buoy to jump down and hop onto the other.

"What's wrong with your bed?"

"I didn't want you to have to move. Once you're done, I'll go join Buoy."

I don't know why I was so worried. How much trouble could I get into with him in this position anyway? I straddled his backside, placing most of my weight on my knees and squeezed and rubbed his neck and shoulders until my hands and arms ached. Dillan had moaned a little more than I thought necessary, but I could feel the muscles soften under my touch and knew he must be feeling better. After a while I heard his deep restful breaths and knew he was fast asleep. I was going to move to the other bed but Buoy had stretched out across the middle and I didn't want to disturb him. I awoke in the morning cradled in Dillan's arms.

We ate a continental breakfast in the hotel then headed toward the highway, making a quick stop at a Krispy Kreme shop. I'd never had one, that I could remember, and Dillan insisted it was something not to be missed. My belly was full, but he swore that if I could eat it now, fresh out of the fryer, I'd be tasting melt-in-your-mouth perfection. I hated the fact that he was right! I looked down at the box on my lap and wondered how many would be left by the time we reached Cocoa Beach.

The rest of the day was a repeat of the previous: sun, heat, hours in the car with frequent pee breaks. When we got near Jacksonville, Dillan asked me to search his phone for a good spot to stop for lunch. After some discussion, we ended up at a place called Akel's Delicatessen where we ate huge sandwiches at a cafe table in the courtyard. Dillan said there must have been a cold front moving through because it was only eighty-five degrees and quite pleasant in the shade. Even our furry friend looked perfectly comfortable after a nice long drink of cold water and a couple of Milk-Bones.

"We're getting close," Dillan said as we crossed the Indian River onto Merritt Island. "Captain Sandy No-Last-Name, are you prepared to complete this mission, ma'am, or abort?"

"Ready to complete the mission, Commander Sir!"

"Affirmative. Please make appropriate adjustments to the landing instruments," Dillan responded with a chuckle. "I spent many hours at the Kennedy Space Center when I was a kid."

"Did you want to be an astronaut when you grew up?"

"Yup, for like five minutes. Then I wanted to be an archeologist, like Indiana Jones and then a pro surfer, but unless you're amazing you can't make a living that way. Dad wanted me to become a lawyer, of course, while Mom suggested I become a doctor or physician's assistant. None of that was in my blood."

"Everyone has their own path and I think you're on the right one."

"Thanks. You're like my own personal cheerleader."

A little further south I spotted a Ron Jon Surf Shop. "Dillan, look! It's just like home."

"Yeah, I was stoked when I saw the one in Ship Bottom. That's where the original one opened, way back in the sixties! There's other Ron Jon shops too, but this one's the largest surf shop in the world! There's a museum inside and they even have a surfing school – one-stop shopping, not a bad deal."

"The sign says it's open 24 hours – that's crazy."

"They take their surfing pretty seriously around here."

"Hey, I just realized you didn't bring your board!"

"I . . . um, I didn't want to spend time away from you," he replied, sounding sweetly sincere.

"Oh, Dillan, I'll be fine. I can swim or lie in the sun and read a book. I don't need twenty-four hour companionship."

"I see," he said, sounding hurt.

"I didn't mean it that way. I know how much you love to surf and you certainly didn't have time for it at home. You should take advantage while we're here."

"Well, since you're twisting my arm, maybe I'll rent a board."

"I'd love to watch you."

"I'd love to *teach* you."

About ten minutes later, we found the Beach Place Guesthouses tucked between much taller buildings and hidden behind a small grove of trees. If not for the decorative dolphin and palm tree signs we would have missed it completely. The Krispy Kreme box sat partly crushed on the floor by my feet. As Dillan sighed and turned off the ignition, I opened it. "How many donuts did *you* eat?" I asked curiously as he opened his door and a wave of heat flooded in.

"One, maybe two at most," he answered straight-faced.

"That's not possible. You're lying!" I accused, as he laughed guiltily. "Honestly I don't know – they go down way too easily."

The whole trip south, I'd felt nervous about meeting Dillan's parents, which was totally unwarranted. I didn't feel at all slighted when they bypassed Dillan and I for Buoy, who was overjoyed with unbridled puppy passion at seeing them again. I couldn't help but shed a tear or two along with Margie who showered us with hugs and kisses while her husband, Richard, was only slightly more reserved.

The family caught up during a relaxing dinner, served on the patio overlooking the ocean. Even though there were more guest rooms nearby, it felt like we were the only people for miles. As the sun was setting, Dillan proudly scrolled through the before-and-after photos of the inn and discussed the more difficult projects with his dad. I was happy to hear him say what an amazingly fast learner and helper I'd been. If he said, "*I never could have done it without her*" one more time, I was going to bust.

We talked about Jack and Carole's heartbreaking secret and his newly found daughter who, as fate would have it, happened to design our beautiful murals. My eyelids were getting heavy as we chatted about our friend Henry, the famous author, whose books we were planning to read on the beach.

"It'll be interesting to finally hear what *Michael Stocks* has to say," I said to everyone.

"Agreed! I can't wait to see what all the fuss is about," Dillan replied.

"He has quite a following," Richard added. "I read two of his books after I retired – most enjoyable mysteries. I hope your friend's not done writing yet."

"Well, there was mention of a collaboration with Lucas but I don't know how serious it was. Plus, Sandy's been keeping him rather busy, what with the new boarders and animals she's coerced him into adopting."

"He was lonely before. If you heard the way he spoke of Naia . . . I think it's great he has new friends."

"You worked your magic again, girl. He seems very happy. I mean, I didn't know him before but he certainly has a spark for life now."

By ten p.m. and a few drinks later, the discussion came around to my mysterious appearance on Long Beach Island. I was completely honest with them, but afraid that every time I answered with "I can't remember" or "I don't know," they'd think I was lying. I recounted in detail what I could about waking up in the inn, how Buoy had saved me from drowning, those first few weeks on the island and the happiness I felt when Dillan finally appeared.

"That's surely a once in a lifetime experience!" Richard said enthralled.

"I certainly hope so. I wouldn't want to do it again."

"So, you have no idea where you came from?" Margie, who was on her third rum punch, asked me for the umpteenth time.

"I wish I did. I whacked my brain, then wracked my brain for months," I giggled tipsily.

"Couldn't your friend Jack find out *anything*?" Richard asked Dillan, disbelievingly. "I mean, in this day and age, with all the advances in technology and unlimited information readily accessible on the internet?"

"He tried but the few leads we had didn't pan out."

"It's almost as if I don't really exist at all," I added.

"That's a strange thing to say," Margie commented, as she reached for the delicious rum and juice mixture. "Here dear, have a little more."

I held out my glass, not wanting to offend her, "Thank you – it's even stranger to feel," I answered.

"I'm sure you'll find your family soon," she said encouragingly.

"Sometimes I feel like I already have," I replied as I looked across the fire pit at Dillan and Buoy. The big old Lab immediately got up and came to lie by my side.

Margie winked, nodded and raised her glass to me. Either she'd had too much to drink or she honestly liked me. I hoped it was the latter.

We shared a few quiet moments listening to the blissful ocean waves and as I drifted off, I had a vivid dream. "*I hope I will see you again, my dear,*" the old man said as I took his frail hand in mine.

"*Of course you will. I won't be long away,*" I replied as he held me in his loving embrace.

"Just listen to that surf," Margie said, rousing me.

A deep feeling of sadness came over me, but I tried to ignore it. "Yeah, there's nothing like it," I sighed, wondering if the dream was merely that, or memories rising, like bubbles in the sea, into my subconscious.

"Is it this nice in New Jersey?" Margie asked as she lowered the back on the lounger and stretched out.

"It's different. The winter can be dreary but it's lovely this time of year. The hydrangeas, hibiscus and butterfly bushes are starting to burst open. In fact, the whole island seems to be coming back to life after the winter and the destruction from the storm."

"I saw a few videos on the internet. It looked horrible – so much devastation," she shook her head sadly. "Thank God Dillan made it home safely – but we really thought we'd lost Buoy."

"I'm grateful every day," I said as I reached down, yawned and scratched Buoy's head.

"So are we, Sandy."

"I'm afraid I can't keep my eyes open," I said as I yawned again.

"Would you like me to show you to your room?" Margie asked.

"That would be wonderful, but I was going to help with the dishes."

"I'll do them," Dillan said. "You get ready for bed."

"But . . . ."

"No arguments."

"Thanks for everything; dinner was delicious," I said as Margie led me to the guest bedroom.

"You have no idea how thrilled we are to have you, Sandy.

Dillan's a very special person and we're happy he's finally found the *right* girl."

Obviously, Dillan hadn't mentioned the complication known as Waimoku.

"That's very kind of you to say."

She left me sifting through my duffle bag, looking for my PJs.

Dillan knocked on the door as he peaked in the room. "How ya doin'?"

"They're very nice."

"What did you expect?"

"I thought they'd be a bit wary, I guess."

He stepped inside, shut the door and came close. "Well, I told them all about you. What's not to love?"

"You didn't mention Waimoku, did you?"

"I didn't want them to worry."

"I won't say a word either, but it kinda feels like lying."

He kissed me on the forehead and said, "We'll get to the bottom of this Waimoku thing. Try not to let him ruin our vacation."

"I won't give him a second thought."

"Good. Sleep tight and sleep in as late as you want. We have two whole weeks to chill and have fun!"

I wanted to sleep in, I really did, but I was awakened the next morning by a noisy seagull. I padded over to my window and peaked out as a cool breeze caressed my face. The sun was barely up and I didn't want to miss the opportunity for a quiet stroll on the beach. I threw on my bikini, covered up with shorts and a tank, grabbed my flip-flops and headed quietly down the hall. I found Dillan sprawled upon the pull-out couch and Buoy looking at me sleepily from his place in front of the sliding screen – looks like I'd have company after all. As I gently pulled the screen door open, Dillan rolled over. I would've invited him to come along, but after all that driving, I felt he deserved his rest.

I wandered down a stone path, through a dimly lit garden, made unique by the addition of colorful sculptures, large crystal formations, gazing spheres, water fountains and small pools of water. Tall wooden fences made the space seem secluded and storybook worthy. I peered among the flowers and plants for the fairies I imagined living there. I did spot a butterfly, slowly beating its wings, in a ray of sunlight. "Good morning little friend," I whispered.

I heard the waves as I emerged on the beach where we'd hung out the night before. Upon the many decks that overlooked the ocean were a variety of umbrellas, tables and chairs, loungers, firepits, grills, water features, sculptures and hammocks. We came upon a large colorful sculpture that functioned as a shower, where we could rinse our sandy feet.

Buoy and I followed a long, narrow path past the dune shrubbery and grass, then across the wide beach to the water's edge. The gentle surf was cool for the briefest moment, then felt like bath water. Though I had come to love Long Beach Island, this was something else entirely. As I looked back, it was hard to believe that our quaint two-story guesthouses and gardens sat between two good-sized condos.

We headed south, Buoy leading the way, enjoying the rising sun as it brought the world back to life. Somewhere along the way, a feeling of familiarity had crept over me. I knew, almost certainly, that I'd been here before. Was our plan of going to Hawaii a total misreading of the clues? I stopped and looked around, hoping a more specific memory would emerge, but nothing came. I looked at the ocean, wishing for answers, then stripped off my clothes and waded out into the gentle surf. Buoy followed and began paddling joyfully. When the water reached my waist, I held my breath and dove under. Immediately I felt the seductive pull of deeper waters. I swam out a bit then back quickly, not wanting to tire my old friend out. I could get used to this place.

Everyone was up when we returned, though Dillan was in the shower.

"I'm so glad you're back!" Margie said as if she was afraid I might have skipped town. "Did you two have a little swim?"

"Just a dip to cool off. I hope you don't mind that Buoy and I took a walk."

"Goodness no, of course not! We want you to be happy while you're here. You kids come and go as you please."

"I know I said we were going to relax today," Dillan said during breakfast, "but I really want to show you my old stomping grounds."

"Sure, I'm game for whatever you want to do," I replied as I finished a good-sized portion of juicy tropical fruit salad.

"You guys want to come along?" Dillan asked his parents who were sitting on the nearby lounge chairs, shaded by bright canvas umbrellas.

"No, you two go have fun. We'll watch Buoy today," Margie replied, "Do you think you'll be home for dinner?"

"Of course, Mom. What time do you want us?"

"How about seven? We'll grill some shrimp and veggies – nothing fancy."

"I love shrimp," I gushed.

"We were hoping you'd say that. Weren't we, Richard?"

"You bet," he replied, barely looking up from his newspaper."

"Living with Sandy's given me a whole new appreciation for seafood. It's practically all she eats!" Dillan said jokingly.

"That's not true!"

"It most certainly is!"

"Well maybe," I conceded.

"Would anyone like more eggs or coffee?" Margie asked.

"I've had plenty, Mom, thanks."

"I'm stuffed," I replied. "Breakfast was delicious."

"Thank you, Sandy. Anything you need, pretend that you're at home."

Oddly enough, I did feel at home, though I felt at home on LBI, too. I had this undeniable feeling that wherever Dillan and Buoy laid their heads at night was my home.

"I'll go load the dishwasher, then we'll head up to the pier," Dillan said as he pushed back his chair.

"That's not necessary, hon. I'll do it in a bit. You're on vacation, remember?"

"So are you, Mom."

"Yes, but we're retired. Every day's a vacation for us."

"You can say that again," Richard said sounding bored.

Dillan got up from the table and took my hand. "Let's go grab some towels and sunscreen, girl. I think you're gonna love it around here."

"I already do."

A few minutes later, Dillan peered in my bedroom. "This place has a whole storeroom of beach stuff we can borrow, so I've loaded up the

Jeep. Are you ready?"

"Almost. I just need to finish packing my bag."

"I forgot women need to take everything but the kitchen sink."

"Well, I wanted to bring one of Henry's books. This one is called *Obsessed in Key West*," I said as I held it up for Dillan to see.

"I thought about that too. I've got *Slow Burn in Bermuda*."

"I feel kinda bad leaving your parents. I mean we just got here last night. Don't they want to go to the pier with us?"

"I asked again but they said they just wanted to relax today."

"Okay, if they're sure. I'll be ready in a couple of minutes."

We said good-bye to Margie, Richard and Buoy then headed north in the Jeep. It was only about five miles to the pier, but there was a lot to see along the way. Dillan pointed out the places that held special memories: where he took surfing lessons, learned to paraglide, Sykes Creek where he kayaked, his favorite restaurants and bars, and the walk-in clinic where adventurous little boys who hurt themselves go to be stitched up.

Dillan paid five dollars to park near the pier; then, laden with our beach stuff, we walked past Trader Ricky's Beach Supplies and Sea Dogs hot dog stand toward the beach.

"Things haven't changed much since I was here last," Dillan said as we trekked toward the pier, "Oddly, it hasn't changed all that much since I was a kid."

"Sometimes it's nice when things don't change."

"Yeah but I think the pier is due for an upgrade."

"It looks fine to me, even with all the signage. When were you here last?"

"Um . . . five years ago – the year I turned twenty-two. After that I headed out to California."

"You didn't come back for the annual birthday celebration vacation?"

"No, well, I'd met Anna by then. She wasn't interested in coming here or vacationing with my parents so they took cruises and went other places. I should've taken that as a warning sign but well . . . love is blind, so they say."

I dug my toes in the sand as we stood, enjoying the simple sensation. "Love is patient, Love is kind," I retorted.

"Love is friendship set on fire."

"Love is a cuddly doggie."

"Love is looking into someone's eyes and seeing your true self for the first time," he said as he peered in my eyes.

"All right, you got me."

"Do I?" he asked excitedly.

"Oh Dillan, what do you want me to say?"

He cleared his throat and pointed over to the pier unfazed. "At the end of the pier is the Mai Tiki Tavern. It's just a kiosk thing with barstools, but on my twenty-first birthday I went straight there. I thought I was a Big Kahuna when I ordered a beer. I kept looking out to sea, trying to act cool and collected when inside I'm screaming *BEING LEGAL IS SO FREAKIN' BOSS!*"

"Gosh Dillan, you're too funny! I suppose without ID I can't even enjoy one with you."

"I never thought of that. What's worse, how are we going to get you to Hawaii without ID?"

"Shoot! Maybe we won't be able to go!"

"I'm sure Dad can offer some advice."

We walked down the beach a bit to get away from the crowd.

"This good?" Dillan asked.

"Perfect."

I watched his lithe but strong muscles ripple as he inched the umbrella pole into the sand. I could tell he was excited about being back because he never stopped talking, not even to take a breath.

"Over there is where I sat wood for two summers."

"Sat wood?"

"Yeah, on the bench – lifeguarding."

"Oh, right."

"Next to the pier, right under the Miss Cape Canaveral sign, is where I kissed this amazing wahine named Julie. God, that girl could surf! Never heard from her again after the summer though."

It was five whole years ago but it still made me cringe. "Want to cool off?" I asked, dying to change the subject before he shared the story of losing his virginity.

"Sure! Wanna boogie board?"

"Yeah, I'd like to try!"

"That's right – you don't know if you've done it before! It's easy – even little kids can do it."

It was super fun and easy just like he said. We spent two hours just playing in the surf. I felt comfortable and at home with Dillan at my side. Even when we discussed going to the pier for lunch, I hated leaving the water.

"There's actually pretty decent food up there. The Atlantic Ocean Grill, Oh Shucks, Boardwalk Cafe and Marlins. It's your pick; I've eaten at them all . . . numerous times."

"Well, which one do *you* like the best?"

"The one with the coldest beer."

"Seriously?"

"Honestly, I like Sea Dogs. I've been craving one for weeks now. When we walked by it before and that smell hit me, it was heavenly."

So, Sea Dogs it was. Dillan went to get lunch while I got comfortable under the umbrella and cracked open Henry's book. There were quite a few people around but none infringing on our space. I was really getting into the story when I felt a presence and looked up. Ten feet in front of me, looking out to sea, was the embodiment of a shirtless Waimoku. Very muscular shoulders and back narrowed down to a trim waist and brightly colored hibiscus print board shorts. I gasped and lifted the book to partially cover my face. Slowly he turned and looked directly at me. I let out an audible sigh of relief – some other dude completely. He gave me a once-over and with a cocky smile said, "Haven't I seen you at the gym?"

"Um no, sorry. I'm not from around here."

"You sure look familiar. I never forget a pretty face, and you, gorgeous, have a very pretty face!"

"Thank you," I said, as I lifted my book to cover it up.

When Dillan returned I was still shaking. "What's wrong?"

"Nothing. I'm fine," I lied.

"Sandy, something happened. Did you have a memory?"

"No, it's this book! It's so intensely engaging. I'm on the edge of my beach chair."

He handed me a hot dog, a container of cheese-covered nachos and an iced tea, then he sat in the chair next to me. "Wanna bite of my turkey leg?"

"No thanks, this is plenty."

"We can get a shaved ice or frozen chocolate-dipped banana later."

"Sounds good but I want to save some room for shrimp."

"I've seen you eat – don't worry about that."

I ignored his comment, picked up my book and continued reading while nibbling. Dillan's two hot dogs and turkey were gone in a matter of minutes. I couldn't help myself – "Wow! You *were* hungry!"

"I burned a lot of calories in the water."

"Boogie boarding's fun."

"Wait till you try surfing!" he said with incredible enthusiasm. "I think I'll try and get into *Slow Burn in Bermuda*," he added as he pulled the book from the beach bag. "We can go back out when the food settles."

"That might take longer for you," I giggled.

I'd only gotten to page forty-six when my eyes wouldn't stay opened. The sun was in the western sky, the crowd had thinned and the beach had quieted considerably. I looked up at Dillan who was thoroughly engaged in Henry's book and my fear of being tracked down by Waimoku had slipped away with the ebbing tide. I laid my chair back and drifted off to the sound of the gentle waves.

***

We spent most of the vacation swimming, eating, reading, hanging out with Margie and Richard and *surfing!* I completely surprised Dillan and myself by riding a wave on my first try. I guess I *had* done it before. His mouth hung open as I paddled back to him feeling amazingly *stoked*!

"Oh my God! That was fantastic! How did you do that?"

"I don't know. It just came naturally. I must've done it before. *Let's go have a dig*!" I said, winking.

"You're too much!" he yelled with laughter.

There wasn't enough time to experience all the things Dillan had wanted to share with me but we stopped at some of his favorite places. We enjoyed a family dinner at The Fat Snook, tried numerous flavors at Oasis Shaved Ice and met up with two of his old friends at the Sandbar Sports Grill. Dillan had spent a couple summers sitting wood with Frank and Eddie during college breaks. Frank was now managing his father-in-law's appliance store and Eddie was in his first year of residency after graduating medical school. They seemed enthralled as we told them about life on LBI after Superstorm Sandy and of my mysterious arrival in Beach Haven.

Frank took a slug of beer and looked at me with an inquisitive eye and stated, "You look awfully familiar. Haven't I seen you on the pier before?"

I answered honestly, "Not that I can remember, but some things seem familiar about Cocoa Beach."

Dillan looked at me with a surprised and hurt expression and said flatly, "Maybe because I've told you so much about it."

Later, on the way back to the guesthouse, I explained that I felt a vague sensation of familiarity while walking on the beach but there was nothing concrete about it.

"You still could have mentioned it."

"I'm sorry. You're right. I'm just so torn lately. All this time I've wanted to find my family but I'm afraid that finding them will take me away from you."

"You said once that we will always be friends, no matter what happens."

"Friends isn't good enough for either of us."

"It isn't?"

"Of course not."

"Then just forget you had a life before you came to LBI. Pretend you were born that day."

"It'd be easier if Waimoku didn't keep reminding us."

"I hate that guy. I want him out of the picture for good," he growled as he slammed his fists on the steering wheel.

"You're scaring me. That doesn't sound like the Dillan I've come to care about so deeply."

The next day was dark and gloomy, but luckily our relationship was status quo. If the weather had been nicer, Dillan planned to take me on a catamaran tour of the Thousand Islands or the Banana River Lagoon to look for manatee in the mangrove channels. Instead we went to the Astronaut Memorial Planetarium and Observatory. It was so peaceful lying back in my chair, watching the constellations move slowly through the sky and the moon as it changed phases. I almost felt its pull as it rose on the horizon.

When the show was done, we went into the IMAX Theater and watched *The Living Sea*. The combination of music and ocean scenery made my heart ache, especially when the narrator spoke about the challenges the seas and their inhabitants are facing. Dillan reached over and took my hand during the surfing scene and we both cringed when the dude went *over the falls* and had a terrible wipe out.

On the way home, we stopped at the "One of a Kind" Ron Jon (largest watersport emporium in the world) Surf Shop. We'd spent an hour and checked out thousands of surfboards when Dillan said, "Sandy, when we get back to New Jersey, I'd really like to buy the first board for your quiver." He was a super generous person.

Nearing the end of our second week, I had finished *Obsessed in Key West* and had started reading *Slow Burn in Bermuda*. Such exciting adventures the protagonist, Detective Alexander, was having! I felt so proud of Henry. I turned off the bedroom light at twelve-thirty and tossed and turned for an hour. Finally, I decided I'd go out and lie in a hammock under the stars as I was sure the muffled roar of the waves would lull me to sleep. I padded quietly past Margie and Richard's bedroom door and found Dillan and Buoy fast asleep in front of the TV. I was about to turn it off when I heard voices coming from the deck and headed to join them. At the screen door, the conversation became tense and I stopped in my tracks.

"How can you be so sure?"

"I was a lawyer for many years. I know when someone's lying," Richard said firmly.

"But what's the point of telling him now?"

"He's not a child any longer, Margie. He needs to know the truth so he can move on with his life."

"But we don't know the truth."

"We know what we saw and what we did."

"We *don't* know what we saw. He's never going to believe us," Margie said sadly.

"That be as it may, it's time this charade comes to an end!" Richard said resolutely.

There was a pause in the conversation and I took a step back toward my room.

"Now don't start crying, Margie. I'm sure it won't change the way he feels. For twenty odd years you found the strength and courage to come back here, never knowing what would happen. Don't lose that strength now."

Then there was a scraping of chairs as they stood up. I scrambled back to my room and jumped into bed, completely baffled by what I'd heard. I was desperately trying to work some meaning into their conversation when I heard my door creak as someone pushed it open. Oh God, they must have seen me! I clamped my eyes shut and forced myself to breathe slowly and deeply. Suddenly I felt the familiar thump-thump of Buoy jumping on the bed and lying down. What a relief! I didn't have a clue what would happen if I'd been discovered eavesdropping on such a private exchange. I reached over and rubbed Buoy's belly. Whatever they were talking about meant Dillan's whole world was about to go *over the falls* and I couldn't sleep a wink all night.

"What happened to you?" Dillan asked the next morning. "You go out partying after I fell asleep?"

"I had trouble sleeping."

"Bad dreams?"

"I couldn't get my brain to quiet down. The thoughts kept spinning like a waterspout."

"I wish you wouldn't worry so much. Every little things gonna be all right. Have a little faith."

"I know – you're right," I sighed, totally not buying it. "I'll nap on the beach later. I'll be fine." *But you won't*, I thought sadly.

For the next two days, I couldn't look Dillan in the eye. I wanted to warn him that his parents were about to drop a devastating bombshell on him but there was the possibility I'd misinterpreted their strange conversation. As our visit was coming to a close, I became more and more concerned for my best friend and he took notice.

"What's been bothering you, girl? You seem preoccupied lately."

"I need to find out who I am and be done with it," I answered distorting the truth. "You know I've come to really care about you, all of you, but this charade has got to come to an end!" I couldn't believe I'd parroted his father's words. Thank God, his parents weren't around to hear it!

Later that afternoon, Dillan surprised me by saying we would be going to Hawaii directly after we completed the inn and therefore we would be leaving Buoy with Margie and Richard for a while. I teared up immediately. Buoy was so old and who knew if I'd be returning from Hawaii. I had this horrible feeling that I'd never see him again.

"It's better that he stays with my family than leaving him in a kennel in New Jersey."

"Couldn't he stay with Henry? It's gonna break my heart to leave him behind."

"He loves my parents and they'll take good care of him. They'll take him home to Cincinnati and we'll go out and pick him up when we get back from our trip."

When *we* get back. Obviously, Dillan hadn't entertained the idea that I might not be returning with him.

Once I had conceded that Dillan was right I realized we had another problem. "What about my ID?"

"How good a liar are you?"

"I don't like lying unless it's absolutely necessary. It's not in my nature."

"Well, it's not like it's going to hurt anybody. Dad has friends, like the one who got Buoy the service dog papers. You'll have an ID in a few days."

"I wonder what my name will be."

"Sandra something, I'm guessing."

"Wow! I don't know if I should be impressed or worried."

"It'll be okay. It's not like it's a passport or anything. Kids get fake IDs all the time. There's no other way to get you there, unless we swim," he laughed.

I took Buoy for a long walk while Dillan packed the car. I wanted some time alone with him, to say a proper thank-you and good-bye. The thought of never seeing him again made me incredibly sad. We sat on the beach and stared out to sea together, my arm resting around his shoulders. Then he lay down and placed his head on my leg as he often did. I didn't want him to suspect that anything was amiss but I couldn't help letting a sob escape now and then.

The next morning, we tried not to make a big deal of saying good-bye, because Dillan and – hopefully – I would be seeing everyone in a few weeks. Buoy tried once to get into the back of the Jeep but didn't seem too distraught when Dillan took him back to his mother. Dillan got down on one knee, wrapped his arms around Buoy and gave him a Milk-Bone. Then he whispered something in his ear and kissed the top of his head. We thanked Margie and Richard for a wonderful time and gave them hugs and kisses. I bent down to kiss Buoy one last time, right where Dillan had.

"You're my dog, too," I whispered.

I was still crying as we drove west over the causeway. Dillan looked at me and smiled. "Everything's gonna be alright, Sandy. You'll see."

Suddenly it dawned on me; we had escaped Cocoa Beach without his world being turned upside down. I let out a sigh of relief and smiled back. Maybe when Buoy had come in my room and jumped on my bed, he'd simply roused me from an incredibly vivid dream.

DILLAN

JUNE

I MISSED BUOY, BUT I knew Mom and Dad were enjoying his company. We were down to the wire with the renovation so thankfully it left me little time to dwell on my furry friend. I had no trouble finding things around the inn that needed tweaking, which made being a perfectionist both a blessing and a curse.

All the blood, sweat and tears I'd spent in this beat-up old inn made me wish it was my own, but all I'd end up with was memories. The most notable of course, the heartache of losing Buoy, the miracle of his return and discovering the love of my life right in my own bedroom. There were times full of laughter, tenderness and pure joy, like watching the music overtake Sandy as she worked. First her toe would tap, then her curvy hips would sway. Her shoulders would follow and then her arms. Before long she'd put down whatever tool she was working with and she'd just dance, completely entranced by the song. I waited each and every day to see her dance. There were also times of great frustration, dealing with a wounded ego and feeling helpless as Waimoku loomed nearby. Where would we go from here?

As I adjusted the pneumatic closer on the screen door, I remembered the way Sandy looked as we walked along Cocoa Beach. I knew without a doubt she was the one and only girl for me. When she rode that surfboard, I thought I was gonna blow a gasket. She was so graceful, as if she'd surfed her whole life – and maybe she had.

I'd be totally disappointed if we didn't have an opportunity to surf in Hawaii, but that wasn't the purpose of the trip. If I was ever going to have this woman, we'd have to get to the bottom of things. Waimoku was one huge, crazy mofo. It didn't seem possible that she'd been in a relationship with him, but if she had, it needed to end. There was no way I'd let her return to an abusive asshole. Hopefully we'd find her parents or other *loving* family members who could fill in all the blanks.

We labored extra hard for a few days so we'd have time to attend the Thank You Festival on the weekend. The whole island was throwing a three-day block party to thank the dedicated people and their families who had helped secure and rebuild the island after the storm. Over the last eight months, I learned just how many organizations and individuals had been involved. The island was forever indebted not only to our own United Emergency Services: firemen, auxiliary members, EMTs, police and government officials but also the 177th and 108th Fighter Wing of the New Jersey Air National Guard, the New Jersey National Guard, State Police from Louisiana, 195th NJ Air National Guardsmen, the Army Corps of Engineers, 150th Engineer Company, 328th Military Police who had patrolled the island, hardcore utility crews, the Red Cross and countless volunteers from far and wide.

Friday evening, we headed up to Waterfront Park at the base of the causeway to listen to After The Reign play *Jersey Strong* among other country ballads. There were people paddle boarding and building sand sculptures on the bay along with food vendors and information booths. We visited with friends from the ALO and ReClam the Bay before we went over to watch Shorty Long perform. They always put on an awesome show. It wasn't long before Sandy's pretty little pout coerced me to dance. As the sky changed to a deep orange, we walked over to the dock and watched another epic LBI sunset, holding hands – not a bad day.

Saturday started with an early walk on the beach and a relaxed breakfast at the little table in our front yard. The morning was crisp and refreshing compared to the heat of Cocoa Beach. As we read our various sections of the newspaper, we heard the constant jingle of dog tags as people paraded by with an array of interesting breeds.

Sometimes it seemed that there were more dogs on LBI than people. Three retired greyhounds, a Boston terrier, St. Bernard, a pug and two Yorkies had all passed by within the hour.   How happy Sandy was to finally see Sherlock appear with Jacqueline Rose at the other end of his leash!

"Hi guys!"

"Oh my gosh! It's so great to see you! When did you get back?" Sandy asked as she jumped out of her chair.

"Yesterday. I'm home for the summer."

I gave her a quick hug and Sandy grabbed her next, holding on for dear life.

I reached down and pet the old pit bull, wondering if Buoy missed me.

"What's new in the big city?" I asked the tattoo queen as I took Sherlock's leash and offered her my chair.

"Well, I've been very busy studying art history and with various projects. I've met a ton of talented people over the last few months. A couple of them work in galleries so I was able to squeeze in a few openings."

"That sounds exciting!" Sandy said.

"It really is. I love the city vibe, but I don't think I'd want to stay permanently."

"I can't remember if I've ever been there."

"It's a totally different atmosphere there, literally and figuratively," she laughed. "Salty sea air versus exhaust fumes. I know which I prefer."

I sat on the front step and Sherlock sat next to me, placing his head on my leg. He stared up at me with big adoring eyes, jonesing for a treat.

"Hey, we're heading to the Thank You Fest in a little while. Do you want to come along? We can catch up," Sandy said.

"Sounds like fun. I'll take this guy over to the park to do his business and I'll be back in a bit."

Though I felt a bit awkward, Sandy insisted that we both wear our LBI IS ALIVE T-shirts. I swear I'd do anything for that woman. She'd cut off the neckband, rolled up the sleeves and tied a little knot at the side of hers changing the style completely – hell, she'd look sexy in a paper bag.

The three of us got in the Jeep and headed up to the Brant Beach town hall to check out the festivities. On the stage was a British singer named Katy Tiz singing a kind of hip-hop/rap/pop catchy mash-up. There was a dunk tank, craft fair, food vendors, ice-cold beer and an array of other booths including one with FEMA representatives handing out information on home rebuilding and mitigation. Talk about a buzz kill! I guess there were still plenty of people dealing with that shit and unfortunately, it would probably last for years. We walked around for a while, listening to The Guy Smiley Band play a variety of songs from Elvis to Cee Lo, Gin Blossoms, Bruno Mars, the Beatles and Aerosmith, to name only a few.

On the way home, Sandy asked if we should work for a while before it got too late but I wasn't in the mood to lift a screwdriver or a level.

"I think we should just chill out tonight. It's our weekend off, remember?"

"Hey, I rented *The Hobbit* from RedBox 'cause Henry raved about the book. I guess Tolkien is one of his favorite writers. You guys wanna come over and watch it with us? We can get pizza or something."

"Sound good to you, Sandy?" I asked.

"Sounds like a plan, man," she said with a smile.

Lucas fell asleep halfway through the movie, while Henry was literally quoting Bilbo Baggins. Sandy and Jacqueline Rose seemed to enjoy it, along with Sherlock, who got an occasional bite of pizza crust and any popcorn that fell on the floor. Mrs. Holmes fell asleep on Lucas's lap. Sandy mouthed the words, *I miss Buoy* to me and I mouthed back, *Me, too.*

When we were leaving, the girls planned to hit the sidewalk sale in town the next day.

"You don't mind that I asked Jacqueline Rose to go with us tomorrow, do you?" Sandy asked on the way home.

"Nothing bad 'bout being accompanied by *two* hot women," I said.

"You think she's hot?"

"Yeah – in a naughty-girl kinda way."

"I don't think she's naughty at all."

"Maybe not anymore, but she sure looks the part."

Sandy didn't say another word on our short walk home. "You alright?" I asked as I unlocked the door.

"Sure, but I was thinking: I don't want you to be bored while we're shopping tomorrow."

"I was thinking the same thing. I'll call some of the guys and see if they'll meet me at the beer garden."

"Don't forget there's a wing-eating contest at the CHEGG."

She was seriously trying to ditch me! "Yeah, but they don't sell beer there," I replied, feeling slighted.

The next morning, I group-texted Mitch, Dave, Joe and Jimmy, who were stoked to meet up at the beer garden. I needed to tell them that I wouldn't be guarding this season, unless Chief Gavin could make a position for me when we returned from Hawaii. I was sure that after a few beers their disappointment would fade and I'd find them involved in a heated discussion regarding training exercises and this season's competitions.

The girls and I walked to town and started the day off by riding the Ferris wheel at Fantasy Island. Sandy balked a little about getting on at first but after Jacqueline Rose confirmed the fun factor, she conceded. She squeezed my hand, hard, but never closed her eyes as we traveled around and around. Jacqueline Rose distracted her by reminiscing about spending numerous hours at the amusement park when she was a kid. When we left, she said sadly, "I miss my grandmother."

After an hour or so of shopping the sidewalk sale and flea market, I left the girls and headed for an ice-cold beer with my bros which was a few blocks away. There were plenty of people milling around the beer and food vendors. The tables were crowded and the line for brew was long. I couldn't spot any of my friends so I headed for the shortest line and texted Mitch who appeared in seconds.

"Shit, it's great to see you again, bro. How's the job coming?"

"Just about done."

"Cool, leaves you more time to surf!"

"I can't imagine anything tasting better than an ice-cold beer right now," Joe said as he and Jimmy fell behind us in line.

"I'll second that. I got parched shopping with the girls and hoofing over here."

"I'm high and dry unless one of you guys takes pity on me," Jimmy said.

"Go have a seat, wee one," Mitch teased.

"I ain't wee – just ask my babe!"

"Everyone's seen you in a Speedo, Jim," I teased.

"Yeah, they look 'cause I'm hung like a donkey!"

"More like a jackass!" Joe spewed, rolling his eyes.

Jimmy dismissed him with, "Yeah, whatever bro," as he walked away.

We stood in line for quite a while, ordering two each from the keg. I guess if Jimmy happened to lift one off the table, it wouldn't be the end of the world. He wasn't driving and his mother let him have his fill the night we'd crashed at his place.

"Hey guys, you aren't gonna believe what I just heard!" Jimmy said as we approached the table.

"What, Taylor Swift dumped another boyfriend?" Joe snickered sarcastically.

"Hey, say what you want but that girl's HOT!" Mitch added.

"No, nothing like that, you idiots."

What could possibly be so interesting? I wondered as we sat at the table with Jim and some geeky dude wearing a *Doctor Who* T-shirt, khaki shorts, black socks and sandals.

"This Dwayne Johnson look-a-like sat down," Jimmy said. "He was huge and *plastered*! The whole time he was talking, he was trying to get this pink Ron Jon cap to stay on his fat head. Man, he said some off-color shit!"

"Like what?" Mitch asked.

"Like, 'she never loved me or gave me the time of day.'"

"What's so bad about that?" Joe questioned.

"Well, then he slurred, 'Have you ever been so screwed over by a woman that you just wanted to frickin' drown her?'"

"No shit?" Joe asked.

"He said he came here to find her and take her home but she wouldn't go. She was being a *slutty bitch* and *playing games*. He sounded super pissed!"

I felt a heaviness settle on my chest and I sprung to my feet. **"Which way did he go?"**

Jimmy pointed toward Bay Avenue.

I ran in Waimoku's wake, into the crowd where he'd seemingly disappeared into thin air. I didn't bother to go back and explain to the guys. I called Jack as I ran back to the flea market where I'd left the girls.

SANDY

MAYBE IT WOULD BE as simple as someone recognizing me as we walked the streets in Hawaii. Maybe some sight, sound or smell would jar my memory and everything would come flooding back. It was a daunting thought – if they included Waimoku, my memories might be terrifying.

Henry kindly offered to store the Jeep and all our belongings while we were away and promised that if we needed a place to stay upon our return, we'd be more than welcome. I held his hand and with tears in my eyes, explained that I might not be coming back.

"But this is your home, Sandy!"

"Is it?"

"It feels that way to me."

"Me too," I said as I wrapped my arms around his neck.

"Wear your necklace."

"What?"

"When you are wandering around Hawaii, wear the necklace. It might bring you luck."

"I will, I promise."

We'd spent the two weeks since we returned from Florida making sure that everything was perfect for Mac and Shona. The last chores were vacuuming, dusting, window washing and packing: duffle bags for Hawaii, cardboard and plastic boxes for Henry's. Buoy's toys, brush, nail clippers, bandanas and bowls were packed together and clearly marked for quick access.

We made time to enjoy some of the Thank You Festival. It was a way to celebrate all the people who secured and protected the island and her inhabitants, those same folks that I hid from when I first arrived. Friday night we listened and danced to live music by Shorty Long and The Jersey Horns at the Waterfront Park in Ship Bottom. Man, those guys could get you movin' and groovin'. Saturday Jacqueline Rose accompanied us to a sidewalk sale where I was outvoted and forced to ride the Ferris wheel. I have to admit that although I was scared, I did enjoy the view. Dillan left us to have a beer with his friends but arrived looking frantic only a short time later. Apparently, there was a shark sighting and he was afraid we might ditch shopping for swimming! Go figure! Later, for dinner, we got takeout BBQ for everyone from the fire station. We ate our meals on Henry's deck, enjoying the ocean breeze and the end of a fun-filled weekend.

The night we declared the inn complete we celebrated with a clam-topped pizza from Panzone's and a few bottles of lovely rosé wine. We sat at the small metal table in the front yard and admired our little fairy garden and the flowering bushes and ornamental grasses which the landscapers had just planted. They made the inn look extra inviting.

"Mac made good choices," Dillan said, motioning to the plantings and the new wooden *Seafarer's Inn* sign that hung by the roadside.

"He most certainly did," I replied, feeling incredibly proud of Dillan's work.

"I declare this, *one mother of a job!*" he said as he held up his wine glass.

"Hear! Hear!" I responded as I clinked it with mine.

"I never could have done it without *you*."

"I'm glad you didn't have to."

"It's been a hell of a ride," he said as he downed what was left in his glass.

"I have a feeling it's just beginning," I responded, emptying the bottle into it.

"Don't *you* want more?" he asked, not completely sure he was talking about the wine.

"I think three is my limit," I said, feeling woozy and warm in all the wrong places.

"Sandy . . . " he uttered as he took my hand and leaned toward me, his lips just inches from mine.

"Please don't."

"How can you fight against the force that's been drawing us together? Certainly, it's more powerful than anything you might have had in your previous life."

"My heart is breaking."

He grabbed me then and kissed me hard, deeply and wonderfully. I felt a rush of waves crash upon me like high tide under a full moon. This unrestrained kiss took me to a place I never knew existed – a place I never, ever wanted to leave.

"Dillan . . . I, I . . . ."

"Yeah, me too. It doesn't get any more real than this."

I looked into his deep blue eyes and knew he was right. I just nodded consent because I couldn't speak. He took my hand, led me into the house and up the stairs to my bedroom.

"At least we don't have to share the bed with Buoy," he said with a smile as he removed his shirt and closed the curtains. "I feel like I've been waiting all my life for this moment."

This was my cue to get undressed but I was oddly paralyzed. He came slowly toward me, never taking his eyes from mine, unbuttoning his jeans along the way. He placed his fingers gently in my hair and ever so softly kissed my forehead, my cheeks, my eyelids and then my neck. My legs became weak and buckled.

***

"Good morning, my love," Dillan said as my eyelids fluttered opened.

He was lying next to me under the sheets with the sweetest look on his face.

"Were you watching me sleep?"

"Yes, for hours. Wondering how you could pass out on me like that when I promised you a night of blissful passion."

Oh my God! I remembered but it was fuzzy. "We didn't make love?"

"I hope you'd remember if we did!"

"I'm sorry."

"I never should have plied you with so much wine. I forgot what a lightweight you are!" he laughed.

"You certainly didn't force me to drink it. We were celebrating."

He climbed over me, one arm on each side and lowered himself to lightly kiss me.

"I'd like to pick up where we left off, but I fear we may be interrupted by the movers. Some of Mac's belongings are supposed to arrive this morning." He climbed off the bed and left the room, whistling.

As he went. I ran my fingers through the hair at my crown and took a deep breath. Was I disappointed or relieved? Whatever I was, sometimes things happen for a reason.

Though Dillan had hinted at it every evening since, and daytime too for that matter, I blew off any attempt he made to get us back into bed. I knew he was terribly disappointed; I could see the hurt in his eyes, but I imagined a much bigger hurt as he boarded a plane alone back to the mainland.

Mac and Shona started moving into their apartment and graciously offered to let us stay until our trip. It was nice to spend some time with them, talking about the work we did and how we overcame the problems we'd faced. Their daughter Fiona would be spending the summer with them to help get the inn up and running. The location was perfect, so close to the beach, the shops, Bicentennial Park, the historical museum and Surflight Theater. Who wouldn't want to stay here? I had a feeling it was going to be a very successful endeavor for Mac and Shona as they finally lived their dream and yet my heart ached.

On Thursday, Jack called Dillan and invited us over for dinner Saturday evening. I was happy to have a chance to spend time with them before leaving. They were such nice people and I was lucky to know them. When I asked Dillan if anyone else was invited he said, "I think it's just us."

"I'm surprised they didn't invite Jacqueline Rose."

"I guess we'll find out when we get there."

When we arrived at their house Saturday, we were surprised to see Chief Bob's command truck parked on the street outside their house.

"I hope Carole didn't burn dinner!" Dillan joked.

"More likely Jack with the grill," I replied, standing up for my female friend.

"I don't smell anything burning."

We found a note taped on the front door:

HEY KIDS,
COME ON UP
TO THE BEACH!

"I don't think these two bottles of wine are gonna cut it," Dillan said as we crested the dune.

"Looks like a party."

There was a tent set up, a long table covered with dining paraphernalia, people standing around drinking and chatting, and a huge mound on the sand covered with canvas.

"Oh! Look at that. It's a clambake!" I squealed excitedly.

"Right up your alley, girl."

I looked at the people and realized I knew everyone! Carole was waving at us to come on down and everyone yelled, "**Surprise!**"

"Isn't your birthday next month, Dillan?"

"Yup, the thirty-first. This party's for you."

"Why me?"

"Because everyone knows your story; they adore you and want to thank you for making LBI a better place after the storm."

"You knew about this?"

"Didn't know I could keep a secret, did you?" he replied proudly.

I was so surprised that Jack and Carole would go to so much trouble just for me. Everyone gave me a hug and said, "Thank You" as we wandered around saying "Hello".

It felt wonderful to see so many friends enjoying a lovely evening on the beach together, including Henry, Jacqueline Rose and Lucas, Mac and Shona, Chief Gavin and his wife Sellina, Katie and Mitch, Chief Bob and his wife Alice, Phil and Bette from the Hud and Janine and little Ellie!! Oh my goodness, Liam must have taken something I said to heart! Dillan went to the cooler to get a beer and I walked over to chat with Janine.

"Hi!" Ellie said happily.

"Well hello there, little one. What a wonderful surprise!"

"I'm not little. I'm a big girl!" she retorted with a pout as she held the hem of her Ariel dress and twisted back and forth adorably.

"You certainly are. Thank you for coming to my party."

"Sandy, I can't thank you enough," Janine said as she hugged me. "What for?"

"Ellie told me all about the lady who came to her playground. I knew right away it was you."

"I hope I wasn't meddling. I mean, I knew I was but . . . ."

"Whatever you said made a difference."

Ellie sat in the sand and started digging with a toy shovel. We were just out of earshot when Janine said, "Liam called me out of the blue and invited me to lunch – just the two of us. After some polite small talk, he apologized for being careless with my feelings and confessed to being overwhelmed as a husband and father, not to mention trying to keep on top of the bills. 'The weeks just fly by. We don't feel like **we** spend enough time with the kids as it is.' I was sad to see so much of his father in him, so much stress. I tried to be brave and not cry because I knew he wouldn't like it but my throat tightened and my eyes welled up with tears anyway. He said he'd try harder to squeeze me into their insanely busy life but I still felt like I was just adding another burden – but he did call a few weeks later," she said as she stepped over to Ellie and bent down to kiss her cheek, "and here I am with my little mermaid girl."

"Well, that's fantastic! I think you'll all be better for it."

"I am not little!" Ellie said firmly, "Mommy says I'm a *big* girl!"

"And Mommy's always right!" Janine added, her voice filled with sincerity.

"Where's Connor?" I asked, missing the little guy.

"With Mommy and Daddy," Ellie said, "Probably playing monster-trucks."

"He's spending some one-on-one time with his parents. I'll have a visit with him in a couple weeks," Janine added sounding thrilled.

"Well, it's a step in the right direction. I hope someday you'll have the type of relationship you truly desire with your family."

"I'm praying for that every day. I hope you'll find your own family soon."

"Well, we think I might have ties in Hawaii, so we're going there in a few days."

"Ohhh . . . Hawaii! That sounds so exotic. I can see that for you."

"I'm sure it's beautiful there, but my heart is here with all of you. I hope to come back if it's at all possible."

"Then I'll pray for that too."

"Sandy! Did you see him?" Ellie asked excitedly as she jumped up from her digging.

"Who, sweetie?"

"The merman! He was right over there! He jumped out of the water!" she shouted as she pointed out to sea.

"Oh, I'm sorry, Ellie. I wasn't looking."

"Grammy, did *you* see him?"

"Oh, yes! He was a big one!" she answered with a wink.

"She's got a wonderful imagination," I whispered.

Chief Bob was supervising the pit, with his fire extinguisher, first aid kit, shovel and buckets of water at the ready. His wife Alice was chatting with Carole as they dug appetizers out of a cooler. Dillan and I enjoyed some jumbo shrimp and cheese and crackers as we mingled with the guests.

When it was time to eat, the men helped Jack pull the canvas off the bake and I felt my knees go weak! Once the rockweed was removed, I donned some oven mitts and was right in there, helping pull out the littleneck clams, crabs, lobsters, mussels and corn. Everything that was loose was piled into big metal pans and set on the table next to pots of melted butter, soft dinner rolls and pitchers of fruity sangria. Next, we removed the foil pouches from the pit and unwrapped potatoes, kielbasa and onions.

People sat on the benches and lawn chairs around the table, talking and eating, taking no notice of the butter running down their chins and wrists or the bits of seafood stuck to their fingers. I got lost briefly, staring out to sea while counting my blessings. The ocean looked perfectly inviting while behind us we still dealt with blown-out garages, decimated lots, empty storefronts, and an occasional home resting in an undesirable location.

Once everyone had eaten their fill, we were offered a melty S'more, which was somehow impossible to resist. As the folks were leaving, I walked Henry and Lucas back to their car and returned to help with the cleanup. Chief Bob was tending to the pit. Carole and Dillan were packing up the tableware and Jack looked like he needed help with the tent.

"You aren't going to hurt him, are you?" he asked bluntly as I joined him to disassemble one of the poles.

I was rather stunned. "Hurt Dillan? I certainly don't intend to. Why would you ask such a thing?"

"It's just your type usually does – not that they mean to. It just happens that way."

"My type?"

"You can level with me. I'm not going to expose you. You seem so genuine; no one would believe me anyway."

"I don't mean to be rude, Jack," I said, feeling hurt and confused, "but I assure you, I would never intentionally hurt Dillan. I love him."

"That's what I was afraid of."

"We're ready to take the first load up to the truck," Carole said as she came over. "How are you guys making out?"

"We're almost done here," Jack replied.

"Thank you, Carole, for doing all this for me. It must've been a ton of work."

"It was well worth the effort to see your face light up as you two came over the dune. Anyway, everyone pitched it. We're all the better for knowing you, Sandy. I hope you'll find the answers you seek in Hawaii."

I gave her a great big hug and besides Jack's strange comments, which I attributed to his beer consumption, the evening had been a true celebration of friendship, perseverance and resurrection.

Two evenings later, we ran like crazy kids down toward the shoreline, sand flying out from under our feet, laughing and grabbing at each other. Dillan got a hold of my Unite+Rebuild T-shirt and pulled me to him. We fell under the momentum and couldn't stop laughing. We had said our good-byes to Jack and Carole earlier in the day. They wished us luck and were more emotional than I expected. Jack hugged Dillan with tears in his eyes while his words from the party echoed in my head. I guess he truly considered him the son he never had.

We had an early farewell dinner with Henry, Jaqueline Rose and Lucas at Howard's Restaurant, hence the French fried lobster tail and wine-induced euphoria we were now feeling. As the sinking sun turned the sky a deep red-orange, locals and visitors alike headed to Bicentennial Park with their lawn chairs and blankets to watch *Ferris Bueller's Day Off* on a big blowup screen. The ocean breeze carried the sound of live music south from the Sea Shell Motel, but for us it was a quiet time to simply enjoy the deserted beach and each other.

Dillan got up and found a piece of broken dune fence and started scratching a message in the sand. "I bet you know what I'm writing," he said.

"That you think I'm amazing?" I joked back, feeling a bit flirty.

"That is true, but it's not that."

I got up and swayed to the bass beat of the music though the song wasn't recognizable. "You know, your hair really suits you now that you've had it styled," I said, imagining my fingers running through it as my lips lingered on his neck just under his ear.

"Yeah, I'll admit it. You were right. I'm glad to be free of the wonder mop," he replied as he continued to write.

What did I have to do to get his attention? "Wanna dance?" I asked hopefully.

"Can we wait until it gets a little darker?"

"Where's your spontaneity?" I pulled my T-shirt over my head and stripped off my shorts. Dillan whistled appreciatively at my bikini but wouldn't abandon his project.

"I'm gonna take one last dip," I said, defeated.

"I'll join you once I've poured my heart out for the whole world to see."

"It will be gone in a few hours; the tide is coming in!" I yelled as I jumped into the surf and swam out past the sandbar. I turned around and looked at Dillan bent over his masterpiece and sighed. I loved him more that I could fathom and I prayed that I'd be free to be with him, once I *finally* discovered my true identity. I lie on my back, floating under the fading blue of the east and the darkening red of the west. So relaxing, peaceful and lovely.

Without warning, I was slammed by a force so lightning quick that I had no time to take a breath. Panic set in as I realized I was trapped in the jaws of a shark that was pulling me deeper and further away from the shore. I struggled to free myself, but my legs were trapped in its vice-like grip. I flailed my arms, fighting to get to the surface and life-giving oxygen – to get to Dillan, to Buoy and Henry, to Jacqueline and Lucas, to Jack and Carole and Janine and her grandchildren, every person who had touched my life. Their faces drifted into and out of my consciousness one by one, but the last face I saw was that of Waimoku. He glared up at me from below where his vast arms of steel had rendered my legs useless and smiled hideously as the last traces of oxygen escaped my lips. Lifelessly, I slipped into the watery abyss.

DILLAN

AFTER I FINISHED MY heartfelt message to Sandy, I pulled off my shirt and tossed it in the sand. I couldn't wait to get my arms around her. I looked north then south but didn't see her. She said she was only going to take a dip – not swim a marathon. I waded out, hoping to see her emerge, but nothing. Suddenly this feeling of panic came over me. Had something happened? Had she had too much to drink? "**SANDY!**" I yelled.

I gauged which way the current was flowing and dove in, coming up every few strokes to yell her name. Finally I heard her coughing and sputtering in the distance.

"I'm over here! I'm okay," she responded unconvincingly.

I let out a massive sigh of relief. "Jesus, I thought you'd drowned!" I yelled, as I swam toward her. "Don't ever do that again!"

"I did, and I won't," she answered strangely.

All I could think about was getting her safely into my arms but when I got about fifteen feet from her she yelled, "Dillan! Stop!" in a forceful voice.

"Let's go in; I don't like this game anymore."

She had caught her breath and sounded oddly tranquil, when she said, "Look, the Super Moon's cresting the horizon."

"It's a lovely sliver of red moon," I conceded, as we bobbed delicately in the ebb and flow of the tide, "Now let's go in."

"There's something wonderfully magical about it, isn't there?"

"Have your memories returned?" I asked anxiously.

"No, not exactly but I've discovered the answer to some of our most puzzling questions!"

"Can't we discuss this inside?"

"I don't think we can."

"I know we've had quite a few drinks, but you aren't making any sense."

"We should just stay out here awhile and enjoy the moon as it rises. It's extraordinary, don't you think?"

"I guess I can appreciate it, now that my heart's no longer pounding out of my chest! I thought I'd lost you and my life was over."

"You shouldn't worry about me in the water. I'm a *very* good swimmer."

"And a pretty good surfer," I added as I floated on my back.

"You're a great swimmer, Dillan. The strongest swimmer I've ever seen."

"You know how much I love the water, always have," I answered as I watched the watery horizon release its hold on the largest moon I'd ever seen. I could feel Sandy float up beside me. She reached over and found my hand in the water. I felt oddly wonderful as I rocked gently on the waves, like a baby in its mother's arms. "This is awesome," I uttered peacefully.

"I have something strange to tell you – I really hope you'll take it okay."

"Girl, you always say the strangest and most wonderful things. Every word from your lips is like a siren's song."

"I see the moon's having an effect on you too," she giggled. "You're mesmerized!"

"I've been mesmerized from the moment I found you in my bedroom!" I replied from the depths of my soul.

"I'm not sure you'll still feel the same way now."

"You know I'm *crazy* about you! There's nothing you could say that would change the way I feel."

"Remember how I always felt that there was someone out there, someone special, someone that I was truly in love with?" she asked, sounding like she was preparing to drop a bombshell.

"How could I forget?" I replied, "It's what kept you at arms' length all this time."

"There is someone – but *it's you*. It's always been and it will always be *you*."

"I don't understand. How is that possible?"

"I don't have all the answers yet. I just know what I know."

"And you know that you love me; you're absolutely sure about that?"

"I do love you, Dillan. I feel like I've been searching for you my whole life."

I felt engulfed by a wave of ecstasy. I pulled her closer so our bodies were almost touching, but I couldn't take my eyes off the breathtaking red-orange moon rising slowly in the sky.

"There's something more," she said timidly. "I seem to have grown a rather large tail."

"You can't scare me away with a little fish story like that, girl," I replied.

"But Dillan . . . ."

I wasn't one to believe in miracles or mythical legends and such, still as strange as it was, I didn't find myself the least bit shocked by her admission. "Why don't you take me for a little swim around the island?"

"I was hoping you'd say something like that!" she chimed as she wrapped her arms and tail around me, pinning me helpless in her embrace. I kissed her and she kissed me back with the reckless abandon I'd been desperately waiting for.

"You know," I uttered breathlessly, "I wasn't that far off when I joked about swimming to Hawaii."

"Why don't we start in Florida and see where the tide takes us?"

"You want to ax our trip to Hawaii?" I asked, as I brushed a strand of hair behind her ear.

"No, but there're answers in Cocoa Beach, I just know it; and we can visit with Buoy and your parents before we head to the Pacific."

"I love the way you think, girl. Now show me what you got!"

I used to think I was a pretty good swimmer, but as she took my hand and we sped toward the northern tip of the island, I realized – I ain't got nothin' on a mermaid.

THE END FOR NOW